THE FAMILY

THE FAMILY

RIC PERROTT

Mirelune Press

First published in the United States by Mirelune Press 2025

www.mirelune.com

FIRST EDITION

ISBN: 979-8-9995624-9-4

Library of Congress Control Number: 2025920053

Front Cover Design: Diren Yardimli

Back Cover Design: 100covers

vP,1.3

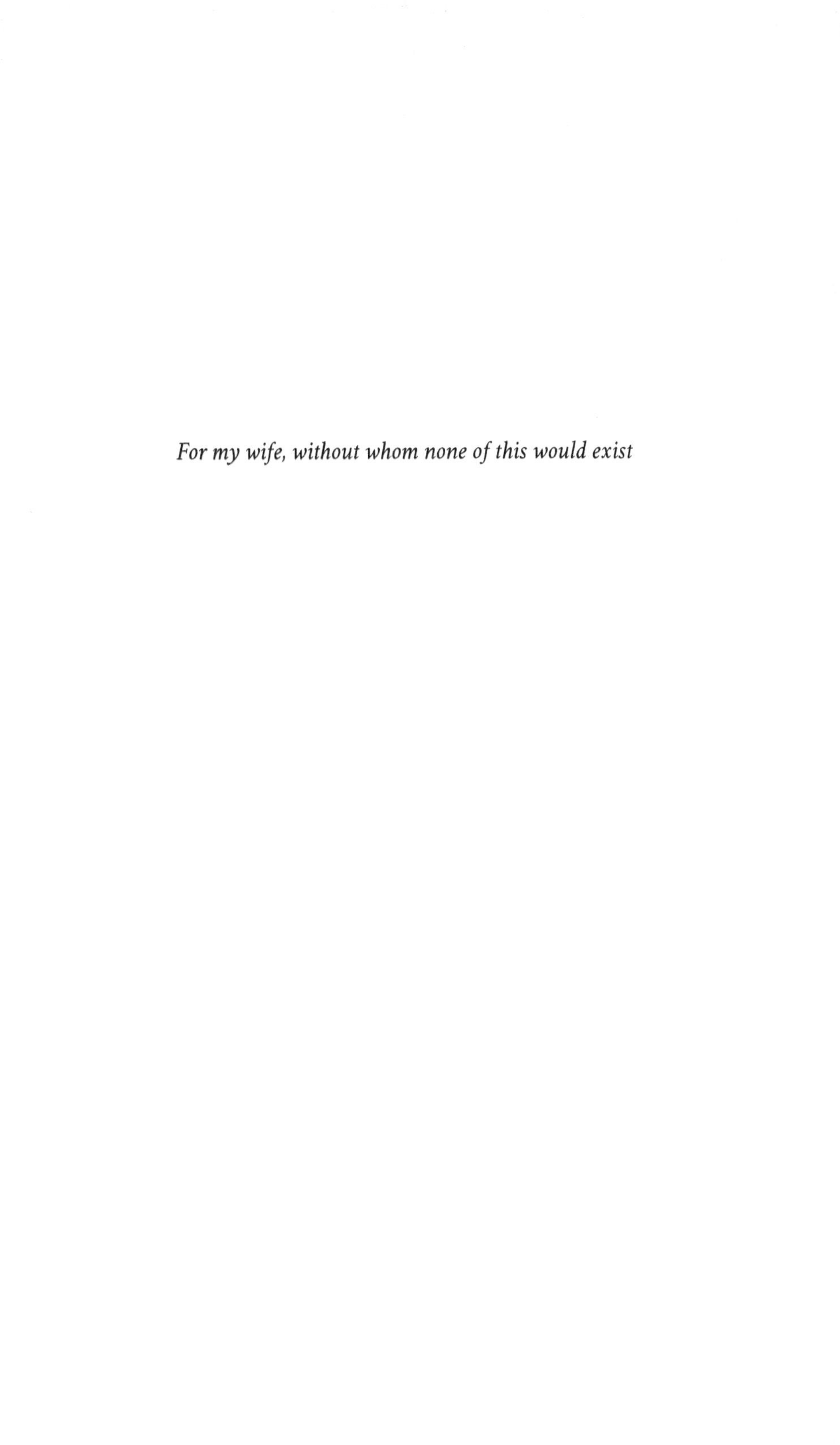

For my wife, without whom none of this would exist

Strong Tails In Stormy Waters

— SILLY LOVE

Prologue

The stupid purple pen was dying again. Esther shook it harder this time, and the ink sputtered back to life. It came from the cheap plastic set her sister had given her last year on her fourteenth birthday. None of the pens had ever worked that well, but she loved them anyway.

Amber light from her bedside lamp bathed the room in a golden warmth. Fantasy paperbacks lay scattered across the floor, spines cracked and pages softened, while a pink Bluetooth speaker sat next to her on the bed, playing a lo-fi indie song.

She paused and stared at the ink-smudged paper. She'd written the same sentence and crossed it out three times: *How do you tell someone you miss them if you'll never see them again?*

A faint *tink* at the window caught her ear. Soft at first, like rain, but then sharper, more insistent. She set her notebook on the pillow, jumped down, and stepped to the sill.

Outside, barely enough moonlight fell over the rusted fire escape for her to make out the hooded figure crouching there. A face peered at her from the shadows.

Her heart thumped.

The figure waved.

Esther didn't care if her mom heard. She threw the window up so hard it rattled, then crawled halfway over the ledge before Amelia could say, "Careful, you dork." She landed in a tangle, knees banging against metal and hair whipping in her eyes. But none of that mattered because Amelia was back. In the flesh, and her arms wrapped around Esther like the strongest safety harness in the world.

"Missed you too, Sprout." Her voice was rough and more alive than the memory Esther replayed every night in her dreams. She squeezed tighter.

"You said you'd call." Esther pressed her face against Amelia's chest. "I waited. Every night."

When Amelia pulled away, she seemed older, more tired, her skin looser where laugh lines used to be. A new tattoo—a sharp, bold diamond with flares—curled from her wrist toward her thumb.

"I'm sorry. Things got…busy," she said, not even trying to sound convincing. "But I'm here now."

A moment passed as traffic and conversations drifted up from the street. But on the second-floor fire escape, under the night sky, the rest of the city faded away until only they remained.

Amelia reached into her hoodie and pulled out a Mounds bar, Esther's favorite. "Don't say I never bring you anything."

Esther took it, ripped it open, and popped half into her mouth. Bliss.

They sat, balancing their feet on the slats—Amelia's ratty sneakers and Esther's bare toes side by side. Amelia's hand rested absently on Esther's hair, twining a strand and letting it go.

"What are you doing here?" Esther asked between chews, her coconut breath and exuberance filling the space between them as Amelia smirked.

"I'm leaving early tomorrow, and I'll be gone for a while. So, I figured we could hang out. Like before."

Esther's belly squirmed. "Where are you going?"

Amelia smiled, revealing the chip in her left incisor, the one she'd gotten from chasing Mrs. Tedesci's cat down 179th Street. She'd taken the corner too tight, lost her balance, and bounced her face off the sidewalk. She couldn't eat anything but pudding and applesauce for three days.

"You know. New places, big adventures." But her eyes said: *Don't ask—not yet.*

"Is Mom pissed at you?"

"She's always pissed at me." Amelia shrugged. "But you need to be there for her, okay, Sprout?"

Esther nodded.

She draped an arm over Esther's shoulder and held her close. They didn't need to say anything more.

The glow of the streetlight caught the fresh ink of Amelia's tattoo and made it shine. Esther reached out gently to touch it.

"Did it hurt?"

"Like a son of a bitch, yeah," Amelia chuckled. "But I love it."

Esther ran her finger over the lines.

"It looks like a—"

"STAR!" A VOICE CALLS out—female, crisp, commanding.

The sound snaps me from the daydream. No longer barefoot. No longer on the fire escape. Was that really five years ago?

Candles flicker around me like a creepy ritual scene from the old movies Amelia and I would stay up late to watch. She'd poke me during the scary parts and roar with laughter when I freaked out. I'd slap her and pretend to be mad, but I'd give anything to be lying there in my pajamas with her right now.

Instead, I'm standing up here, in front of all these people with this shimmering black dress drooping so low on my shoulders, they could hang me right in the closet when this is all over. A blister from these heels keeps screaming, as if I had a say in it. *Your feet are so thin. These may be a little loose.* Yeah, no kidding.

The last time I'd worn heels was for the ninth-grade dance, after Tyler Reynolds asked and I'd said "Okay" without understanding the expectations my answer carried. Come to think of it, I had a blister then too.

"Stand proud, Sister, and receive your name." She sounds so dramatic, like a community theater production of *Hamlet*. Though perhaps *The Taming of the Shrew* would be more appropriate in this instance.

The woman takes a black pendant necklace off the table and holds it up. Just like she did with Amy—Athena now, I guess. Is that how this works?

My lips are so dry. The deep red lipstick looks pretty, but it's like a melted crayon coating my mouth. I keep licking them, which probably makes me look like a nervous Jack Russell terrier.

Leaning my head forward like the other girls did, I let her slide the chain over my hair. *Please don't mess it up.* Three hours in a salon chair for this. The stylist took one glance at my matted, split-end mop and wished she'd taken the day off.

To her credit, she turned it into salon-perfect layers falling past my shoulders—blonde with amber highlights. I never imagined having a haircut which cost more than the electric bill we "forgot" to pay every other month, but now that it's mine, I have to admit it's great.

The woman lays the pendant beneath my collarbone and smiles. It's so cold. The smile I return is half-formed, but with lips on the verge of cracking, it's the best I can offer. Hushed voices swirl all around, adding to my anxiety.

"From this moment on, you are Star."

My body remains motionless. A feeling of change is supposed to come over me, right? I'm getting nothing other than: *I don't belong here.*

Her tone softens, becoming almost warm. "Welcome to the Family."

ONE

It's as if I've been cast in the starring role in someone else's life. If this is a makeover montage, I'm definitely more Vivian Ward than Holly Golightly.

The crowd claps politely, like I've finished performing "Chopsticks" at a piano recital. My cheeks are burning. Taking a bow seems appropriate, but the fear of face-planting in these shoes is too real, so I manage a little curtsy and regain my balance.

Star. It sounds like someone else's name. Like I'm a kid playing dress-up in her mother's clothes.

Melody waits at the bar, luminous in a teal dress that clings to her like water, her dark hair a contrast of shadows against bare shoulders. She holds up a champagne flute and wiggles it from side to side, teasing me. I mouth, "I'm trying," and turn sideways to avoid a girl whose gown makes her look like she's being consumed by a fancy mushroom.

The thing I love about Melody is that when she says something, you believe her. It's not her words alone but the absolute certainty behind them. She believes in me with such conviction that I can almost see myself through her eyes—confident, capable, and worthy of this name.

I wish I could bottle that feeling.

Barely off the stage, I'm swallowed by a sea of faces. Some familiar, most not. Everyone is beaming and beautiful—so many perfect teeth.

Breathe. Take it all in. The swirls of music, laughter, and the dizzying sparkle of the room surround me. This place is all gilded edges and soft, golden light. It's over the top, like we're inside a giant Fabergé egg. I keep expecting to hear a director yell *Cut!* and the extras to peel off their fancy clothes. The marble floors are so glossy, I can see up the skirts of the girls three paces ahead of me.

Melody squeezes my hand when I arrive at the bar. She's been my compass since my second day here—a necessity in a place where losing your bearings is not only common, it's anticipated.

"I knew you could do it, Star."

"You mean I didn't pass out?"

"Never," she teases. "Think about all the champagne you'd miss out on."

I laugh, and the knot between my shoulders loosens.

She hands me her glass. "You look like you need this more than I do."

"Is it obvious?"

"Only to me." She links her arm through mine. "Everyone else thinks you're a natural."

I snort. "A natural disaster, maybe."

"Star, you belong here as much as anyone."

A gentleman in a crisp suit brushes past, his cologne leaving a cloud of expensive musk in his wake. He glares at us like he's trying to figure out how we taste. "See you around, Star." His stare lingers a beat too long.

"Ugh." Melody grabs my arm and tugs me away.

"So, this is what it's like to be famous," I say, stumbling in my shoes.

She raises a glass I didn't see her pick up. "To new lives!"

"New lives." The words are strange but exciting on my lips. My stiff, waxy lips.

"This place is wild." I tilt my head and take in the gaudy ceiling.

"Don't worry, it gets wilder," someone calls from the bar. "You should see the bathrooms."

A girl with curly brown hair and a crooked smile is perched on a barstool as if she were born on it. She raises her glass.

"Come have a drink with me." She turns toward us. "Welcome to the freak show."

"Kora," she says as though she were introducing a luxury sports car. "I hope the best middle-of-the-road champagne is good enough for you."

"You haven't been around much this past week," Melody says, her tone playfully accusatory.

Kora grins. "I like to skip the boring stuff and get straight to the party. After all, if you've seen one naming ceremony…"

"I'll have to take your word for it," I blurt out, sharper than I intended.

She arches her brow but remains silent.

Champagne bubbles tickle my nose as I take a sip and try to hide behind the glass.

"So," Melody teases, "tell Star how long you've been a Sister."

Kora chuckles, leans behind her, and grabs another champagne flute from the display. "Too long." She downs it in one smooth motion while I stare at her.

"I'm just teasing." She sets the empty glass on the bar. "Been doing this seven years now."

"That's amazing," I say. "It's been less than a month, and I've thought of running for the exits seven times."

Melody grabs my shoulder as a hush falls over the room, like a sudden drop in barometric pressure. Girls straighten their backs, skirts get yanked down, and bras are adjusted.

An older woman moves past us like a monarch. Her presence is magnetic, attracting all attention her way. Bottled-blonde hair gleams under the lights, and she's a portrait of control—elegant, aloof, and scary as hell.

"Natalia." Kora tilts her head in the woman's direction. "Here comes the speech. Betcha it's still the same."

Natalia addresses the room with a Russian accent, which makes her even scarier. "Congratulations to our newest Sisters," she says, throwing a glance at me. It's not warm but calculated. "You are valuable now. Remember that. You are part of the Family. Some of you will have the honor of serving something far greater than yourselves."

My eyes are pinned on her, mesmerized by the way she holds herself, how the other girls react—some with reverence, others with fear.

"In this business," Natalia trumpets, smooth and confident, "true luxury and success are about more than money. It's about earning your name, building a legacy." Her focus lands on each person, driving her message home. "Loyalty is rewarded handsomely, but never forget the cost of failure."

"She's a force of nature," Melody says.

"A legend," Kora replies. "And she never forgets a face, or a speech."

"So, enjoy tonight," Natalia continues. "But understand who you are now. You've been given your names. Earn them."

Natalia claps fervently, starting a chain reaction of applause that fills the room. She sweeps the space one last time, the queen dismissing her court, then smiles and walks away.

My heart quickens, like the school principal walked by and I'm chewing gum. The enormity of it all presses down on me. This is bigger than I'd imagined.

"Her bark is worse than her bite. But try not to fuck anything up," Kora says with a devilish smirk.

Melody and I giggle.

Kora hands me another glass. This time when she smiles, she exposes a snaggletooth, and it's the first genuine human flaw I've seen here tonight. It endears her to me even more.

"Oh boy, watch out," Melody says.

A living doll waltzes past the bar, straight out of pristine plastic packaging. Her blonde hair is curled into precise waves, makeup bold and immaculate. A pink satin dress sparkles under the lights and hugs every curve of her body. In her hands, she's clutching a little gold statuette.

"That," Kora says, "is Barbie."

Avoiding the spit take, I cough out, "Get the hell out of here."

"Just like her namesake."

She floats past us, her stride bouncing between catwalk and strut. Each movement radiates intentional superiority.

"Whatcha got there, Barbs?" Melody asks, tilting her head.

Barbie turns, her megawatt smile dripping with triumph. "Oh, this little thing?" She holds the statuette higher, letting it catch the light. "Only this quarter's highest earner. Again."

Kora rolls her eyes and mouths, "Bimbo." I bite the inside of my cheek to keep from laughing.

"Something to aspire to," Barbie squawks, with enough edge to sound like a dare. "Tell the new girl, Kora. Tell her all about me, won't you? Mmm-hmm." She flashes another dazzling grin and is swallowed by the crowd.

I mouth, "Wow," as I turn to Melody, who is trying to stifle a laugh.

Kora leans toward us. "Barbie thinks she's a big fish," she says, "but she's really the shrimp they keep around to clean the tank."

Melody and I share a glance, and the three of us collapse into laughter. It's nice—the pressure of the past month, training, and initiation, had been getting to me.

What have I gotten myself into?

Kora reads my expression. "You'll get used to it. Just like the first day of school. A fancy, fucked-up private school."

She nods toward someone at the far end of the room. "Speaking of, there goes Miss Popularity."

I follow Kora's gaze, and my knees lock. A vision in white glides through the crowd, her fiery red hair falling to mid-back. People part for her as if by instinct. It's like spotting a snowy owl in Central Park —you know they exist, but seeing one close up is a treat. And yet there's something familiar about her.

"That's Sage," Kora says matter-of-factly. "She's kind of a bitch, but also my best friend."

"She's not a bitch," Melody chides. "She's just a bit…intense."

A cool tickle starts at the top of my head and works its way down my neck. Captivated, enchanted, awestruck—my internal thesaurus spins, searching for the words, but in the end, what comes out is "Pretty."

Kora chortles. "You noticed that, huh?"

Sage is looking directly at me, and I'm caught, like a raccoon in a trash can. She raises her glass, smiling with the confidence of a woman who knows she was being admired from afar.

"Star?" Melody nudges me. "You there?"

"I'll be right back," I say. Melody says something, but her words don't register. I'm a nervous terrier, and Sage is the squirrel.

She threads through the gathered attendees, and I follow, weaving my way around guests. I catch up to her in the corner of the room, where the lighting is softer, more intimate.

She turns, and her gaze zaps my circuits. My face contorts into something between a smile and a seizure.

"Star," she says, soft and weightless. "Settling in, are you?"

Words try to form, but they jumble on the way out. "I—uh—well…" Real smooth. I sound like a malfunctioning robot.

She laughs. "I know it seems like a lot at the moment." Glancing over at Melody and Kora, she adds, "I trust my friends are being nice to you."

Her proximity is electric. I'm not sure if I want to be her or be with her, or if I even know the difference right now.

"I saw you from across the room," I say, the words sounding like a line from a bad rom-com. "You're—"

"A lot to take in?" she finishes, her lips curving into a sly smile. "I know."

There's no embarrassment, only a disarming directness in the way she fills the space with her contagious confidence.

"I'm glad you came over." She moves closer, touching the pendant around my neck. Her fingers are cool, sending a jolt through me. "That name…Star. It suits you." She lifts it gently from my skin like she's a mystical shaman blessing my soul.

"Hey, Sage, do you have a sec?"

We both turn to her left, and a Sister I don't know is waving with vigor.

"Duty calls." Sage releases my pendant, letting it settle like a promise. "Welcome, truly."

It's overwhelming. The lights, the voices, the teeth. It's like the walls of the room are closing in, compressing the air in my lungs. I drag in a shuddering gasp of breath, trying not to dissolve on the spot. A perfect time for a panic attack.

Desperate for an escape, I glimpse Melody at the bar talking to Kora. Her smile is bright and easy, and it calms me enough to put one foot in front of the other and lurch back toward them, my heart a wild drumbeat in my ears.

A hand lands on my shoulder and startles me, but I recognize the kind eyes, the warm smile, the familiar scent.

"You okay, my dear?" Caron asks, his voice like honey steeped in chamomile, his accent a calming panacea.

Part benevolent king, part trickster, Caron's eyes let you in on his secret, and his smile makes you feel like the only one in the room.

The sharp sting of tears surface, and I blink them back. It's only been a month, but it feels like a lifetime. The memory is fractured.

"Esther, right?" he'd said back in the park.

How he looked at me, with pity.

"You must be freezing."

Why did I go to the diner with him?

Part of me wishes I hadn't. But where else could I have gone?

"I said, are you okay, my dear?" That same velvet voice shakes me from my fog.

A tear rolls partway down my cheek before I wipe it away, hoping it hasn't ruined the makeup we'd spent forty minutes on. "I'm fine. Just a little overwhelmed, that's all."

"I completely understand. That is to be expected." He steps back, his gaze sweeping over me softly. "You look…" I blink at him, waiting for the punchline, but instead, he puts on a smile. "Enjoy yourself. This is a big day for you."

He pats my shoulder with his enormous hand and turns away as Natalia and Sage walk by.

"Are you through scaring my girls?" Caron asks loudly, still smiling.

"You'd do well to give them something to be afraid of," Natalia retorts, unfazed by the jab. "Softness makes them sloppy."

This exchange—it's more than friendly banter. There's a history there, something deeper.

Melody waves me back to the bar. I raise my hand and smirk, already wobbling toward her.

Kora chirps at me. "You all right? Is she everything you thought she'd be?"

"Okay, I deserved that."

"Any veteran advice for her?" Melody asks.

"First month's the toughest. If you survive that, you're golden." Kora winks.

"Your first month," I ask, "were you scared?"

"Like a nun at Chippendales." Kora looks across the room. "But I had Sage. She's like a bulldozer—helps clear the path."

Kora said "survive" as a joke. But looking past her at the sea of perfect, smiling faces, I can't help but wonder how many girls didn't.

Two

The alarm on my phone chimes, jostling me from a dream about a life I don't want to remember—a life still right behind me, waiting to snatch me back if I stumble. A tap brings silence, and a realization.

I'm in my own room.

Sitting up, I take it all in, yawning in the soft morning light filtering through the sheer curtains. *My room.* The words don't seem real. A plush comforter pools at my waist, cool and smooth against my skin. The sofa in the corner is an exact match of one in a Fifth Avenue window, comfortable and inviting, and a long wooden wardrobe takes up half the wall, stuffed with more clothes than I've ever owned in my life.

I haven't had a room of my own since Mom died and they kicked me out of the apartment. *You're an adult now,* they said. *Here's your shit, good luck, and have a nice day.*

My bare feet sink into the thick rug as I walk to the window. Below, Manhattan sprawls, endless and glittering in the low sun. Being a Queens girl, I never spent much time on the Upper East Side, so overlooking Central Park feels illicit. My palm rests against the cool glass, and the memories surface. The bench in the park, the way my back ached from sleeping on wood slats, the constant gnaw of hunger, the *smell.* Once it got in you, it wouldn't go away. It became so bad that CVS started putting those little Vicks inhaler sticks behind plastic because they became currency on the street.

It's amazing how fast you can adjust to ridiculous living conditions when you have no other choice. I've been given a gift—even if it comes with some pretty thick strings wrapped around it—and I can't let it slip away, not after everything that's happened.

How long before they decide I'm not worth it?

That girl from a month ago wouldn't recognize this one: clean hair, clearer skin, and bed linens nicer than the Roosevelt Hotel's. We stayed there when Mom won an all-inclusive Broadway package once, and we saw *The Lion King*—the only show I've ever seen—and ate at Ellen's Stardust Diner, where a waitress sang "A Million Dreams" to me. That girl would want this one to put some weight back on. Living on the street is a surefire crash diet no one wants to talk about. She would think I look like someone who belongs here. I don't. At least, not yet.

The little desk in the corner is gorgeous—overkill for something that only needs to hold my old notebook, but it's okay by me. The striking swirly pattern on the wood probably has some fancy name I don't know, with small metal bits of actual brass my mom would try to polish if she were here to see it. These surroundings let me pretend I have my life in order, even if I'm still writing outside the lines.

My notebook is up there, beckoning. Part of me needs to write about last night—about Sage, the ceremony, the surreal, electric feeling of it all. But coffee comes first. And a moment to figure out who the hell I'm supposed to be.

Screw it. Coffee can wait. I pull out the chair and plop down. The leather exhales as I open my notebook and scribble.

April 7, 2025

My first proper day in the Family, and a first assignment to go along with it, which scares the shit out of me. Do I want them to like me or leave me alone? A little of both, maybe? Melody and I joked while I was in training about what today would feel like. Well, it's terrifying. Kora was right. It's just like a private school. One with a very eclectic curriculum.

In the middle of the paragraph, my phone comes to life with the sound of bubbles. It's Melody's ringtone, given to her in honor of the little seahorse tattoo on her ankle. I'll have to get the full story of it someday.

She's summoning me to breakfast.

THE CAFETERIA IS A BARELY CONTROLLED chaos of chatter, clattering silverware, and the hiss of an espresso machine. It's a five-star hotel restaurant with the energy of a college dining hall.

Melody is near the windows, waving me over with a piece of toast.

"Star!" she calls out. The name is still awkward. "Got you a plate—scrambled eggs and bacon, right?"

"You're the best." The eggs are fluffy and buttery. Nothing like the rubbery disasters I used to get from Gino's deli. He'd give them to me for free, hoping for a reward I never planned on granting. Still, I appreciated the gesture.

"So," she says, "did you sleep at all? I didn't on my first night."

"A little." More truth than not. "But I'm okay."

The din around us blurs into a meaningless hum of designer brand comparisons and boys with "boundary issues." The banality makes my head spin.

"Checked the app yet?" She pulls out her phone. "I'm so excited for you to get your first assignment."

The eggs in my mouth turn to boulders. "What if I'm not ready? What if I screw it up?"

"Hey." Her hand covers mine. "You've been training for almost a month. You know what you're doing." Her lips twirl up. "Right? Unless they ask you to explain derivatives. Then you're totally screwed."

We both crack up. She's been here six months longer than me and is already so polished. Will I ever be like that?

"Morning, ladies." Kora slides into an empty chair at our table. She's holding a massive mug emblazoned with *World's Okayest Sister* and wearing oversized sunglasses.

"Rough night?" I ask.

"The roughest," she groans. "Someone thought it would be fun to keep the party going until dawn. That someone was me, but that's not important." She lifts her sunglasses to reveal bloodshot eyes. "But enough about my poor life choices. How are my favorite newbies feeling?"

Melody takes a huge bite of her toast. "I'm nervous for Star." She makes a classic nervous face, and Kora chuckles.

"That's totally normal," Kora says, taking a long sip from her mug. "First-assignment jitters are a rite of passage. I threw up twice before my first client."

"That's oddly reassuring," I say.

Kora studies us over her sunglasses. "You'll be fine. Better than fine. You've got good instincts, and you've got her." She gestures to Melody with her mug. "She's a natural. And you've got me, naturally."

Melody beams as she chews.

"Remember, you're in control," she continues, "even when Natalia's giving her dramatic speeches. You're in charge of you."

"Hey, Kora!" a tall brunette yells from across the cafeteria, waving frantically. "Massage? I'm totally destroyed."

Kora groans and finishes the rest of her coffee in one gulp.

"And that's my cue," she says, easing out of the chair. "But seriously, breathe. Eat. Don't overthink it." She pats my shoulder as she passes. "You've got this."

As she weaves through the tables, other Sisters call out to her with little waves and inside jokes. Kora responds to each one with her crooked smile. Everyone's favorite Big Sister. She reaches the brunette and starts kneading her shoulders; the girl melts, practically purring under her touch.

"It's reassuring," I admit. "If she can survive this place for seven years and still be normal…"

Melody's toes tap on the floor, and she leans over the table. "So? Did you write any of it down?"

"What?"

"Last night, the ceremony, Barbie. Did you journal it?"

"A bit. It got late, and my hand cramped up…" I'm embarrassed by how dorky I sound. "I will, though. Not just for me. For posterity."

Her eyes light up. "Perfect! You have to let me read it. Unless it's about, you know…" She tweaks her nose. "Sage."

"It's not like that. You should do it too."

"I already do. A few thoughts here and there when I can." She straightens up. "In a month, we should go back and read them. Not lame, right?"

"Very us," I say. Every moment with her is like discovering a new flavor of comfort.

A klaxon blares, piercing the cafeteria din. It's less school chime and more prison alarm—engineered authority. Forks rattle onto plates, and conversations fade away.

Then, as one, the room stands. Chairs scrape back. Phones are raised to check reflections, clothes are smoothed, and last sips of coffee are downed. The casual breakfast becomes a single-file migration toward the exit, a shift from relaxed disarray to controlled efficiency.

"Meeting time," Melody says, already on her feet, grabbing my sleeve. "We can't be late."

She tugs me into the stream of bodies. No one rushes; no one dawdles. The discipline is eerie.

We pass through a corridor and into the auditorium with its chrome, leather, and carafes of cucumber water. The air has no scent, which is both calming and uncanny.

Sage stands at the doorway, arms crossed, sizing up the Sisters like a drill sergeant at reveille. She catches my eye, tips her chin without a smile, then lets her gaze move on. A tiny part of me hopes for one more glance back. It shouldn't matter. But it does.

Inside, rows of seats fill on a gradient of seniority: veterans close to the head table, rookies like me toward the back. We find two empties and settle in, hands folded on the table like good little students. My knee bounces, a nervous habit I cover with a placid look. A trick from the street: Appear calm, be ready to bolt.

Kora stands out immediately. Feet up on the table, rainbow socks like flags, and her sunglasses perched atop her head like little panda ears.

A hush falls over the room as Natalia enters from a side door. She strides purposefully toward the raised platform at the front, her heels clicking against the polished floor. Sage follows a half step behind, hair catching the light like in those shampoo commercials where everything is in slow motion. They move in unison—a superbly choreographed dance of power and elegance.

Sage's blouse is so perfectly tucked into her pencil skirt, it's as if the fabric is afraid to wrinkle. My brain short-circuits, and I scan from the pendant against her collarbone to the arch of her back. She exudes a confidence usually reserved for movie stars. Every detail is committed to memory.

A sharp smack on my knee breaks the trance.

Melody's face twists with amusement. "You look like the cartoon wolf—eyes bulging, tongue rolling out, the whole thing."

Heat rushes to my cheeks as I straighten up. "I do not!"

"You absolutely do—*Ahwoo-Gah!*" She makes the horn sound under her breath while popping her eyes wide.

Mortified but chuckling, I bury my face in my hands and elbow her lightly in the ribs. She snorts.

I force my gaze away from Sage and onto Natalia as she takes center stage. She commands the room without saying a word.

"Good morning, Sisters."

The room sends back a unified "Good morning, Natalia."

Well, that's not creepy at all.

She looks out—taking in the room—and everyone sits up straighter, trying to seem worthy.

"First, let me begin with congratulations to the newest members of the Family," Natalia says, her accent adding flavor to each syllable. "Athena, Lilac, and Star—welcome to your first official day as Sisters. You will each have a Big Sister assigned to you today. They will be your point of contact for any questions you have during your first six months."

A smattering of polite applause ripples through the room. Sinking a little lower in my seat, wishing invisibility were one of the perks of this job, I roll my eyes as Melody mouths, "Big Sister, wow," at me.

"Now, to business," Natalia continues, tapping her tablet. "Project Wakefield has exceeded quarterly projections by 17 percent. Excellent work, Diamond."

A striking blonde in the second row glows.

Natalia scrolls through her notes. "The Rulani portfolio requires additional attention. We've seen a significant decrease in engagement. Jade, please see me after the meeting."

Two rows ahead, a thin girl with ebony skin stiffens, her hand rising to her temple.

"Our goals this week are clear." Her tone sharpens. "We need to finalize arrangements for the Harrington gala and prepare for the Ukrainian delegation arriving on Thursday. Be ready, Denali."

Natalia smiles at a girl in the front row. Her complexion is flawless—a deep, glowing brown, like it's been kissed by sunshine her entire life. Denali puts her thumb up in response and flashes her pearly whites. Great, more perfect teeth.

"The strong serve a legacy. You would all do well to remember that," Natalia says.

"Does she always talk like this?" I ask, but Melody shushes me.

Natalia's smile fades, and her eyes narrow. "A reminder to all about professional standards. Your security badges are not accessories or suggestions. They are requirements."

The sound of uncomfortable shifting in seats.

"Amber," Natalia snaps.

A girl with pink hair freezes, her face draining of color.

"This is the third time. Rules exist for a reason. One more incident, and we will have a serious conversation about your future here."

Amber nods frantically, looking like she wants the floor to swallow her whole.

Note to self: Superglue badge to body if necessary.

"Remember," Natalia continues, "we are only as strong as our weakest link. Each of you is responsible for keeping her house clean."

A peek around the room, and all the Sisters are locked in. The precise blend of halftime rally speech and warden's lecture is impressive.

"Meet your appointments promptly. Dress impeccably. Discretion is key," she says. "You are the Family. Wear your name with honor."

She straightens up. "Bring your best today, Sisters."

She steps back and gestures to Sage, who moves forward gracefully.

"Thank you, Natalia." Sage smiles, and the room softens around her.

"Before we dive into assignments," she says, "let's celebrate our Sisterhood. Today marks five years since Denali joined the Family."

Denali raises her hand and waves to a dash of applause as Sage looks on with a bright smile.

"And tomorrow is Caroline—I mean Kora's birthday," she laughs, glancing across the room.

Kora mock-scowls. "Don't you dare!"

"Too bad," Sage teases. "Twenty-nine looks good on you, babe."

"Start the final countdown!" Kora calls back, grinning with an edge as laughter rustles through the room.

Leaning toward Melody, I whisper, "What does that mean?"

Her stare is part pity, part exasperation. "You age out at thirty."

A blink. "You *what*?"

"Can't be a Sister after that. Natalia's rule." She shoots me the it-is-what-it-is look. "Some stay on as staff. Sisters Emeritus."

"And the others?"

Her shrug is an answer in itself. She turns her attention back to the front of the room.

"And a special mention—Ruby's mother's surgery went well. She's out of the ICU and expected to make a full recovery." Sage glances at the first row.

A dark-haired girl dabs at her face, nodding gratefully as light applause ripples around.

"We're Sisters," Sage reminds everyone. "We celebrate and grieve together; we support each other. Always."

She talks about a weekly get-together, but Melody's words are still in my head: *You age out at thirty.* The Family has an expiration date.

"Your newly booked assignments are being uploaded to your portals as we speak," Sage says, tapping her tablet. "Any questions before we close?"

Silence.

"Then let's make it a great day, Sisters. Meeting adjourned."

The room comes alive with movement and conversation. The girls gather their things, hurriedly checking their phones for new assignments. Melody is already deep into the app.

"Anything there?" I ask her, desperate for a clue about what to do next.

THREE

S played diagonally across my duvet, I'm doodling a cat in my notebook when my right leg goes numb. There's a purple pen in my hand and a red one in my mouth. I exhale, knowing that waking the leg means suffering the vengeance of pins and needles.

A knock on my door. My teeth clamp down on the pen as the sensation kicks in.

"Come in," I say—louder than necessary.

It's the tech guy. I was expecting Melody.

Here I am, akimbo on my bed in a camisole and boy shorts like the Vitruvian Man of oversharers, and yeah, moving means being tasered by my nervous system.

"Oh, hi," I mumble.

Standing in the doorway, he is a walking contradiction—mid-twenties but looks older, clean-cut but disheveled. Tech-bro uniform of khakis and a polo shirt. His fragrance is cedar and citrus, and I like it more than I should.

He stops dead and blinks a few times behind his glasses, his eyes trying to land anywhere but on me while his foot partially closes the door. Impressive.

"Hello. I—Star, right?"

Off to a wonderful start. I spit the red pen onto the bed and smile through my grimace.

"Sorry, my leg's asleep. Well, technically it's waking up again, so..."

"Oh, yeah, I hate that," he shares. "It happens when I've been gaming too long and—"

His words cut off as I rub my leg while flexing my calf.

"Tech, right?" I prop myself up on one elbow, stretching the tingling leg slowly to give him time to avert his line of sight. "They said you'd be coming by."

"Jeremy Tallinder, director of systems," he says. "There's a ticket about you having trouble logging in to the portal?"

"Pretty sure I rage-tapped until it locked me out," I say. The truth is, I'd panicked after three failed passwords and typed *"Not Working!!!"* in the "Help" field.

Jeremy sets a black iPad on my desk and stands as far from the bed as the room allows, which is not far at all. He opens the case with cautious, deliberate movements, folding it into a stand.

"Okay, let's get you reset." He glances up to check if I'm paying attention and musters a half smile. His Adam's apple bobs, and I decide to make this my midday entertainment.

"Don't be shy," I say, rolling myself upright. The duvet drapes off my hip like a toga that's passed out. "I'm not dangerous until after lunch."

Jeremy's immune, or at least too distracted to notice.

"Right." He taps in credentials with the speed of someone who makes very few mistakes in life. "This is your dashboard. If you ever get locked out, tap 'Need Help'—it pings me directly," he says, turning the iPad around. "See? You're back in."

Leaning in to grab the tablet puts our heads closer. A trace of sweat and cologne drifts up from under his shirt. Frozen in place, it's possible he's stopped breathing.

"So, how do I check my next assignment?" My finger hovers over the sparkly "Inbox" icon. The Family's brand aesthetic bleeds through everything—pastels, gold foils, and typography that's one stolen font away from a luxury makeup campaign.

"Good question." Jeremy regains his stride. "Assignments post at 10 a.m. daily, but you can always check the pre-briefs for a heads-up."

His hand lands with deliberate care on the bezel, finger floating over the screen in an obvious effort not to touch me. "And here," he continues, "you can see your Big Sister info, rules, cafeteria schedule, and wellness report."

Nodding, I pretend to digest this, but mostly I study his face as he cycles through the menus. He's clearly run through this tutorial a thousand times. How many Sisters has he done this for? I picture him in every room: nervous, earnest, and trying not to stare. The proverbial rooster in the henhouse, but he doesn't seem to care.

"Do you ever get a day off?"

"Technically Wednesdays," he says, "but no one really respects the 'off' part."

Standing there with his hands clasped awkwardly, he looks as though he's posing for his LinkedIn headshot. "Any other questions?"

I shake my head. "Think you covered it. But if I lock myself out again, you'll be the first to know."

He smiles—an honest-to-god, dimpled smile—as if this is the best thing anyone's said to him all week. It almost makes me want to mess up my password tomorrow, just to see it again.

"Great, so…ping if you need me. That's what I'm here for."

Jeremy pivots toward the door and walks directly into the edge. The thud is soft but unmistakable.

My lips press together to stifle a giggle. He offers a quick, awkward bow, mutters, "Sorry," and shuffles out. The door closes with a breathy little sigh that makes me like him even more.

A WALK around the building this afternoon is a chance to familiarize myself with the layout. During training, they kept us penned in like veal, but this place is massive. Five floors of over-the-top opulence and layouts so confusing, I got lost twice trying to find the stairs. The top floor is executive row and Caron's office, where I signed my Family contract. Below that, the floor with the cafeteria, auditorium, and gym—some hotels aren't this full-featured. The lowest is tech and maintenance, and the two in between are the residence floors where the Sisters live. Everyone calls them "the dorms," which would be fitting if dorms had marble floors, Persian rugs, and crystal chandeliers worth more than my entire ancestry.

There's something else too. An odd institutional vibe that makes my skin crawl. It's like a sorority house designed by someone who's only seen sororities in movies—prison movies.

Rounding the corner, I nearly collide with a tiny human cannonball. A mop of black hair with bleached ends surrounds her face like a halo.

"Star!" she exclaims with breathless enthusiasm.

Aura. I remember seeing her in training. She's smaller up close, barely passing my shoulders, but her presence fills the hallway.

"It's your first day—that's so exciting!" Her accent has a warm Latina lilt.

"It is!"

"I'm headed to Kora's yoga class. You going?"

"Maybe next time? Have fun, though."

"Fun is my middle name," she quips, tapping her temple with a wink. "Actually, it's Marisol, but whatever." She gives me a quick hug—surprisingly strong for someone so tiny—then spins away toward the gym.

Continuing down the hall, I arrive at Melody's room and plant three quick raps on her door. As my hand falls away, the little seahorse sticker in the corner catches my eye—so shiny. So her.

"*Entrez!*" a fake snooty French accent calls out, dissolving into giggles before I can turn the handle.

The door opens, and she's standing in the middle of her room, surrounded by a jumble of clothes and makeup. Her hair is banana-clipped on top of her head, and she's wearing three different shades of eyeshadow.

"What happened?" Stepping over a pile of shoes, I rescue a crumpled silk blouse from the floor. "It's like a bomb went off in Sephora, and then a second one hit Saks."

There's a mascara wand in one of her hands and an eyeliner in the other, like a makeup artist gone rogue. Her emerald eyes sparkle under the haphazard layers of shadow.

"I need to be perfect," she says, spinning back to her vanity mirror. "I have an important client tonight."

"The Keller guy?" The blouse falls from my grip, and I teeter on the edge of the bed.

She tosses the makeup onto her already cluttered vanity and grabs her tablet, tapping frantically at the screen before turning it toward me.

"Some big shot at a high-class bank," she says. The photo shows a professional headshot of a middle-aged man with salt-and-pepper hair and a practiced smile. Richard Keller. There's a rating alongside: 4.6 stars. "Kora says he's harmless and low ick."

"That doesn't sound so bad."

"I know, right?" She turns to her mirror and applies more eyeshadow. "One review said he tips well and isn't too handsy."

A deep green dress in her pile catches my attention. I pick it up and hand it to her. "First, you'll wear this—it matches your eyes."

"What about you?" She takes it and holds it against herself. "Did you check your portal yet?"

The question sends a jolt of panic through me. With Jeremy's visit and everything else, I hadn't thought to.

I open the app. When the screen loads, my face goes slack. "What is it?" she asks.

On the screen, under "Big Sister," is a picture of Sage. I can't process this right now.

Melody snatches the phone from my hand.

"Holy shit. Sage is your Big Sister?"

My legs give out, sending me collapsing back onto her bed, where an eyeliner pencil jabs me in the thigh.

"Gah, sorry about that." She grabs it and tosses it aside. "That's great, isn't it?"

"Great? I don't think so." I stand back up and pace the room, crunching various makeup items beneath my feet. "Sorry, sorry," I mutter, kicking a crushed palette aside.

I grab the phone back from her, Sage's sublime face staring at me. There's a blinking message icon next to her name.

"I can't do this," I blurt out, tossing the phone onto the bed like it's on fire. "She's going to hate me and think I'm an idiot. She'll tell Natalia I'm incompetent, and they'll kick me out. I'll be back on that park bench—"

"Star!" She grabs my arms, forcing me to stop pacing. "Breathe."

I suck in a ragged breath and meet her eyeline.

"This is a good thing," she says like she's explaining to a child. "Sage is like queen bee around here. If she's your Big Sister, that means they see something in you."

"Or they're setting me up to fail." I scrub my hands across my face. "Maybe it's some kind of sick test to watch me crash and burn."

Melody rolls her eyes. "Now you're being ridiculous."

"Am I, though? You saw how she looked at me. Like she was sizing me up."

"No, but I did see how *you* looked at *her*," she counters. "Like she was chocolate cake, and you were on a diet."

My face burns hot. "That's not—I didn't—"

"You totally did," she chuckles and sits back down at her vanity. "And now you can spend quality time with her. Other Sisters would kill for that."

"That's easy for you to say. You have serotonin on legs for your Big Sister."

"Don't talk about Kora like that," she snorts.

"Can I ask for a swap?" I let myself fall backward onto her bed, arm crossing my face like a distressed Southern belle.

Melody clicks her tongue, sorting through her makeup bag. "No way. Besides, this is perfect for you."

"Perfect how? Disaster? Humiliation?"

"Opportunity," she says, her face serious. "Look, Star, you've been practically orbiting around her since the ceremony. Now you have a legitimate reason to talk."

"That's the problem. What am I supposed to say? 'Hi, I'm your new project. Please don't notice how I can't form two coherent sentences when you're in the room'?"

"You're catastrophizing." She pats my knee. "Have you read her message?"

Stretching over, I pick up the phone, my finger hovering above the blinking icon. Melody leans in like she's observing me defuse a bomb. With a final surrender, my finger falls.

Dear Star,
I wanted to tell you how excited I am to be your Big Sister. I know there is something special about you. Your uniqueness is your greatest asset. I remember how overwhelming the first days can be. I want you to know that you belong here.
Please reach out with questions. Even the things you're embarrassed to say out loud. I'm sure I've felt them too.
With warmth and sisterly affection,
Sage

"What does it say?" she asks.

My throat clamps shut. I hand her the phone, turning away so she won't see my face.

"Oh, Star, this is beautiful."

Tears come quickly without permission. My face crumples, and I cover my mouth, trying to force them back, but they refuse.

"Hey, hey," she coos. "What's wrong? This is a good thing."

I shake my head. These words of kindness shatter me more than any cruelty ever could. "She doesn't know me. How can she say these things?"

Melody slides onto the bed beside me, tucking one leg beneath her, the seahorse tattoo on her ankle peeking out from under her pink sock. It's simple and beautiful, with delicate lines that curve and flow. She notices me staring at it.

"You want to hear a story?" She pulls her sock down.

I nod, grateful for the distraction. I'd listen to her read the instructions off a shampoo bottle right now.

"Well, in my first year at The New School, some fellow thespian ladies and I had the idea to get matching tattoos. We were going to get little narwhals, and—"

"Nar—what?"

"Narwhal. It's the school mascot. A toothed whale with a large tusk?" She extends her hand out from her nose.

I have no idea what she's talking about, but I smile. "Okay."

"Anyway, they were set on the matching narwhals, and I'm scared of needles." She pokes my thigh for effect. "But I was more scared of being left out. So I went with them to this sketchy place in the East Village, sweating bullets the whole time."

"But you didn't get a nar-whole," I butcher the word.

"I chickened out at the last minute. Couldn't bring myself to get the same thing as them. The artist had this flash sheet with other sea creatures, and this little guy just spoke to me." She smiles down at it. "The others were pissed. Said I ruined the whole point of matching tattoos."

"Sounds awful."

"At the time, it was. But then something weird happened. I loved it more than I ever would that mascot. It became a reminder that I didn't have to be like them."

She runs her finger over the tattoo. "I chose a seahorse because it doesn't swim like other fish. They're built differently, move differently—they're special. They use their tails to anchor themselves when the water gets rough."

Her eyes shine as they flick over to me. "Strong tails in stormy waters."

The metaphor isn't lost on me. My finger traces the tiny seahorse, feeling the raised lines of ink under her skin.

"I call him Silly Love," she says.

"Silly Love?"

"Yeah." A shadow crosses her face. "Because it's the only type of love I've ever had, I guess. The kind that feels fun for a while but doesn't last." She shrugs, but the hurt beneath the gesture comes through. "Silly, but not the real thing."

Silence hangs between us for a moment as her words settle. "That's…kind of profound."

"Right?" She wipes my cheek.

I don't deserve her.

WRITING in my notebook passes the time, but the actual show is Melody wrestling her reflection into submission. She's been standing there for at least thirty minutes, turning side to side, spreading the green dress over her hips, tugging at the neckline as if desperation might magically change its shape. Her hair's styled in loose, hopeful curls—the kind you get from a curling iron and prayers. She keeps fussing with the ends, trying to make them fall *just right*.

"You look amazing," I repeat for the fifth time. It's the truth, but also an experiment. Can positive reinforcement penetrate her thick Midwestern skull? So far: inconclusive.

"I look like a Muppet."

"Kermit would be offended. Anyway, it's much more Ninja Turtle, don't ya think?"

She throws her lip gloss. I duck, but it almost hits me. That's talent.

Setting the notebook aside, I scoot closer and catch her wrist. "Melody, please. Relax."

"I want to look sexy, you know?"

Her phone buzzes on the vanity and she picks it up, frowning. "Just spam."

Before she can end the call, I snatch the phone from her hand, hit Accept, and channel my best sultry starlet voice. "Penny's Pleasure Palace, what's your pleasure?"

Melody's jaw drops, and I cover the mic, trying not to crack up. A moment passes, and they hang up.

"Crap. I wanted to keep going."

Melody takes her phone back and giggles. "You're pretty good at that. Maybe you should have joined the phone-sex family instead."

"It should be part of the app."

We both laugh, and the tension breaks.

Pushing her boobs out, she turns to me. "Too much cleavage?"

"There's no such thing. But if it helps, I can Sharpie on a chest tattoo. How about an actual horse this time? Really lean into the theme."

She grins and elbows me. A brief war of nudges breaks out, ending only when her phone buzzes again and she grabs it like it owes her money.

"It's time. Car's here."

Pulling her into a hug, I crush her dress a little and murmur against her hair. "You'll be fine. You're a pro."

"Not really." She hugs me back, trembling slightly.

"Then fake it. These guys are used to that, right?"

A smile, but she doesn't let go of me.

"Promise we'll always be here for each other?" She raises her pinkie like we're eight years old and not professional escorts.

Without hesitation, I hook our pinkies together. "Always."

"Even if I accidentally seduce the chef tonight and run off to France?"

"Especially then."

She grabs her purse, checks her makeup one last time, and starts the metamorphosis—shoulders back, chin up, mouth set in a smile that could sell milk to cows. This is how an actor becomes her character. It's mesmerizing.

On the way to the elevator, Melody walks like she's always belonged here. Maybe she has. Maybe they all have.

THE NIGHT STRETCHES as thin as my patience. The clock on my desk says 12:45 a.m., but the world outside is so silent it doesn't matter. My room is lit only by the soft glow of the desk lamp, and the notebook in front of me is half-filled with cats in bow ties and a single repeated phrase:

She's fine. She's fine. She's fine.

Each time I write it, my hand grows less certain.

The dorm is so quiet that the air-conditioning sounds loud. Down the corridor, someone sneezes, a mug clinks, and muffled laughter floats through the air. It's soothing yet revealing how little the world cares if I'm sitting here, worrying.

I write something to pass the time:

What Melody is doing, sorted by likelihood:
Having mind-blowing, consensual sex.
Dissociating and counting ceiling tiles.
Sleeping, covered in room service fries.

Why does caring about someone feel like I'm inching toward the edge where something I have turns into something I could lose?

One more check of my phone. Nothing. Flipping to a new page in the notebook, I write a letter I'll never send.

Dear Melody,
Do you remember my first week here? You promised you'd
never let them eat me alive, even if they started nibbling at
my ankles. If I could be anything to you, I'd be the person
who made you feel safe, not just the one who made you laugh.
I wish I knew how to be that.
Love, Star

The pen is still on the paper when the door handle clicks and the hall light floods the doorway.

Melody stands there—mascara smudged and hair wild, lips parted in a gentle O of surprise, like she forgot this isn't her room. For a suspended moment, she stares at me like she's not sure whether to laugh or cry.

So she does both—and stumbles into the room.

There's no script for this, only instinct.

Jumping up, I nearly take the chair with me and catch her before she falls.

"Hey, hey." I steer her blindly toward the bed. "I've got you."

We collapse onto the comforter, legs tangled, half on and half off. The dress she spent two hours perfecting is smeared with fingerprints and memories; her clutch slips from her hand and plops to the floor, spilling its contents—lipstick, a room key, a crumpled napkin. A thick envelope slides free, landing on the floor with a thwap.

She shakes, face hidden in my shoulder, crying harder now that it's safe to do so. The sound is raw and beautiful.

Rocking her, I shush her with nonsense words, combing my fingers through her hair. Anything to calm her down. Questions can wait.

When the storm eases, it leaves her as empty as a spent wave. She rolls onto her back, wiping her cheeks with both hands. Makeup streaks her palms like war paint. I want to tell her she's still flawless.

"Are you okay?"

Her laugh is raw, punched-through. "I am." She sits up straight, grabs my hands, and exhales. "That was so crazy."

"What happened?"

"He was lonely. But like, professionally lonely? He wanted to talk about his kids and how he misses his dog. We sat on that stupid hotel bed and watched Animal Planet for like two hours."

"For real?"

"And we cried—like, from the gut. We held each other and let everything out."

"Oh, so, nothing weird, then?"

She chuckles, kicks her heels off, and snuggles closer.

"That's the thing. It wasn't weird at all. It was like the most natural thing ever. Like, raw human contact, you know? I'm thinking of dropping my therapist and seeing him again."

I pull her to me, letting her head fall against my shoulder. I'm happy.

"Star?"

"Yes," I say as endearingly as I can.

"Could I stay with you? I don't want to be alone tonight."

"I don't know," I joke. "Can you behave yourself?"

She playfully slaps my arm. "Goof."

A contented smile crosses my face as she settles against me, her breathing already slowing toward sleep. It's been so long since I've had someone to worry about. I pull the duvet over us both and listen to her drift away.

Will I ever have someone waiting up for me like this? Someone who'll catch me when I stumble through the door?

Four

Am I in an aquarium?

The sound of bubbles chases away a dream, and I groan, flailing for the phone like it's personally betrayed me. The screen says 9:09 a.m., and my mind is filled with words inappropriate for Sunday school.

"Hello?" My voice is pure gravel.

"Where are you, snoozy?" Melody's way-too-cheerful tone chirps in my ear. "We're in the cafeteria. Everyone's here."

A mumble that sounds vaguely like "Five minutes," but could also be whale song, leaves my mouth. Tossing the phone down, I drag myself out of bed. She must have woken up and left early, leaving me unconscious and snoring.

"Shit, shit, shit." My vocabulary is on point this morning as I grab the clothes nearest me—a faded blue T-shirt and black leggings. No makeup. Rinse of mouthwash. Lip balm swipe. Slides on. Go time.

They spot me skidding into the cafeteria like a cartoon character and wave me over. Kora, Melody, and Aura, plus surprise guest Sage, hair done up in chopsticks, sipping herbal tea like it's sacred.

"Hey! You've rejoined the living," Kora calls, wielding a spoonful of Greek yogurt like a magic wand. "Cute bedhead, Star."

"At least she made it here." Sage smirks at Kora. "Remember your first week? I had to physically drag you out of bed."

Kora blushes as laughter flitters around the table.

My eyes land on the nearest seat, but Aura slides her tray over with practiced triumph, as if she's been saving this move all morning. The only option is next to Melody and directly across from Sage.

Oh good. A spotlight.

When I drop into the seat, what I'm aiming for is *cool*. What I deliver is *hostage video*.

Melody grabs my arm like it's a prized petunia. "Can I tell y'all how sweet this girl was to me last night?"

My cheeks overheat.

"I was so wrecked when I got in, I forgot my own name, but this girl? She held me and let me cry 'til I fell asleep in her arms." She sighs. "Have you ever heard of anything more tender?" Her head lands on my shoulder.

Full-on clown cheeks. The chorus of "Awws" crashes over me like a wave. I peek at Sage, who's smiling—crinkled-eyes, adorable smiling—and it's possible I may spontaneously combust.

I grab the coffeepot, with dignity already a memory. "You all would've done the same."

Kora musses my already tragic hair. "You've got Big Sister energy. It's giving Hallmark."

Coffee sloshes into my mug, my hand trembling. My obituary will probably leave out my edgy side.

"Be careful, though. This place eats sweet girls for breakfast," Kora adds.

"You don't have to scare the girl before her first date," Melody says.

"Yeah, well," Kora chides, "I'm just saying, coddling doesn't help you survive."

An awkward chuckle trickles across the table before Aura changes the subject.

"So, Mel." She leans forward. "After the crying...did you?" She waggles her eyebrows.

Sage cuts in. "Aura, what did we say about boundaries?"

"Aight," Aura says, popping a grape into her mouth.

"Star." Sage turns to me. "We asked you here to give you some news."

"News?"

"You've been assigned," Melody says, practically vibrating. "Your first client!"

The coffee nearly comes back out. "What?! Already?"

She squeals and grabs my arm. "Isn't it exciting? You're official now."

"Who is it?" I try to sound like I'm not going to puke or cry—or both.

Sage slides her phone across the table. On-screen: a man in his late thirties, clean-cut, expensive haircut. "Gideon Telluride. He's a regular client. Very respectful. Very generous."

"What do I have to do?"

"Dinner, Le Bernadin. He's hosting investors from Macau and wants someone charming on his arm."

"I'm not charming."

"You're great. I recommended you," Sage says.

I blink, caught somewhere between flattered and dumbfounded. "You did?"

"I think you'll be perfect. And he'll be good for you—for your first time."

The way she says "first time" makes my skin go electric. I gulp some orange juice to stay conscious.

"The dinner's tomorrow night. The formal briefing is this afternoon. We wanted to give you time to process."

"Thanks, I'll be ready." Then, under my breath, "I hope."

"So." Aura stabs her fruit cup with unnecessary force. "Did you guys see Step-Sister's latest rant? She's going off about how 'they don't take your name, they take your memories too.'" She rolls her eyes dramatically. "Like, hello? I still remember the Vuitton in my closet."

My body freezes mid-sip. "Step-Sister?"

Kora leans in. "Some ex-Sister with a blog. Total doomsday energy. She thinks we're all brainwashed clones in some elite sex cult."

"She's butthurt," Aura continues, popping a grape into her mouth. "Says we're all being used as pawns in some game we don't understand." She snorts. "Like, whatever. I understand my bank account just fine."

I set my mug down. "So...she was here? In the Family?"

"Yep," Kora says. "And now she thinks she's gonna take it down from behind a keyboard."

"But what if—"

"Trust me," Sage interrupts, calm and certain. "Step-Sister is a cautionary tale, nothing more. Someone who couldn't adapt, couldn't evolve. The Family gave her every opportunity."

"You know who she is?" I ask.

Sage's smile tightens almost imperceptibly. "No. But she's clearly someone who couldn't handle the life. You see for yourself how everyone is treated here. She wants attention. Best not to give it to her."

"The saddest part," Kora adds, "is that she thinks she's a hero. Saving us from ourselves." She laughs, but there's something brittle in it.

"How do you know it's all lies?"

Four pairs of eyes lock onto me.

"I mean," I backpedal, "it just seems smart to know what your enemies are saying, right?"

Melody squeezes my arm. "Don't waste your energy. It's some sad girl in her mom's basement making stuff up."

"Besides," Sage says, her gaze lingering on me, "we have more important things to focus on. Like getting you ready for your first client."

The conversation shifts. They talk about outfits, shoes, and the bathrooms at Le Bernadin.

But the echo of the girl who left lingers. A girl who's gone but won't stop writing.

THE DAILY MEETING DISMISSES, and Sisters scatter like marbles across the polished floor. I'm halfway through the door when Piper—my dorm neighbor with the impossibly magnificent eyebrows—catches my elbow.

"Surviving so far?" she asks.

"Barely. Still feel like I'm wearing someone else's skin."

She snickers. "Three weeks in, you'll forget you ever lived anywhere else."

That's what I'm afraid of.

We part with a meaningless promise to grab coffee soon. I sink into an armchair near the bookshelf and stare out at the jagged skyline. Did I make the right choice? The streets down there had teeth, but at least I knew their bite.

Phone in my hand, I open an incognito browser and load the Step-Sister blog.

Blog Entry #38

The Hollow Girls

Here's the truth about the Family. You're not an escort; you're a toy molded to their specifications.

They start with your name. A new one, sleeker, sexier, and different enough from your real one that you start forgetting who you were.

Then, a wardrobe. A schedule. A philosophy. You think it's liberation. But it's replacement. Piece by piece, they strip you down. Your history. Your voice. Your instincts. And in their place, they build something beautiful and hollow.

The rules come next. An app that tracks your time, clients, and mood. Constant check-ins and coaching. Reviews. Notifications. Your value is measured in scores, seduction, and silence. Asking questions is a bad look. Having boundaries is "bad for business." Saying no makes you a problem.

I've seen brilliant, vibrant women become soft-eyed mannequins. Saw them laugh at jokes they didn't understand and fawn over men they despised, pretending that this was the dream.

If you're already inside, I'm not judging you. I was you. But know this: You are not crazy for feeling like something's wrong. You're waking up.

Stay sharp, Stay free.

—Your Step-Sister

The words glow on the screen. My thumb hovers, not scrolling, not moving.

This morning's coffee crawls back up my throat.

I lower the phone to my lap, but the words remain, burned into my vision. It's as if someone reached into my head and pulled out the half-formed doubts I've been pushing away since arriving.

"This is stupid," I say out loud. It's just some pissed-off girl who didn't make the cut.

But my hands are shaking.

Kora's dismissal at breakfast—a casual wave of her hand.

And Sage. When Aura brought it up, something flashed across her face for a second. Anger, but also…fear? She shut the conversation down so fast.

The phone is in my hand again, my thumb scrolling back through the post.

Your value is measured in scores, seduction, and silence.

Is that what's happening to me? To Melody? Are we those "soft-eyed mannequins" she describes?

At the ceremony, Sage and Kora were so natural, working the room. My clumsy attempt to mimic them—was that being hollow? Or trying to fit in?

The worst part is the truth: A month here has been more like home than anywhere since Mom died. Sleeping in a real bed and eating real food. People know my name—well, my new name.

The browser window vanishes. A second later, I open it again to read the last lines one more time.

You are not crazy for feeling like something's wrong.

That's the thing. Nothing feels wrong. Everything's better. Easier. Like I have a place to be.

Unless this is exactly what they want.

Great, now a strange blog is twisting my thoughts.

The phone flips from my hand and lands in my lap with a soft flop. I press the heels of my hands against my eyes until stars burst behind them—real ones, not me.

Maybe this is bullshit. Maybe the Family is genuinely what Caron promised: a second chance for girls like me.

Maybe Sage knows something she's not telling us.

I'm going to figure out which.

THE DOOR to Sage's room is ajar. A soft push on it, and I step inside. She's on her bed, laptop sitting on a fortress of pillows. Her room is immaculate, of course, straight out of a magazine, and it carries a scent of citrus and fresh rain.

"Hey, little Sister," she says, barely looking up. "Look at you, all settled in. You wear it better every day."

"Thanks. I wanted to ask you something." A tight-lipped smile is the most I can manage.

"What's up?"

"Why is the Step-Sister blog so taboo?"

She takes her glasses off and puts them on the side table, then pats the bed beside her. An invitation or a command—impossible to tell. I sit, and she exhales loudly. "Star, listen to me. Nothing good comes from chasing conspiracy theories on the internet. That blog is poison."

"But—"

"No buts. Do you think you're the first Sister to wonder about that garbage? It's designed to do one thing: make you miserable with the best life you've ever had. It wants to turn your champagne into vinegar. Don't let it."

"But there's truth in it. The way she describes how they change your name and—"

"Every organization has initiation rituals," Sage interrupts. "College sororities, Wall Street firms, even Starbucks baristas get new names on their tags. That doesn't make us a cult."

Her tone is light, but something's hiding underneath it—something tense.

"I just don't know what to believe."

She scoots closer and takes my hand. Her palm is warm, and her manicure is impeccable.

"There was a Sister a couple of years ago. A friend. Smart, beautiful, could charm the pants off anyone—literally and figuratively."

My back straightens. "Yeah?"

"She believed the conspiracy theories too. Became obsessed with them." Sage's fingers trace patterns on my palm. "Started asking questions, poking around in places she shouldn't. She'd sneak into offices after hours, copy files, listen in on private conversations."

"What was she looking for?"

"Proof, I guess. That we were all secretly evil." Sage shakes her head. "She'd corner other Sisters, demanding to know if they felt 'controlled' or 'manipulated.' Started seeing shadows where there weren't any."

"Did she find anything?"

"What she found," Sage says carefully, "was that paranoia is a sickness. She lost friends, and clients started complaining. Natalia warned her, but she wouldn't stop."

"What happened to her?" I press.

Sage studies my face, moving her eyes between mine. "She left. Walked away from it all—the safety, the security, everything we built here."

"And then what?"

Her eyes keep probing, like she's analyzing me, waiting to see if I'll flinch. The patterns she was making on my hand stop.

"Something terrible," she whispers.

An icy ripple starts at the base of my neck. "That's it? That's all you're going to say?"

"What more do you want, Star? This isn't a game. The Family gives you everything. It asks for one thing in return: loyalty. You question that, and you're not just putting yourself at risk. You're putting *all* of us at risk.

"Think about it," she says, softer now. "Do you want to be the girl who couldn't let it go? The one who let her curiosity ruin it all?"

Silence. I can't answer. Because the truth is, I *do* want to know. I want to peel back the layers of this place until I find what's underneath. Is that being too curious?

"You're smart, Star. Don't waste your energy on nonsense."

A protest dies on my lips as she cuts me off with a big smile.

"Come on, let's go get some Froyo—my treat." She jumps up from the bed. "They have a new boysenberry I've been dying to try."

Her smile does me in. I nod, her hand closing around mine to pull me up. We're off to the yogurt shop. The conversation is officially over, and Sage is offering a sweet, cold bribe to make me forget. For now, I'll take it.

But I won't stop asking questions.

ESTHER
HOLLAND

"Esther, right?" the man said as he sat next to her on the derelict park bench. He wore a wool coat with a scarf draped elegantly around his neck. "I've seen you here a few times."

He was an older man with a warm, fatherly voice that carried a European accent, though Esther had no idea from where. She'd noticed him feeding squirrels the past few days but thought nothing of it. He appeared relatively harmless, but she couldn't be certain. She pulled her knees close to her chest and turned aside, breath visible in the air. She nodded once.

"Caron." He extended his hand.

She didn't take it.

"You must be freezing," he said, and pulled his hand back. "How long have you been out here?"

Esther side-eyed him with guarded suspicion. "I'm fine."

"Fine," Caron repeated. He pointed to the bruises on her arms, the dark marks splotching her pale skin. Some were fresh—angry and swollen—while others had faded to sickly green shadows. "Those don't look fine to me."

"I told you." She pulled her sleeves down. "I'm fine."

"I'm sure you are," he replied, "but how about a warm meal? Surely you would enjoy that."

His eyes appraised her—a clinical assessment that made her want to disappear. She wrapped her legs tighter, and the oversized jeans she'd stolen from the back of the Goodwill slid down her hips, the worn denim catching on a hip bone that felt sharp enough to cut through the fabric. Her cheeks grew hotter as she hitched them back up. He was taking inventory, she knew: the hollows beneath her cheekbones, the limp, greasy hair, the wrists that looked fragile enough to snap. She was a ghost of the person she used to be, haunting a park bench in someone else's clothes.

Esther hesitated, weighing the proposal, her hunger winning over her reluctance. She couldn't remember the last time someone had offered her anything without expecting something in return. She held her paper notebook against her knees like a shield.

"Just a meal," Caron said. "No strings."

She glared and tried to read him, but she was *so hungry*. Against her better judgment, she nodded.

He stood and offered his hand again. "There's a diner a few blocks down. It's not fancy, but I promise the coffee is hot, and the pie's not terrible." He waited, arm outstretched, palm up.

Esther stared at it like it might disappear, then slipped her thin, chapped fingers into his. The warmth—surprising and steady—startled her.

"Friends?" he offered with a lilt. "For now?"

Esther eyed him nervously and nodded.

They walked in silence, Caron matching Esther's uneven pace, never rushing. She kept one eye on the passing cars and the other on the man beside her. Every thirty steps or so, she waited for the catch: the question, the hook, the price. When it didn't come, unease crawled up her skin.

The diner was nearly empty, bathed in a weathered yellow light that made the cracked vinyl seats seem jaundiced and tired. He sat her at a booth, went to the counter, and returned with a mug of coffee. She cupped her hands around the warmth, her gratitude so fierce she had to fight to keep it off her face. Esther stared at the silverware, the napkin, the table itself, like they were all part of an elaborate trick. She studied Caron carefully, waiting for the other shoe to drop.

"Here we are," Caron said, and as if on cue, an older waitress slid a plate before her. The sudden, rich smell of bacon and fried potatoes made Esther's breath catch. *Proper food.*

"Eat," he urged, an order. The waitress glanced subtly at him before stepping away.

Esther pushed her notebook aside and picked up her fork, the metal cool in her hand. The first bite was tentative, testing. The second, ravenous. Caron observed and waited.

"What do you want?" she asked.

"Conversation," he replied, tearing off a piece of hash brown and popping it into his mouth. "I'd like to know about you, if you're willing."

Esther's fork paused midair. She'd heard that line before. She'd heard them all before.

"Why?"

"Maybe I see a bit of someone in you. Maybe I want to help."

She shook her head, scooping a forkful of eggs. "I don't need help."

"Then tell me what you do need."

Esther glanced at the plate. She took another bite, buying time. As the warmth spread through her, the defenses she'd spent so long building up shifted uncomfortably.

"I need…" She stopped, catching herself. She didn't know this man or what he wanted. Didn't understand why she was sitting there. She should leave, should—

But where?

Esther sighed. "I need a place to stay."

"And your family?"

The question stung. A lump rose in her throat. "I don't have one anymore."

"Anymore?"

Esther nodded reluctantly. "My father left us, my sister ran away, then my mom got sick and…yeah, it's just me now."

Caron wore an expression that said he'd heard a thousand stories like hers, but his heart still broke every time. "That's a lot for a young girl to handle."

"I'm not that young."

"I suppose you're right," he said with a gentle smile. "Certainly old enough to make your own decisions."

Esther picked at the eggs. "You still didn't say why you're talking to me."

"I've spent a long time building something." He sipped his coffee. "Some might call it unconventional, but I call it a family."

Esther froze. There it was. The catch. The hook she'd been

waiting for. That word from a stranger's mouth always meant something twisted.

"What kind of family?"

"One where you'll be important. Where you'll belong."

She let out a sarcastic laugh. "I'm not important."

"Also, one where you won't have to be alone anymore, Esther."

She swallowed hard, her breath catching.

"I can offer you a place to sleep tonight. A proper bed. Clean sheets." He tapped a finger against his coffee cup. "And a full breakfast in the morning. Then we can talk about everything."

She stared at the half-eaten plate before her. The food sat heavy in her belly as her mind deconstructed the offer. *Don't take it. Don't be stupid.* But the same thought kept circling back: Where else could she go?

"No strings?" she asked, hating how weak she sounded.

"No strings," he confirmed. "Just sleep, food, talk."

Something about him made her want to believe. It wasn't only desperation, but something in the way he looked at her, something she couldn't quite place.

"I sleep alone, right?" She raised her gaze to meet his.

His belly laugh shook the table. "Yes, Esther. Alone. Your own room."

"Okay," she said, and bit off a piece of bacon.

When she was finished, he left money on the table—too much, she noticed—and guided her outside. A sleek black car waited at the curb. Esther hesitated.

"It's all right." He gestured toward the door. "I promise."

She slid into the seat, the leather cool against her skin. Every nerve screamed at her to run, but she forced herself to stay still. Caron settled beside her—close enough to claim her, far enough to let her breathe. The car pulled into traffic, and there was no turning back.

"Where are we going?" she asked.

"Upper East Side. The Family has a place there."

"This family of yours," Esther said, trying to sound casual. "What is it? Some kind of cult?"

Caron laughed with a broad smile. "No, not a cult. Though I

suppose some might see it that way. We'll talk more in the morning. For now, let yourself relax."

Esther pressed her forehead against the cool glass, city lights smearing into ribbons as they passed. Her stomach, though finally full, twisted with doubt. She'd need to stay alert tonight—ready to run if necessary. She stole a glance at his profile, the sharpness of his jawline and the clasp of his hands. Something in her whispered that this man might be different from the others who'd made her promises. How many poor decisions had led her here? And why did this one—potentially the worst—feel right?

The car stopped in front of a stately glass building across from Central Park, and Esther stood at a crossroads. Everything about this screamed danger, and yet...

"Just one night," she said, more for herself than him.

Caron nodded. "Just one night."

THE ELEVATOR DOOR retracted to reveal a corridor bathed in bright, crisp light. Esther followed Caron, her filthy sneakers leaving dirt on the gleaming marble. The walls were a rich cream, adorned with tasteful artwork.

Stopping at a door, Caron slid a key card into the lock. "This will be your room for tonight."

Esther stepped inside, and her breath stuck in her lungs.

The space wasn't big, but it was made to order. A queen-size bed with a fluffy white comforter and a dozen pillows dominated one wall. Floor-to-ceiling windows showcased Manhattan's skyline on another. The comforting scent of fresh linen swirled around her as she suppressed a smile.

He stood in the doorway. "Is it suitable?"

"It's fine. Better than a park bench." She shrugged, crossing her arms.

"The bathroom is through there," Caron said, gesturing. "A shower, toiletries, the works."

She nodded, still playing it cool.

"Consider this your space."

"For tonight," Esther reminded him—and herself.

"For tonight."

She ran her hand slowly over the bed.

"Get some rest. In the morning, we'll talk more about the Family. What we do, what we could offer you."

"And what you'd want in return," she added.

"Yes," he said. "That too."

The door clicked shut behind him.

Esther stood silent for a moment, then spun in a slow circle.

"Holy shit," she whispered, a grin breaking across her face.

A giddy energy rose in her as she bounced on her toes and took a running leap. She flew onto the bed, sinking into softness so complete, so absolute, it was dangerous. A genuine laugh bubbled up from inside, her first in months.

Her smile faded as she looked at the door. Esther slid off the bed and walked over to it, pressing her ear to its cold metal surface. Nothing there. She flipped the lock and tested it, then turned and jumped back onto the bed.

Rolling onto her back, she made a snow-angel gesture. "Just for tonight." It already seemed like a lie.

Whatever this "family" was, whatever Caron wanted, tomorrow she'd find out the catch. Tonight, she'd pretend there wasn't one.

Tonight, for the first time in years, she was content.

ESTHER, freshly showered and wearing name-brand clothes for the first time in her life, sat in a leather armchair that seemed to swallow her whole. Caron's office exuded old money and class. She took a bite of a buttery croissant, the flakes melting on her tongue, and viewed him over the rim of her coffee cup.

"Does that make it any clearer?" Caron put his arms on the massive mahogany desk. The morning light sharpened the silver in his hair.

Esther swallowed and wiped a crumb from her lip. "So, it's like prostitution for really rich people?"

Tightness pulled at his mouth, and he exhaled through his nose before settling into something more composed. "That's a crude word, and not what we do." He stabbed the desk with his index finger. "The

Family's clientele are the richest and most powerful people in the world. They travel often and sometimes wish someone to accompany them to a show, or dinner—"

"Or their bedroom?" The words came out sharp, but something about his phrasing made her want to poke holes in it.

Caron pinched the bridge of his nose, the surrounding skin whitening under the pressure.

"You're smart," he said. "Too smart for such simplistic thinking. What we offer is companionship. Which yes, sometimes includes physical intimacy. But these are not street transactions." He gestured around the opulent office. "We provide safety, luxury, and education. Our Sisters receive clothing, housing, and healthcare. They learn languages, social graces, and financial management."

Esther took another sip of coffee, using the moment to study him.

"And in return?"

"In return, they represent the Family with discretion and excellence." He leaned back in his chair. "They become part of something larger than themselves. They find belonging."

The word hit her in the gut. Belonging. How long had it been since she'd belonged anywhere?

"I'm not sure." She looked down at the pastry in her hand—the best thing she'd eaten in months.

"Perhaps this will help." Caron stood, beckoning her to follow.

She hesitated, then trailed him out of the office and down two flights of stairs, stopping before a heavy door. Muffled sounds leaked from behind it—not one voice, but many. The kind of carefree laughter she hadn't heard in a long time—like girls at the beach, top down, wind in their hair. The sound of friendship. Of belonging.

Caron paused, glancing back at her. "This is the Family."

He tugged the door toward him, and Esther stepped through, the wall of sound and life hitting her so hard she physically recoiled. A vast open-concept living area took up half the floor. Plush couches, armchairs, and a gleaming kitchen opened to one side. But it wasn't only the luxury that stunned her. It was the girls. At least twenty of them, all beautiful, moving with a serene confidence she couldn't fathom. They were everywhere, like a scene from a college movie where no one ever studied and everyone had fun.

A girl in a green beauty mask danced by, singing dramatically into a hairbrush. On a nearby couch, three girls sprawled across one another like puppies, giggling at a tablet. Another sat cross-legged on a barstool, typing furiously on a laptop while sipping from a giant pink mug.

"Is this real?" Esther blinked rapidly, trying to process the scene. It didn't seem fake. It seemed like joy, not pretense.

That stung the most, because she wanted it.

"They all live here?" She clutched her arms around herself.

"This is one of our residence floors," Caron said. "Each Sister has her own room, but they share common spaces."

Esther nodded, half listening, but taking in everything—the expensive coffee machines, fresh flowers on every table, the glass-doored fridge with its neatly arranged shelves.

Then she appeared.

At the kitchen island, a tall girl with red hair twisted into a high bun swayed to music only she could hear. Slicing pineapple with white AirPods nestled in her ears, she moved her hands with an easy, confident rhythm. Sunlight caught her hair, setting it ablaze.

The chatter of the room compressed into a dull hum, and everything but the girl with the red hair fell out of focus. Her eyes were closed, and a small smile curved on her lips—private, content, like she existed in a bubble no one could burst.

A warmth bloomed from within Esther, an ache built of part awe and part agonizing envy. She didn't want to just be *in* this room. She wanted to *be* that girl. To move like the world couldn't touch her.

A voice in her head screamed that it was all a lie, a performance for her benefit. But the one in her heart, the one that was cold and starving and so terribly alone, whispered back: *I don't care.*

"Esther?"

Caron broke her focus. She blinked, startled. "I'm sorry, what?"

"Would you like to see your room?" He glanced toward the redhead before looking back at her.

The flush on her cheeks was evident as she nodded quickly and followed him across the floor.

They stopped at an unmarked door, and he opened it, revealing a small studio. Esther eyed the pale blue walls and the inviting queen bed heaped with pillows, but glided right past them to the massive mirrored wardrobe against the far wall.

"Go ahead," he urged.

She crossed the room and pulled the panels apart. The wardrobe sat empty, waiting.

"The Family provides clothing," Caron said. "Designer apparel, shoes, accessories—everything you need for any occasion. We also offer a monthly stipend if you prefer to shop for yourself."

Esther ran her fingers along the smooth wood. "How much?"

"Four thousand dollars."

She dropped her hand and stared at him. "A month?"

He nodded.

Walking to the bed, she sat on the edge. The mattress was just as decadent as last night's. Staring at her hands, at the worn-down nails, the grime she could never quite scrub away, she finally asked the question.

"And what would I have to do? Exactly?"

The bed dipped as Caron joined her, keeping a respectful distance. "You would be a companion. Our clients are powerful men. They want charm, intelligence, comfort."

"Sex," Esther said flatly.

"Sometimes, yes." Caron folded his hands. "But only if you choose. No Sister is ever forced into anything she doesn't choose."

She wanted to balk at the absurdity, to call him a liar. But the image of the redhead dancing in the kitchen replayed in her mind as the sound of uninhibited laughter still swirled in her ears.

Thoughts of the park bench waiting for her, of the cold seeping into her bones, of the gnawing fear of tomorrow, which would be the same as the day after that. Her eyes took another trip around the sunny room.

This was a choice, she knew. Just not the kind most people ever had to make.

"Okay." A single word, like a door slamming shut on her old life.

THE THICK STACK of papers on the desk was as intimidating as the legalese swimming on its pages. Esther barely ate her lunch, turning everything over in her mind. She'd taken a book from the tall shelf and was reading in the corner when Caron came by with coffee, a knowing smile, and a contract.

"Kari here can answer any questions you have about the language in the contract, but it's pretty straightforward," Caron said, gesturing to the woman standing beside his desk. "You'll be an official employee of the Family. Taxed. Documented. Entirely aboveboard.

"Training takes three weeks," he continued, fingers steepled. "You'll move into the dorms after that, along with the other girls."

Esther flipped through the pages, skimming sections about confidentiality, code of conduct, and compensation.

"What's this about my name? Why can't I keep my own?"

Caron rose from his chair and walked to the window, hands clasped behind his back.

"It's for your own protection," he said, gazing out at the skyline. "The anonymity allows you to take on a new persona and become someone else—someone, perhaps, you've always dreamed of."

She stared at him.

"It's symbolic to shed your old life and take on a new name as you join the Family."

"Did you change yours?"

A smile touched his lips. "Yes. Long ago."

"What was it before?"

"That person no longer exists."

"Do I get to pick my new name?"

Kari dipped her head. "You may offer suggestions, yes. If it's acceptable to the Family, you can use it."

"And if it's not?"

"Then you will be assigned one that suits you," she said with a trained smile.

Esther ran her fingers over the embossed letterhead. *The Family.* Such a simple word for such a complicated decision. She'd lost her real family piece by piece, and now a replacement dangled in front of her, wrapped in shimmer and shadows.

"What happens if I want to leave?"

Caron returned to his desk, sitting down with deliberate calm. "You're free to go whenever you wish." His tone became firmer. "But understand, everything you have here stays here. You leave the way you came in."

"That's in the contract too," Kari added, tapping a manicured nail on page four. "Section seven."

Esther nodded, studying him. There was more than he was letting on, but whatever secrets he kept, whatever haunted him, he held out a lifeline, and she was drowning.

She picked up the pen; it felt substantial in her hand. With one signature, Esther Holland would disappear. She'd become someone new, someone with a future.

"Okay." She signed her name with a flourish—perhaps the last time she would do so.

Caron took the contract, his fingers brushing hers. "Very good."

He stood up and stretched his back. "Do you have any suggestions for your new name?"

Esther combed her memories for something that would hold meaning for her. It came to her immediately.

"I'd like to be Star."

Five

Three twenty. The chair is too soft. The silence is too loud. Ten minutes early, and I already regret it. My notebook is on the table, but I'm staring out at the skyline, trying to pretend my nervous system isn't staging a full-on revolt. The conference room is like a movie set—all sleek glass and polished chrome, the kind of place where world-changing decisions are made over bottled water and notepads nobody writes on.

The door opens, and Aura bounces through, all five feet of her radiating pure energy. Her curly hair is pulled back in a puff that's wider than her face.

"Thank God I'm not the only one who's early." She drops into the chair beside me. "I couldn't sit still. I've changed outfits three times already."

The distraction is welcome. "You look great. I'm trying not to throw up."

"Girl, same." She pulls a pack of gum from her pocket and offers me a piece. "Kora says gum tricks your brain into thinking you're calm. I say it's candy for quitters."

"Is she coming?" I take the gum.

Before Aura can respond, Kora saunters in, carrying a tray of coffee.

"Ladies! Pregame fuel." She sets the tray down and hands each of us a cup. "Figured we'd need the caffeine."

"Legend," Aura says, taking a grateful sip.

The door barely closes before it swings wide again, and Jeremy steps through carrying a laptop and a tangle of cables. He looks like he'd rather be anywhere else—which, knowing him, is probably true.

"Need to hook up the presentation display," he mutters, kneeling beside the massive wall monitor.

Kora grins. "Jeremy, sweetie, you have an entire department for this, right? Or do you need an excuse to hang around gorgeous women?"

He blushes. "I, uh—it's faster if I do it myself. Hi Star."

"Hey," I say, taking another sip of coffee.

He finishes connecting the monitor and practically sprints for the door.

They're both staring at me. "What?"

Aura snorts. "Girl, that boy has it bad for you."

"Jeremy?" I chuckle. "No way. He's awkward with everyone."

"If you say so."

Kora kicks her feet up on the table and grins. "So, first-client jitters? On a scale of one to 'might pee yourself'?"

"Hand me the Depends," I say.

"Excellent. That means you care." Kora leans forward conspiratorially. "Secret time: I still get nervous to this day."

"But you're so…confident," I say.

"Oh, honey, that's just good packaging." She winks. "The nerves never go away. You just get better at using them."

The glass door groans yet again, and Sage walks in—no, glides in, like gravity works differently for her. She's in a silver tweed pantsuit that shimmers in the bright lights, and her hair is swept up in an elegant twist.

"Sorry I'm late," she says, though she's precisely on time. "Natalia needed something."

"We were discussing pregame jitters." Kora slides a coffee toward Sage. "Our baby is nervous."

Sage takes it with a grateful smile. "That's normal. I'd be concerned if she weren't."

She sits at the head of the table and displays her tablet on the screen behind her. "Let's get started. Star, tomorrow night, you'll be meeting Gideon Telluride at Le Bernadin at seven thirty."

My hand shakes more than I'd like as I write:

Gideon. Le Bernadin. 7:30.

"Forty-two, divorced, and has no children. Executive director of international relations at Pinnacle Investments. He's been a client for three years and has a reputation for being respectful and generous." Sage swipes through her tablet. "He's hosting potential investors from Macau and wants someone who can be charming, intelligent, and make him look good."

"Arm candy with brains," Kora says.

"Exactly." Sage looks at me. "You'll need to be familiar with basic investment terminology. I've uploaded a cheat sheet to your portal."

Investment terms. Cheat sheet. Don't sound like an idiot.

"What is he…expecting from me?" I say.

Kora snorts and almost loses her coffee. "Don't worry, he wants arm candy to wow his clients. He's too worried about closing the deal to be handsy in public."

"Kora," Sage says, but there's affection in her reprimand.

"Just stating facts." She puts her hands up.

"What should I wear?" I ask.

"I've selected three options from the Family closet," Sage says. "They're being delivered to your room as we speak. The silver Valentino would be my recommendation."

I blink. "You picked out clothes for me?"

"Of course. That's what Big Sisters do." She smiles, and I have to look down at my notebook again.

Kora cups her hands under her boobs. "You may want to pad up a little. You know, to fill it out."

Sage exhales. "You don't have to make her feel bad."

"It's okay," I say, but no one hears me.

"I'm not," Kora says. "But let's be honest, she's no Aura." She flicks her thumb at Aura, who's trying to decide if she should be offended.

"That's rich coming from the girl who showed up for brunch topless in Maui." Sage winks.

Kora points at Sage. "That was one time, and you promised never to bring up Maui."

"Okay, can we focus?" Sage taps her stiletto against the floor—a tiny, controlled gesture that commands more attention than shouting. Kora straightens up, and they're both grinning.

Smiling behind my notebook, I absorb their banter—Sage, the consummate professional, Kora the irreverent truth-teller. They're a buddy cop movie where both characters got cast as the cool one.

"Aura, you'll be observing from the bar," Sage continues. "Standard procedure for first assignments is to have a shadow. You'll be there to support Star if needed."

Aura nods eagerly. "Got it. Fly on the wall."

"More like backup dancer," Kora corrects. "Present, but not the focus."

"What if I mess up or say something stupid or—"

"You won't," Sage interrupts me. "And even if you do, he's not looking for perfection. He's looking for someone genuine who can hold a conversation."

"Men love talking about themselves and their money," Aura chimes in. "My mama always said that's the secret to dating rich guys."

"Facts." Kora holds out her fist for a bump, which Aura fulfills.

Keep him talking $.

"After dinner, he'll most likely invite you for a nightcap at The Champagne Bar in his hotel. This is expected. You'll have up to two drinks maximum. Flirt appropriately, but maintain professional boundaries."

"What if he wants more than that?" I ask.

The room falls quiet—my pen hovers over the page. Kora sets down her coffee.

"What did they teach you in training?" Sage looks at me.

A cold sweat forms on my neck. Was I paying attention that day?

"That the Family doesn't officially require anything other than companionship?" The lilt at the end of my sentence does some heavy lifting.

"Right. If you choose to extend the evening, that's your decision. If not, you thank him for a lovely time and leave."

"Will he be expecting me to sleep with him?"

Kora spins in her chair and points at me. "Yes."

Sage exhales sharply. "Kora."

"I'm being honest," she continues. "They always want to sleep with you. That's part of the job. Sometimes you'll want to, sometimes—"

"The choice is always yours," Sage says firmly. "If it's not something you want, stand up, thank him, and go."

"And if he pushes?" I ask.

"Then you use the Family weather app on your phone like we showed you."

Aura chuckles. "I thought that shit was the coolest thing when they showed me. 'Oh, let me check the temp.' Meanwhile, fam is on the way."

Kora chuckles. "All kidding aside, Gideon's not that guy. He's more worried about his reputation than getting laid. But if anything —and I mean *anything*—feels off, you bail. Got it?"

Sage turns to Aura. "If you see Star press two fingers to her Family pendant, what does that mean?"

"Meet her in the ladies' room," Aura answers.

"And if she taps her pendant repeatedly?"

Aura looks up as if she's reading from an invisible prompter. "She's a friend from college, and I'm a little tipsy. I drape myself over her until extraction arrives."

Sage smiles and turns back to me. "See, you're in good hands, Star. This is what we do."

I nod, and my anxiety recedes slightly.

Sage swipes to a new slide showing the evening's schedule.

"You should expect to be done by ten thirty, eleven at the latest. The car will be on standby all night."

"And if it goes later?" I ask.

"Then you're probably having a pleasant evening." Kora grins.

Sage glares at her. "Or you're not following the exit strategy we discussed."

My eyes flit between them, tag-teaming this briefing—Sage all precise information and procedure, Kora translating into real-world wisdom with snark. It's like viewing a perfectly choreographed dance. Maybe someday I'll know the steps too.

"He's a good first client," Sage says. "Safe, respectful, clear expectations. Remember your training, and you'll be fine."

"Okay."

"Any other questions?" she asks.

"What's he like? As a person, I mean."

Sage's face softens. "He's quite charming. Intelligent, well-read, dry humor. He collects first edition books and speaks four languages."

She leans in. "Word has it, he recently acquired a rare Fitzgerald first edition. So, do what you will with that tidbit. The car will come at seven. I'll stop by before you head out to check on you."

"This is so exciting! Like prom, but we get paid," Aura says.

Kora stretches her back. "Girl, if your prom was anything like this, I want to know where you went to school."

We all laugh, and the tension eases in my neck. The nerves are still there, but they're mingling with excitement.

"One last thing," Sage says. "When you're with a client, you're not just Star—you're the Family. Every word you say is our reputation."

"I understand."

"Good." She closes the tablet. "Then we're done here."

Grabbing my notebook, I stand and turn when Sage stops me.

"Star, could you stay for a moment?"

My throat gets a mighty lump. Kora catches my eye as she leaves, giving me a subtle thumbs-up that does nothing to calm my nerves. Aura bounces out after her, and the door clicks shut, leaving me alone with Sage.

She moves with that fluid grace of hers and perches on the conference table, close enough that her perfume surrounds me— something expensive and subtle, like the scent of fresh spring rain.

"Melody mentioned my message surprised you," Sage says. "She was concerned."

My cheeks burn. *Traitor.*

"I—" My throat clenches. "I wasn't expecting it, that's all."

"I'm glad it meant something to you," she continues, her sincerity disarming me. "I see something in you, Star. That's why I asked to be your Big Sister."

My neurons flicker in and out. "You…you asked for me?"

"I did. I recognized something in you. In how you carry yourself, like you're always ready to run if you need to."

My pulse is thudding in my ears. This doesn't feel like just a compliment; it's personal, almost invasive.

"I was pretty down-and-out once." Her confession disarms me. "Before the Family found me. Before all this." She gestures around.

"You?" I say, unable to imagine this polished woman being anything other than pure elegance.

Sage's smile twists. "We're cut from the same cloth, Star. Survivors. The kind who don't just make it through—we transform."

She keeps watching me, and for a moment, the cynical part of my brain registers the quiet perfection of her performance. Like it's been rehearsed, designed to build a bridge between us. One that I desperately want to cross, even if I'm not sure what's on the other side.

"We're a team now," she says, turning for the door. "Don't forget that."

And God help me, I want to believe her.

THE SILVER LACE Valentino catches the light like it knows it's the winner—which is why I'm suspicious of it. Its open back taunts me.

Melody bounds into my room, carrying two cans of Dr Pepper. "Emergency caffeine delivery. You're welcome." She tosses one my way. "Ooh, is that one of your options?"

"Yeah. Sage picked them out."

She flops onto my bed with zero regard for the red dress lying there, rolls onto her side, and props her head in her hand. "Show me everything."

Holding up the sleek black column dress with a slit that goes somewhere north of decent, I pose. "Option one."

"Very Audrey Hepburn plays dominatrix." She nods approvingly. "What else?"

I point to the red one she's currently crushing. "That one. And the one Sage recommended."

Melody sits up and notices she's squishing couture. "Oh crap, sorry." She smooths the red dress, a silky wrap number with a plunging neckline. "This one's trouble. But like, cultured trouble."

"Is that good?"

"That's good." She sips her soda. "So, which one are you wearing?"

"I'm not sure. Sage said the silver one, but—"

"You're thinking red?"

"Yeah. It's more…me?"

"You should wear the one you feel confident in." She pauses. "Though Sage knows the client."

"That's what I'm worried about." The red dress goes back into the wardrobe. "I don't know when to follow advice and when to trust my gut."

"Welcome to the Family," Melody says with a chuckle. She pats the bed beside her. "Come sit. You're overthinking."

Flopping down next to her, we press our backs against the headboard in synchronized exhaustion.

"Can I ask you something?" I say.

"Shoot."

"Are you happy? Being here?"

She turns to me, eyes bright. "God, yes. Aren't you?"

"I guess so. I'm still figuring it all out."

"Well, I love it here." She sits up straighter. "Do you know where I'd be without the Family? Back in Ohio, married to some boring insurance salesman, having unfulfilling sex twice a month, and watching HGTV until I die."

"That's…oddly specific."

"It's true. My high school boyfriend, Todd, is literally selling insurance now. He sent me a friend request last month." She shudders dramatically. "Instead, I'm here, living in Manhattan, wearing clothes I couldn't pronounce before, and not failing at something."

"And the sex is good?"

"Exactly!" Her can clinks against mine. "Plus, I have Sisters now. Real ones, not like those fake college bitches who dropped me the second I didn't conform."

Her enthusiasm is infectious, but my doubts nag at me. "You never worry about the other stuff?"

"What other stuff?"

A moment of pause, my mind on the Step-Sister blog. "Just… everything that comes with this life."

Her smile dims for a second. "Sure, maybe I traded one cage for another. But at least this one's got Gucci pajamas."

"I guess you're right."

"I know I'm right." She bumps her shoulder with mine. "Now, back to important matters. The dresses."

"Honestly, as a seahorse…which one?"

She laughs and studies them thoughtfully. "The black one is sexy but safe. The red one is you, but it might be too bold for a first impression." Jumping up, she grabs the lacy silver dress. "This one, though...this is the middle ground. It says, 'I'm sophisticated and confident, but I still have secrets worth discovering.'"

"When did you get so wise about fashion?"

"Sweetie, have you seen the stack of *Vogue* in my room?" She holds the dress out. "Trust Sage on this one."

The fabric is impossibly soft. "Okay."

"Good choice." Melody flops back onto my bed. "Now, tell me everything about this Gideon guy. Is he hot? Rich? Both?"

Laughter bubbles up, easy and warm, before I collapse onto the bed beside her. Melody's rock-solid certainty is my stable ground in this whole glittering mess, and precisely what I need right now—someone who believes in this life completely, without questions or doubts.

Even if I can't quite get there myself.

"HOLD STILL," Melody says, bobby pin between her teeth as she secures a loose strand of my hair. "Almost done."

"It's almost like I belong here," I say to my reflection.

"You *do* belong here." She steps back to admire her work. "There. *C'est parfait.*"

She's spent the last forty minutes helping me prepare—styling my hair into a sleek updo with enough loose tendrils to appear effortless, and coaching me through makeup application. I've never worn a backless dress in my life, and I feel indecent.

"Seriously, Star. You're incredible." She pulls a curl down. "Like you walked out of a magazine."

I turn away from the mirror, my face flushing. "Thanks to you."

"No." She twists me back to face my reflection. "This is all you. I helped with the wrapping paper, but the gift was already there."

"Was that one of your mother's sayings?"

"No, all mine. I have my moments." She grins, adjusting the thin diamond bracelet on my wrist—a loaner from the Family's jewelry collection. "Nervous?"

"My stomach has more knots than a pretzel factory," I admit. "What if I say something stupid? What if he hates me? What if—"

"Stop." She squeezes my hand. "Remember what Sage told you. You're not selling desire tonight. You're selling the fantasy of *you*."

"Right. The fantasy of me." A quick breath to settle myself. "Whoever that turns out to be."

"She's right here." She taps my chest lightly. "Just be you. The you who doesn't apologize for taking up space."

A loud knock interrupts us, and the door flies inward.

"*¡Ay, Dios mío!*" Aura spins in, a whirlwind of nervous energy in a black cocktail dress. Her curves are criminal, but she keeps tugging at the hemline.

"What's wrong?" I ask.

"What's wrong? *¡Todo!*" Aura paces, her hands making random gestures. "My dress is too tight, and my hair won't behave."

Melody and I exchange amused glances.

"Knock knock!" Kora sings from the hallway as she floats into the room. Her simple black dress appears almost painted on. "Pregame checklist."

She holds out her hand, revealing two sticks of gum. "Breath check. Nonnegotiable."

Aura and I each take one.

"What about me?" Melody pouts.

"You're not on duty tonight, sweetie." Kora winks, then steps back to examine us. She looks at Aura first, nodding approvingly. "The black is perfect with your skin tone. Good luck keeping the waiters off you."

Aura preens a little under the praise.

Kora turns to me with soft eyes. "And you..." She pauses, tilting her head. "Truly...*gorgeous*."

Something about her sincerity makes my cheeks flush. "Thanks."

"The Valentino was the right choice," she continues. "Guess I owe Sage a dollar."

As if she were summoned, Sage waltzes into the room, radiant in a deep emerald dress. Her hair scatters over it like flames in a forest fire.

"Is this where the party is?" she asks.

Sage moves through the throng and stands directly in front of me, placing her hands on my shoulders. Her touch is light but grounding as she stares into my soul.

"Listen," she says, speaking only to me. "Tonight isn't about being perfect. It's about being *present.* You'll make mistakes—we all do—but what matters is how you recover. Remember, you belong there as much as anyone does."

This isn't the lieutenant or the trainer. This is Sage, the Big Sister.

"If you make me cry right now, I swear…," I warn, blinking rapidly to keep my mascara intact.

A smile plays at the corner of her mouth. "Can't have that. You look exquisite."

She squeezes once more before letting go, and her touch lingers on me. I shouldn't care what she thinks. But I do. I really do.

"Heads up," Melody announces with a crisp clap. "Your car is waiting. Time to shine."

Six

My shoes tap out an awkward Morse code against the floor as Aura and I wobble toward the front door of the building. "I'm going to break my neck in these things," I mutter, my fingers finding the wall for support.

"Please," Aura says. "Try doing this since you were thirteen. *Mi abuela* made me practice with books on my head."

"Did it work?"

"Hell no. I dropped her Bible in the toilet." She tips forward in an exaggerated stumble.

We slide into the car, and I replay Sage's instructions in my mind. *Make him feel like the most powerful man in the room. Be the mirror that reflects his greatness back at him and his guests.*

No pressure, then. My entire future in this place is riding on one dinner.

The car glides to a stop at Le Bernadin, and we step out. The hostess greets me with a rehearsed smile. "Good evening, miss."

"I'm with Mr. Telluride's party," I say, my tone steadier than my nerves.

"Of course. Right this way."

Aura heads to the bar as I trail the hostess through a sea of whispered wealth. The word *impostor* burns on my forehead, but no one cares. I'm just another woman in an expensive dress in a city full of them. Anonymous. Interchangeable.

We approach a corner table where they sit, sipping their drinks. Two Asian men in severe tailored suits and Gideon Telluride—three-figure haircut, chic watch, eyes glued to his phone. He doesn't stand up as I arrive.

"Ah, Star. Wonderful," he says, gesturing to the empty chair beside him with a quick, transactional smile. "Join us."

Sliding into the chair, I cross my ankles the way Melody taught me.

"You look lovely." His gaze slips over me like someone assessing the value of a painting.

"Gentlemen," Gideon says, "this is Star, my guest for the evening." He offers a brief, polite smile. "This is Mr. Fan and Mr. Lei, the founders of Golden Peak Capital. From zero to a billion, isn't that right?" He titters pretentiously and toasts Mr. Lei, who returns the gesture.

Mr. Lei, the older one with wire-rimmed glasses, gives me a slow, deliberate appraisal. "Gideon," he says, slick as oil, "you always acquire the finest…assets."

Cold needles walk up my spine, and I shoot a brittle smile at Gideon, waiting for him to object, to correct, to say anything. But he only gives a short, hollow laugh and takes a sip of his drink.

Okay, I'm on my own. Gideon appears weak. I need to fix this.

"Your English is excellent," I say to Mr. Lei, trying to steer the conversation onto neutral ground.

"We studied at Harvard," the younger one, Mr. Fan, replies.

Oof, I'm not making this better.

Mr. Fan's eyes are sharp, analytical, and haven't left my face. "Tell us about yourself."

"Well, I'm quite the literary enthusiast."

"Is that so?" Gideon asks.

This is it. The lifeline Sage handed me. My chance to drive.

"Yes, I'm especially fascinated by first editions. Holding a book that has become a part of history…" I trail off, letting the image hang in the air.

"What a coincidence," Gideon says. "I've recently acquired a first edition of *This Side of Paradise*. Fine condition."

Tingling at the base of my neck, a welcome stroke of luck. When Sage mentioned the Fitzgerald, I assumed it wouldn't be the popular one, so I guessed and picked the rarest one. Now, to breathe and not forget the details I crammed in the car.

Leaning in, I feign excitement. "Oh? Haven't most of the dust jackets been trashed on that one?"

His eyebrows shoot up. "Exactly right."

"Does it have the original…" My hand goes to my head as I try to remember. "Was it red boards?"

"Blue actually, but—"

"Red rules. Yes, that's right." I smile as if it had momentarily slipped my mind.

"Precisely." He almost looks impressed.

Holy shit, I did it. Wait, how many did the article say were left?

"Less than three hundred of those survived, I think? Compared to what, twenty thousand of *Gatsby*?" I squeak out a pretentious chuckle.

The effect is immediate. He beams, looking validated. Mr. Fan looks at me with heightened curiosity. And Mr. Lei raises his glass.

"Beauty and brains." Mr. Lei's gaze drops to my breasts. "A dangerous combination."

Wrong. Wrong answer. My insides twist. He turned my calculated move into a comment on my appearance. They only see a talking doll.

Mr. Fan's knee brushes mine under the table. My reaction is reflexive as I pull back, bumping into Gideon, whose hand lands firmly on the small of my back, a gesture of ownership.

"Tell me, Star," Mr. Fan says, leaning closer. "What other… interests do you have?"

Gideon smiles, his hand still on my back. "Gentlemen, we should order another round before our main course arrives."

Mr. Fan swirls his whiskey. "You Americans have such… fascinating women. So beautiful and eager to please." His eyes slide over me like I'm on the dessert menu. "I find it refreshing compared to the restraint of women in my country."

Mr. Lei laughs with a low, guttural sound. "Perhaps, Gideon, you might consider sharing your prize later this evening? My hotel has an excellent view of the park."

The air leaves my lungs, and my fingertips start to numb. They're trading me like a stock tip, and Gideon, my client—the man I'm supposed to be propping up—smiles a placid, diplomatic smile.

"Gentlemen," he says, as if discussing traffic, "Star is a delightful companion, but I'm afraid we have plans after dinner."

Not *she's not for sale*. Not *she's a person*. Only *she's already booked*. He sounds merely regretful, like he's turning down a cigar.

Half of my water glass disappears, forcing down the lump in my throat. My new room flashes through my mind—then the streets before it, the hunger, the fear. My sight blurs. I need to get out of here.

Aura is at the bar, laser-focused on me as I place two fingers across my pendant.

"Excuse me, gentlemen. I need to visit the powder room."

Gideon glances at me. "Don't be long, dear."

My legs are like stilts as I walk to the ladies' room, fueled by pure rage.

The bathroom door bangs open behind me, and Aura sweeps in. "What happened?"

"They're disgusting." I'm trembling. "They asked Gideon if he would share me. Like I'm a rental car." My breath hitches. "And he just sat there! He didn't say anything!"

I will not cry and ruin this makeup. I will not.

"I can't do this. I'm not cut out for this. I don't belong—"

Aura grabs my arms. "Hey. Hey! Look at me." Her pupils are pinpricks. "You think this is bad? Let me tell you something."

Her intensity makes me gasp.

"When I was sixteen, living under the bridge near Hunts Point, these junkies found me. Four of them. Big motherfuckers. Passed me around like a crack pipe for two days."

My insides lurch. "Aura—"

"No, *escúchame*," she commands. "I was too scared to fight. Too scared to scream. I just...survived. *Porque eso es lo que hacemos.* We survive." She swallows hard, her own memory a phantom in the room. "When they got tired of me, I walked two miles to the clinic, bleeding. You know what the nurse said? 'At least you're alive.' So don't tell me you can't handle some crusty old fucks in a fancy restaurant. This ain't the streets, Star. You got power here."

"What power?"

"They see a doll. Go back in there and show them a queen." She smirks. "You can't play their game, so make them play yours. You're smarter than them. Run the table."

She straightens my pendant, her touch surprisingly gentle. "You're Star now. So go shine, bitch."

A shaky laugh. I'm still rattled, but now I'm pissed off too.

"Okay," I say, straightening my spine. "Okay."

Aura grins. "That's my girl. Now fix your lipstick."

I walk back to the table with steady, sure steps. Every inch of the floor belongs to me now—or at least that's what my body language is desperately trying to sell to anyone looking on. The men stand as I approach. A courtesy they hadn't bothered with before. Progress.

Sliding back into my seat, I catch Gideon saying, "...the volatility in the currency market makes that a significant risk." He turns to me. "What do you think, Star? Would you consider it a promising investment?"

He's testing me, putting me on display again. But now the rules have changed.

I smile, a slow, deliberate curve of my lips. "With all due respect, gentlemen," I say, my voice as smooth as my legs, "my opinion on finance is hardly relevant." I turn my full attention to the older man, ignoring Gideon. "I'm far more fascinated by real power. Mr. Lei, Gideon mentioned you built your company from nothing. In a market like Macau, that's more than an investment strategy; that's a legacy. How does a man develop that kind of vision?"

The table goes quiet. Mr. Lei, who had been ogling my neckline moments before, now meets my eyes directly. Pride lights his face from within, and a slow, satisfied smile unfurls. Gideon sits back, eyebrows raised. I've elevated him.

For the rest of the meal, I become the hostess, drawing out their stories, moderating their little pissing contests, giving each one of them time in the spotlight so everyone feels like the guest of honor. Which is impressive because I usually just burn the toast.

When we stand to leave, Mr. Lei takes my hand. "It's a pleasure to meet such an intelligent and perceptive young woman," he says, kissing my knuckles. His gaze meets mine, my smile an impenetrable mask.

Mr. Fan looks at me, and his eyes hold a question I have no intention of answering. "Perhaps we will meet again when I am back in New York."

"The universe has a way of leading you to where you're supposed to be, at the moment you're supposed to be there," I say. It's from a *Men in Black* movie I saw a couple of years ago. I've always thought it sounded profound.

Mr. Fan nods at me, and I hope the look on his face is confusion.

Gideon walks them out and then returns, glowing. "They are quite impressed with you," he says, his hand planting a quick pat on my ass. "I knew you'd be great."

"Thank you."

"What do you say we continue our evening at my suite? The Plaza has a beautiful view."

My hand covers his, halting its journey. "That's a very kind offer, Gideon," I say, warm and final, "but my evening is complete."

He deflates.

My purse slips over one shoulder and I give him a coy smile. "That Fitzgerald is an amazing find. I hope it brings you a lot of joy."

His smile is resigned. "Thanks. I think it will."

Cool night air hits my skin when the doors swing away, and Aura comes up from behind me.

"You killed it in there, *chica.*"

"I just shined, bitch."

Aura cackles, "They never even seen you take the crown."

We duck into the car, my dress feeling less like a costume and more like couture. This was more than survival; it was learning how to fight in their world, with their weapons.

That's a victory.

THE CAR HUMS BENEATH US, a cocoon of black leather and tinted windows. Aura is curled up on the far side of the seat, breathing deeply, her head resting against the window. She passed out so fast—maybe it's her superpower. Perhaps it's easier to sleep when you've already learned how to survive these kinds of nights.

I haven't.

I should be proud. After all, I played the part, said the lines, smiled the smile. Gave them enough without giving anything real.

But the feeling crawling up my spine and making my teeth clench isn't pride. It's a particular brand of humiliation reserved for those who've been played.

My fingers move before I've made the decision. Phone unlocked. Browser up. The link still lives in my history: *Step-Sister.*

A tap on "Previous Entries," and I scroll. I shudder when the title appears.

Blog Entry #17

The Night You Realize You're Just a Prop

Being a Sister in the Family isn't glamorous. It isn't empowerment. It's performance. There will come a night when you understand you're nothing more than decoration. Not a person, but a carefully selected accessory designed to stroke a powerful man's ego.

You aren't there to speak. You're there to glow. To reflect. To make them look better simply by existing in their orbit. Your intelligence becomes a prop, your conversation a carefully rehearsed script where every word is measured, every laugh calculated. They don't see you. They see a status symbol they can display like an expensive watch.

The Family trains you for this. Not just to execute, but to excel at being invisible while simultaneously being the center of attention. A magic trick where you're both everywhere and nowhere. And the worst part? You learn to love it. To crave it. To believe this is freedom instead of a cage.

You are worth more than this. So much more.

Stay sharp, Stay free.

—Your Step-Sister

Each line hits and leaves a bruise. I shift, unsettled, as the words reinforce things I haven't dared say aloud—or even to myself.

I want to believe all of this. The safety. The sisterhood. The transformation. But right now, I'm like an understudy who got shoved onstage before learning the lines. Expected to perform, but scared shitless that I'll trip over the words and get tossed into the back alley where I belong.

You are worth more than this. So much more.

I don't know if that's true.

But I want it to be.

The phone goes back into my bag, and the passing lights make warped shapes on the window. We pull up to the building in silence. Aura doesn't wake until the driver opens the door. His look to us says, *You'll be okay.*

Melody's waiting at the entrance for me, because of course she is. She pulls me into a hug and says, "Aura was texting everyone all night. I'm so sorry you had to deal with that."

Her sincere sweetness pushes everything aside for a moment. She keeps her arm linked through mine, her fingers giving occasional reassuring squeezes as we walk to the elevator.

I want to put the night behind me. To shed this dress like snakeskin, stand in the shower, and tell myself everything will be fine.

But the stench of Step-Sister's words still clings to me like cigar smoke.

Melanie Caderea

The envelope felt heavy in Melanie's hand—thick red cardstock, almost bulletproof. As if the registrar's office thought padding the rejection might soften the blow. She held it up to the window—sunlight bled through, illuminating the official gold crest, making the words *The New School College of Performing Arts* look as if they'd been lifted from the Vatican library instead of a Manhattan office annex.

Her father, sweating in a generic-brand polo, hovered in the hallway, pretending to fiddle with a broken hinge. "You gonna open it, princess?"

The word *princess* represented his highest praise—after *slugger*, which he reserved for boys—though what Melanie desperately wanted was for him to stop treating her like a fascinating doll and show overt pride so she didn't have to do all the emotional heavy lifting herself.

Her mother, a former ballet teacher who lost her career and gained a limp in the same BMW T-bone accident, sat on the couch. She'd dressed up for Melanie's audition video—blue skirt, good pearls, a spot of lipstick—like her outfit might lend the application some extra credibility. "Let her breathe, Thomas."

The address on the front read:

Melanie Caderea
22 Hickock Drive
Rocky River, Ohio 44116

Melanie wouldn't blame the mailman if this turned out to be

another rejection. Her stack of those was growing steadily, with NYU's crest the latest to join the pile.

She turned to her mom one more time before holding her breath and flipping the envelope over.

Melanie unsealed it with her thumbnail, slow and torturous, like peeling sunburn.

Inside, the letter was printed in a serif so serious it might have been a funeral announcement. Her dad made a small, involuntary sound as his eyes hit the first word—*Congratulations*—but she hadn't registered it yet. Her mother teared up immediately, one artist's pride in another's accomplishment.

For a fleeting moment, Melanie morphed into a new identity—a version of herself that thrived in New York, sipping iced espresso in winter, tucking hastily scribbled lines on index cards into her boots. She envisioned herself captured in black-and-white photos, immersed in scripts under the shade of Central Park's American elms. But then the familiar skin tightened back around her, and she wondered whether any of it would be as good as her parents being happy in this moment.

"You did it," her dad said, voice tinny and thin, like he'd recorded it in the back of his throat rather than said it out loud. Her mom touched a hand to her cheek and smiled, which made her face briefly, heartbreakingly beautiful.

Melanie let the letter fall onto the table and spun in a little circle—not as gracefully as in her mother's old home movies, but enough to feel dizzy.

"I'm going to New York," Melanie whispered, the words transforming from impossibility to reality as they left her lips.

Her father wrapped her in a bear hug, rich with the smell of WD-40 and the cheap aftershave he'd been using since before she was born. "My little princess in the big city."

Her mother dabbed at her face with a tissue. "You'll need a new coat. The wind there cuts right through you."

Melanie nodded, though she wasn't listening. In her mind, she was already walking down Broadway, script in hand, becoming someone else entirely. Someone worth noticing. Someone special.

Rocky River had always felt like a waiting room to her. A place you existed until your real life started. The town's very name suggested movement, but nothing really flowed there except time, slowly eroding dreams until they resembled acceptable compromises.

She'd spent eighteen years being Melanie Caderea, the quiet theater girl who teachers praised but classmates overlooked. The girl who won awards for performances nobody came to see. The girl who played the lead in every school production but never got invited to the after-parties.

New York wouldn't see her that way. New York would see the real her.

$\mathcal{S}$EVEN

$\mathbf{M}$elody's tongue pokes out in concentration as she paints her toenails a deep cherry red. I'm sitting in her swivel chair, resisting the urge to fidget with the little glass seahorse on the desk. Acetone and her fruity lotion fill the air—a small island of calm in my day. Her room is cozy and personalized, with colorful scarves draped over lamps and Playbills tacked to the walls.

"So then," she continues her story, "Professor Merrick tells me I sound like I'm 'acting an equation' instead of feeling the emotion of the scene." She rolls her eyes dramatically. "Like, excuse me for taking time to analyze the text, right?"

I snort. "What an asshat."

"Are you going to Sister Wednesday tonight?" she asks. It's the weekly "no staff allowed" party the Sisters throw in the common room.

"Wasn't planning on it."

"Oh, come on. It'll be good for you to mingle more." She rolls the final stroke across her big toe. "Be seen by the older Sisters."

She caps the polish and wiggles her toes, admiring her work. Then her eyebrows sink as she studies my hands in my lap.

"Girl, your fingers are looking rough." She gestures for me to show her. "Let me do your nails."

My hands jerk back. "No thanks. I'm good."

"You sure? Because we can't have you at Sister Wednesday looking like you just clawed your way out of a dumpster."

A glance down reveals she's right—bitten to the quick, cuticles ragged—definitely not Family standard. I had to use the press-on kind for my date with Gideon. "Fine. You win."

The bed dips when I sit down across from her, and a pillow flops down between us.

"So, what color?" She opens a makeup bag filled with tiny bottles.

"Whatever's least likely to make me look like I live in a dumpster."

Her hand dives into the bag, and when it emerges, she's holding a subtle mauve. "This is the one. I call it 'the magician.'"

She grabs a small red file and gets to work.

"You know, before all this, I did this avant-garde production on a Bushwick rooftop," she says, filing the edge of my thumbnail. "It's eighteen degrees outside, and I'm standing there topless for five whole minutes while the audience stares."

"Jesus. Did they at least pay you well?"

"Three hundred bucks total for six performances." She chuckles. "But I felt so alive, you know? Like we were making real art or something. One night, the audience was three guys and a German shepherd. God, I was so naïve."

She applies the base coat, and I flinch.

"Have you ever had your nails done before?"

I shake my head.

"Not even by your sister?"

"No, she wasn't exactly the 'nail polish' type." An image flashes in my mind—Amelia with her combat boots and perpetually dirty fingernails, showing me how to hot-wire a scooter *just in case*. I miss her so much.

"My roommate used to do mine. Ray was this wild music student who'd get me into all kinds of trouble, but boy, could she do nails."

As she talks, the throbbing in my neck eases. Her voice is a low, steady rhythm against the usual static in my head.

My left hand finished, she holds it up, inspecting her work. "What do you think?"

My transformed fingers catch the light, and the subtle color is elegant. Too elegant, like they belong to someone else—someone whose life hasn't been a series of spectacular disasters.

"It's amazing." I mean it.

She smiles widely at me, already taking my other hand. "Now for the matching set."

This girl, who's sharing her stories and skills so freely, holds my fingers, and it hits me that two months ago, I was sleeping on park benches. Now I'm sitting in a ritzy dorm while my nails are being done by a failed acting student turned elite escort, and somehow, that's perfectly normal.

As the polish dries, a heaviness settles over me. A question I've been turning over in my head for days tumbles out.

"What do you really think about the Step-Sister blog?"

Melody's hand stops mid-stroke.

"That trash? Some bitter ex who couldn't hack it here." She rolls her eyes. "Just jealous that we get to live like this while she's back to slinging cocktails at some dive bar."

"But don't you think there's some truth in what it says?" I follow the brush along my nail. "About the Family being more than…you know."

"More than what?"

"The secrets? The extra services? The way they—"

"I don't read it," she cuts me off with a shrug. "Why spend precious energy on someone else's misery? That's what my mother always said."

Taking my hand again, she resumes her work with enthusiasm. "Life's too short to dwell on haters, Star."

Maybe she's right. Or she's better at not asking questions. I have to learn how to do that.

"Thanks." My voice is quiet.

"For what? The manicure?"

"For this. For…" I make a sweeping gesture. "You, I guess."

She squeezes my hand gently. "That's what we do. Patch up and keep going."

I tilt my head down but look up at her. "Strong tails?"

A warm smile blooms on her face. "Strong tails."

LIFE WOULD BE SIMPLER if I could just stop reading. The questions keep coming, and my obsession with the Step-Sister blog has become something unhealthy—scripture for someone who shouldn't be believing. The pain bleeding through those posts touches something in me. Sure, some of it reads like melodrama cranked to eleven, but it's laced with just enough truth to make my skin crawl.

Everyone else floats through this place like they're living in some glossy magazine spread. But there's a wrongness scratching at the back of my brain, demanding attention. Why does nobody else see it? Or maybe they do and simply don't care. Step-Sister noticed. The archive proves it—every single post from day one now lives in my head, memorized like some kind of masochistic homework assignment.

Blog Entry #1

Don't Believe the Family: A Warning from Inside

It's taken me months to write this. Just typing these words feels dangerous. I can't use my real name—or my Family name. They'd find me. The Family has eyes everywhere. Their network is merciless. And that app you all use? It tracks everything.

I was one of them—a Sister. I believed the lies about choice and power. But the Family isn't what you think. It's not empowerment. It's a machine that grinds you down until you are unrecognizable.

The glamour is a trap. The luxury is a gilded cage. What you think is freedom is the most elegant and subtle control imaginable. You don't even feel the leash as it tightens around your neck.

To any girl thinking about joining: Run. Run so fast their promises can't catch you.

They'll try to discredit me. They'll say I'm bitter, crazy, or another girl who couldn't handle "the lifestyle." Let them. The truth has its own weight. I'm doing this so they can't hurt anyone else the way they hurt me.

—Step-Sister

The fear in the first post is raw, honest. What kind of next-level trauma pushes someone to write this? The posts are erratic, dropped at random over the last two years. I've developed a new habit—refreshing the page, hoping for an update—but it's been weeks. A dry spell.

Reading them over and over, though, I noticed things. A shift in the writing. At first, it's subtle, but then it hits you. It's like a different person behind the keyboard. The phrasing, the rhythm—it all changes. There have to be at least two of them. The tonal whiplash is a dead giveaway.

Blog Entry #14

The Mask Slips: The Real Family Exposed

Listen close. This is what they never want you to see.

The Family may seem perfect from the outside. Glossy. Polished. Like a high-end finishing school where beautiful young women get "opportunities." But perfection is always a lie, especially when someone's working that hard to maintain it.

I've seen how they recruit. Young and vulnerable. Women who think they're getting a golden ticket to something better. But golden tickets have razor-sharp edges, and the Family knows how to slice you open without leaving a mark.

They sell you on luxury, but you are not the product. You are the tool. For what job, you ask? You don't want to know. There is a rot in the foundation of this Family, a purpose far uglier than selling sex. You think you know the rules of the game, but you're playing checkers on a Monopoly board.

The Family isn't a family. It's a trap. Get out while you can.

Stay sharp, Stay free.

—Your Step-Sister

The first dozen entries are missives from the past, desperate pleas from someone trying to warn people away. The voice in post fourteen isn't frightened; it's furious. It's a manifesto.

And post thirteen? It just…doesn't exist. Superstition? Maybe. But the change happens right there, straddling that missing number. That can't be a coincidence.

Of course, the bit about the app being a leash? I'd already figured as much. Denial can be a very cozy blanket, though. You don't pull at that thread when you're busy trying to convince yourself you've finally made a positive life choice.

I checked my room for cameras and everything but came up empty. Not that I'd know what to look for, anyway. My electronics skills begin and end with knowing which end of the phone to talk into.

Good thing there's a certain tech genius who likes me.

FINDING JEREMY's office is like a quest in a fantasy novel. The tech floor is a maze of identical, unmarked corridors filled with the hum of servers that sounds like the world's most expensive white noise machine.

Three wrong turns later, a dip into a janitor's closet, and the urge to give up getting stronger, I stumble across a door with a tiny paper sign in what must be eight-point font—"J. Tallinder"—because why make things easy?

Two knocks, and something crashes inside the office.

"Come in?" Jeremy's voice lilts up at the end like he's not sure if visitors are allowed.

When the door opens, he's frantically shoving empty Red Bull cans into his desk drawer like a teenager hiding contraband from his mom. His eyes widen behind his frameless glasses as he springs to his feet, sending a stack of papers spilling over the side of the desk.

"Star. Hi. You're—you're here." He adjusts his frames. "Did I miss a meeting? I check my schedule obsessively. I would've remembered."

"Relax, Jeremy. I come in peace. Finding your office is like discovering the final level of a dungeon. Do they purposely hide you guys down here?"

An embarrassed laugh. "Security protocol. Keep the tech nerds where no one can find us." He casually sweeps a collection of chip bags into his trash can. "Sorry about the mess. I wasn't expecting... well, anyone."

His little cave is a tech genius cliché: three massive monitors, walls covered in sticky notes with cryptic codes, and enough snack wrappers to suggest he lives here. Well-read paperback books line one shelf; an army of energy drink cans lines another.

"I love the 'bachelor pad meets mission control' aesthetic."

Jeremy blushes, heat virtually radiating off him. "It's functional. I mean, most of my time is spent here, so…" He trails off, staring at me like I'm a unicorn that wandered into his zoo. "Is there something wrong with your app? I could have sent someone up if you're having technical issues."

"No, the app works fine. Too well, actually." I drop into the only other chair in the room. "That's kind of why I'm here."

"Oh?" His eyebrows shoot up like they're trying to escape his forehead.

"Yeah. The Family portal. Like, how much information does it collect? And who has access to it?"

Jeremy's jaw tightens, and he glances at the door like he's checking for eavesdroppers.

"That's an interesting question. Why do you want to know?"

My skirt—chosen for this exact purpose—rides up my thigh as my body settles back into position. It's a costume for a role that I loathe having to play. "Idle curiosity?"

Jeremy's laugh comes out strangled, like a hiccup that took a wrong turn. His eyes fall on my legs, dart away, then come back again—a ping-pong match of desire versus professionalism.

"I, uh—" He swallows hard. "Star, I can't discuss the backend systems with users." The pen in his hand clicks repeatedly.

I pout, sticking out my lower lip. "Come on, Jeremy. It's not like they're nuclear launch codes. I only want to know who can see what I'm doing on there." Leaning forward to push up what little cleavage I have takes actual effort. "Don't you trust me?" The words taste like acid.

The grimace on his face makes it seem like I've asked him to choose between his favorite computer and his mother.

"It's not about trust." He clears his throat. "It's about security. Natalia would literally skin me alive and use my hide as a statement piece in her office if I started giving away secrets to the Sisters." He nudges his glasses into place, a nervous habit I've noticed he uses when he needs a moment to think. "She's made it very clear that tech stays with tech."

Sitting back, I let the pout fade and my cleavage relax. He might be awkward, but he's not stupid, just paranoid. His gaze flicks to the security monitor in the corner, as if he expects Natalia to walk through the screen.

"Fair enough," I say. "Can't blame a girl for trying."

His face relaxes, but immediately tenses up again when I ask, "Are you familiar with the Step-Sister blog?"

His hand is suspended in midair over his keyboard. The flicker of recognition on his face is unmistakable.

"The Step-Sister blog?" He blinks rapidly. "I mean, yes. I'm familiar with it. Security rules require monitoring of all external references to the Family. Why do you ask?"

Scooting the chair forward, I monitor his face carefully. "What's your take on it? Crackpot? Or is there something to it?"

Jeremy looks from his monitors to the door, then back to me. The flustered boyishness drains from his face, replaced by a sudden, unnerving stillness. It's like he's switching to a different operating system.

"The official position," he says, "is that a disgruntled former Sister writes it. Fabricated, but peppered with enough truth to seem credible."

My eyes roll, and the chair creaks. "Okay, Natalia. Now let's hear what Jeremy thinks."

His posture corrects, the *nervous tech guy* mask falls away, and he smiles.

"Okay, you got me," he admits, running a hand through his hair.

"So? Real Jeremy's thoughts?"

Reclining in his chair, he lets out a long sigh. "Look, I'm not supposed to have opinions about these things. I just maintain the systems."

"And yet you do?"

"Everyone does." He glances at the door again, types something on his keyboard, and the sound from the hallway is now in the office as well. "White noise generator," he explains. "Makes it harder for anyone to listen in."

"You're paranoid?"

"I'm cautious," he corrects. "There's a difference."

"And that caution suggests the blog isn't total bullshit."

"What are you looking for, Star?"

The question hangs between us, and I don't have an answer. Am I looking for validation? Or someone to tell me I'm overreacting?

Time to drop the flirty act. Because this is about something that matters, and he deserves the truth if I'm going to ask him to risk his neck for it.

"Jeremy, between you and me, okay?"

"Okay."

"There's a lot of truth in those posts. I've read them all multiple times. She knows things that only a Sister would know. There's an undercurrent of fear in them. You see it too, don't you? Help me find out who it is."

Jeremy exhales like I asked him to jump off the Brooklyn Bridge with me. His fingers stop their nervous tapping, and he stares at me with an odd intensity.

"You're asking a lot here. Do you know what I'd be risking?"

I do, but I need him. Not because he's the only tech genius in the building, but because there's something underneath all that nervousness that feels trustworthy.

"No one will know," I say, leaning across the desk to touch his hand. "The person who built the system is the only one who knows how to move through it unseen, right?"

He draws his hand back and slips off his glasses, fingertips pressing into his eyes. "It's not that simple."

"Why not?"

He's quiet for a moment, then slides his glasses back on. "Do you know what I did before the Family? I worked at Google. Normal hours, benefits, never worried if what I was building would—" He stops himself.

"Would what?"

"Nothing." He shakes his head. "I've spent years convincing myself that I just maintain systems here. That's it. Just infrastructure. I don't ask questions."

I look into his eyes. "Maybe it's time to ask some?"

Jeremy turns toward his monitors, staring at them like they might offer an escape. His nose wrinkles, the conflict playing out across his face—a war between the safety of ignorance versus the pull of truth.

"It would take time," he says. "And I'd need to be careful. Use a secure channel, route everything through proxies."

Thinking through the logistics—a good sign.

"I'm not asking you to expose yourself," I say. "Help me find the source. That's all."

He studies my face. "Why is this so important to you?"

It's a fair question. One I'm not entirely ready to answer. "Because I need to understand what I've gotten myself into."

Sitting back in the chair, he closes his eyes, and I get the sense that he's been waiting for this. The twitch of his cheek says that something inside him has been wanting to do the wrong thing, but just needed the right reason.

He exhales. "Give me a day. I'll see if I can do anything."

I smile.

"But Star, if this gets too risky, I'm out. I mean it."

I nod, still smiling.

EIGHT

Aura's hip-hop playlist bleeds through the common room door before I even reach it. I push inside to a wall of noise—Wednesday night Sister time. Mandatory fun.

The room is a collage of the usual cliques: Sage holds quiet court with the veterans in one corner; a trio performs yoga poses near the TV, hoping to find Zen amid the noise; and Aura's crew is sprawled on the main couch, laughing as they scroll through their phones.

"Where's Barbie?" someone calls from the poker table, where the betting chips appear to be chocolate truffles.

"She's working," Sage cuts through the chatter without looking up.

"On a Wednesday?"

"Hey, those awards don't win themselves," Aura shouts.

A wave of laughter ripples through the room.

The can of hard seltzer I grab sweats cold against my palm as I eye the giant beanbag chair. Big mistake. The thing swallows me whole the moment I fall into it—apparently "sitting" was too ambitious a goal. I'm sinking into furniture quicksand. Every attempt to adjust only makes it worse.

Movement down the hallway catches my eye. Melody and Kora stand near the elevator, and even from here, I can tell something's off. Kora's arms are crossed, her frame tense. Melody's gesturing with her hands in small, controlled movements that don't match the strain on her face. They're speaking low—Kora keeps shaking her head, Melody's fingers clench and unclench at her sides. This isn't their usual banter.

Shifting in my beanbag prison, I try to get a better view without being obvious about it. Melody's saying something, her face pinched with worry. Kora responds with what I think is "No way," based on her lip movements, then glances over her shoulder like she's checking if anyone's there.

What the hell? They've always gotten along great. I can't recall seeing them at odds before.

Kora checks her watch like it's a lifeline, says something clipped, and walks toward the elevator. Melody stands there alone for a moment, her posture slumped. She exhales, straightens up, and plasters on a fake smile before heading into the common room.

Turning my head away, I pretend to be fascinated by my drink. What I witnessed was private and raw. Melody's always so bubbly, so eager to please. Seeing her upset like that makes my insides curl up.

Maybe it's paranoia. They could have been arguing about borrowed clothes or half-eaten yogurt left in the fridge. I put it aside and wave at her across the room. Melody weaves through the clusters of Sisters, her smile widening as she approaches.

"Look at you," she says, putting her hands on her hips. "Like a turtle stuck on its back. You planning to stay there all night, or should I call for a salvage team?"

I wiggle helplessly. "I think this thing is eating me. I'll be nothing but shoes by morning."

She laughs, but it lacks her trademark lightness as her arms extend down to me. "Come on, let's rescue you from certain doom."

My hands find hers, and she yanks with the kind of strength that makes you reconsider everything you thought you knew about tiny people and their deceptively powerful grip. With a lurch, I pop free from the beanbag's clutches and nearly topple into her.

"My hero," I say, faux swoon and all.

We head to a small love seat in the corner. Her smile is flawless—too flawless, like someone pressing on a wound and pretending not to feel it. "Hey, you okay?" I ask.

Her eyes flicker away for a second before returning. "I'm fine. Just nervous about tomorrow. Some big shot from D.C., real high-level. Kora likes things exact."

"She said that?"

"Yeah, no biggie." She grabs my can of seltzer and takes a long sip. "Really, I'm good."

The urge to push harder is strong—to tell her I saw their argument. But the fragile expression on her face puts the brakes on my interrogation. Melody's been my rock since day one in this place. If she's not ready to talk about what's bothering her, I can respect that.

Across the room, Sage is observing us, missing nothing. She raises her glass in our direction with a mysterious smile.

"Sage is looking over here," I say without moving my lips.

Melody glances up, then away again. "She's always watching." It doesn't sound like admiration.

"What do you me—"

Before I finish my question, the music is cranked louder, and several Sisters start dancing in the center of the room. Melody jumps up, taking me with her.

"Come on, Star. Let's dance!"

"What? No… I'm not—"

Kora steps into the common room, head down as she walks toward the yoga girls.

"I don't dance," I protest, but she's already dragging me by the wrist. "I have a medical condition. Doctor's orders."

"What condition?" She laughs, not slowing down.

"Acute rhythmic deficiency. It's terminal."

But it's too late. We're in the middle of the floor. Melody finds her groove immediately, eyes closed, lost in the rhythm. I look like I'm fighting off invisible insects.

"Just feel it!" she shouts.

"Feel what? My dignity leaving my body?"

She spins me around, but the move only throws me off-balance. As I'm contemplating faking an injury, Aura bursts into the center of the floor. Everyone steps back and surrounds her.

Holy shit.

Aura drops to the floor, spins on one hand, then flips back to her feet in a move that defies physics. Her tiny frame becomes a blur of motion—popping, locking, spinning. This isn't just dancing; this is destroying gravity's entire thesis.

"Go Au-ra! Go Au-ra!" The singsong chant starts with Melody and spreads through the crowd. Sage joins in from her perch, full of enthusiasm.

"Where did she learn to do that?" I shout.

"Dance crew in the Bronx. Before, you know…"

Before the Family. Before all this.

Aura finishes with a dramatic freeze pose, and the room erupts. She pops up, takes an exaggerated bow, and for a moment, the hierarchy of the Family dissolves.

"*¡Así se hace, perras!*" Aura laughs, high-fiving everyone around her.

"I think I pulled something watching you," I say.

"Girl, you dance like you're being electrocuted," Aura replies, but her smile takes the sting out of it.

The music shifts again, and for a few minutes, nobody's thinking about clients or portfolios or whatever Kora and Melody were arguing over.

We're a bunch of girls dancing, laughing at ourselves and one another. It's almost normal.

Melody throws her head back, smiling, and all traces of her earlier worry are gone. That's the point of this, isn't it? The mandatory fun, the Sister bonding—it's anesthesia, a painkiller for reality.

Because when the music fades, we all remember where we are and what we do here.

Nine

The cafeteria buzzes with morning energy, but I'm fixated on Aura as she demolishes a stack of pancakes like she's refueling after a marathon. Which, given last night's performance, isn't far off.

"I still can't believe those moves." I stab at my eggs. "Where did you learn to dance like that?"

Aura grins, syrup on her chin. "My cousin Rico taught me when I was twelve. Said I needed something to keep me out of trouble."

"Did it work?" Melody asks, picking at her toast and tearing it into small pieces without eating any.

"Hell no. Just made me better at running away." Aura giggles.

"Where's Kora this morning?" I ask, glancing around the cafeteria. "Leaving her little Sisters to fend for themselves?"

Melody's fingers stop tearing. "She had an off-site meeting. Left early."

"Everything okay?" I lean in. "You seem—"

"A little nervous, that's all. I'm good."

"Not surprising with Kora as your Big Sister," Aura says.

"What's that mean?" I ask.

Aura chuckles. "Let's say her mentoring style can be a little... aggressive. Right, Mel?"

Melody gives a half-hearted smile and nod.

"Kora's idea of being a Big Sister is tossing you into the ocean and calling it a swimming lesson." Aura laughs and pops a strawberry into her mouth.

The buzzer cuts through the air like a chainsaw, drowning out what I was about to say. Around us, Sisters gather their plates, conversations switching from lazy morning chatter to business mode.

"Time for the grind," Aura says, pushing back from the table.

We fall in line and walk single file into the conference room. Girls are missing, at least six or seven, and that doesn't include Kora. The side door opens, and Natalia steps onto the stage.

"Good morning, Sisters," she begins.

The room responds in unison, "Good morning, Natalia."

It's weird participating in these synchronized responses, like being in some fancy boarding school run by a corporate cult.

"First, I'd like to announce that several of our Sisters are working off-site today," Natalia continues, tapping her tablet. "They're preparing for the upcoming Harrington gala."

Next to me, Melody shifts in her seat. No excitement at the mention of a gala; her face is blank, posture still.

"I trust everyone enjoyed themselves at our Wednesday gathering," Natalia says with a thin smile. "Sage will collect suggestions for future themed nights."

Sage turns and smiles from her seat toward the front.

"Next," Natalia barks, "we have two special clients visiting from Washington, D.C., this evening." She looks up. "Jade, Melody, these gentlemen are significant to the Family. I expect you both to be exceptional."

My head snaps toward Melody. This is huge—a direct assignment from Natalia herself. But instead of bouncing in her seat or flashing her goofy grin, she nods, fingers locked around her pen.

When Natalia hands the floor to Sage, I whisper to Melody.

"Hey, big night, huh? You okay?"

Her smile is all teeth and no soul. "I'm fine, Star."

I want to believe her. But her eyes don't match her mouth.

She turns away, focusing intently on Sage as she reads out assignments. But the muscles in her jaw are twitching; her breathing is too controlled.

That look is familiar. I've seen it in shelters, on the streets, in my mirror. Something's tearing her up inside.

My plan? Find out what happened, even if it means trailing her all day like some bargain-bin private detective.

A vibration hums against my thigh. When I slide the phone from my pocket, there's a notification I've never seen before.

You have a new encrypted message.

That's odd. Everything usually comes through the Family portal. This is new—and not at all suspicious.

I tap the notification, and a message window appears.

JEREMY

Come see me.

He's found something.

I promise my guilty conscience that I'll catch up with Melody after this is done. For now, I'm off to see the wizard.

JEREMY'S HUNCHED over the desk when I stroll in, three monitors glowing around him like a digital altar. His hair is messier than usual, which means he's been running his hands through it. Must be a stress habit.

He gestures toward the door, saying nothing. I push it closed, the staccato *click* locking it into place.

He nods at the chair across from his desk. "Sit."

The chair catches me, and my knee bounces immediately. Can't help it. When the nerves hit, my body moves on its own.

"You found something, didn't you?"

Jeremy holds up a hand. "Don't get too excited. It's not much, but it's a start."

He turns his center monitor toward me. The screen shows the Step-Sister blog, but it's wrong somehow. Older. Crappier. The layout is basic, the font is different, and I don't understand any of this.

"What is this?" My knee bounces faster. "Like a prototype or something?"

"Close," Jeremy says. He clicks his mouse, and another window pops up—this one is all text. "It's an old version. I think the first one. It was posted on the dark web before they moved it to the one they're using now."

I blink. "Dark web?"

Jeremy exhales, runs his hand through his hair—*I knew it*—and leans back in his chair. "Okay, how do I explain this…" He thinks for a second and then swivels his chair to face me.

"Okay, so imagine the regular internet we all use is New York City. Except it's everything at street level and above you can see, right?"

"Uh-huh."

"So, the dark web is like another level of the internet, underground—the tunnels and passages. They're always there, but hard to get to unless you know where to look."

"So, like a…secret internet?"

"Yes." He smiles, and it's like I've gained a few brain cells. "For instance, the Family's main site is on the dark web because, well, you can imagine the shitstorm if it were out there next to Amazon and your local church. It's hidden and anonymous, so it's harder to track who visits and where they're coming from."

"Okay," I say, trying to keep up.

"Whoever launched Step-Sister originally put it on the dark web to protect themselves. But at some point, it got moved to the regular public internet. And when it did, they forgot to remove this version."

"Oh, I get it." I totally don't. "And that means…what exactly?"

Jeremy's eyes widen. "It means they made a mistake. They ultimately exposed the IP address of the server, so I looked into it. And that's what this window is here." He points to the screen for emphasis. "It's a simple WordPress site, and like most amateurs, they didn't patch it, so I was able to gain admin access to it."

Now *that* makes sense to me. "Admin access? So, you can see… everything?"

"Well, on this old version, yes. But this hasn't been touched or updated in well over a year."

My heart sinks a little.

"But we have all the dates of the first twelve posts and the IP addresses used to post them."

My body moves before my brain can catch up, launching into his arms. "Thank you—you didn't have to."

He stiffens like he's been hit with a taser. When I pull back, he's doing the blinking-glasses-adjusting thing again.

"I'm sorry. I didn't—"

"No, Star, it's okay. Thank you…er, you're welcome." He fixes his crooked glasses. "I found something else as well."

"What?"

He opens a file on his monitor. It's text, but garbled.

"This appears to be part of a post that was never published." He points to the monitor. "It was deleted, but I did a deep recovery on it. During the process, it was corrupted, but there's still some readable text."

"So, what can we do with this information?"

"That's a good question. The first eleven posts are from the same IP address here in the city, but post twelve and this deleted one are from a public Wi-Fi in Hoboken. Then they must have moved to the new server. I checked it out, and it's locked down tight. So, they've gotten smarter. I'll send all the data over to you."

"Thanks again. Dinner is on me." My smile is genuine this time— no flirty nonsense required.

He turns back to his monitor, stops, and looks over at me. "If you find anything interesting, let me know, okay?"

I've successfully recruited the wizard.

TWO TORN-OUT notebook pages sit in front of me, Jeremy's data scribbled across them: twelve posts, a corrupted file, dates, and locations. My pen traces the timeline, trying to force a pattern to reveal itself—because patterns always exist, right?

"Come on," I mutter, tapping the pen against my teeth. "Give me something."

The earliest post is from two years ago. Eleven posts from the same IP, but not the last two. Why the change? Was the writer running? Hiding?

I close my eyes, and I'm sitting cross-legged on our living room floor. Amelia, sixteen and impossibly cool, is sprawled beside me with a 1,000-piece puzzle scattered between us.

"Start with the edges, Sprout," she'd said, flipping pieces right side up. "Make your frame first, then work your way in."

"That's boring," I'd replied, pouting.

"Yeah, but it works." She'd flicked my nose. "Sometimes the boring way is the smart way."

My eyes open, and I blink down at the scattered notes. The edges. The frame.

The corrupted file opens, displaying a bunch of zeros and funky characters I've never seen before. It's like every language on Earth puked into a word processor.

As I scroll, I find fragments of text—not complete sentences, but remnants from the original file.

```
.e.f..t .n..y.o..  .ea..n.. Sp.c..l A.s.t.
.ex .n. .e.r.t.
.la..i..e. .n.e. .o.p..a.e..s.i.n..e
P.l..i.a. .l.c..ai. .o. e..o.t..w.a.o..
```

A couple of paragraphs are like this, and I can't make heads or tails of them.

If there's something here, I'll find it. If Amelia taught me anything, it's that every puzzle has a solution if you find the right way to look at it.

The edges first. Then work my way in.

I scroll to the last line in the file.

```
.ou. S.ep..is.er
```

My breath catches. It's her sign-off, "Your Step-Sister." This is a blog post. This was going to be entry number thirteen, wasn't it? Why did she delete it and then never repost it?

The buzz of my phone startles me.

MELODY

Heading out

Shit. How did I forget?

The door swings wide, and the potted fern outside my room becomes an unfortunate casualty of my momentum—again. "We have to stop meeting like this," I say.

They're waiting by Melody's door—pure elegance. Jade is wearing midnight blue, while Melody's crimson red dress clings and flows, aging her beyond her years into something fierce and refined.

"Damn, look at you two," I call out, breathless from my sprint. "Mel, you're absolutely gorgeous."

She twirls slowly, the dress catching the light. "You think? It's not too much?"

"Not at all."

"I've never had to prepare this much for a client," Jade says, checking her clutch repeatedly. "Three separate briefings, two wardrobe consultations, and Natalia reviewing my file? It's intense."

Melody nods as she fidgets with her bracelet, twisting it around her wrist.

I give her shoulder a gentle squeeze. "You're both going to be amazing. Seriously, they'll be putty in your hands."

"Thanks, Star." Jade's confidence is genuine, while Melody's face doesn't radiate the same.

The elevator chimes, and the doors slide open.

"Don't wait up for me," Melody says, stepping inside. "This is definitely going to be a late night."

"No problem. We'll catch up in the morning. I want all the gossip." I wink at her, trying to lighten the mood.

She laughs, but there's no joy. As Jade steps in beside her, she adjusts the Family pendant hanging from Jade's neck, centering it perfectly.

"There, that's better."

It's such a Melody thing to do—fussing over someone else when she's the one who needs reassurance. I've seen her do it so many times.

The doors start to slide over, and my stomach knots.

"Hey, Mel—"

Her eyes meet mine, wide and questioning.

"Never mind," I say, forcing a smile. "You've got this."

She nods, and the doors close with a soft thud.

My legs stay rooted in place, and I'm not thinking so much as vibrating with thoughts. I *should've* said something.

Back in my room, the notes are still scattered where I left them.

The edges first. Then work my way in.

TEN

My phone screams in the dark.

Notifications hit like machine-gun fire—*ping-ping-ping-ping*—dragging me from a deep sleep. My eyes won't focus. The screen burns white spots into my vision, but through the blur, one word crystallizes. Repeated in message after message.

Melody.

My heart stops, then restarts, a frantic drum against my ribs.

I am numb as I get out of bed, my bare feet hitting the carpet. Then I'm running, camisole twisted, shorts riding up, brain lagging a few steps behind.

The common area is already crowded. A crush of sisters, all staring. Too many faces. Too much knowing—that terrible, pitying look that says everything before a word is spoken.

Sage stands at the center of them all, hair still tidy, but her face... God, her face.

My legs won't carry me farther than the doorway. Tears build, hot and urgent. I shake my head. Small, desperate movements. *No, no, no.*

"Star." She's moving toward me, arms opening.

"Don't." The word comes out broken. "Please don't tell me—"

"Melody didn't come home last night." There's a tremor in the gentleness. "Her phone is off. No tracking."

The room warps, my knees buckle, and I'm in her arms, my face pressed against her silk blouse, sobbing so hard I can't breathe.

"Shhh, shhh." Sage's hand strokes my hair. "Caron's already sent a recon specialist. They're trying to trace her steps, and we're waiting for information."

"Jade?" I choke out.

"Jade came back early this morning." Sage speaks slowly. "We've talked to her. She saw Melody heading upstairs with her client, and she seemed in good spirits."

Good spirits. The words are a needle in my head. The fear that was on her face in that elevator. I should have said something. I should have—

"What time?" My lip quivers. "When did Jade come back?"

"Around four."

Four. The ornate clock on the wall says it's almost seven. She's been on her own for three hours.

The other girls are watching me—Trixie with a hand to her mouth, two others I don't know huddled by the window. Everything is too small, too hot.

"I need to see Jade."

"Star—"

"I need to see her!" I shout. "She has to know something."

Sage looks behind me. "She's in the conference room. They're going through her information, trying to piece together—"

"Her information?" I grab Sage's arm. "What about the client? Where is he?"

"We're still looking into that. There were some…irregularities."

Irregularities. The word makes me want to heave. In the Family, *irregularities* mean wrong—really wrong.

"I can help. I've been working on something—these posts. There might be a connection—"

"Star," she says firmly. "The best thing you can do is let the specialists handle this. Caron has people—"

"Fuck Caron's people!" I wrench away from her. "This is Melody!"

The room goes silent. I've crossed a line. You don't talk about Caron like that, not here.

Sage's face hardens. "You're scared, Star. We all are. But losing control won't help her."

She's right. But standing here doing nothing while Melody is…

"Can I wait in there? Please?" I'm blubbering like a toddler. "Please?"

Sage studies my face and takes my hand. "Come on. But stay quiet. You don't interfere. Understood?"

I nod, my bare feet slapping the floor as I follow her. Heart drumming so loud I'm sure everyone can hear it. A jumble of scenes in my mind: Melody's red dress. The twist of her bracelet. The way she adjusted Jade's pendant so carefully.

Never mind. You've got this.

My last words to her. Why didn't I say to be careful? Why didn't I say I had a bad feeling? Why didn't I say I loved her?

The door to the conference room pushes open, and Natalia's head snaps up from the massive oak table she's standing over. She grimaces when she sees me.

"Absolutely not. Get—" She bites off the command.

Sage raises her hand, a gesture of power, and her eyes lock with Natalia's in a wordless conversation I'm not privy to. Natalia's jaw tightens, and after a long moment appraising my tear-streaked face and bare feet, she turns away with a dismissive flick of her wrist.

Sage guides me to a leather chair against the wall, a place for observers. "Try to stay calm." She crouches, her face softer now, her own fear leaking through. "We'll get through this." She squeezes my shoulder and joins the others at the table.

I pull my feet up on the chair and curl in on myself. Jade isn't the composed goddess from last night. Her makeup is smeared, with dark trails down her cheeks. The midnight blue dress is torn and stained. She's in mid-conversation when I'm able to overhear.

"...it was okay, though." Jade's timbre wavers. "Everything went like the briefing. We got to the bar and stayed a couple of hours. Neither of us was drunk."

"And then?" Natalia paces, Louboutins clicking a brisk rhythm on the floor.

"We split up. Like we discussed." Jade wipes her face. "Melody went with Daniels, and I went with Cortez. Daniels even said something about meeting for coffee in the morning."

Jeremy is hunched over his laptop. "App data shows Jade's phone at the hotel bar at 11:47 p.m. Remained until 1:23 a.m., then moved to the Bentley Suite. Correct?" He glances at Jade. She agrees, sniffling. "And Daniels was in the Dior Suite?"

"I waited for her." Jade coughs. "When I left at three thirty, I tried to check on her, but her location didn't show in the portal."

"Her phone," Jeremy cuts in, "stopped transmitting data at 3:10 a.m." He looks at Natalia.

3:10 a.m. Where could she have been?

"The phone was either turned off," he continues, voice clinical, "or the battery died."

"Then why isn't it there?" Natalia's composure finally cracks. "The room was empty. Daniels checked out at 3:30 a.m. The surveillance footage—"

"Shows nothing useful," Jeremy finishes. "According to the hotel's security, the cameras had 'technical difficulties' between 2 and 4 a.m."

Technical difficulties. The phrase hammers in my head. How convenient. There's no way that's a coincidence.

Sage glances back at me, and I bury my face in my knees.

"What about Daniels's background check?" Sage asks.

"Clean," Natalia spits. "Too clean in retrospect. Jeremy's running deeper searches."

Their voices fade. The sleek, cold room is like a mausoleum, all money and death. Somewhere out there, Melody is frightened. Or Hurt. Or worse.

"Not again," I pray into my knees. "Please not again."

First, Amelia vanished into the night. Then my mother, eaten away by cancer. Now Melody—bright, beautiful Melody. My seahorse.

Strong tails in stormy waters.

The leather of the chair creaks as I sway back and forth to comfort myself. Phone calls are made, databases searched, and contacts leveraged. The Family's vast network grinds into action around me, but the hole in my heart grows wider with every passing minute.

They're all focused on the data. On the *how.* But there's something they won't say out loud: In this city, in a world like ours, girls who disappear at three in the morning don't come back.

No, I can't think like that. I won't.

The edges first. Amelia in my memory. *Find your boundaries.*

But what do you do when the puzzle keeps getting bigger and the pieces keep disappearing?

THE BLANKET IS soft against my skin, but it can't stop the trembling. My teacup shakes as I gently guide it to my lips—chamomile, though

I can't taste anything. Everything in the common area feels different now, like all the warmth has been sucked out of it. Aura's hand moves in slow circles on my back, steady and rhythmic.

Around us, Sisters drift aimlessly. Trixie stands by the window, gazing out into nothing. Two other girls lean against the wall, whispering in hushed tones that fade whenever I glance their way. Someone moves toward the chair across from me, hesitates, then backs away. We're all waiting for something. News. A miracle.

The main door bursts open, fracturing the silence.

Caron enters first, and my breath catches. His usual warmth, that paternal energy that swirls around him—it's gone. His shoulders are slumped, and his face is drawn and gray. Behind him, two men follow like shadows, dressed in dark suits and surveying the room like searchlights. Ex-police or military for sure. One has an earpiece, the thin wire disappearing into his collar. The other carries a metal briefcase that looks like it could survive a bomb blast.

They move with purpose toward the conference room, and for a split second, Caron's eyes find mine.

His expression—God, I've never seen him like this. It's more *finality* than sadness, like a doctor about to deliver terminal news.

My fingers twitch. The cup tips. Falls. Shatters on the marble floor in a spray of ceramic and lukewarm tea.

I'm on my feet in an instant, the blanket sliding to the floor. "Caron—"

Strong arms wrap around me from behind, pulling me back. I struggle, desperate to follow him, to demand answers, to make him tell me she's okay, that this is all a misunderstanding.

"Star!" I twist to find Kora with bloodshot eyes and a runny nose. Her gym clothes are rumpled and creased. "I know, honey. I know."

"No!" I try to pull away, but she's stronger than me. "I need to—he has to tell me—"

"You can't." Her tone splinters. "Star, you can't. Sit here with me and Aura. Please."

The fight drains out of me. My knees buckle, and Kora guides me to the couch, her arm tight around me. Aura is quiet but supportive, rubbing careful circles on my back again. The shattered cup lies forgotten on the floor, tea seeping into the throw rug.

"They found something," I whimper.

Kora's silence agrees with me.

Through the glass walls of the conference room, Caron and his men join the others. Natalia stands abruptly when they enter. Jeremy's fingers freeze over his keyboard. Jade's face crumples.

One of the dark-suited men sets the briefcase on the table, and I imagine the click of the latches sounding like gunshots.

"Don't look," Aura says. "Whatever they're doing in there, you don't need to see it."

But I can't turn away. Caron's lips move, and Natalia's hand flies to her mouth. Jeremy pushes back from the table like he's been shocked. And Sage—always composed—sinks into the chair like her legs have melted.

The sob builds inside me like a tidal wave. "She's dead."

"We don't know that," Kora says, but there's no conviction.

"She's dead." The words come out louder this time, and then I'm screaming. "She's dead!" I knew something was wrong, but I didn't stop her—I *let her go*.

Kora holds me while I thrash. I'm wailing my throat raw and beating my fists against anything within range. The other Sisters back away, giving us space, but they're staring at me. Their pity. Their relief that it wasn't them, wasn't their best friend, wasn't their—

"Breathe!" Kora commands, her coach voice cutting through my hysteria. "In through your nose, out through your mouth. Come on, Star. Do it with me."

Each inhalation scrapes like broken glass down my throat. In the conference room, the dark-suited man pulls something from the briefcase. Small. Metallic. I can't see clearly through the tears.

Sage's head snaps toward us, and she rushes through the conference room door.

"Take her to her room," she orders. "Now."

"What did they find?" I demand, trying to look past her. "What's in the case?"

"Star—"

"What did they find?!" I bellow, more gravel than words.

Sage kneels, her hands gripping mine so hard it hurts. "Evidence. They found evidence. That's all you need to know right now."

Evidence. The word is clinical, cold. Evidence of what? A struggle? Blood?

"I want to see—"

"No!" Sage snaps. "You don't. Trust me on this, Star. You don't."

My mind races, filling in the blanks with every horrible possibility. Melody's red dress is torn. Her careful makeup smeared. Her eyes—those bright green eyes that crinkled when she laughed—empty and staring at nothing.

"Come on, honey." Kora pulls me to my feet, and I can't muster the strength to resist anymore. "Let's get you somewhere quiet."

They guide me toward my room, and I turn to peer back through the conference room glass. Caron is sitting, his head in his hands. The dark-suited man repacks the briefcase, and on the table, barely visible, something glints—black and gold, catching the light.

A Family pendant. Melody's pendant. Like a dog tag from a soldier who's never coming home.

My legs give out entirely, and I fall back into Kora's arms. The heaves come again, quieter now but somehow worse. Deep and agonizing, like they're tearing me apart from the inside.

"She's supposed to come back," I sob into Kora's shoulder. "She always came back."

But not this time. This time, all that came back was evidence in a metal briefcase and the knowledge that somewhere out there, in this city of millions, my best friend is gone.

Kora drags me away—from the evidence, from the truth. But not from the memory of Melody's nervous smile, or the way she always had my back, or the last words I said to her.

You've got this.

The biggest lie I've ever told.

ELEVEN

The cocoon of blankets can't keep out the cold that's settled in my bones. I've been staring at the same spot on the wall for what must be hours. Time isn't working right anymore. Aura sits beside me, strong and quiet, her presence the only thing keeping me from falling apart.

The door opens, and Kora walks in carrying a tray of food. The smell hits me like a wall, and a flash of nausea follows.

"Try to eat something if you can." She sets it down next to me.

All I see in the food is Melody at breakfast yesterday, that worried look on her face as she tore her soggy toast into strips.

Melody, who isn't coming back.

"I was supposed to protect her." It comes out with more air than sound.

Kora's fingers find mine. "No, Star. We were all supposed to protect one another."

Their kindness is like a fake medal—one more thing I don't deserve.

The door pushes in, and Sage crosses the room, kneeling in front of me. She's disheveled, no makeup, eyes red-rimmed and puffy. She takes my hands in hers. They're cold and trembling.

"There's going to be an all-hands in a few minutes, okay?"

I nod.

"Star…" She squeezes my hands tighter. "Look at me."

Raising my head takes more effort than it should, but I meet her eyes.

"I promise you, everyone from Caron on down is here for you."

Something about her—the raw sincerity—causes fresh tears to well up. For a moment, the glamour and armor dissolve as she pulls me to her, and we're just two people drowning in the same grief.

Kora's strong arms slide beneath us, interrupting the hug and lifting me with ease. Sage stands up quickly, fixing her blouse with shaking hands and looking around the room as if she's forgotten why she's here. Her eyes meet mine again, full of something I can't name.

Then she turns and walks out, closing the door quietly behind her.

The buzzer cuts through the haze of my grief. I don't move, can't move, but Kora is already guiding me forward.

"Come on, Star. We need to go."

The hallway is a blur of faces. Sisters stop as we pass, their conversations dying mid-sentence. They're looking at me—pitying, curious, afraid. Word travels fast in the Family. Everyone knows.

Melody is dead.

I'll never hear her laugh again, never see her face light up when she talks about musicals, never feel her hand in mine while we sit on her bed and share our dreams.

Someone steps into our path. I take a moment to focus, to recognize the flawless blonde hair, the hourglass figure.

Barbie.

She covers my hand with both of hers, and it's surprisingly warm. Her face—usually set in that practiced, superior smile—is soft with genuine concern.

"Oh, child, I am so sorry," she says, her Southern accent thick with emotion. "If you ever need anything at all, you let me know now, ya hear?"

Throat too tight for words, I can only nod. She squeezes my hand once more before stepping away, and we continue our slow procession to the auditorium.

The room is already half full when we arrive. Kora steers us toward seats in the back, and I'm grateful.

Sisters file in silently, filling the rows. The usual morning chatter is absent, replaced by a heavy, suffocating silence. No one's on their phones, no one's gossiping. They sit with hands folded, waiting.

Natalia takes the stage, and the difference is striking. The immaculate, intimidating woman who commands every space she enters is diminished.

Kora's hand slips into mine on one side while Aura's does the same on the other. We sit like that, connected, as Natalia steps up to the podium.

My eyelids close briefly, and for a second, I swear Melody is here too, our pinkies linked in that promise we made.

Natalia's fingers tremble as she adjusts the microphone. I've never seen her anything less than perfectly composed. It's terrifying, like the foundation of a building cracking.

"Good morning, Sisters," she begins. "I stand before you with the heaviest of hearts."

The room holds its breath. Some already know. Others are only now realizing this isn't a regular meeting.

"Last night, we lost one of our own." She pauses. "Melody was on assignment when a tragic accident occurred."

Accident. The word slices through me. Is that what we're calling it?

"The details are still being gathered," Natalia continues, "but what we know is that she suffered a fatal fall."

A sob erupts from somewhere in the front rows. I think it's Jade. I try to block out the image of Melody falling, of her body broken on the pavement.

"We are bringing in grief counselors starting this afternoon," Natalia says. "I encourage all of you to speak with them. There is no shame in seeking help during this difficult time."

Kora squeezes my hand. She's trying to encourage me to take advantage of this, but how could I possibly explain this to some stranger? How could I tell them about the gnawing suspicion that Melody's death wasn't an accident at all?

"In the coming days, we will arrange a memorial service to honor her memory. All assignments for today have been canceled. Take this time to process, to grieve, to be there for one another."

Natalia scans the room. Her focus lands on me, and her gaze is unnerving. Is it worry? Fear? I can't tell.

"Caron and I are here for you. Our doors are open."

She straightens up, trying to regain her composure.

"It is the worst thing imaginable when we lose a colleague, a friend, a Sister." She trembles on the last word. "But the Family endures, and so will all of you."

The room hushes as she steps away. No one moves, no one speaks.

It's like we're all frozen in this moment, unable to step forward into a world without Melody in it.

My insides are scraped out like a jack-o'-lantern, but there's no candle to warm the void. Natalia's words stick in my mind. *The Family endures.*

But what if the Family is the reason she's gone?

Kora stands first, pulling me up with her. "Come on, let's get you back to your room."

She leads me out, and I let her, Aura trailing behind us. As we pass the rows of Sisters, I catch fragments of whispered conversations.

"…just like Sparrow…"

"…wasn't she with a senator or something…"

"…third time this has happened…"

Third time?

What did they mean?

Kora's grip tightens, pulling me forward.

The Family endures, Natalia had said. But at what cost?

And who pays it?

Twelve

Purple and blue construction paper confetti whipped through the anarchy of the Holland sisters' bedroom, where Esther lay sprawled upside down across the foot of her bed. Head hanging over the side, her hair swept the carpet like the giant, thrilling flaps she loved to watch at the car wash.

Amelia, sixteen and the undisputed grand empress of the household, reigned from the headboard, legs crisscrossed in her favorite flannel pajama pants, with an old, chewed-up Bic pen poised above a spiral notebook and a bag of gummy bears next to her. The lamp between them cast everything in a honeyed light, and the room was thick with the scent of old books and not-so-fresh laundry.

"Okay, you ready to start?" Amelia asked.

Esther chuckled and proclaimed, "Once upon a time, in the Kingdom of Glass Animals, there lived a magical chicken named Prince Eggward the Third, even though there wasn't any First or Second." Her eyes sparkled with mischief.

"Every hero needs a sidekick, Sprout. Eggward's is a meaty goose who goes by Professor Honkington, who wears glasses." Amelia barely finished before dissolving into laughter.

Esther snorted so hard she nearly choked on her grape Jolly Rancher. "Prince Eggward and his trusty Honkington lived in a glitter castle, ate only jellybeans, and dispensed justice."

"Where does a ten-year-old learn the word *dispensed*?" Amelia raised a single eyebrow, the way older sisters and villains could.

Esther shrugged upside down, arms flopping in dramatic indifference, but inside her chest, her heart wiggled. "Mrs. Finkel said it in social studies. She was talking about, like, kings and taxes and stuff."

"Anyway," Amelia said, twirling the pen, "Prince Eggward wore a red cape made of the curtain from the Theater of Swirling Mirrors."

"And he had a horse named Pancakes who was afraid of syrup," Esther added, smiling.

"Pancakes liked it when Prince Eggward rode him through the brown hash field." Amelia winked and popped a red gummy bear into her mouth.

An uncontrolled giggle bubbled out of Esther. "Pancakes could smell lies. If you fibbed near him, he'd scream like a teapot."

She slid off the bed with a soft thud, rolling across the carpet in a fit of laughter. Amelia tossed a balled-up sock at her head. Esther batted it away, scrambling back onto the mattress, her breath catching in giddy gasps.

"So, Prince Eggward discovered a hidden tunnel where the whistling wind said, *You're dirty!*" Amelia leaned on her elbows.

"Prince Eggward jumped into the bathtub and found a secret door in the drain." Esther lowered her voice to a conspiratorial whisper. "It was shaped like a question mark and smelled like oatmeal."

Amelia laughed, her whole face going soft and brilliant. "Inside, he met a talking sandwich, who said, *Beware the velvet foxes—they teach you how to vanish.*"

Esther folded over, clutching her knees, joyful tears in her eyes. "But Prince Eggward wanted to vanish, because the queen kept stealing his secrets and putting them in the soup."

"He told the sandwich, *No one controls a chicken with a cape!*" Amelia plucked a yellow bear from the bag and tossed it to Esther, who caught it on the fly. "And then he stole the moon."

"But the moon is secretly a disco ball," Esther said between chews, "so everyone got dizzy from the sparkles."

"Especially the velvet foxes." Amelia grinned. "So, they made Prince Eggward a deal: Disappear, and they'd give him a map to the truth."

A lull settled between them, leaving only the soft tick of the radiator and the scrape of the city outside their window. The playful energy dissolved, and the last of Esther's laughter faded away.

"Did he do it?" Esther asked.

Amelia looked at her, and for a second, she wasn't just the greatest big sister in the universe—she was the only other person who knew the same heave and tremble of Esther's insides.

"Yeah." She popped a red bear into her mouth. "He left the cape behind so someone else could wear it."

Esther didn't answer right away. She didn't have to. But after a moment, she whispered, "I'd totally wear it."

Amelia leaned over and flicked her gently on the forehead, smiling. "I know you would, Sprout."

THE WALLS ARE QUIETER TODAY. Outside, the city sings its usual glass-and-concrete lullaby. Aura left the room a few minutes ago. She's feeling it as much as I am but has acted like my pain is somehow more important than hers, which is so damn sweet of her. It's been a steady parade of visitors today. Most of them mean well, but my appreciation wars with the desire to be alone. There's a hole right now that no number of Sisters could fill.

Folding open my notebook to a blank page, the lines blur for a moment before I press my pen down and sketch something from the archive of my childhood. A chicken. With a cape. And a tiny sword. Prince Eggward the Third.

The drawing is stupid.

Juvenile.

Still, a crown takes shape on Prince Eggward's head, complete with the wobbly jewels Amelia always insisted were "totally necessary for royal chickens." God, she'd find this so funny. We used to spend rainy days creating this ridiculous comic story about glass animals with superpowers. Prince Eggward was my creation—the runt of the coop who became a hero.

Heart heavy, I close the notebook, unable to draw anymore.

Melody would've loved these stories. I never got around to telling her about them. So many things I never got around to telling her.

It's funny how death makes you catalog all the things you never said, the stories you never shared. With Amelia, it was different—she just vanished. I got to keep hoping. With Melody, there's no room for hope—only this crushing certainty.

My phone buzzes with a notification.

JEREMY

Didn't want you to stumble across this yourself.
Hope you're okay.

It's a link to an AP article. My gut drops before I even read it.

Young Woman Found Dead Outside Midtown Hotel

The headline steals my breath. I scan the article, each word a chore to read.

An unidentified young woman believed to be a sex worker… found dead… St. Regis Hotel… Friday morning… unresponsive near the rear service entrance.

My throat closes up.
The last line of the article mocks me.
No arrests have been made.
Of course no arrests have been made. The Family doesn't leave loose ends.

My arm cocks back, the impulse to hurl my phone against the wall so strong it makes my muscles burn. They've reduced her to nothing —a nameless body, a statistic, a cautionary tale for parents to tell their suburban kids.

Her name was Melanie. She was from Ohio. She loved seahorses. She snorted when she laughed too hard. She could recite all fifty states in alphabetical order in under a minute. She always saved the marshmallows in her cereal for last.

The desire to fling open my window and scream it all into the void is so strong. To make the whole city stop and acknowledge that someone *real* is gone. Not "unidentified." Not "a sex worker." *Melanie.* My friend.

My phone buzzes again.

"Leave me alone!" I snap at the screen as if it can hear me.

SAGE

"Can you please come to Melody's room?"

PART of me wants to ignore it, to curl up in my grief alone. But it's Sage asking. And it's about Melody.

The sleeve of my sweatshirt drags across my face, and I force myself up. My legs are wobbly, like I've forgotten how to use them. Snatching a tie from my nightstand, I pull my hair back. No need to check the mirror—it would only confirm I look like hell.

When I approach Melody's room, the door is ajar, spilling light into the eerily silent hallway. The last time I was in there, she was alive. With a mournful sigh, I step inside.

Sage is sitting on Melody's bed with her hair done up in a loose bun—no makeup, no jewelry. Only her. She looks up at me, and her eyes soften.

"Oh, Star," she says.

My arms cross over my chest, hands rubbing my elbows. "You wanted to see me?"

Sage stands up.

"I let myself in. Wanted to see if I could find anything…odd. Out of place." She hesitates, twisting her hands together. "I needed to do something, you know? I couldn't sit in my room staring at the wall."

"Did you find anything?" I ask, glancing around.

The room is exactly as Melody left it—clothes draped over a chair, makeup scattered across the vanity, her silly stuffed frog sitting on the pillow. She called it Mr. Ribbit. God, that was so Melody.

"Actually, yes." Sage points toward the desk by the window. "Over there."

A crisp white envelope sits in the center. It's sealed, with a single word written on the front in Melody's loopy handwriting.

Star.

My name. Only my name.

"What is that?" A stupid question. It's obviously a letter.

"I don't know," she says. "I didn't open it. It's addressed to you."

The walk to the desk is slow and unsteady. As my fingers hover over the envelope, it seems to pulse with importance, with finality.

"When would she have had time to write me a letter?"

"Maybe she planned to give it to you when she got back?"

It's light when I pick it up, like there's nothing in there. A message from a phantom.

"Sage," I ask, my throat closing, "would you mind if I took this back to my room?"

She looks at me, and her chin trembles.

"Of course not. I just wanted to show you."

"Thanks." The moment sits between us—because this isn't only a letter. This is a goodbye.

BACK IN MY ROOM, the envelope flutters onto my bed like it's a butterfly wing. My name stares up at me in Melody's handwriting—one big loopy *S* and a textbook little *r* that trails off and curls. So perfectly *her*.

Pacing around it gingerly, like it might explode if I touch it again, I run through the possibilities. What if it's nothing? Just a silly inside joke she wanted to share? Or what if it's everything—all the answers about what happened?

"This is ridiculous," I mutter, snatching it up.

But I don't open it.

What if I don't want to know? What if it changes everything I thought I knew about her? About the Family?

I press the envelope to my chest and exhale. Melody's voice floats around me: *Stop overthinking, you goof. Rip the bandage off!*

My finger slides under the seal. The paper tears with a sound that's too loud for its size. A scent floats up from inside the envelope; it's her perfume. A deep inhale. The tears rise, but no…not this time. I have to be strong for her.

Inside is a small Post-it note, the pale yellow kind Melody always kept stuck to her mirror. My heart sinks a little—I'd expected a letter, pages of explanation, not this tiny square.

Three lines in Melody's curvy handwriting:

Seahorse Memories
Safely within cloud's embrace
Remember the name

"What the hell?" Nothing on the back of it.

I read it again. And again. A haiku? Since when did Melody write poetry?

Which memories?

"Cloud's embrace? What embrace?" My mind runs through our conversations, trying to remember if she ever mentioned anything like this.

The tiny note trembles between my fingers. This isn't closure; it's the opposite—a riddle when I need answers.

"Remember the name? Whose name, Mel? What are you trying to tell me?"

The words blur the longer I stare at them. My guts twist into a pretzel of confusion and dread.

Did she know? Did she sense she wouldn't come back that night? The thought makes me nauseous.

"You planned this," I say to the empty room. "You clever, paranoid girl." If she'd written something direct—about the Family, about why she felt afraid—it might have been seen by the wrong eyes.

A riddle keeps secrets safe. Keeps *me* safe.

"Seahorse Memories," I repeat.

I drop to the floor, hugging my knees. My brain is splitting apart. What if I'm overthinking this? What if it's Melody being Melody— cryptic and dramatic?

But what if it's not?

What if the last words my best friend left for me could unravel everything about her death?

Blog Entry #12

The Pretty Dead Ones

In the Family, Sisters are disposable. Replaceable. Like designer shoes or outdated phone models. You're shiny and new until suddenly, you're not.

Two names. Two girls. Two absences.

Sparrow is gone. She was 22, from Wisconsin. Her mother

is still putting her missing person's poster on Facebook. The Family knows where she ended up, but nobody's talking.

Before her, Ivy, 21. Bright-eyed, desperate to escape her dead-end hometown. She believed in the glamour, the promise of transformation. Now she's another statistic in the system.

The cleanup crew always comes fast. They scrub, and the walls pretend not to remember. Then the handlers arrive. They absolve the Family, leave the girl. Just another statistic. Another disappearance that gets filed and forgotten.

To the Sisters still inside: Pay attention. Count the empty beds. Ask who used to sleep there. They want you to forget. Don't let them.

Not until the truth comes out.

—Your Step-Sister

THE FIRST TIME I read this Step-Sister post was over a week ago—back when it was just another conspiracy theory among dozens. Now it's like she was standing right there in that meeting room, when Natalia's mask slipped as she announced Melody's "accident."

Third time this has happened. That's what the girl behind me whispered. Third time. Three Sisters. Gone.

Ivy. Sparrow. Melody.

I flip through my increasingly tattered notebook—where I've been obsessively tracking Step-Sister's posts like some discount Nancy Drew with anxiety issues. My handwriting's gone from "barely legible" to "raccoon with a pen" with each new page.

The timeline of this post fits perfectly. I checked the original post date against news archives and found an article about an anonymous sex worker's death two days before Step-Sister wrote this. That had to be Sparrow.

Step-Sister knows things, specific things, about the Family. About the "cleanup crew." About how they operate. What secrets hasn't she written about yet?

There's someone else who knows secrets about this place too.

Kora's room is upstairs, and with any luck, she's through with CrossFit sessions for the day. She acts bulletproof, like she's made of sarcasm and protein shakes, but I saw the argument in the hallway and how Melody's loss affected her. She knows something. She has to.

THE DOOR to Kora's room swings open, and she's standing there in gray shorts and a sports bra, her curls pulled back. She blinks at me like I'm a hallucination.

"Star?" Her tone has a careful neutrality I've heard her use with difficult Sisters. "What's wrong? It's late."

"I'm sorry." The words spill out. I try to pitch them just right—fragile, desperate, like I'm a younger Sister seeking guidance. "I couldn't sleep. I keep thinking about Melody. Did I do something wrong? On Wednesday night, was she upset with me?"

Kora's face relaxes for a moment, exactly what I wanted. She leans against the doorframe, slipping into her Big Sister role like a well-worn sweater. "Oh, honey, no. Melody adored you. You know that."

"But she seemed off. I thought maybe I'd said something…" I trail off, scanning her face.

"Look"—her tone shifts to gentle condescension—"everyone has off days. Even Melody. She was stressed about her client. Those government types can be demanding."

"You're right." I step forward, crowding into her space. "I just miss her so much, and I keep replaying that night—"

"Star." Kora straightens in the doorway, using her height advantage. "You need to let this go. Trust me, obsessing over it won't help."

I push into the room and stick my elbow out enough to catch her water bottle on the side table. It crashes to the floor, and the cap pops off, spreading liquid across the carpet.

"Shit!" Kora drops to her knees, grabbing a towel from her dumbbell rack. She mashes it into the carpet, her movements jerky and frantic. "God, *of course.*" Her fist digs into the terry cloth. "This will never dry."

"Kora."

She doesn't look up. "You should go."

"I saw you."

Her hands go still.

"Wednesday night. I saw you with Melody by the elevators." I fold my arms. "You looked upset."

"I wasn't upset." She stands back up deliberately, the wet towel dripping onto her bare feet. "We were discussing her client. That's all."

"What about her client?"

"Jesus, Star, does it matter? She's gone." She tosses the towel into the bathroom. "I know you two were close, but sometimes it's better to let things go."

"Let things go?" My volume rises. "She's dead, Kora."

"Lower your voice." Her eyes dart to the door.

"What were you arguing about?"

She puffs herself out, hackles up. "A word of advice from someone who's been here a lot longer than you have: In this house, there are things you don't understand yet. Don't go down this path, Star. Not now. It won't end well."

It's not a suggestion. It's a warning.

I step closer until we're toe to toe. I've never confronted anyone like this in my life, but fury makes me brave. Stupid brave. She's got five inches on me, but we stand there like two magnets repelling each other for a good thirty seconds.

"What. Happened. To. Melody?" I enunciate each word slowly. My hand rises, fingers clenched, the suggestion of something more.

"Don't do something you'll regret."

"You're her Big Sister, Kora. She's dead! Doesn't that matter to you?" I snarl through gritted teeth.

Something breaks in her, and she flops down onto the bed.

"She got special instructions from Natalia. For the D.C. client. She didn't want to go through with it."

"What instructions?"

"I don't have the details. She asked me to talk to Natalia for her. I told her to handle it herself." She wrings her hands together. "I didn't want to get involved."

"You didn't want to get involved? But you pushed her to do it, didn't you? Like a swimming lesson in the ocean."

"What?"

"It wasn't an accident. The assignment from Natalia? That got her killed, didn't it?"

"You need to stop this, Star." Kora's face hardens again. "You don't want to lift this rock, believe me."

She rubs her hands across her face. "Whatever you think you're doing, whatever crusade you're on, you won't find what you're looking for. Not here, not now."

"What happened, Kora?"

"I don't know," she yells, falling back onto her bed. "I swear to God, I don't. But I should have helped her. I was her Big Sister, for Christ's sake." She chokes back a sob. "I never meant for this to happen to her."

And there it is—the truth, or at least part of it. The Family isn't just corrupt. It's deadly. And Melody got caught in it.

My chin trembles because she's telling the truth. She doesn't know what happened to Melody. But she knows enough to feel guilty about it.

Without another word, I turn and walk out of the room, closing the door behind me. The click of the latch releases the anxiety in my chest. In the hallway, the wall is cool against my back, supporting me as my legs give out and I slide to the floor.

This place killed my best friend. And yet I'm still here, sleeping under their roof, eating their food, playing their game.

What does that make me?

Melody's poem flashes in my mind. Step-Sister's warnings. The guilt on Kora's face. Sage's painted smile. Caron's promises.

Documentation—that's what I need. I open my notebook and scribble down names, dates, connections. If something happens to me, I want there to be a record of it. I want someone to know the truth—

The realization sucks the air from my lungs.

—just like Melody did.

Seahorse Memories.

It's her journal. I need to find it.

Caroline Tenning

The treadmill whirred, a punishing, monotonous sound. Forty-five minutes. Caroline's feet fell in a relentless rhythm, a metronome counting down until she could let herself rest. Sweat slicked her skin. The rule was simple: Keep moving. Don't stop, because that's when the darkness catches up.

But today, it was keeping pace.

The rhythm summoned up the old ghosts, a steady, choreographed beat of a life that wasn't hers anymore.

Thud. The sharp *pop* of a tennis ball. Her father yelling across the court: "Follow through, Caroline!"

Thud. The slam of a locker in the halls of Vandale Academy. Perfect grades on a flawless transcript.

Thud. Her mother's Back Bay accent from the driver's seat, as crisp and clinical as the scrubs she wore, quizzing her on SAT words. "Sanguine."

"Optimistic in difficult situations," her own twelve-year-old voice recited, the manicured lawns of Greenwich blurring past the window.

Thud-thud-thud. Field hockey captain. Valedictorian. Yale acceptance. "They'll be lucky to have you," her father had said, beaming, as if fate had ever offered another path. An exemplary daughter, polished like a trophy, running perfectly in place.

Caroline adjusted the volume of her earbuds, not the expected pop beats or dance tracks the other Sisters favored. Instead, she lost herself in the delicate cascade of an instrument her father had brought back from Senegal when she was fifteen. A kora, with twenty-one strings that sang like water over rocks. She'd taught herself to play it during stolen moments between debate tournaments and college prep courses—probably the only thing she'd ever learned without some greater purpose in mind. Just because it sounded beautiful. Just for herself. Her own private joke now in the Family.

She slammed her palm onto the Stop button, and the belt slowed under her feet with a final groan. The solid floor was unstable beneath her trembling legs as her labored breathing settled. The air was redolent of sweat and rubber as she wiped her forehead and moved toward the weight rack. The treadmill was for endurance, but the iron—that was for resistance.

The metallic scrape of the plate sliding onto the bar was a comforting sound. Lying back on the bench, she gripped the cold steel, lowered it to her chest and pushed. The clean burn in her muscles was honest, and it reminded her of a different kind of honesty—the kind she'd first tasted in a Philosophy 201 lecture.

The girl's name was Lexi, and the spice of her body lotion combined with the defiance in her grin floated through Caroline's mind. She'd leaned across the aisle, whispering, "You know none of this matters, right? It's all bullshit designed to keep us in line."

The words were like a key opening a door she'd kept locked all these years.

A part of her had always known she'd open it someday—the lingering glances in locker rooms, the inexplicable flutter when certain girls laughed. But there'd never been time for it between studies and debate tournaments, never permission to want anything her parents hadn't preapproved. Until Lexi made wanting feel like breathing.

The bar was heavier now as her pecs contracted to push it up again, remembering not the lectures on inequality, but the night she'd found a worn copy of *Winnie-the-Pooh* on Lexi's nightstand. She'd looked away. "It's my brother's. He's in rehab. I was his Tigger." It wasn't just her defiance that made Caroline fall for her; it was the way she carried someone else's pain alongside her own.

Re-racking the bar and stretching out the tightness exhausted the memory, ground it out of her muscles. She swung her legs off the bench and added more weight. One more set. Heavy this time.

Lying back down, the cold of the bar shocked her palms, and the final Sunday morning came unbidden, sharp and clear with the strain. Lunch in the bistro just off campus. Her father suggested, "Turks and Caicos," while she smiled and nodded, already knowing she'd find an excuse. Her mother's hands, cool against her cheeks. "You look better. More rested." A charade. She'd been up all night with Lexi, and her real life, the one waiting for her back at her apartment, pulled at her like a secret tide.

Caroline grunted and pressed the bar up, her shoulders trembling.

The tactile sensation of her father's wool coat on her skin as she hooked her arms through theirs, walking them to the car. She kissed her mother's cheek and breathed in her unique scent—a mix of HibiClens and Chanel No. 5.

"Drive safe," she'd said. The automatic words. "Love you."

Her father had honked twice as their silver Mercedes pulled away. A gut-deep twist of guilt for wanting them to leave—for wanting to get back to Lexi, to the tequila, and the night that stretched ahead like a promise. She hadn't thought about black ice or sleeping truck drivers.

The burn in her triceps broke her form, and the barbell dropped, crashing down onto the safety catches with a deafening metallic *THRANG.*

The sound was the same. The same as her phone slipping from her numb fingers, clattering down the metal stairs of Lexi's building. She was pressed against the cold concrete again, the state trooper's voice bleeding through the shattered glass.

"...Miss Tenning...terrible accident...struck on I-95...I'm so sorry..."

Caroline didn't move from the bench. Her adrenaline receded, leaving only a familiar, cavernous emptiness, and the silence dragged her back to her father's study. A suffocating mix of leather and old paper filled the air as the attorney stood before the giant teakwood desk, his words a meaningless drone. The blue binder in her lap lay open, and her finger traced the raised lettering of her name—*Caroline Tenning*—but the person on the page was a stranger, a fiction of her parents' imagination. *Sole beneficiary.* The term wasn't a gift; it was a brand on her skin. A future designed for a daughter who had died on that interstate just as surely as they had. It was blood money, each penny a tiny betrayal.

She recalled signing a check to her mother's hospital as a way to get rid of it, the zeros swimming before her eyes. It was useless. The wealth, their intricately planned legacy, kept growing, accumulating like interest on her guilt.

Caroline squeezed the bottle over her head, letting the water run down her neck. Every face had reminded her; every place was haunted by memories.

So she ran. Not from the money, but from the demons that chased the girl who had inherited it. Fleeing Yale, she ghosted Lexi without a word—her brand of rebellion offered only hollow platitudes now. A train to Manhattan with no plan but to be somewhere else was her escape. She walked until her feet ached, then ducked into a swanky hotel to elude the autumn rain.

Sitting down, shaking the water from her pants, she looked across the lobby and spotted her. Tall, red-haired, and impossibly composed —the antithesis of her own frayed edges. Something in Caroline, broken and adrift, recognized both a kindred spirit and a portrait of control in a world that had spun her off its axis.

Her movements were slow and deliberate as she crossed the marble floor and held out a hand, offering the only thing that remained of her old self.

"Hi, I'm Caroline."

The redhead's smile was small and pure. She met Caroline's palm, her grip gentle but firm.

"Shannon. Shannon Maroney."

The towel swept across her face, drying the sweat and letting the vision of that chance meeting linger. Seven years had passed since their friendship gave her purpose—since the Family gave her structure—a place to live a life that soothed but didn't heal. She'd found somewhere to be, if not someone to become.

THIRTEEN

Two days since Melody died, and the entire building is like a museum after hours—people moving quietly, talking softly, avoiding eye contact. At least down here, the hum of the computers provides some companionship.

Jeremy opens his office door, glasses slightly askew. "Star. Hey. Come in." He steps aside, nearly tripping over a box of cables. "I wasn't expecting—how are you doing?"

"Still breathing."

His office is a mess of laptops, cables, and blinking lights beyond my comprehension. A little black box sits on his desk with cables extending from it.

"What's that?" I ask.

He looks at it, then pushes it aside. "Nothing, just something I have to fix."

Easing into the chair next to his desk, I lift my arms into a dramatic yawn.

"Hey, I'm sorry about Melody," he says, fidgeting with a pen. "I really liked her. She was…kind to me."

"Jeremy." My mouth is dry. "What happens to all her files? On her Family drive?"

The wrinkles on his forehead vanish as he glances at me. "Standard procedure. After thirty days, all personal data is wiped. Work-related information is archived."

"Thirty days. So, her drive is still…accessible?"

He shifts in his chair. "Technically. But access is restricted to admin level."

A slow nod, attempting to look casual. "So…you?"

He smirks. "Yes. Why?"

My fingers find a loose thread on my sleeve, picking it. "She had some photos. Of us. I'd like to have them."

His eyes soften, and he grabs the mouse, ready to spring into action. "I could recover specific files for you. If you tell me what you're looking for."

"Actually…" A sharp inhale. "I need to see all of it, Jeremy. Her messages, her notes—everything."

He stiffens. "Star, you know I can't do that."

"Jeremy, please, I need to. I won't even download anything. You can watch me the whole time."

He runs a hand through his hair. "It's not that simple. There are logs and security rules. If anyone found out—"

"No one will find out." My hand hovers near his before I pull it back. "This is Melody we're talking about."

He checks his monitors, then swivels back to me. "Why, Star? Why risk it?"

I wait a second before tossing the grenade.

"Because Melody was murdered."

"What?" He recoils, shaking his head. "That's—" He recomposes himself. "That's insane. It was an accident."

"You sure?"

"Star, grief does things to people. Makes them find patterns that aren't there." The pity in his eyes makes my blood boil.

"She knew she was in danger."

"She told you that?"

I take the folded note out of my pocket, dropping it onto his desk.

"She left this for me. *Before* her last assignment. Like she knew she might not come back."

Jeremy stares at the paper, adjusting his glasses as he reads the haiku.

His brow furrows. "I don't understand. What—"

"It's a clue."

His puzzled gaze jumps from the paper to me. "Seahorse Memories?"

"A journal." My finger stabs the note. "She must have had one."

Jeremy sits back, and the chair's leather squeaks. He stares at the haiku, rereading it under his breath. "Safely within cloud's embrace." He looks up. "Maybe cloud storage?"

"Yes! And 'Remember the name'—it's telling me where to look."

"This doesn't prove anything, though."

"She was my best friend, Jeremy. If someone hurt her..." I swallow hard. "I have to know."

His fingers hover over the keyboard.

"Please." The word is barely audible. "I know this is a risk for you."

Jeremy closes his eyes, exhales through his nose, then opens them. "Ten minutes. I'll stay with you the whole time."

"Thank you."

"Don't thank me yet," he mutters, typing in his password. "We might both regret this."

Before he can stand, I'm sliding into his still-warm seat. Our bodies brush awkwardly in the exchange, and a clean scent of mint and laundry detergent floats between us. Jeremy stumbles, his glasses slipping.

"Sorry," I murmur, already focused on the screen.

"It's fine," he says. "Just be careful."

The cursor hovers over Melody's user folder. I open it. Photos, documents, calendars. My heart sinks. Where do I start? Folders fly open with rapid clicks—*Pictures, Downloads, Documents*, a recipe for banana bread. Normal.

"There's nothing here." I throw my hand up in irritation.

"Maybe that's all there is," Jeremy suggests. "It's just...a poem."

"No." I shake my head. "She wouldn't have left the note if it didn't mean something." I click faster, opening and closing folders, desperate.

"Star, slow down. You'll miss—"

"I'm not missing anything because there's nothing to miss!" I snap. "Sorry. I thought..."

Jeremy's hand lands on the back of the chair, close but not touching me. He points to a folder named *SM*. "That?"

A double-click opens it. Inside is a single file: *Seahorse Memories.docx*.

My breath catches. "Jeremy..."

"I see it."

My hand trembles as I click twice. A dialog box appears.

This file is password protected. Please enter password:

I turn to Jeremy, hope and doubt fighting inside me. "What's the password?"

He stares as if I've asked him for the meaning of life. "How would I know? It's her file."

Slumping back, I exhale. So close. "Think. Remember the name."

Melanie.

Incorrect password.

"Dammit."

Seahorse.

Incorrect password.

"You only have one try left before it locks you out for an hour," he warns.

I turn to him with thinly suppressed rage. "Your design?"

He shrugs like a toddler with his hand in the cookie jar. "I never thought someone would use it against me."

Concentrate. Think like Melody. What name?

"Wait." My fingers hover over the keyboard. "Her tattoo." A smile spreads across my face as the memory clicks.

My fingers carefully tap out *Silly Love* and press the Enter key.

The password dialog box disappears. The document opens. Pages of text fill the screen.

"Holy shit," he says. "That was it."

Scrolling past her early entries, I stop at my first day of training.

March 7

I thought it would be fun, so I volunteered to help train the recruits. There's this one girl, Esther. Well, her Family name will be Star. I think we're going to be fast friends, I can tell. She's so nervous. I want to help her get through this.

Jeremy peeks at me and says, "Esther?"

The glare I give him could flatten cities.

"Sorry."

Scrolling through pages and pages full of notes, journal entries, and meeting minutes, I say, "Jeremy, she documented everything!"

The chair flies across the floor as I vault out of it and fling my arms around him. He goes rigid. Tears prick my eyes, but they don't fall. I've found her voice in the digital void.

Our awkward hug breaks, and he bends around me to grab the mouse. He drags the file into the folder with my name on it. It vanishes with a satisfying little *thunk*.

"This never happened," Jeremy says, not looking at me.

For the first time in two days, an honest smile lights up my face. "What never happened?"

BACK IN MY ROOM, cross-legged on my bed with my laptop balanced precariously on my knees, I'm ready to open it. Melody's journal, now disguised with the most innocuous filename I could think of.

"*Star's Menstrual Tracker*," I snicker, reveling in my cleverness. "Nobody's gonna open that."

After some googling on how to change the password on a protected Word document, it has a brand spanking new password as well. Can't be too careful, after all.

Starting at the beginning, I deliberately scroll through the document, overwhelmed by the sheer volume. There must be over a hundred entries here, dating back to her first day. Each one is meticulously labeled with dates, sometimes multiple entries per day. Personal stuff, notes on the Sisters, assignment logs, and more. Strange little details I wouldn't have remembered.

"Jesus, Melody," I say, "when you journal, you really journal."

An entry from last fall catches my attention.

October 15

It's funny the things that stick in your head sometimes. Today I remembered the Bowery Poetry Club. Ray was sick one night, so I went by myself. I remember just sitting there with a beer, feeling a bit invisible.

This guy with a patchwork guitar and a head of messy black curls sang a Tom Waits song, his voice so much gentler than I expected. Afterward, he just came over and sat down. No agenda, no angle. He just…did it. "Ezra," he said. We ended up leaving and getting pancakes at like 2 a.m. somewhere in the Village. And once it started, I couldn't stop. Maybe I'll write more about it another time.

Ezra. A flicker of a life I never knew she had, a world of cheap pancakes and gentle singers, is a million miles away from this Fifth Avenue fortress. A world she lost. It makes the ache in me sharpen.

A wave of heat rises up my neck as I page to the last entry, dated the night before she died. My fingers hover over the trackpad, afraid to read her last words. But I need to know.

April 11

Don't have a great feeling about this one. Something feels off. Natalia was super specific about what I need to do, and it's not my usual thing. If it doesn't go well—I don't know. I might be paranoid, but Natalia's been different lately. Colder. Like she's on edge all the time. This one is important to her.
I asked Kora what I should do, but she just kept telling me not to worry about it, that it'll be good for me. That she believes in me and I'll be great. I guess she's numb to all this already. I wonder if I'll ever be the same.
Think I'm going to do the haiku thing after all, just in case. I'm probably being silly, but better safe than sorry.
Anyway, big day tomorrow. Gotta try to sleep.

Pressing my palm against the laptop, I try to feel her through it. The cold of the metal, the heat in my face—nothing helps. I fall backward onto the bed, staring up at the ceiling.

She knew something was wrong. Melody trusted me to figure this out. She gave me seventeen syllables to find out what happened to her.

No pressure.

Fourteen

Ninety minutes of sleep. That's all. For the rest of the night, it was me and Melody whispering secrets in the dark.

Upper Manhattan in the early morning has its own kind of magic. The sidewalks aren't packed yet, the honking hasn't hit its full crescendo of rage, and there's this brief window where you can hear yourself think. Cool morning air slips across my skin, hinting at the spring warmth to come as the sun creeps up between the buildings. Pulling my jacket tighter is more for comfort than necessity.

I dodge a delivery guy on a bike who gives exactly zero shits about the sidewalk being for pedestrians. Typical. The city is waking up. Traffic. Motion. Faces. Another day without Melody.

Her journal entries catalog themselves in my mind. Names, dates, places—puzzle pieces that don't all fit yet. But they will; they have to.

Stopped at the crosswalk, the woman beside me is wearing Melody's perfume. The scent surrounds me, and I turn away, blinking hard.

Five more blocks to the internet café. Not a hipster spot with pour-overs and avocado toast, but an old-school twenty-four-hour place with flickering lights and archaic machines that haven't been cleaned since Y2K. The kind of place where nobody asks questions, and you pay in cash.

My phone is back at the dorms. Working offline is essential—no digital trail. The Family app tracks everything. Where we go, what we search. Jeremy might say they don't monitor our history, but I'm not taking chances. Not with this.

One thing I didn't expect to do this week: mail a letter to parents who don't know their daughter is dead.

A letter she had written, discovered while I scrolled through her journal last night. Addressed to Mr. and Mrs. Caderea in Rocky River, Ohio.

Dear Mom and Dad,
I know it's been a while, and I'm sorry for that. I just wanted you to
know I'm okay. Better than okay, actually...

She filled three pages, telling them about her "exciting job in hospitality" and "amazing new friends." Not a word about the Family or what she did there. Just reassurances. She ended it with *I'll call soon, I promise. Love you both, Melanie.*

Dated two months ago. As far as I can tell, she never sent it. Never called.

Sending that letter now wouldn't do much good, so I did what I thought a friend should do: I wrote a new letter.

Dear Mr. and Mrs. Caderea,
You don't know me, but I was a close friend of your daughter
Melanie. I have some unfortunate news to share with you.

I told them what a wonderful woman she'd become, how her laugh could fill a room, how she'd make up these ridiculous country sayings that perfectly fit the moment, how she made me welcome in a strange new place, and the contagious nature of her kindness.

I couldn't tell them how she died; I didn't have the words. Only said that she "isn't with us anymore" and that she'd been "deeply loved by her friends." It was a betrayal not to say more, but it's best if they don't get all the details right now.

Halfway through writing it, the tears fell and smudged the ink, making it look like purple watercolor. I had to start over.

The second attempt came steadier. I signed it, *A Friend*, and slid it into a fresh envelope I'd bought at a bodega, along with a stamp and this morning's paper.

The internet café still looks like it's waiting for someone to tell it the '90s ended. Fluorescent lights buzz and flicker overhead, casting everything in a sickly glow.

Every surface gleams with a dubious shine. I'm not a germaphobe, but I'd bet if you brought a blacklight in here, it'd light up like Times Square on New Year's Eve.

The man behind a scratched plastic barrier glances up from his phone with the enthusiasm of a DMV worker. He doesn't make eye contact.

"Ten bucks for an hour."

I slide a crumpled bill through the slot. He pushes a USB fob toward me with chipped fingernails painted black.

"Computer five," he mumbles.

Back corner, far from the windows. Perfect. The chair squeaks as I slide into the sticky seat. Best not to think about why. I plug in the fob, and the screen flickers to life.

Notebook open on my lap, angled away from any potential cameras. There's probably no one watching, but paranoia is my new best friend.

Two incognito tabs. My fingers hover over the keyboard for a second. This isn't illegal, necessarily. Melody gave me this information. Left it for me in her journal. It might have been a little too trusting of her to write down her banking credentials, but then again, what other option did she have?

If anything happens, she'd typed, *use the money for what's right.*

What's right. Such a simple phrase, but it carries a lot of baggage. What's right is making sure her parents understand she was happy, even if only for a moment. What's right is finding out why she died. What's right is not letting the Family toss her aside like yesterday's newspaper.

The bank's web address goes into the first tab, Melody's email service into the second. The credentials from my notebook go into the fields to sign in to the bank.

A security prompt: *We've sent a verification code to your email address.*

Switching tabs, I log into her email and hold my breath.

The inbox loads. At the top, an email from the bank. I copy the code, flip back, and paste it in.

The account opens.

Balance: $87,630.

Stare. Blink. Refresh. But the number doesn't change.

"Holy shit, Melody."

No time to dwell on it now. I initiate a transfer to my account, typing in the full amount. My fingers shake as the transaction confirms. For a moment, I'm worried the bank might flag it, but it goes through almost immediately.

Transfer complete.

A deep exhale. Step one: done. Now, for step two.

I close both tabs and sign off. The fob slides out with a gentle *click*, and I tuck my notebook inside my jacket.

"Thanks," I mutter as I pass the desk, tossing the fob under the barrier. It skitters across the counter and lands by the attendant's elbow. He doesn't look up. My work here is done.

Outside, the city's in full stride now—commuters clutching coffee, earbuds in, their faces locked into that classic New York don't-talk-to-me stare. I join them, another body in the flow.

Melody had foresight. Not just clever, but strategic. The day after my first client, she dragged me to a bank and helped me open a second account, one separate from the Family.

"Every week," she said, "move your earnings. Like clockwork."

I'd laughed. She once made coffee for everyone and forgot the grounds. But with this, she wasn't playing around.

"Never keep all your eggs in one basket, Star," she'd said, her Midwestern accent peeking through. "The Family's got its fingers in everything. But your money? That's yours. You earned it. Don't let them touch that too."

It seemed like paranoia.

Now, it's like she saw it coming.

At 8:30 a.m., the bank opens. I walk straight to a middle-aged teller with graying temples and a flat-lipped smile.

"Good morning, how may I help you today?" He's polished, professional.

"Cashier's check, please." I slide my ID and account information over to him.

His eyebrows lift. "Ten thousand dollars?"

"Student loan." The words are accompanied by a pout and a flutter of my eyelashes. Ridiculous, but it greases the wheels.

It'll wipe me out until Melody's transfer clears. But that's fine. What do I need that I don't already get at the dorm? Food, clothes, shelter—all covered. Money is only numbers on a screen until you do something with it.

And right now, Melody needs it. Rather, her parents do. I'll send this now, then the rest next week.

Five minutes later, the check is in my hand. It slides into the envelope with the letter, and I seal it. The glue tastes bitter on my tongue. You'd think they'd flavor it by now—grape or something.

The envelope is heavy as I walk down Lexington Avenue, like it's carrying more than ink and check stock. I pass three mailboxes before finding the right one—a standard blue box on a secluded corner.

I stand there a moment, letter in hand, hovering.

Then it falls to the bottom.

The metallic clunk is louder than expected. Final. Like a door closing behind me. A period at the end of Melody's story.

Let it give her folks something—closure, comfort, anything that helps. It's more than the Family would've given them. To the Family, Melody was an asset. A line item. Gone and forgotten.

But to her parents, she was their little girl, who got swallowed up in the big city.

And to me? My best friend.

Who told me to do what's right.

THE ELEVATOR back to the dorm groans like it knows where I've been. My mind keeps replaying that metallic clunk of the mailbox, like I've set something irreversible in motion.

Lost in thought, I almost walk past my door and miss Aura leaning against the wall beside it, scrolling through her phone. She looks up. "Oh, that's why you weren't answering your door. I thought maybe you'd taken an extra Ambien or whatever." Her smile is friendly but guarded, like most of ours are these days.

"Wanted to get some air, clear my mind a little." Fishing my key card from my pocket, I avoid her gaze. The less she knows about my morning activities, the better—for both of us.

Aura stretches her tiny frame, the gesture almost comical. "Well, I'm starving. Let me buy you breakfast."

"Such generosity. How can I refuse?"

"How're you holding up, for real?" Aura asks as we head to the cafeteria.

I shrug, keeping my face neutral. "Taking it day by day."

She nods, not pushing further. That's why Aura is great—she understands when to back off.

"Got a client tonight," she says, changing the subject. "Some tech bro with more money than rhythm. Dude doesn't look like a dancer, but he wants to take me to some club in Tribeca."

"Sounds thrilling," I deadpan as we push through the cafeteria doors. The waft of fresh coffee and French toast fills the air.

"I was looking forward to dancing tonight," she sighs. "Now I'll be stuck watching this guy flop around like a fish on the beach. *¡Carajo!*"

Something about her pouty cheeks brings out my silly side. "Then make him a dancer, *chica*," I say, mimicking her accent terribly.

Aura yelps, genuine and bright. "Oh my God, never do that again!" She playfully shoves my shoulder and for a moment, things are almost normal again.

"Have you seen Jade around?" I ask, grabbing my tray. "I haven't glimpsed her since…" I trail off, not wanting to finish the sentence.

Aura grabs a yogurt parfait. "They gave her a week off. Girl was falling apart."

"Makes sense." I grab a banana. "Is she staying here, though?"

Aura shrugs, her tiny shoulders rising and falling dramatically. "I dunno where else she could go. Not like any of us have actual homes to return to, you know? That's kind of the point of this place."

As we weave between tables, Kora eyes me from across the cafeteria. She's sitting alone, coffee in hand, staring into the distance. She tips her chin, and I return the gesture, relief washing over me. No hard feelings from the other night. At least that's one relationship still intact.

"You wanna sit with her?" Aura asks, following my line of sight.

"No, let's grab a table for ourselves."

We fall into our own little world, trading empty observations about clothes and weather like we're playing some bizarre game of small-talk tennis.

The buzzer cuts through our conversation—that familiar, jarring sound that herds us like cattle to the daily meeting. We dump our trays and join the stream of Sisters flowing toward the conference room.

"Sit in the back?" I'm angling toward the rear seats.

"Always."

We slide into chairs as the lights dim, expecting Natalia to emerge, but Sage glides to the front of the room, silencing it.

"Good morning, Sisters," she says with a blend of authority and warmth. "Natalia is off-site today attending to Family business, so I'll be handling our morning briefing."

She moves through announcements with ease—client satisfaction rates, upcoming events, and reminders about discretionary conduct. I'm barely listening until her tone shifts, becoming softer.

"And finally, a small memorial for Melody will be held tomorrow afternoon in the auditorium. Please stop by and pay your respects."

For a split second, I'm convinced that every eye in the room swivels toward me, a spotlight of collective attention that makes my skin crawl. But when I blink, everyone's still facing forward, expressions neutral. Just my paranoia working overtime.

I bite the inside of my cheek hard, fighting the urge to stand up and scream about the hollowness of this gesture. A "small memorial" for a murdered Sister? How generous.

Aura's hand finds mine under the table and squeezes.

The room empties, bodies filing past me in a blur of colors and perfume. I'm halfway to the door when Sage calls out. "Star? Could you stay a moment?"

My body tenses. Aura waits.

"Go ahead," I tell her. "I'll catch up."

Sage gestures to a small table near the doors, away from the few stragglers still gathering their things. Her movements are graceful, like she's performing for an audience of one. I follow her lead, sliding into a chair across from her.

She searches my face, probing for something, and I stare back. Whatever she's looking for, she won't find it. I've gone numb, like someone's pulled my emotional plug.

"You've had a booking come in for tomorrow night. Are you okay to go?"

I nod silently.

Sage leans forward, her perfectly manicured hand almost—but

not quite—touching mine. "I'm concerned about you, Star. Is there anything I can do?"

The question hangs between us, so earnest it almost sounds genuine. With Sage, it's impossible to tell where the performance ends and the real person begins.

My chair slides against the floor, and I push myself up. "Not really, Sage, unless you can bring my friend back…"

Her lips press into a thin line. "Would you like to say anything at Melody's memorial tomorrow?"

A bitter laugh. "There's a lot I'd like to say, but…" I look directly at her. "No."

The words hang between us like a challenge. She doesn't flinch. Just analyzes me.

If I opened my mouth at that memorial, I'd burn the whole damn place down like Godzilla.

I turn and walk out, not waiting for her response. The door closes behind me with a *thud* that sounds ominous, like I've closed a door on more than a conversation.

In the hallway, I press my back against the wall and shove my shaking hands into my pockets.

Tomorrow night, I have a client. Tomorrow afternoon, a memorial.

But tonight—tonight I have a date with what Melody left behind.

🦄

IT'S EMBARRASSING how technical illiteracy can prevent you from seeing something that's right in front of you. I've been buried in Melody's journal for the past two days but only just realized that the client assignment notes weren't in the main document. They were embedded in a separate Excel file. You can do that? Apparently. Who knew? Not me.

"God, Melody, you were smarter than people gave you credit for." I click the file, and it opens with a soft chime.

Client names. Dates. Preferences. Special instructions. Personal notes. Everything color-coded. Melody's modest brilliance laid out in rows and columns.

The first couple of entries are normal enough—champagne brands, outfit preferences, euphemisms for kinks. Escort stuff.

The next tab had a lot more:

Client #4 – Michael Alderman *Special Instructions: Covertly record intimate encounter. Equipment provided during prep meeting. Return device immediately after assignment.*

A slow crawling sensation starts at the top of my head.

Client #5 – David Litierri *Special Instructions: Obtain replica of client's phone. Mechanism will be provided with training. Process takes under five minutes. Best performed while target is showering or otherwise indisposed.*

My chair almost topples over as I jump up, my insides sinking fast.

This can't be real.

Stumbling back to the laptop before I lose my nerve, I sit down and force myself to scroll.

Client #6 – Andrew Daniels *Special Instructions: Use supplied vial in client's beverage, preferably wine. Entertain the client until he passes out. Connect device to client's satellite phone as demonstrated in training. Process should take 30–40 minutes.* ***Process cannot be interrupted. Keep client occupied in case of premature resuscitation.***

"What the actual fuck."

Backing away from the screen, I grab my pillow and scream into it until my throat burns.

They had her drugging clients. Hacking phones. She was a kid from Ohio.

My vision swims, and I pound the side of my fist into the wall. Not hard enough to break anything. Just enough for the pain.

"This got her killed." I swallow. "This is what got her killed."

My breath won't come. My arms get pins and needles, and I'm floating inside my skin.

Then:

Breathe, Star.

Melody. Clear. Impossible.

Inhale. Exhale. Again.

Start at the edges, Sprout.

Amelia this time.

Back to the laptop.

"Okay, let's figure this out."

Not what happened to her. Not who gave the order. But how to make it mean something. How to place the last piece.

I can't go straight at this. If I push too hard, too fast, they'll know I'm onto them. I have to be smart. Be careful. I have to build slowly.

Start at the edges.

I work backward. The first special assignment occurred three months after she began seeing clients.

The personal notes confirm it:

Didn't feel right about this one. Asked Sage if this was normal. She said exceptional Sisters get exceptional assignments. Told Nat I felt uncomfortable. She said I should be grateful for the opportunity. That I was a "Special Asset," whatever that means.

The words stop me cold. *Special Asset.*

Where did I see—

I glide the cursor to the *Documents* folder, and a double-click opens Step-Sister's corrupted blog post. Near the end of the file, there it is.

Sp.c..l A.s.t.

I've watched enough *Wheel of Fortune* to solve this puzzle:

Special Assets.

This can't be a coincidence. Natalia called Melody a "special asset," and Step-Sister used the same term in a blog post that was wiped from the internet.

My jaw clenches.

Andrew Daniels. Her final client.

Off to the Family's client database to search while trying not to think about the consequences of doing so. I enter his name.

Nothing.

They've scrubbed him. Covering their tracks.

"I'm not going to let them get away with this," I promise her. "I'm going to find out what happened to you."

Back to the spreadsheet, methodically working through each entry, building my frame. The edges first, then inward. I have to solve this puzzle.

I need a wizard.

Fifteen

The spring air is electric. Today, I am a spy.

The setting sun throws shadows across the path as I turn into Central Park. A jogger passes by with her dog, both moving with the easy rhythm of a daily ritual. The day's warmth is giving way to evening's cool embrace, and the city is gentler here. The beauty of it is so melancholy, I take a moment just to breathe it in.

Before leaving, I sent Jeremy a message with the latitude and longitude coordinates for the Conservatory Garden. No explanation. Only numbers. I read it in a book once.

Part of me hopes it confused him. All of me hopes he shows up.

The yew hedges in the Italian section are pretty, and I pretend to admire them while watching for surveillance. Well, that's a line right out of Mom's paperback thrillers.

Fifteen minutes of feigning interest in foliage before I spot him—Jeremy's unmistakable gait, hunched over, hands in pockets, lumbering toward me across the lawn. A warmth I dismiss as relief spreads through me as he approaches.

He stops in front of me, adjusts his glasses, and glares at me like I've lost my mind.

"Why?"

"Let's walk."

We fall in step along the perimeter path. Not too many people now, only a few tourists taking twilight photos.

"You're making me nervous, Star."

"Join the club. I've been the president for days."

Everything I've compiled, I lay it all out for him—the spreadsheet, the blackmail ops disguised as dates. He remains stoic.

"They had her drugging people. Hacking their phones."

He says nothing.

"She was from Ohio. She did high school musicals, and they turned her into—"

"A spy."

I stop walking and turn to face him. "Why would they do this to her?"

He removes his glasses and pinches the bridge of his nose. "Because she'd do it."

"What?"

"Because she wanted to belong. Because she'd do anything they asked." He puts his glasses back on. "Because she was ideal for it."

"That's brutal."

"But efficient."

We come to a stone bench partially hidden by overgrown shrubs. I sit, and he remains standing.

"Andrew Daniels. The client from the night she died. He's been scrubbed from the client database," I say.

"Completely?"

"Not a trace."

"Unusual. Even for them."

"Could you find him? Outside the system?"

He sits beside me, leaving a careful gap between us. "Maybe. If he exists."

"What the hell does that mean?"

He sighs. "I have no idea why I'm telling you this. Do you know what I'm risking here?"

"You're the only person who can help me." Sliding over, I close the gap a little. "I need to know what happened to her."

I need more than that. I need to tear down whatever corrupt machine chewed up my friend and spat her out. But that can stay my secret for now.

A silence builds between us. I glance at him, and a narrative forms in my mind. "Everything here runs on your systems, doesn't it? The app, the portal, the client database—you built the whole machine." I lower to a whisper. "Did you know they were using your little devices for this? To have girls like Melody do these things?"

"I didn't build those devices," he says with defiance.

"That black box I saw on your desk? Is that one of the things she used?"

His jaw tightens, and he looks down at his hands. "All those 'devices' are from Natalia. She brought them in a few years ago. I didn't build them; I just maintain them. I don't ask questions."

"So, you're okay with it?" I press. "You bury yourself in your office, maintain, and let it happen?"

I hit a nerve. Jeremy's back straightens. "No, Star, I'm not okay with it. I'm not okay with any of it." The words come out strangled. "But this is my job—no, it's my life. They have my life in their hands."

He's talking rapidly.

"Do you honestly think they'd ever let me leave this place with what I know? They'd rather 'disappear' me." He makes air quotes.

A fresh wave of guilt washes over me, and his words hit me hard. In all my righteous anger, I never considered that Jeremy might be trapped too.

"I'm sorry, I didn't think—"

"They don't let people like me out. You think I'm some hacker with a weird office and a funny screensaver, but I understand everything. Names. Faces. Where the money goes. I've seen things… If they suspect I'm helping you—" He stops, jaw clenched.

As if on cue, a cool breeze rushes through the garden.

My voice softens. "You say they'll 'disappear' you if you help, but aren't you already disappearing? You sit in your cave of an office while they use what you build to hurt girls like Sparrow and Melody. Doesn't that bother you?"

His legs shift, and his knee bounces.

"I think it does," I say. "I think it bothers the shit out of you that they took your genius and used it for this. There's nothing altruistic here. This can't be the life you want."

He stares at the ground and says nothing, knee still bouncing.

"Help me, Jeremy. Help me change it. Make what you know matter." I take his hand in mine; he doesn't resist. "Don't let them decide your fate. You built the systems, so make them work for us. You can ensure no Sister ever has to go through this again."

He runs his other hand through his hair, exhaling slowly. The conflict is plain on his face, but then his knee goes still. I hold my breath.

"Okay," he says.

The tension melts away as I slouch back, a tentative smile creeping across my face.

His laugh is hollow. "I've always hated that office."

I squeeze his hand tight. He squeezes back a little. It's enough.

He sighs, takes off his glasses, and rubs his face. "Andrew Daniels won't be in any database because he doesn't exist. It's a cover name."

"A cover? For who?"

"No one. Anyone. It doesn't matter. Melody's op was a setup. I'm almost sure of it."

It's like I've been hit with a cattle prod.

"What? Who set her up?"

He glances around, then leans closer. "Do you really want to hear this? Once I tell you, there's no going back."

I bite the inside of my cheek to prepare myself, then nod.

"The Department of Defense."

"DoD? Like, the fucking government?" A shot of adrenaline sends me to my feet.

"Yeah, the Family isn't small-time bullshit. Do you think they pay for all this stuff through escorting alone?"

My mouth drops open as the pieces click into place: the building, the tech, the money. So much money.

"But why would the DoD be involved? What *is* this place?" The scale of it all is making my head spin. "Some kind of blackmail operation?"

"Among other things," he says. "Information brokering. Corporate espionage. Political leverage. Sex is a foot in the door. Someone you'd never suspect."

"That…that's illegal, isn't it?"

"Didn't they tell you this in training?" he asks, a confused look on his face.

"No?" The hair lifts on the back of my neck. What else haven't they told me?

His brow furrows, and he shakes his head. "It's only illegal if you get caught, and they're meticulous. They package it all up nice and neat, anonymize it through shell companies, then auction it off to the highest bidders on dark web marketplaces."

The look on my face must tell him I'm struggling to keep up. He moves closer to the edge of the bench.

"They monetize trust," he continues. "Think about it. Who expects the escort they hired for the night to not only understand the data on their devices but also have the skill to hack them?"

My head drops into my hands. How is any of this real? "But all that money. Wouldn't there be traces, audits?"

"Sure, but they won't lead anywhere." He counts on his fingers. "There are crypto wallets and hidden bank accounts in the Caymans."

"Like in the movies?" The absurdity of it forces out a puff of incredulous laughter. "You're kidding."

"It gets better," he says, with no trace of humor. "They launder it through legitimate businesses like catering companies and cleaning services, things no one pays attention to."

I cover my mouth with my hand to keep from laughing in shock and crying in disbelief.

"The information never comes directly *from* the Family, and the money never goes directly *to* them. It's actually quite elegant." He smiles.

"That's the craziest shit I've ever heard."

"Welcome to information brokering."

In my daze, I try to sit back down next to him, forget the bench doesn't have a back, and almost fall over. His hand catches me. I take a breath and refocus. "But it doesn't explain why the DoD would try to set them up."

"Natalia believes one of the Sisters got sloppy on a previous mission," he continues. "Left digital fingerprints. She had me investigate it for a week. That must have put the Family on the DoD's radar."

"They sent someone to check us out?"

"More like confirm what they already suspected." He adjusts his glasses. "They set up the perfect honey trap—a client profile they knew would trigger Natalia to send in one of you for intelligence gathering."

"And Melody drew the short straw," I say. The words hang in the air, cold and final. "But why her? Why not someone more experienced?"

"Could be the point. Fresh face. Less likely to be recognized."

"And they killed her?"

Jeremy shakes his head. "That's the only part that doesn't make sense. They should have just arrested her. Killing her…that's not the play. It means something got screwed up."

"Screwed up how?"

"Not sure. Melody saw something she wasn't supposed to, or recognized someone?" He sighs. "Maybe it was an accident they couldn't explain away. The whole thing went FUBAR."

"FUBAR?"

"Fucked Up Beyond All Recognition."

"That should be the Family's motto."

"It's mine, at least." A frail smile crosses his face.

"If the DoD knows this, why haven't they come after us? Why are we still operating?"

He shrugs. "Maybe they're building a bigger case, or watching to see who the Family connects with. Or maybe…" He hesitates.

"What?"

"Someone inside is protecting the Family."

"Would explain a lot."

We sit in silence for a moment as the last of the tourists filter out.

"Jeremy, what happens if they find out we're talking about this?"

His answer comes slowly and quietly. "Nothing good."

"Are we being watched right now?"

"No. Not yet, at least."

The light may be dim, but the strain on his face is clear.

"Thank you for helping me," I say, "even if you won't say why."

He scratches his ear and gives a half smile. "I don't know why. I've been asking myself that since you came into my office."

"Is it my rapier-like wit and dashing charisma?" I say, trying to lighten the mood.

His half smile turns full. "Could be."

"About the Step-Sister blog data you gave me. It looks like the corrupted file was a post that got deleted and never republished."

"Were you able to tell what was in it?"

"Not completely, but in her journal, Melody said that Natalia called her a 'special asset,' and the term 'special assets' was in that blog post."

The corner of his mouth twists. "Could just be a coincidence, could be a connection. Step-Sister is the only one who knows for sure."

"There's more than one writer," I blurt out.

"I agree with you."

Boom. Someone else sees it too.

"But we have no way of finding her. Or even talking to her," I say.

"Let me see what I can do."

We sit in silence as a cool breeze rustles the leaves.

His face has gone slack, and he looks lost. Trapped by the same machine that's consuming me. In this empty garden, he's the only other person who understands. With a spark of a thought, an impulse takes over, and I lean in, pressing my lips to his. It's brief, gentle.

No training. Just me.

When I pull back, his glasses are fogged.

"So, what's next?"

"Wh-What do you mean?" he stammers.

"For us, dumbass. What's our next step? We have to look out for each other."

He blinks, his face softening as if no one's ever included him in a *we* before.

I extend my pinkie finger between us. "Promise me, whatever happens, we have each other's back?"

Jeremy stares at my extended finger for a moment, then hooks his pinkie with mine. The gesture is childish and sacred all at once.

"Promise."

Melanie Caderea

Melanie stood on the sidewalk outside Penn Station, flanked by two suitcases and a duffel bag, and watched her father try to hail a taxi. He conducted an orchestra of honking cars while a storm of city life broke over her. Sirens, construction, a dozen languages, and the subterranean rumble of subway trains all fused into a single deafening roar. The air, thick with exhaust, hot dogs, and the lingering stench of trash, was dense enough to chew.

This was it. This was where she belonged.

"Got one!" her father yelled, waving at a cab that had taken pity on him.

They loaded her bags, and her mother grabbed her arm. "Promise me you'll be careful. People here aren't like people back home."

"I will, Mom."

"And don't forget where you come from," her father added, sliding onto the back seat beside her. "You're still our little princess."

She nodded, not listening. The taxi's window framed a world in motion, a vast stage set with neon signs and a cast of millions. The energy intoxicated her, vibrating through the seat and up her spine.

The cab pulled up to Kerrey Hall. Its face of angular glass and steel seemed to buzz with the same creative energy as the students who milled about its entrance, their instrument cases and artfully messy hair marking them as members of a tribe she ached to belong to.

They took the elevator to the fourteenth floor—suite fourteen. A promising sign, she thought. The door pushed open to reveal a small, bright space. On the left bed sat a girl with hair the color of grape Kool-Aid, her fingers dancing silently across a miniature piano keyboard on her lap. Melanie could almost hear the notes hidden in the soft plastic clicking of the keys.

The girl raised her head, pulling off a pair of oversized headphones. Piercings dotted her face, which broke into an amused smile. "You must be the roommate." Her voice sounded like she'd walked off the set of *The Sopranos*. "I'm Ray."

"Melanie," she said, keenly aware of her father's wrinkled polo and her mother staring at Ray's hair as if it were contagious.

Ray's eyes flicked to the parents, then back to Melanie. "First time in the city?"

Melanie laughed. "Is it obvious?"

"You're clutching your suitcase like it's a life preserver."

The bag dropped to the floor with a thud.

"It's okay." Ray smiled. "The city doesn't swallow you up all in one bite."

The goodbye to her parents was an awkward, tearful affair. When they were gone, she saw her future laid out before her. One of Ray's friends stopped by, long dreadlocks swinging as they gawked at Melanie like she belonged in the "World Outside New York" exhibit at the Natural History Museum. Back home, she'd been the creative one, but here, next to Ray's purple hair and effortless cool, she was just another Midwestern transplant with big dreams and nothing new to say.

A MONTH LATER, Melanie learned her roommate didn't ask—she announced. Tonight's came while she read her *Advanced Scene Study* textbook.

"Open mic at the Bowery Poetry Club," Ray said, pulling a black crop top over her head. "You're coming."

"I have this paper due—"

"When?"

"Friday."

"It's Tuesday. You're coming." Ray grabbed a battered leather jacket. "Trust me, this is education too."

The club was dark, cramped, and thick with smoke that wasn't entirely tobacco. Ray floated through the crowd, leaving Melanie to trail behind like a puppy. The other students wore their art like heraldry—portfolio cases covered in stickers from galleries and exhibits, enamel pins clustered on their bags like medals of honor. "Ray!" A guy with gauged ears and tattooed sleeves waved them over. "Who's your friend?"

"My roommate. Melanie, Jayson. He's a genius with a camera when he's not high."

Jayson laughed. "Nice to meet you. You performing?"

Melanie's eyes widened. "Oh, no, I'm—"

"She's just getting warmed up," Ray interrupted, shooting her a look.

The first performer, an impossibly thin girl with a shaved head, delivered a spoken-word piece on gentrification—her words cutting and poignant—and the gathered bohemians snapped their fingers in appreciation. Next, a guy named Ezra sang with an unpolished tone that made Melanie's throat tighten. His lyrics spoke of poverty and addiction. Genuine pain. Authentic stories.

"You should get up there," Ray said during a break. "The monologue you were practicing? The one about the woman waiting for her husband to come home from war?"

Melanie's insides twisted. The piece felt powerful in the safety of the acting workshop. Here, it was like bringing a plastic sword to a gladiator fight. But Ray pushed her forward, and then her name came over the speakers.

She climbed the steps and stood behind the mic. The words came out clear, powerful, technically sound. She hit every beat she'd practiced.

When she fell to her knees at the climax, the crowd clapped. Polite, appreciative clapping lasting precisely the right amount of time before trailing off into the silence that meant "*next.*"

"Very nice," Ray said when she returned, like she was describing a haircut.

Jayson nodded. "Yeah, really great technique. You've got good training."

Training. Technique. The words were consolation prizes.

THE NEXT MORNING, Professor Merrick slid his glasses to the top of his head and exhaled through his nose. "Quite proficient," he announced to the Advanced Scene Study class after Melanie's Lady Macbeth. "But where's your fear, Ms. Caderea? Where's the pain?"

The class shifted in their seats. A few exchanged glances—some sympathetic, others barely concealing their delight. Melanie's face flushed as she returned to her chair wearing the wet cardboard of his backhanded compliment. She'd nailed every technical element, hit every mark, modulated her voice exactly as trained. And they'd felt nothing.

He gestured to Jessica Chaisse, the sophomore with three off-Broadway showcases under her belt. "Show her."

Jessica took the floor, and with the first jerk of her arm, she became Lady Macbeth. Her voice hitched and cracked, as her body contorted with guilt. When she whispered, "Here's the smell of blood still," goose bumps broke out along Melanie's arms. No one moved for three full seconds. Then the class erupted in applause. Someone whispered "holy shit" from the back row.

"That," Professor Merrick said, with a slow clap, "is how you make Shakespeare your bitch."

LATER, in a studio space, her scene partner, Chris, held up a hand. "Stop. You're saying the words, not feeling the emotion. She's lost everything. You sound like you're looking for your cat."

A few students snickered. Melanie bit the inside of her cheek.

"Think about the worst thing that's ever happened to you," Chris said. "Then double it."

She frantically dug through her mental filing cabinet of tragedies. The broken arm in fourth grade? No, she'd gotten a neon pink cast and attention from even the cool kids. Her grandmother's passing? She'd been five—all she remembered was extra ice cream and getting to stay up late.

Chemistry, junior year. The B+ had been a personal apocalypse. She'd cried in the bathroom for twenty minutes, lamenting the loss of her 4.0 GPA. The red mark on her report card was a scarlet letter.

"I'm waiting," Chris said, arms crossed.

Her eyes closed, and she summoned the memory of that grade,

inflated the pain into something usable, imagined the B+ as a lost lover, a dead child, a burned home. She reached for the emotions, stretched them like taffy, but they snapped back in her face, thin and insubstantial.

"Still sounds like you're looking for your cat," Chris sighed. "Are you sure you really want to find it?"

IN THE EVENING, Ray was at her keyboard again, no headphones. A haunting melody filled the room. It built to a crescendo that made Melanie's soul ache, then hung in the air like a question.

"Ugh." Ray shook her head. "This is garbage."

"Are you kidding? It's incredible."

"The flat second to major seventh isn't working. It's not ready."

Melanie glanced at her own homework, at the neat, honor-roll handwriting. At the notes she'd jotted in the margin: *Where's the pain?*

Slipping out of bed, she left the room. In the shared bathroom, the fluorescent lights hummed to life. Her reflection looked smaller, prettier in the way that had always worked for her.

She grabbed the cotton pads.

One swipe at a time, she erased herself. Eyeliner—the soft wing she'd perfected in ninth grade—smeared into gray. The subtle shimmer on her cheekbones, meant to catch the stage lights, disappeared. Gloss faded, revealing thin and pale lips. The "Rocky River Special," the flawless face that had gotten her cast as the ingenue in every production.

She scrubbed until only skin remained. Exposed pores. A small scar on her nose from when the cat scratched her. Water splashed across her face as she leaned closer to the mirror, close enough for her breath to fog the glass in small, disappearing circles. Her mouth twitched; water droplets ran down her cheeks. She didn't blink.

"You're not special."

The words hissed out like quiet venom. She took her bag, turned out the light, and left.

Sixteen

Aura tugs at the ends of my turquoise scarf, her brow creased in concentration. "Girl, I could never wear these things." She scrunches her face. "They make me itch like crazy."

"It was Melody's favorite color," I say. The silk is cool against my skin, a welcome relief from the nervous warmth in my face.

"You look good. Really put together."

My laugh is sharp and bitter. "That's ironic, considering I'm about to fall apart."

We leave the room and head to Melody's memorial, Aura's hand in mine. "If you need to cry, girl, you let it out, okay?" She squeezes. "No shame in it."

So many Sisters file into the auditorium alongside us, all dressed in elegant black with their faces composed in solemnity. I expected a handful of us huddled in a corner somewhere, not this full-blown event.

I lean over to Aura as we settle in. "She wasn't here that long. How did she know all these people?"

Aura's face pulls taut. "That was Melody. Girl never met a stranger."

The front of the room houses a table arranged with framed photographs. The largest is a professional headshot of Melody, her smile radiant and carefree. Then a candid photo of her and Kora, both laughing as Melody points to her tattoo. And in the center, surrounded by flickering candles, sits Mr. Ribbit, the stuffed frog she kept on her bed.

The sight of that worn green toy almost breaks me. It's so undeniably her—silly and sweet and utterly out of place in this fishbowl of fake glamour.

The piano music playing in the background fades to silence, and Natalia rises from her seat. She walks to the podium with measured steps; her face is a mask of composed grief.

"Sisters," she begins, "we gather today to honor one who left us too soon."

Here come the corporate platitudes—the hollow words of a boss who lost an employee.

"Melody exemplified all that the Family stands for," Natalia continues. "Not only beauty and charm, though she had both in abundance, but loyalty. Warmth. The ability to make everyone feel like they belonged."

This doesn't sound like the emotionless Natalia I'd expected.

"Everything a Sister should aspire to be." Natalia gestures to the audience. "I spoke with her only a week ago about her future here. She was eager and full of plans."

Her composure cracks on the last word, and she clears her throat.

"Each of us should carry a piece of Melody in our hearts when we walk these floors. Remember her laughter in these hallways. Her kindness in our daily interactions. A beautiful soul taken much too soon."

I don't understand. These words sound so genuine, so heartfelt.

She steps away from the podium, and for a second, something raw and unguarded surfaces. Is the monster I've built up in my head just a woman after all?

Sage walks up next, her poise clearly fraying. She tucks a strand of hair behind her ear.

"Thank you, Natalia, for those beautiful words," she says. "I have so much I could say about Melody. In her short time with us, she made an impression on everyone she met. I want to share one small example of her heart."

She takes a breath, her fingers wrapping around the podium. "A couple of weeks ago, Denali and I were talking outside the cafeteria. We noticed Melody browsing the donation rack and thought nothing more of it." She pauses. "I was telling Denali about a pair of pearl earrings I must have misplaced. I'd looked all over but couldn't find them, and I was upset about it."

Her breath catches, and she takes a second to compose herself.

"When I got back later that night, taped to my door was a little plastic bag with a pair of pearl earrings in it and a Post-it note that said: 'Couldn't help but overhear. These will look much better on you than me. Love, Melody.'"

Sage stops speaking, tears dripping from her face. The auditorium is silent.

When she leans back toward the microphone, she wavers. "That is the person Melody was—and that I hope to be someday."

She steps down from the stage, shaken, and my heart breaks. That's the Melody I knew—always giving, always noticing the little things that would make someone else happy.

Kora rises from her seat. She walks to the podium without the boundless energy she usually carries. Her curls are pulled back, and she's wearing minimal makeup.

She adjusts the microphone, clears her throat, and looks out at all of us.

"I'm not real good at this, so it may get sloppy."

A polite laugh ripples through the room.

"I've been in the Family a long time," she continues softly. "And I've had the privilege of mentoring many Sisters."

She takes a steadying breath.

"But I never had one quite like Melody."

Something in her tone puts a lump in my throat. This isn't the cool, aloof Kora I know—the one who handles every crisis with a quip and a plan.

"She was so eager to learn, to keep getting better." Kora pauses for a moment. "We had so many late-night talks in my room, drinking chai and sharing stories, our laughs, our tears."

I blink in surprise. They were close, sure. But Melody never mentioned these late-night sessions.

Behind me, there's a stifled sob. I turn to see Sage breaking down, hand pressed over her mouth, tears streaming down her face. Her entire body shakes with the effort of containing her grief. I've never seen her like this—raw and unguarded.

I turn back to Kora, who's gripping the podium like a guardrail.

"I tried—" She pulls in a breath. "—tried to encourage her, to help her see the greatness in herself."

Her posture drops, but she pushes through.

"She used to worry she wasn't special enough for this place. Can you believe that?" Kora huffs a laugh.

She looks over at the picture of Melody on the table. "I'm so sorry." She chokes up, fighting her tears back. "I'm so sorry I failed you."

The last words come out as a broken rasp, and Kora falls apart at the podium, shaking with sobs she can no longer contain. Sage rushes to her, wraps an arm around her waist, and helps her off the stage.

Frozen in my seat, I'm dumbfounded. These women are shattered with grief. Actual grief. Not the wooden performances I expected, but honest pain.

A sharp elbow catches my ribs, and Aura leans in close. "You have to say something."

I shake my head. "I can't."

"Yes, you can," she insists, giving my shoulder a gentle push, and I'm on my feet, legs moving against my better judgment. The walk to the podium is like crossing a minefield—so many faces. My throat tenses.

"I, um…" The words stick in my mouth like peanut butter. "Melody was my best friend."

Was.

"Not just in the Family, but in life. I only met her a month ago, but it felt like I'd known her forever."

Heads nod, faces soften with recognition. Everyone knew—our instant connection, our constant togetherness.

"She saw the good in everyone. Even when they didn't deserve it."

Natalia's face remains composed, and something hot and dangerous flares inside me.

"She should still be here," I seethe. "But she isn't. And that's something we all have to live with."

My implication hangs in the air, unmistakable, as Sage shifts uncomfortably in her seat.

Blinking back tears that burn like acid, I turn toward her picture. "I love you, Melanie," I say to the photo, to Mr. Ribbit, and to wherever she might be now. "And I always will."

The words are inadequate—a penny tossed into a fountain of loss—but they're all I have. Before I even leave the podium, Sage is already moving to the microphone.

"That's all for now. Thank you for coming. You may continue to pay your respects throughout the day," she says.

The polite dismissal makes me want to scream. As if this were a corporate luncheon, and the potato salad is starting to turn.

"Come on," Aura says. "Let's go before someone tries to give you a pep talk."

She pulls me away, and I'm grateful for her understanding. I am surrounded by shared grief, but I've never felt more alone.

KARI'S perfectly manicured nails click-clack against her keyboard. She hasn't looked up once, except to tell me it'll be "just a few more minutes" three separate times. The woman's a human gatekeeper and a former Sister, according to Kora. Regardless, she enjoys watching me squirm.

My plan is simple: convince Caron I'm on the verge of a breakdown. Not exactly Oscar-worthy acting, considering I wake up most mornings expecting it to be the day I crack. But this isn't about me falling apart—it's about buying time, which Jeremy and I need if we're going to figure out what happened to Melody.

"Shouldn't be long—he's finishing up a call." Kari leaves her chair and walks down the hall holding a file.

Caron's voice rises from his office as though he's chastising someone. I slink to the door and press my ear to it, keeping my eyes on the hallway. He's not speaking English, that's for sure. The words are sharp, clipped, and the emotion translates even if I can't understand them. I've never heard him angry before, in any language. Kari rounds the corner, and I slip back into the chair.

Ten more minutes pass in this purgatory of a waiting area while I pick at my cuticles and mentally rehearse my lines, hoping no residual hostility carries over to me.

"You can go in now, Star," Kari says. She doesn't look up from her screen, just waves toward the heavy oak door.

My hands tremble enough to be visible, and it's not acting. There's something about Caron that makes me five years old again, standing before some mythical deity who can see right through my bullshit.

He's sitting behind his massive desk, bathed in natural light from the enormous windows. When he sees me, his face attempts to soften, like smoothing out a crumpled sheet of paper. Whatever anger remains is beaten back, but not absent.

"Star," he says, rising to his feet with surprising agility for a man his age. "Come in, please."

My posture falls a little as I step forward. Not too much— overplaying grief always looks phony.

"Sit, sit." He gestures to the plush chair across from him. "Water? Tea?"

"No, thank you."

He sits and leans forward with his elbows on the desk. The concern on his face reads as genuine, which makes this harder somehow.

"My sincere condolences." The emotion is apparent in his tone. "Melody was…special. A bright light."

The mention of her name blindsides me. I'd rehearsed this whole thing, but now I have actual tears to contend with.

"Thank you." I look down at my hands, milking the emotion. "Can't say I'm doing that well. Hard to sleep. Food tastes like nothing. I keep seeing her face."

He nods slowly.

"I have a client tonight, but I'm worried I'll…" I swallow hard. "I don't want to give a poor impression of the Family."

The irony of those words coming out of my mouth almost makes me lose it. Like I give a shit about the Family's reputation when they're responsible for my best friend's death. But I keep my face composed, vulnerable.

Caron sits back, scrutinizing me. For a terrifying moment, I think he's seen through the charade. But then he sighs.

"Of course you're struggling. This is normal, healthy even." He waves his hand dismissively. "Don't worry about your client tonight. I will take care of it."

Relief floods through me, but I hold it back. "Thank you."

"Go back to your room, Star. Try to be at peace." He's gentle, almost paternal, but a muscle in his jaw tightens and releases in a frantic rhythm that betrays the calm. "Grief can be…a labyrinth. Be careful you don't become lost searching for things that aren't there."

I'm not sure what to make of that, but he's smiling, so I'll take what's offered and move on. I'd wanted a little more time, but it's a start.

As I get up to leave, the guilt gnaws at me for having lied to him.

But then I think about everything.

He might act like everyone's favorite grandfather, but he built this beast. He's the architect of it all, whether or not he gives the orders himself.

SEVENTEEN

Jeremy swivels in the chair as he downs the last swig of his energy drink. "I checked again, but the Step-Sister server is still locked down. There's no obvious way in, and the admin controls are secured. She doesn't leave an email, a Dropbox, or anything. It's one-way communication."

I slump against the wall of his office, arms crossed. "So that's it? Are we screwed?"

"Not necessarily." He spins his chair in a full circle, a nervous habit I've come to recognize when he's debating whether to share something questionable.

"Spit it out, Wizard. I'm not in the mood for dramatic pauses."

He stops spinning. "There's another possibility, but I'm not sure you'd want to do it."

"Try me."

"If you can't get to her, then you have to make her come to you."

"And how do I accomplish that?"

"With a response post," Jeremy says, like it's the most obvious thing in the world.

My face goes blank. "A what now?"

"Step-Sister thrives on insider information that compromises the Family, right?" His fingers drum against the desk in a nervous rhythm. "So, give her some."

"Like what?" I ask, but understand as soon as the words leave my mouth. "Oh."

Jeremy stares at me.

"No, I can't do that," I say, pushing off from the wall. "Are you insane?"

"She'll see through any attempts to bullshit her." He swivels to follow my pacing. "It has to be something true, something real."

"It'll stir up a hornet's nest. Natalia will know the leak came from inside."

"Indeed," he says. "That's why Step-Sister will believe it's real. If you drop that, you won't have to search for her anymore." He leans in. "She'll find you."

The logic of his plan resonates but also sinks my stomach. It's dangerous, crazy, and undeniably the only path forward. "Okay."

Jeremy's face lights up, and he spins back to his computer. "I can set up an anonymous identity for you outside of the Family network. You make a post on the same forum where the first Step-Sister post appeared. Call yourself—I don't know—the *real* Step-Sister or something antagonistic."

"Cinderella."

"What?" Jeremy's fingers pause over the keyboard.

"The foil to the Step-Sisters, right? Cinderella." I smile at the literary symmetry.

"That's perfect. You're good at this."

I shrug. "Fairy tales were my jam."

"Cinderella it is." He starts typing again. "I'll cover the tracks. Even if they trace it, they'll end up in some internet café in Jakarta."

"And you're sure she'll respond?"

Jeremy stops typing. "No. But it's the best shot we have."

"What do I say?"

"It has to hurt," he says. "But be careful how much you reveal. Step-Sister might be our ally in finding out what happened, but she's not our friend."

Our eyes meet—silently acknowledging the risk.

My phone buzzes against my hip, and I nearly jump out of my skin.

SAGE

At your room, wanted to talk, are you down at tech?

"Shit." The color drains from my face. "It's Sage. And she knows I'm here."

Jeremy's focus narrows on his monitor as he clicks the mouse a few times.

"I paused your tracking," he mutters, typing. "But I only bought you a few minutes."

I turn toward the door, shoving my phone into my pocket.

"Star, wait." He leans down, opens the bottom drawer of his desk and pulls out what looks like a generic smartphone. He copies something off the sticker on the back and hands it to me.

"And this is?"

"A burner phone. It'll keep you off the Family's radar. Leave your Family phone and use this when you need to go somewhere or talk to someone you shouldn't."

"Like you?" I smile, then touch my neck. "Wait, what about my pendant? I assumed they were tracking us through these too."

Jeremy laughs. "They used to. But the Sisters figured it out and would just leave them in their rooms. So they switched to using the app instead. Much harder to function without your phone than without jewelry."

"Clever," I admit. "Evil, but clever."

"Just be careful, Okay?"

A nod, and then I'm out the door tallying plausible excuses for why I'm down here. Something other than plotting against the Family with the tech guy who's crushing on me.

Rounding the corner, I tap out:

Omw, 2 mins.

THE ELEVATOR CARRIES me to the top floor, and then I take the stairs down to mine. The extra time helps me get my story straight and my breathing under control. Sage is waiting outside my room, a picture of refinement in a pale blue pantsuit.

"Hey, sorry," I say, trying to sound calm. "Was having some trouble with my portal. Rushed back as soon as I got your message."

Sage chuckles, tilting her head. "You know they'll come to you if you ask, right?"

My jaw tightens, but I keep my face neutral as the door unlocks. "It's okay, I could use the exercise anyway."

We step in, and I set my notebook on the desk. She stands while I flop down onto the edge of my bed.

"You went to see Caron," she says, studying me.

"Did he send you here?"

"No, but he expressed concern about you. He's worried."

"That's nice of him."

"How are you doing?" she asks.

I dial in my performance—enough grief to seem real, enough control to keep her from digging. "It comes in waves, you know? One minute I'm okay, the next..."

"I talked about it with Caron, and he thought it might be good to give you the week off. Would that help?"

Inside, I'm practically doing cartwheels—this is what I need to work with Jeremy—but I keep my reaction measured. "Yes, thank you. I think it will."

She walks over to the desk and leans against it.

"He thinks you're falling apart." Her tone is casual, but she's scrutinizing me. "He sees a grieving girl who needs a break." She looks down at my notebook. "But I don't think that's what's happening at all."

My insides drop like I've stepped off a cliff, that sickening free-fall sensation spreading through my core as the top of my head tingles.

Sage reaches down and picks up the notebook. My hands go clammy, trembling enough that I have to clench them to keep still. She doesn't open it, just holds on, feeling its weight.

"What are you always writing in here? Poems? Secrets? A list of all the rules you're planning to break?" She runs her hand over the cover and looks up sharply.

"They're just thoughts. It's a journal," I say. This isn't a casual gesture; this is a move, a deliberate display of power. She's holding my lifeline in this place, and we both know it.

"Be careful what you write in here, Star." She waves it in front of her. "Paper may hold secrets better than people, but it remembers them longer too."

Every nerve ending feels exposed, hypersensitive, like my skin has turned inside out.

"Make good use of your time off." She places the notebook gently back on the desk, straightening it so it aligns perfectly with the edge. The gesture is unnervingly intimate. Her stare lingers a moment, and then her eyes drift to my pen—cracked and chewed. A flicker of disdain crosses her face, like she's looking at a dead insect.

Her hand disappears into the inner pocket of her blazer and emerges with a pen of her own—sleek, black, and expensive. The Family's diamond logo is etched into the side.

I follow her every move, still too nervous to say anything.

She picks up my old pen, holding it as if it's contaminated, and places it into the cup on the far side of the desk. Then she slides her own into the space beside my notebook.

"That's better," she says. She walks to the door and leaves quietly, the latch clicking closed behind her.

MY HEAD POUNDS from staring at the screen in the dark. Each entry in Melody's journal is another paper cut on my soul, but I can't stop reading. If I'm going to lure Step-Sister out, I need to understand how girls like us end up here. How we fall into the Family's web.

The file labeled *Star's Menstrual Tracker* is open on the laptop next to me—a grimly funny name for a book of a dead girl's secrets. Assignment logs and notes about the Sisters scroll by, but buried between them are fragments of my friend's history. There's a long entry I haven't read yet, dated a few months before I joined.

January 10

It's funny to think it all started with a boy. This whole new life, this building, this name. It all started with Ezra. I think I wrote about him before, but I can't remember.

I met him at a poetry slam. He had this beat-up guitar and sang like he was whispering a secret just to me. We ended up at a diner in the Village at two in the morning, eating pancakes. I kissed him right on the street corner. I was stupid and hungry, and for the first time since I got to this city, I felt like the girl in his eyes and not mine.

Kora said the feeling was just a symptom of how I was desperate to escape myself and find a new reflection to look at. It wasn't about Ezra; it was about me wanting to be someone else.
But here, I don't have to look in someone else's eyes to feel worthy. They've taught me to love the girl in my own, and it feels more sincere. That night was a spark in the darkness, but this place is a warm, steady light. You can't live inside a spark, after all.

An ache blooms in my chest. She never told me about Ezra, but I can picture her—wide-eyed and hopeful. The girl eating pancakes at two in the morning, feeling seen for the first time—that's the Melody I knew. But she was starting to sound like them. Like her own memories were something to be cured.

Two months later, I was living in his apartment, a crappy little box that reeked of old weed and Bukowski paperbacks. He called me his Dropout Queen. We were broke and brilliant and totally full of shit, and I thought I loved it. I tanked every class, dodged calls from my parents, and played the role of the tortured artist, too talented for school. Ezra never pushed me. He'd say, "There's no future. Just this. Just right now." He made it sound like magic, but it wasn't. It was just failure.

The words blur as my headache pulses behind my eyes. Where is Ezra now? Does he even know Melanie is gone? The curiosity pulls at me, but this is a path better left untraveled.

After that, it fell apart fast. Dad sent a late Christmas text asking me to come home, but I ignored it. Ray got me a job bartending for cash, and I started dancing at this topless bar off Avenue A. Weirdly, I liked it. Another performance. Onstage, under the lights, I didn't feel like a failure. I felt wanted.

When the man in the tailored suit handed me the card, he said I had "presence." Said I was "special." The next night, I walked out on Ezra, and this life began. I wish I'd made different choices, but they led me here, which has to count for something. When I first started, Kora told me everything I did before was "discovering my power." That I'd been rehearsing for this life all along, and now I could thrive. And I plan to.

Life with Ezra was like that moment in a dream where you're soaring through the air, weightless and free, right until you remember you can't actually fly. The thrill and the crash were always part of the same package. But here? There's real magic, real love, real Sisters. I can just be me, silly and special.

I press my forehead against the cool laptop as Melody's story settles in my bones. Her love, her failure, twisted into a "rehearsal" for this life. The last words are like a sales pitch to herself, but that's the pattern, isn't it? It's how they get all of us: find the cracks, pour in the glue of validation, and mold us into who they need us to be. All the while we're just grateful to be healed.

My temple throbs. Too much screen time in the dark, too little nourishment.

The dorm is subdued tonight. Most of the girls are out with clients or staying in their rooms. Piper is head down in a book, and we exchange waves as I walk by. The cafeteria is empty except for Emma, the night attendant, scrolling through her phone behind the counter. I grab a chocolate meal shake and a cookie-dough protein bar from the glass fridge. Food doesn't hold much appeal, but I need fuel for what's coming.

On my way out, voices stop me cold. They're loud, and familiar.

"—wouldn't let it go." That's Sage, her voice sharp.

I press myself against the wall.

"So, it's all on me, then?" Kora.

"Who else would it be on?" Sage snaps.

The wrapper of the protein bar crinkles in my fingers.

"Bullshit, we all agreed in there. You can't put this on me."

"This is exactly what happened last time, Kora. Exactly."

"It's not the same—she was ready."

"Now it's my ass on the line!" Sage is getting emotional.

"I didn't ask you to do this. I'll deal with the fallout."

"Oh, fuck you. Always the martyr, aren't you?" Sage pauses. "I'm not doing this."

The metal door to the stairwell opens, then clangs shut.

There's silence for a moment, and Kora curses softly as I strain to hear.

Some shuffling, and another door closes.

I lean around the corner, but the hallway is empty. My hands are shaking as I release my grip on the protein bar.

What the hell was that about? I've never heard them fight before. Not once. They're always finishing each other's sentences, presenting a unified front. But whatever happened has cracked something between them.

The Family is going dysfunctional, and I can't say I'm torn up about it.

Once I'm back in my room, I choke down the meal shake and protein bar, then plant myself at the desk. The notebook page is blank, my new pen is twisted open, and my mind is all scattered light and white noise. The words need to light a fuse under this whole place. Once this post goes live, the countdown starts. How long before Natalia, Sage, or even Caron figures out it's me?

Every angle I try is wrong. I'm writing a threat, a plea, and a secret message all at once, and it's coming out frazzled. If I want to sound like Step-Sister, I need to understand her voice. I need to feel her pain. Melody's pain.

I pull out my phone and scroll to an older entry.

Blog Entry #23

The Water's Fine

You know the story of the boiling frog. The Family doesn't just throw you into the fire. That would scare you off.

They place you in a warm pot and slowly, degree by degree, turn up the heat. The warmth is their approval. It's the compliments in the hallway, the expensive gifts, the hand on your shoulder saying "great work." It's the lie that they see you, the real you, in a way no one ever has before. It's slow seduction, and it feels so good, you just…float.

And while you're floating, they teach you to fear the cool air outside. Your old life? It was miserable. Your family? They didn't understand you. That boy who broke your heart? Proof that love outside these walls is a lie. The heat gets a little higher, but you barely notice the manipulation.

That's when the worst part happens. You see the new girl shivering by the side of the pot, and you tell her, "Come on in, the water's fine." It's warm, earnest exploitation. You become the reason the next frog doesn't jump.

By the time you both realize the water is scalding, you've lost the will to leap. It feels safer to boil than to face the cold alone.

If you're in the Family, jump now, before you're in the next bowl of soup.

Stay sharp, Stay free.

—Your Step-Sister

My eyes close, and I let the words sink in. *It's slow seduction.* Step-Sister nailed it with *warm, earnest exploitation.* They don't just take; they keep you comfortable while they do it. It's why the girls stay. It's why I stay. The pot feels like home because they've designed it to, and that's more terrifying than any threat could ever be.

That's it. That's the angle. Step-Sister isn't asking questions; she's delivering judgments and writing with the absolute moral clarity of a prophet. She's a leader offering an escape, not a victim asking for help. She's speaking from truth, not at it.

A bitter little laugh catches in my throat. To draw her out, I don't have to become *her.* I have to become her *equal.* Instead of asking for a seat at the table, I need to claim one.

The pen sits more comfortably in my hand now, and the first line emerges. Not a plea or a threat, but an introduction. A performance. The truth is, I've been playing parts my whole life: poor girl, dutiful daughter, grieving orphan, street rat, escort. What's one more?

The ink glides along the fresh page.

You can call me Cinderella.

Jeremy Tallinder

Jeremy's fingers flew across the keyboard like he was debugging at 4 a.m. for a 5 a.m. launch window. The code scrolled in an asymmetric cascade—meaningless to most but, to him, a lattice of logic and structure. His noise-cancelling headphones blocked out the ambient Starbucks chatter, creating a bubble where only he and his algorithms existed.

Until the cursing began.

At first, it was just a whispered "Shit" from the stranger at the next table. Then a more forceful "Goddammit," followed by the unmistakable sound of someone who wanted to slam their laptop shut but couldn't afford to lose the deposit. He tried to focus on his own work—a side project that challenged him, unlike his day job at Google—but the man's frustration became a distraction.

The man jabbed his keyboard with increasing aggression, muttering profanities that grew more creative by the second. A glance revealed someone in his mid-forties, dressed in an expensive suit that fit too well to be off-the-rack, with a platinum watch peeking from beneath a French cuff. The kind of guy who didn't expect technology to disobey him. More intriguingly, there was code on the screen.

Jeremy sighed, slipped off his headphones, and stood. He shouldn't care. He really shouldn't. But the code was familiar enough that he knew he could most likely fix it in thirty seconds.

"What seems to be the issue?" he asked, instantly regretting the intrusion when the man's head snapped up with irritation.

The well-dressed stranger started to say something dismissive, paused as his gaze drifted to the open laptop on the adjacent table, and held his words. The irritation gave way to recognition—one technologist spotting another in the wild.

"Threading issue," the man said, his tone switching to respectful. "The damn thing won't synchronize."

"Mind if I look?" Jeremy gestured toward the laptop. "I've done a fair bit with concurrency."

The man hesitated, then slid the MacBook across the table. "I appreciate it, but there's nothing you're going to—"

Already scanning the code, Jeremy's eyes darted across the screen with machine-like efficiency. The problem jumped out immediately —so obvious it was almost beautiful in its simplicity.

"Your issue is right here," he said, pointing to a section. "You're accessing the structure pointer too soon on this thread. Put a mutex in there, and that should lock it for you."

The man stared at the screen, shifting from skepticism to astonishment—the look of someone witnessing something they couldn't quite comprehend, like a chicken playing checkers.

"Jesus Christ," he whispered. "That's it." He pulled the laptop back, made the change, and ran the program. His face lit up when it executed flawlessly. "I've been fighting with this for three hours."

Jeremy shrugged and returned to his table. "Happens to everyone." He slipped his headphones back on; social exchanges drained him, even brief ones.

Twenty minutes later, as he was deep in code again, a shadow fell across his keyboard. The stranger had stood to leave but now hovered by his table. Reluctantly, Jeremy removed the headphones.

"I didn't properly thank you," the man said, sliding into the chair opposite. "That was impressive."

"Not a big deal," he replied, uncomfortable with the praise.

"What's your name?"

A hesitation, then, "Jeremy."

"Where do you work, Jeremy?" The man's face took on a measured quality, assessing.

"Google. Data infrastructure."

"And you're happy there?"

He hesitated again. Happy? He was paid well, solved moderately interesting problems, but always had the feeling of being a small gear in an enormous machine. "It's my first year. It's…fine."

The man nodded like he'd just confirmed something. He slid his hand into his jacket and pulled out a business card—not paper, but what appeared to be black anodized metal with an etched design. No name, no phone number. Just a sleek logo and an onion address—a dark web network location.

"Drop by and let me know if you're interested in doing something important." The man placed the card on the table.

Jeremy picked it up, running his thumb over the etched surface. "Important how?"

The man stood, straightening his tie. "Let's just say it's a place where someone with your abilities wouldn't be wasting time fixing other people's threading issues." He smiled, revealing perfect teeth. "And very lucrative."

With that, he turned and strolled out the door, leaving Jeremy with a business card in his hand and the smooth hum of his career rerouting.

EIGHTEEN

Dear Step-Sister,

You can call me Cinderella. Not because I'm waiting for a prince to save me, but because I'm living two lives inside these marble halls. By day, I smile and play the perfect Sister. By night, I document the rot beneath the chandeliers.

I've been reading your posts, watching from inside the tower as you throw pebbles at our windows. Some land. Most don't. While you yell from outside the gates, I'm scrubbing the floors every day. I hear the hushed secrets. I see texts that never make the Family app. I know which Sisters cry themselves to sleep and which ones are plotting their escape.

But I'm not leaving. Not yet. Not until I expose what happened to our Sister who died "accidentally" last week. The sex worker found outside the hotel? Let me be clear: there was nothing accidental about it.

She had secrets. They think they buried them with her. They're wrong. I have the screenshots. I have the timestamps. I have the truth. You claim to want to help us. Prove it. Your blog posts are warnings written in water—they evaporate before anyone can act.

You know how to find me. Look for my glass slipper on the stairs. If it fits, we'll dance. If not, we'll all go down together. Midnight's coming for all of us.

—Cinderella

"So, what do you think?" I nervously chew on my cuticle.

Jeremy's face twitches as he reads, and I study every micro-expression. His eyebrows rise, then furrow, and rise again. The paper rustles in his hands as a gust of wind rushes through the park, nearly snatching my masterpiece. He clutches it tighter, pressing it against his thigh. A few leaves swirl around our bench, a chaotic little vortex, before scattering on the wind.

"This is…good," he says against the backdrop of distant traffic and children's laughter. "Really good. Vague enough that you're not giving anything away, but with enough attitude to get her attention." He adjusts his glasses, squinting at me. "Are you absolutely sure you want to do this? You know what'll happen the second someone from the Family sees it, right?"

I nod, the finality of my decision settling in my bones as Melody's smile flashes in my mind. I owe her this much.

"Yes. Whatever happens, I'll deal with it."

Jeremy folds the paper carefully and tucks it into his pocket. "Okay. I'll set up the account tonight and post it. The DMs will stay open in case she makes contact." He scratches his head, nervous energy radiating off him. "As soon as she responds, I'll take the post down, but by then—"

"It'll be too late," I finish for him. "Someone will have seen it."

We sit in silence for a moment, the gravity of what we're doing settling around us like fog.

"Thanks," I say.

"Don't thank me yet."

An unspoken agreement passes between us as we stand. No lingering goodbyes, no apparent connection. We walk away in opposite directions, two strangers who just happened to share a bench.

JADE KNOWS MORE than she's let on, I'm sure of it. She's been hiding away for days now. Was it her idea to lie low or Natalia's? Either way, someone doesn't want her talking.

There's rustling inside when I knock, but no one answers.

I try again, a little firmer this time. "Jade? It's Star. I want to see if you're okay."

Nothing. Then, after a few moments, the door cracks. Just enough to reveal one eye and a sliver of hollowed cheek.

She looks like hell—frizzy hair, dark circles, and an oversized sweatshirt. Jade doesn't do casual. Hell, she barely does comfortable.

"Star?" Her voice is hoarse, like she hasn't used it in days. "I didn't expect to see you. Is everything okay?"

The question hits me wrong, sideways, like asking someone with a broken leg if they're enjoying their jog. There's something on her face that I recognized in myself after my mother died. Guilt. The kind that eats you from the inside out.

"No," I say.

She blinks, caught off guard by my honesty. Most people would have lied, said everything was fine. But I'm done with pleasantries. Done pretending this is normal.

"Take a walk with me." I put on a smile. "Please?"

Her grip tightens on the doorframe. She's going to slam it shut, disappear back into whatever hole she's been hiding in. But then she exhales. "Let me get my shoes."

We step out of the building, and the city greets us with grace—honking taxis, chattering tourists, street vendors, and delivery trucks. Jade squints in the daylight like someone emerging from a cave. For five minutes, we walk quietly.

"It's been days," Jade says, finally breaking the silence. "The air feels nice."

I smile but don't push. Not yet. We trade meaningless observations about the city, a weird billboard for cryptocurrency, and the price of coffee. All while her hands fidget with her sleeves, pulling them down over her wrists like a security blanket.

We step onto Museum Mile and walk along Central Park's stone wall. Her posture has softened. This is the time.

"Do you think you'll come back to work?" I ask.

Jade stops. Her fingers slide against the rough texture of the stones. She stares into the park—families picnicking, joggers with their dogs, normal people living everyday lives.

"Where else do I have to go?" Her mouth curls downward. "This is all I've got."

The defeat in her words hits me hard.

"Iced oat milk matcha latte, right?"

She snaps her head to me like I've recited a magic incantation. "What? Yes, how did you know?"

"Melody told me. She tried it because of you and loved it."

Her chin quivers.

I wrap my arm around her. She's coiled into herself, but she softens a little at the touch. "I miss her too."

Her breath catches in a choked gasp, almost a sob.

"There's a place on the corner," I say. "Let's get you one."

Ten minutes later, we're seated on a weathered park bench off the main path, where joggers and tourists won't disturb us. My coffee is scalding, and I burn my tongue on the first sip. Jade cradles hers like it's something precious, staring into the swirl of green.

The silence between us isn't necessarily uncomfortable; it's weighted with all the things we're not saying. Jade toys with the straw, pushing it up and down in the lid before taking a sip. Her eyes are clearer now, more present.

"Why did you bring me out here, Star?" she asks. "What do you want?"

There's no accusation, just a tired acceptance, like she's been waiting for this moment, dreading it and needing it in equal measure.

"I want to hear the truth. About what happened."

Jade's fingers tighten around her cup. For an instant, I think she might crush it and send matcha splashing across the pavement.

"What do you want to know?"

"Everything."

She inhales, and when she looks up, tears cling to her lashes.

"The stupid part about this whole thing is…they never assigned Melody to this mission." The words pour out, like she'll lose her nerve if she slows down. "Amber and I originally had it, but she screwed up her birth control and got her period two days before."

The cold knot in my core is back again. "What?"

"Natalia was pissed." Jade laughs nervously. "Like Amber needs more reasons for her to be mad." She draws another sip. "She told Sage to find a replacement."

It's like I've been punched in the mouth. All this time, I thought they chose Melody specifically. That it was part of some plan. But it came down to…random chance?

"Sage chose Melody as a replacement?"

Jade shakes her head. "Not exactly. We had a meeting to discuss it."

"Who?"

"Me, Kora, and Sage."

The knot is getting larger.

"What happened?"

Jade takes a long pull on the straw, like she's fortifying herself. "In the meeting, Sage threw out names—Tiffany, Raven, Denali. Kora shot them down, one after another. She kept insisting it had to be Melody. That it was her time."

"Kora did that?"

"Yeah," she says. "I remember thinking it was strange because Kora hardly ever pushes back against Sage. But she wouldn't drop it—kept saying how Melody could handle it, that she'd vouch for her."

My mind scrambles, searching for an explanation. Kora—who seemed so genuinely shattered at the memorial—put Melody in that position?

"But why would she…?" The thought falls away.

"I don't know, I swear. But she was relentless."

I turn the information over in my mind, waiting for something to filter out. "And Sage?"

Jade shrugs helplessly, her fingers picking at the sticker on her cup. "Eventually, she gave in. I think she trusted Kora's judgment. But right before we left, they both pulled me aside and made me promise not to tell Melody or anyone what they said in that meeting."

The revelation is stunning. Someone Melody trusted pushed her into danger—someone *I* trusted.

"They made you lie to her?"

Jade turns away, her cheeks reddening. "They didn't call it lying. Kora and Sage called it 'protecting her confidence.'" She makes air quotes with trembling fingers. "That she would perform better if she thought she'd been selected on merit."

A mother chases after her toddler up ahead of us. Everyday life continues while mine keeps shattering into smaller pieces.

"Did Melody suspect anything?"

"No." Jade's chin trembles. "She got so excited, Star. So proud to be picked. At first, anyway."

I touch her arm. "What do you mean, at first?"

Jade glares into her matcha as if it holds the answers. Her fingers tremble around the cup.

"It should have been simple," she says. "Just install a device recorder. But at the briefing, they gave her this vial—a sedative, they said. She went pale, like she realized something felt wrong, but they wouldn't let her back out."

The word *vial* wails like an air horn in my mind. Melody's spreadsheet. Andrew Daniels. *Use supplied vial in client's beverage.*

"Vial?" I repeat, trying to keep my cool.

"They said it was something to make the client sleep while she downloaded the data. But Melody—" Jade looks into her lap. "She kept asking, 'Why me?' and saying, 'I'm not ready for this.' But they reassured her that she'd be fine, that she had the skills."

My mind spins, connecting dots I wish weren't there. Kora pushing for Melody in that meeting. The special assignment. The vial. Andrew Daniels, who no longer exists in the Family's records.

I grab Jade's arm harder than I should. "Wait. Did you have the same instructions for Cortez? Or did you not get a vial?"

Her silence makes the answer obvious.

Something snaps inside me—a rush of anger, scorching and raw. My coffee cup crashes to the pavement, brown liquid exploding across the concrete. A nearby couple jumps, startled. I'm shaking, gasping for breath, and very aware of how conspicuous I've become.

"Why her? Why not someone more experienced? Why my best friend?" Each question grows louder until I'm practically shouting.

Jade wraps her arms around me to settle the trembling.

"I don't know, Star. That's what I've been trying to understand."

Kora, who held me while I cried, who mourned Melody right beside me—why would she push her like that? My ears burn with rage.

"What about that night?" I press. "What happened? What did you see?"

Jade flinches, shrinking away from me.

"I told the truth, Star, I swear. After Melody went into that elevator with Daniels, I never saw her again."

"Not even when you left?"

"No." She's trembling. "Cortez rushed me out so fast, I couldn't think. One second I'm on the bed, the next he's throwing my clothes at me, saying, 'It's over, time to go.' I'm telling you, I don't know what happened."

She's full-on crying now, and the guilt fills me. I probe her face; she's telling the truth.

"I have to go."

"Star, wait—"

"No." I back away from the bench. "I just—I can't process this right now."

Jade stands. "Please don't do anything stupid. They're watching us."

Too late for that.

Nineteen

The scalding water I've been standing under for too long has turned my skin pink, and my thoughts circle the drain with the bubbles—round and round, never quite disappearing.

Wrapping a towel around my hair, I grab my phone from the counter. I missed a message.

JEREMY

Post has gotten traction on the forum. No DM yet, no way to know if Family is aware.

Jeans and a loose T-shirt today—the luxury of being off duty. No makeup, no heels, no pretending to be someone I'm not. Just regular old me in casual clothes that still feel too nice and fit too loosely.

The hallway is different this morning. I swear Piper's glare follows me past her door, but when I turn back, she's scrolling through her phone. Two Sisters are gabbing near the elevator, but their conversation dies as I approach. Or am I imagining it?

"Morning," I offer. They smile back, tight and rehearsed.

In the cafeteria, I grab a tray and join the line, hyperaware of every movement. Barbie's cackle carries across the room—is it about me? Is she staring? No, she's pointing at something on Ruby's plate.

I'm losing it, totally losing it.

The scrambled eggs and bacon pile onto my plate, my hands steadier than they have any right to be as I grab a few berries for color.

Our usual table sits empty. Aura's spot is vacant. She's never late for anything, especially not for breakfast. The girl treats meals like sacred rituals.

My Spidey sense tingles—the intensity of someone's stare. I sweep the room and land on Kora, sitting two tables over. She's not pretending to look elsewhere. She's full-on staring at me with an expression I can't decipher.

She doesn't react when I smile and wave. Doesn't even blink. Just keeps staring, reminding me she's a survivor who's made it seven years in this place.

My tray drops onto the table, and I'm not hungry anymore. The water running off the strawberries looks like blood.

Traitors don't get second chances. They get silenced.

What have I done?

"Sorry, *chica*, had to do some extra grooming this morning, if you catch me."

Aura's tray clatters onto the table, making me jump. She slides into her seat with a grin.

"You okay?" she asks.

"Yeah, didn't sleep much. Bad dreams."

Kora's turned away now, laughing with Ruby about something. Not staring. Not plotting my demise. Having breakfast.

Did I imagine it?

"So," Aura says, dumping sugar into her coffee, "you still off duty? You get to sit here and be all casual while I have to let old white men stare at my boobs?"

I manage a weak laugh. "Sorry."

"Natalia's on the warpath this morning. Heard her yelling at someone in the conference room. Probably Amber—that girl can't stay out of trouble."

I nod, only half listening, surveying the room for any sign that I'm being eyeballed, discussed, targeted.

Aura waves her hand in front of my face. "Seriously, what's with you today?"

"Nothing. A little tired."

She shrugs and digs into her oatmeal, talking between bites. "Oh, you gotta check this out…"

Warning. Back of my neck. *This is it.*

"You read that Step-Sister blog, right?" Aura says, her mouth full. "Well, look at this."

She whips her phone around and hands it to me. The adrenaline surges as I look down at the screen—at my own words staring back at me.

"Some *perra loca* posted calling herself Cinderella," Aura laughs. "Can you believe that?"

I keep my face neutral as I read. My hand is clammy against the phone case.

"That's crazy," I say, handing it back. "Do you think it's real?"

"Who knows, but the drama is killer." Aura takes another bite. "Like, who has the *cojones* to post something like that?"

"How'd you find it?" I ask, trying to sound casual.

"Kora showed it to me this morning."

The cafeteria stretches and contracts around me, like someone's playing with the focus on a camera. Kora knows. She's telling people.

"Wonder who it could be."

Aura scrolls through her phone. "My money's on Jade. That girl's been acting off ever since…"

The water glass shakes in my hand. I take a quick sip before setting it down abruptly.

They don't all know. They can't. It's my paranoia twisting every glance into a threat, every word into a warning.

But Kora knows. And that means Sage does too.

BREAKFAST FINISHES UNEVENTFULLY. Aura chatters about her client's weird business-suit fetish while I nod at the right moments, my attention fixed on Kora's table. She doesn't look my way again, just eats her yogurt and scrolls through her phone like any other morning.

Maybe I imagined it all. My paranoia's cranked up to eleven, and I'm seeing conspiracies in innocent glances. God knows I've been jumpy enough lately to suspect my own shadow.

When the buzzer goes off, I help Aura clear our trays and observe the daily march toward the auditorium. Sisters fixing their hair, adjusting their clothes, transforming from sleepy breakfast-eaters into polished professionals.

"You coming?" Aura asks.

"Off duty, remember? Perks of being new and traumatized."

She rolls her eyes. "Lucky bitch."

I wave goodbye and head toward my room, relieved to escape the cafeteria's fishbowl.

The burner phone vibrates.

JEREMY

40.791819, -73.953504

I stare at the numbers, recognition dawning. That sneaky bastard is paying me back for the last time. A smile tugs at my lips.

The map opens when I tap the coordinates, and a pin drops on Central Park. It's a close ten-minute walk.

"What are you up to, Wizard?" I mutter and head to the elevator.

Whatever Jeremy wants to show me, it's important enough for cloak-and-dagger theatrics. And honestly, after this morning's paranoia fest, a walk in the park sounds sublime.

The GPS leads me through Upper Manhattan, dodging commuters and dog walkers, before crossing Fifth Avenue into Central Park. It leads me down winding paths that seem to loop back on themselves. Maybe Jeremy's idea of fun involves watching me walk in circles.

"Esther!"

The shock splashes me like ice water. My real name, spoken aloud in public. I spin around fast and nearly trip over my own feet.

Jeremy stands beside a wall-sized granite monument, hands shoved deep in his pockets, looking like he'd rather be anywhere else. The familiar awkward slope of his shoulders makes me smile as I walk over to him.

"What did you call me?"

He pushes his glasses up. "I can't yell out 'Star' in the middle of the park, can I? I figured it'd be a little less conspicuous this way."

I take a moment to look at the monument he's chosen for our little rendezvous. The granite surface is weathered, but the inscription is still clear: *Arthur Brisbane. American Editor and Patriot.*

"Why here?"

Jeremy's face brightens with the particular glow he gets when he's about to share some obscure bit of knowledge. "One of the major newspapermen of the twentieth century. Seemed appropriate given our current investigative tendencies."

Something about his face—the barely contained excitement, the way he keeps glancing at me like he's got a secret he's dying to share —makes everything click into place.

"She replied," I say.

Jeremy smiles, and I can't help myself. I give him a playful whack across the shoulder. "Wizard!"

He chuckles, rubbing it dramatically. "Ow."

He pulls out his phone. "I took the original post down, so whoever got to see it, did, but it's gone now."

"How long was it up?"

"About seven hours, most of it overnight. Long enough for our mystery blogger to see it and respond."

Seven hours. Plenty of time for night-owl or early-bird Sisters to stumble on it before breakfast. Was Kora the only one who saw it? Well, Aura too, but I'm not concerned about her. Can I get to Kora and find out what she knows before all of this explodes?

I take Jeremy's phone. This could be nothing. Or it could be the beginning of the end of everything.

Cinderella:
Today, 3:30 p.m. 96th Street Library. Second Floor.
Long table by the window.

Wear a pink scarf. Bring a copy of "The Night Sister" by Jennifer McMahon. When approached, you'll be asked: "How many rooms in the hotel?" Respond with: "Twenty-nine, of course."

Bring proof of your Sisterhood. Come alone. No phones. No tracking. No Second Chances.

—Step-Sister

"She doesn't give much lead time, does she?" I hand the phone back, my brain cataloging what I need to do. Three thirty. Four hours from now.

Jeremy studies my face in his analytical way, like he's running diagnostics on my emotional state.

"Are you sure about this? This isn't like digging through files or decoding metadata. This is real-world dangerous."

The question hangs between us, weighted with the implications we both understand. Meeting Step-Sister isn't about satisfying my curiosity anymore—it's about finding answers that might keep other girls from ending up like Melody. It's about meeting the only other person in this city who wants the same thing I do.

"I have to."

His eyes agree, but there's worry etched across his face. He's socially awkward, but not blind to what we're walking into.

"About the 'no phones' thing. Do you think she'll know if I bring one?"

Jeremy adjusts his glasses. "Probably not, but that depends on whether you're willing to risk it." He pauses. "No second chances."

I nod slowly. One shot. That's it.

"Guess I have to go buy a book."

THE CORNER BOOKSTORE on Madison Avenue is bathed in the comforting fragrance of vanilla candles and fresh paper—the sort of place where people honestly browse instead of just buying whatever is on the bestseller table. I find *The Night Sister* in the horror section, a crisp trade paperback.

The walk back to HQ gives me some time to plan what I'm going to say to her. How can I avoid blowing my only chance to make this work?

Three blocks from home, my phone makes a sound I've never heard before—sharp, urgent, nothing like the gentle chimes of regular notifications. I pull it out, and the screen blazes with a red banner that looks like a wanted poster.

THE FAMILY

FAMILY HIGH IMPORTANCE ALERT

MANDATORY All-Hands meeting today at 4:00 p.m. in the auditorium. Attendance Required. No Exceptions.

Four o'clock. That's only thirty minutes after I meet with Step-Sister.

"Shit, shit, shit."

A woman walking her poodle gives me a dirty look. My fingers fly across the phone screen, opening Jeremy's encrypted chat.

> Is this about Cinderella?

I hit send and keep moving, my pace quickening involuntarily—four o'clock mandatory meeting. No exceptions. The timing can't be coincidental. Nothing at the Family ever is.

My phone buzzes.

JEREMY

> Don't know. Alert went to everyone simultaneously.
> Could be anything.

Right. The Family regularly calls emergency all-hands meetings on random Friday afternoons because that's totally normal behavior for an organization that prides itself on smooth operations and predictable schedules.

I'm practically jogging now—like movement might ward off the panic clawing from inside me.

But it doesn't work. Nothing does.

The elevator ride to my floor drags on, and when I step out and turn the corner, Kora is leaning against the door to my room, arms crossed, her perfectly imperfect smile playing on her lips.

My heart stops for a full second. This is it. She's going to turn me in.

"Hey," I say, trying to sound normal. "Want to come in?"

"Sure, doll," she says. "How are you holding up?"

I put the book on my desk and turn to face her. "Not great. What did you expect?"

She sinks into my desk chair with her fluid grace. "Fair enough. How are you handling the time off? Must be weird after everything."

"It's okay." I shrug, dropping onto my bed. "I went out, got a book. Tried to feel normal for a few hours."

"I see." Her eyes flick to the paperback, and there's something in her expression I can't quite read. Amusement? Suspicion?

The silence sits between us, thick with anticipation. I want to ask her about the meeting, about the argument with Sage, but her posture tells me to wait.

"You know," Kora says, "you've got some time before you're back on the schedule. Use it to figure out who you want to be when you come back to work."

I nod. There's depth in her words, layers I'm not sure I understand.

"I mean, we all have choices to make in this life." She stands, brushing off her pants. "About how much we want to get involved in things. How much we want to poke around in places that might be better left alone."

My mouth goes dry.

She walks to the door, grabs the handle, and turns back with the crooked smile I've grown to love as much as fear.

"Oh, and don't be late for the ball today, okay?"

The smirk that follows twists something inside me. My hands go cold. She disappears into the hallway, and I'm left staring at the closed door, two seconds from cardiac arrest.

She knows. She fucking knows.

And I have no idea if that makes her my ally or my enemy.

TWENTY

Almost time to leave for my tête-à-tête with Step-Sister, and I still can't shake Kora's remark to me. Is the mandatory meeting going to be an ambush?

I send Jeremy a message.

> Kora knows.

Time check: 2:46 p.m. Less than an hour to go.

Right. What does one wear to meet a mysterious whistleblower? She might get suspicious if I appear too casual, like I'm not taking this seriously.

A blue-and-white sundress calls out to me—cute but not try-hard, the kind of thing a responsible young woman might don to run errands on a Friday afternoon.

The phone buzzes.

JEREMY

> Shit, you sure? What does that mean?

> 100%, have no idea, she didn't turn me in, so that's gotta mean something?

Okay, shoes. The ballet flats seem like a comfortable choice, but what if there's a mad dash back to HQ for the meeting? I grab a pair of trainers to stuff into my crossbody bag and pluck a scarf from the drawer—fuchsia. Close enough.

Fifth Avenue stretches ahead of me like a runway as I power walk in my flats, weaving between people who've never heard of *walking with purpose*. The bag bounces against my hip with each step, the sneakers inside making soft thuds that sound like a muffled heartbeat. I adjust my oversized Jackie-O sunglasses and keep moving forward.

How many rooms in the hotel? Twenty-nine, of course.

Rehearsing the line under my breath makes me look like one of those people who talk to themselves on the street. The words are awkward, like a password to some exclusive club I'm not sure I want to join.

At 96th Street, I hang a left and scan the sidewalk for anything suspicious. Not that I'd recognize suspicious if it walked up and introduced itself. What does it even look like? A guy in a trench coat reading a newspaper with eyeholes cut out?

Come on, girl. This isn't a spy movie.

Still, I check over my shoulder before going inside.

The familiar aroma of old books and industrial carpet cleaner hits me as the woman behind the circulation desk glances up with her patient librarian's smile. The stairs are directly ahead. My phone is powered down and tucked into a sneaker in my bag. Jeremy's right about the risk, but I need the security blanket.

The wall clock reads 3:25 p.m. I made decent time.

The long empty table is by the window, like Step-Sister said. The afternoon light pours through the glass, bathing the place in a gold tint, making even cheap library furniture look cinematic.

I pull *The Night Sister* from my bag and place it next to my elbow like a talisman. The scarf looks stupid, but it's my signal flare in this sea of anonymity.

Now comes the part I suck at: waiting.

I check the time: 3:32 p.m. Dammit, is she not coming? Did I miss something? Did she spot me walking in and not like what she saw? Is this whole thing a setup? Is—

A kid at the next table over keeps sniffling, and I want to throw him a tissue to make the sound stop. The minutes tick by with excruciating slowness.

There's a prickle at the back of my neck. Someone walks up

behind me, their presence like a specter, silent. I resist the urge to turn around.

"How many rooms in the hotel?" A girl's voice, low and measured.

I swallow hard, my mouth dry. "Twenty-nine, of course." The rehearsed words slip out.

She slides into a chair, leaving one empty seat between us. Younger than I expected, with dark hair tied back in a yellow scrunchie. Nothing remarkable, which is probably what she's going for. "Cinderella," she says flatly.

"Step-Sister?" I ask, sounding hopeful.

"No. But I represent her."

I nod, trying to look like this is all normal to me. So, there's more than one of them. A network, not just a lone whistleblower. I knew it. "Okay."

"Your pendant?"

I pull the neckline of my sundress down to show her the black-and-gold pendant all Sisters receive at initiation. The tiny diamond in the center catches the light as I hold it out for inspection.

She barely glances at it. "So, what do you have for us? Is this about Melody?"

The name stops me cold. My head snaps toward her, and I make a sound somewhere between a gasp and a cough. "How do you—"

"Do you think you're the only insider we have access to?" She's indifferent, assessing.

I'm flabbergasted. This isn't how I pictured this going at all. I'm the one with information they want, not the other way around.

"Tell me something I don't know, or this conversation is over."

I lean in. "Melody's death wasn't an accident, or a client gone wrong. It was a setup by the government. They suspected the Family of stealing classified information and set a trap to catch them."

Her face is unreadable as she sits silently for a moment. "You can prove this?"

"Not entirely," I admit, and she shifts in the chair. I turn toward her, my breathing getting quicker. "But we're close."

"We? Who are you working with?"

"I can't tell you that right now." I try to sound more confident than desperate.

She stands up, and panic floods through me. I jump out of the chair and tear off my sunglasses. "Wait!"

The girl steps back, her face morphing from cold assessment to shock. She stares at me like I've shattered her reality.

"What?" I ask.

"No…that's not…"

The wall clock reads 3:50 p.m. *Shit.* If I'm going to make it back for Natalia's meeting, I have to leave now. Time to make a choice, and fast.

Screw it. Full honesty it is.

"Look," I say, dropping all pretense, "I was Melody's best friend, and I'm close to having proof of the government setup—I just need a little more time. Natalia called a secret all-hands meeting because of the post I wrote, and it starts in ten minutes. If I'm not there, I'll be blown, and everything we both want will vanish."

She's still staring at me, but out of her pocket comes a small white card with a phone number printed on it.

"Text this number as soon as you can." She presses the card into my palm. "There's someone you need to meet."

Before I can ask anything else, she turns and walks away, disappearing around the stacks.

3:52 p.m.

Whatever just happened, I'll have to figure it out later. Right now, I have a meeting to get to.

I tuck the card into my pocket and yank the trainers from the bag. My fingers fumble with the ballet flats, taking precious seconds I don't have. The phone goes into my hand next, and I power it on.

"Come on, come on," I mutter, lacing up the sneakers with shaking hands.

I leave the book on the table and dart toward the stairs, taking them two at a time, the clap of rubber soles far too loud. I get a dirty look as I burst through the door, but I'm already gone—a blur of sundress and desperation.

The phone screen blinks to life as I hit 96th Street. 3:54 p.m. *Shit, shit, shit.*

I tear the scarf from my neck and stuff it into my bag while dodging a woman with a stroller. My lungs burn as I sprint across the intersection, and the crosswalk timer flashes red as my feet hit the opposite curb. A taxi honks, and I wave an apologetic hand without slowing down.

I pump my arms, feeling sweat trickle down my back. A delivery guy with a stack of boxes on a dolly appears from nowhere, and I swerve at the last second, clipping the side of his load.

"Sorry!" I yell over my shoulder as boxes tumble.

He shouts something back that's definitely not "Don't worry about it," but I'm already half a block away.

The Family HQ is straight ahead, its glass front reflecting the afternoon sun. Time check: 3:58 p.m. I might make it.

I pop through the door, chest heaving, and look at the elevator. The digital display shows it stopped at the top floor.

Of course.

"Fuck me," I hiss, and make for the stairs.

By the third floor, my thighs are screaming. By the fourth, I'm questioning all my life choices.

I fumble for my key card, slide it into the reader, and practically fall into my room. The sundress peels off in a single motion, and I use it to mop sweat from my face and back before tossing it aside. My bag lands on the bed as I lunge for the wardrobe.

Yoga pants. Sweatshirt. I yank them on, mess my hair up, and check my phone one last time.

4:05 p.m.

I'm so dead.

I step into the hallway, trying to look groggy rather than flushed, and stop cold. It's Sage. Headed straight for me like a freight train down a catwalk.

My pancreas drops to my knees.

"I was just coming to get you," she says. "The meeting's already started."

Blinking slowly, I force a yawn. "So sorry. Took a nap, and my phone battery died—no alarm. Just woke up."

Sage's gaze moves over me—taking in my messy hair, the oversized sweatshirt, the flush in my cheeks that could be sleep...or Olympic-level sprinting.

For one terrible moment, I think she's going to call me out.

Then she turns and starts walking.

"Let's go. Natalia hates tardiness."

Only once I fall in line behind her do I notice my sweatshirt is inside out.

THE AUDITORIUM FEELS SMALLER than it should, the glass and leather closing in around me like a fist. Every active Sister in the Family sits in neat rows, their faces painted with the same measured neutrality I'm trying to maintain. My hands are folded in my lap, but my right leg keeps bouncing involuntarily—a nervous tic I've had all my life. I cross my legs to keep it under control.

Natalia stands at the podium like a general called to address her troops. Her charcoal suit is impeccable, with a posture so straight you could draw lines with it. Her blonde hair is done up in a tiered chignon, which adds to the dramatic effect.

"Someone in this room," she begins, scanning the assembled faces, "has forgotten what loyalty means."

It's about the post. I mean, of course it is—I knew it would be. So why do I have a grapefruit-sized lump in my throat?

Sisters shift uncomfortably in their seats, and chatter ripples around me.

"The post that appeared online overnight was not just a betrayal of the Family. It was an act of terrorism," she continues, rising in volume, "designed to destabilize everything we have built."

I subtly look around, half expecting all eyes to be on me—but they're not. They're transfixed by Natalia and her passionate speech.

"The author calls herself *Cinderella*." The derision is apparent in her tone. "How quaint. How theatrical. How…utterly foolish."

I'm thankful for the oversized sweatshirt hiding how hard my heart is pounding.

"Make no mistake." She paces like a caged tiger. "This person, this…coward hiding behind a fairy-tale name has endangered every single one of you. They've invited scrutiny we cannot afford. They've painted targets on all our backs."

Kora is in the second row. She knows it's me. What is she waiting for?

"The claims made in this post are not just false—they are malicious." Natalia reaches the end of the small stage and twirls on her heel with grace, pacing in the other direction. "Our beautiful Sister who passed recently died in a tragic accident. The investigation showed that clearly. The case is closed." She stops and scans the room. "But apparently, someone here believes they know better than trained investigators."

The silence is eerie. Even the air-conditioning stops.

"I want to be very explicit," she says, resuming her pacing. "The Family protects its own. We are a haven. A home for girls who have nowhere else to go. We provide safety, security, and opportunity." *Heel turn.* "But protection requires trust. And trust, once broken, cannot be repaired."

Natalia glances at Sage, who offers a look of staunch agreement.

"So, here is what's going to happen now." The hairs on my arms rise. "Our modern-day Cinderella has until midnight tonight—her favorite time, no?—to identify herself. She will come to Sage or me, she will confess, and she will face the consequences of her actions like an adult."

I fight to keep my face blank, but I'm not sure I'm pulling it off. My skin is buzzing, and right now, even blinking feels suspicious.

"If she does not," Natalia says, stopping mid-stage, "if she continues to hide behind her Sisters like the coward she is...then everyone in this room will share in her punishment." She smiles.

She actually *smiles.*

"Allowances will be frozen. Stipends suspended. We will conduct a thorough investigation of every person in the organization who may have had access to the information mentioned in that post. Technology leaves fingerprints."

In my haze, I'd overlooked Jeremy. He's standing against the back wall, partially in shadow. He looks incredibly uncomfortable.

The murmurs grow louder. Girls nattering in hushed tones—the fear spreading like wildfire. They're all going to suffer because of what I did.

"You see," Natalia continues, "Cinderella thinks she's the hero of this story. She believes she's saving you all from a terrible fate." *Heel turn.* "What she failed to account for is that her actions would not only affect her, but every single person who calls the Family home."

Aura sits a few rows down, her face a mix of confusion and anger.

"Loyalty is not just a word we use in ceremonies. It's the

foundation upon which the Family is built!" Natalia pounds her hand down on the podium, scaring the collective shit out of everyone in the room—me especially. "When one Sister betrays that loyalty, she betrays *all* of us. And that comes with a price."

What have I done to them?

"To all the loyal and dedicated Sisters who have nothing to do with this, I am sorry." She holds her hands out. "I am sorry that one of your own has chosen to include you in their fairy tale. Keep your chin up. You will survive this. The Family will look after you.

"Midnight. Tonight." She surveys the entire auditorium slowly, like a predator.

Some part of me wants to stand. To confess. To stop it before they all suffer for me. But I can't. If I do, everything ends—Melody's truth, exposing the corruption, all of it.

"Dismissed."

The dismissal is like a starting gun. Sisters rise in a din of chatter, rustling fabric, and hushed allegations. I stay in my seat. Kora turns back, catching my eye with a gaze I can't read. Is that complicity or a silent warning to run while I still can? I wasn't expecting there to be a clock.

I need a plan.

My phone screen is black, and I'm willing it to light up. Jeremy hasn't responded to my messages. Is he avoiding me? Can't really blame him. I've dragged him into a mess that could cost him everything.

The same helpless spiral returns. Like watching Mom pack for our third eviction, and the certainty that whatever I touch will turn to shit.

Three quick raps on my door—no doubt who it is.

"Come in."

Sage enters and stands motionless for a moment. Her face is calm, but her eyes have a sniper's focus that unnerves me. She crosses to the desk and falls into the chair, crossing those endless legs. The move is deliberate, choreographed. Everything Sage does is choreographed.

She takes a slow breath. "Star, I think we need to talk about what's happening."

"Okay."

"I know you're scared right now. Everyone is. But I'm on your side."

Concentrate.

"I appreciate that."

"The Cinderella post," she says, observing me. "Did you write it?"

The question sparks between us like a live wire. My eyes meet hers.

"No." The lie is bitter on my tongue. "Why would you think that?"

Sage studies me, then leaves the chair to sit on the bed. The mattress dips, her fragrance surrounds me, and I try not to succumb.

"Because you're smart. Because you cared about Melody. Because you've been asking questions since day one."

Her hand grazes mine. "And because I know what it looks like when someone is fighting."

"Sage, it wasn't me," I say reflexively.

"Star, I'm not trying to trap you." She leans in, and I notice a splash of freckles across her nose that she usually conceals.

Her proximity scrambles me. At this distance, she's overwhelming —pristine skin and lips and her damned perfume. She knows what she's doing.

"I didn't—"

She tucks my hair behind my ear. The touch is sensual, purposeful. "I'm trying to protect you."

My breath catches. This is Manipulation 101, but recognizing that does nothing to stop my traitorous body from responding. She's good. She's so good.

If she kissed me right now, I'd let her. Just to feel something other than guilt.

"If Natalia finds out it was you..." She lets the threat hang while her fingers caress my face. "But if you tell me now, I can help. I can make it easier for you."

Her voice nearly makes me confess everything—the post, Step-Sister, that time I stole Amelia's lip gloss when I was twelve, all of it. But Melody's face flashes in my mind—her last night, the fear on her face.

"I didn't write it." I slide away from her touch.

"Goddammit, Star!" she snaps, frustration cracking her veneer. "Stop lying to me!"

My entire body flinches, jumping from the bed. I've never seen her this angry—not at me, anyway—and it's terrifying.

"You're just like the others." She stands up. "You think you can fix things. Expose things."

"This isn't about me," I shoot back. "It's about Melody. Something happened to her, Sage."

"You think I don't know that?" She chokes on the words. "You think I don't feel that loss every fucking day?"

"Then why isn't anyone doing anything about it?" The question bursts out of me, raw and desperate.

"What exactly do you want us to do, Star?" Her volume increases to match mine. "Call the police? Expose the Family? What do you think happens then? To the rest of us?"

I have no answers.

Sage runs both hands through her hair—losing her cool makes her look younger, less sculpted. "I thought you understood what we're trying to build here."

"At what cost?"

"At whatever cost necessary!" She's coming undone. "Do you have any idea what's out there? What happens to girls like us when we have nothing and no one to go to?"

This is personal.

"I lost everything I ever cared about, Star! All of it! And I busted my ass to get back to where I am. I will not sit back and watch you destroy it all."

"I'm not trying to destroy anything," I say. "I just want the truth about what happened to her."

"You already know the truth. You just don't like it."

We both go as still as a photograph.

Then she moves closer, her eyes glassy. "You want truth? I had nothing. The Family gave me everything. That's my truth."

Her vulnerability is mesmerizing, and it holds me in place.

"You should have come to me before blowing the whole fucking thing up." She tosses her arms up. "I could have helped you. Protected you."

"This isn't about protection. It's about justice."

"Justice?" she snaps, wiping angrily at a tear. "There's no justice for girls like us, Star. There never has been."

Her words hang in the air between us, heavy with a truth I don't want to acknowledge.

"Sage—"

"No." She holds up a hand. "You don't get to speak. Not now. This is the only life I have left. The only place I belong."

My body wilts under the intensity of her reprimand.

"I see how you look at me." She wipes her face. "I know what you wanted. And for a moment, I thought maybe I could want that too." Her blue eyes hold mine, devastatingly direct. "But then you showed me who you really are."

My legs give out, sending me to the floor. "I never meant—"

"That's because you don't think before you act."

"—to hurt you."

"But you did." It comes out fierce and wounded. "You're just like the others—willing to burn down the entire forest to save one tree."

She turns toward the door, her body rigid with anger or grief—or both.

"Sage, wait—"

I want to grab her. Hold her. Apologize for everything.

She pauses, hand on the lever. "You know what the worst part is? I thought we were the same once." She shakes her head. "I was wrong."

The door closes behind her with a soft *click*. Gentle as a coffin lid. Her imprint lingers in the air.

My phone buzzes—Jeremy. But it's too late now.

Sage knows. And soon, everyone else will too.

Twenty One

E l Burrito Loco on 103rd Street is a far cry from the Family's luxury: a riot of colors, scents, and questionable health code compliance. The plastic table wobbles under our trays, and the chair makes a plastic groan every time I shift. A violent orange paint covers the walls, and someone's gone wild with the *papel picado* hanging from the ceiling. The air is layered with cumin and fryer oil, and the tinny mariachi music on the radio meshes with the sizzle of the grill.

It's perfect.

"No one from the Family would be caught dead here," I say, unwrapping my carnitas burrito. "Except maybe Aura, but she's with a client tonight."

Jeremy nods, his mouth already full of chicken and guacamole. He's wearing the same rumpled polo he had on yesterday, and his greasy hair matches mine. We're quite a pair.

We eat in silence, and all I can focus on is the squeak of Jeremy's chair and the taste of cilantro. It's so normal, it's unsettling.

"So," I ask, "how bad is it?"

Jeremy wipes his mouth. "Not great. Natalia pulled me into her office this morning. Grilled me for two hours about the post."

"What did you tell her?"

"The truth. Well, most of it." He takes a sip of his horchata. "I showed her what I did to trace the post—all the technical steps. But I stopped just short of the last part leading back to me."

"And she bought it?"

"She thinks even I can't trace where it came from. And since it's been taken down, there's nothing more she can do." He shrugs, but his jaw is fixed. "Technically."

"But she knows it was me."

"She suspects. But she doesn't have proof." He leans forward. "That's the key, Star. No proof."

"Sage knows too now."

"So you said. That must be tough."

"She asked me point-blank if I wrote it, and I denied it." I swallow hard, remembering the hurt on her face. "But she didn't believe me. And Kora knows—she basically said as much."

"And neither of them has said anything to Natalia?"

"Not yet." I put my burrito down. "Maybe I should just confess and take the heat. Let the Sisters get their lives back."

Jeremy leans forward. "Listen. As long as you deny it, you have leverage. Once you confess, you lose everything—any chance of finding out what happened."

"But the others are suffering because of me. Their allowances, their stipends—"

"Yes, and it sucks. But it's temporary if we act quickly."

I take the card Step-Sister's rep gave me and toss it across the table.

Jeremy studies it. "It's a virtual number. Is that from—"

"It is. The whole meeting was weird. She wasn't what I expected."

"How so?" he asks as a few beans tumble from his burrito.

"She was just a scout. And when I took my sunglasses off, she looked at me strangely."

He shakes his head. "Odd."

"Then she gave me the card, told me there's someone I need to meet, and left."

"You should text the number. Find out what they know."

I take the card back. "It could be a trap."

"Can it really be worse than where you already are?"

"Probably not."

Jeremy pulls what looks like a bootleg smartphone from his jacket pocket and hands it to me.

"And this is?"

"A new burner. It's good to rotate them every once in a while. Leave no trail, you know?"

It looks like a detonator as I turn it over in my hands. Which, in a way, I suppose it is.

"Contact Step-Sister with that. The number is clean."

"Wizard," I say with a grin as I hand him back the first one.

He smiles, and it's the best thing I've seen all day.

I finish my burrito and wad up the foil wrapper. Outside, the streetlight flickers on and off.

"Ready?" Jeremy asks.

"As I'll ever be."

THE NIGHT AIR is a splash of cool water after the cloying heat of the burrito joint. We part ways at the corner—Jeremy north, me south. The burner phone is heavy in my hands, and I may as well get this over with. I take out the white card and type carefully, thumbs clumsy on the unfamiliar keyboard.

> This is Cinderella. I would like to meet.

There. Done. I slip the phone back into my pocket and keep walking. Hopefully, I'll have a response sometime tomorrow and can take it from there.

Bodega cats and teenagers on stoops blur past as I walk down 102nd Street. The city at night still feels like home in a way the Family's excess never will. A woman sleeps in a doorway, a cardboard sign propped against her shopping cart, and I lean down to stuff a fiver under her makeshift pillow. Not so long ago, that was me. Back then, every shadow held a threat. Every doorway was a potential shelter. Every passing cop someone to avoid. Now I'm just another well-dressed woman walking alone at night, camouflaged by polish instead of poverty.

"The more things change...," I muse. "Still skulking around after dark, running from something. Just traded park benches for eight-hundred thread count sheets."

The phone beeps in my pocket. That was fast—way too fast. A shudder runs up my back as the message glows up at me.

UNKNOWN

> Can you meet now?

Twenty Two

M y fingers hover over the phone for a moment before typing.

Yes, of course.

The response is immediate, like they were waiting with their thumbs poised over the keys. My nerve endings spark as the screen lights up again.

UNKNOWN

The Blockhouse in Central Park, 30 mins.

The Blockhouse. That old stone fort north of the Great Lawn. Isolated enough for privacy, public enough that I won't get murdered. Maybe.

The street signs say 102nd and Park, and I evaluate my options. I could grab a cab, but my thoughts are pinballing around my skull so violently that I might scream trapped in a back seat. The healthy option is best, I suppose.

The buildings loom above me, windows staring me down. I quicken my pace as I press ahead to 110th, then turn west. Every step is like a tick counting down. This is the part of the movie where the audience screams at the girl to stop and turn around. But now, I get to use one of my favorite SAT words—*perspicacity*, having shrewd insight—and perform a risk analysis. Best-case scenario: I gain an ally who gives me answers. Worst-case: I end up as a cautionary tale on some true-crime podcast. Seems like a coin flip to me.

The Blockhouse comes into view, and the path leads me up the stone steps to the entrance, the weathered structure dwarfing me. The rough stone is cool beneath my fingertips, solid in a way my life hasn't felt lately.

"Look at you, little fortress," I say aloud. "Two hundred years and still standing."

I fill my lungs with cool night air, pick up a small stone, and twirl it around in my fingers. A random factoid from eighth-grade history pops into my mind: The Blockhouse was built for the War of 1812 but never saw combat. All dressed up with nowhere to go. The irony isn't lost on me.

The burner phone beeps, and the stone tumbles from my hand. It clatters down the steps as I fumble to check the screen.

UNKNOWN

Behind you

Chills as I spin around, scanning the area in a slow pan.

Two figures approach from the east path. One of them is familiar, and I take a second to place her: the girl from the library, the one who'd scouted me. Her dark hair falls down over her shoulders now, and she walks with purpose. Beside her is someone taller with close-cropped blonde hair and a denim jacket.

They stop at the bottom of the steps, looking up at me. My mouth is desert-dry as I amble down to meet them.

"I'm Luna," says the library girl, calm and flat. She gestures to her companion. "This is Vega."

Star, Luna, Vega—we're a walking astronomy textbook. My laugh fades quickly as Vega pulls out a phone and begins tapping the screen.

"What's happening?" I ask, hating how my voice wavers.

Neither answer. Vega holds up a phone; they're starting a video call. The screen flickers to life: a darkened room, a hooded figure seated in shadow. Too dim to make out any faces—just the suggestion of features behind the obscurity.

Vega steps forward, holding the phone up to my face like I'm at airport security.

From the speaker: "Bring her here."

The call ends abruptly. Vega pockets the phone and signals to Luna, who turns to me.

"Follow us," she says, already stepping away.

My fight-or-flight system kicks in. "How do I know this isn't a trap?"

"You don't," Vega says. "But you came this far, right?"

They turn to go, and I follow—my heart racing. This is my entire cardio workout for the week. Kora would be proud. I'm either going to find answers or make the biggest mistake of my life. But the line between those two things is pretty thin.

A silver sedan sits at the curb. Vega opens the back door for me with a slight bow that's more mocking than courteous. The windows are tinted dark, almost black.

"Where are we going?" I slide onto the cracked leather seat.

Luna turns from the passenger side, her profile sharp against the streetlights. "To see the Fairy Godmother, of course," she says with a blend of smugness and sarcasm that brings the blood to my face.

Vega starts the car, and we pull away from the curb. No music plays. No one speaks. The only sounds are the soft purr of the engine and my breathing, which is embarrassingly loud in the silence.

Through the dark windows, Manhattan blurs into a neon fever dream. We're heading uptown, but my jangled nerves and the unfamiliar route leave me unsure as to where.

After fifteen minutes, we pull up to a brownstone that's seen better decades. Peeling paint, crumbled steps—a building that screams *condemned* and *haunted* in equal measure.

Vega opens my door with the same mock formality as before. "After you, Cinderella."

Out of the car and down cracked stairs into the basement apartment. Every sound makes me flinch.

The hallway carries a funk of dust and electronics. It's dark, stuffy, and a spot-on secret lair for someone as mysterious as Step-Sister.

Women look on from hallways and door edges. About half a dozen, ranging from twenty to forty. They're dressed in everything from ripped jeans to punk chic. The vibe is more resistance cell than meeting hall.

"That's her," a woman with silver-streaked dark hair mumbles to a younger girl with a nose ring.

It's slightly cultish but not fanatical. More like I've walked into a support group for trauma survivors, unsure if I'm a fellow victim or part of the problem.

At the hallway's end, the hooded figure from the video stands shrouded in shadow. The details are clearer now—medium height, slim build—but the face remains obscured beneath the hood.

"Welcome, Cinderella," the figure says. "I've been waiting for you."

This is it. The person who knew about Melody, who's been exposing the Family's secrets, who might hold answers to questions I haven't figured out how to ask yet.

"Step-Sister, I presume?"

The figure laughs—definitely a woman, younger than I expected. "We're all Step-Sister." She holds her arms out to gesture across the apartment. "You can call me Andromeda."

"You guys sure like astronomy, huh?"

Andromeda chuckles. "Our founder had us cast aside our Family names and take on new ones. She thought the heavens seemed like the ideal inspiration."

She leads me into a cramped converted bedroom. A desk dominates the space, and an open laptop is the primary source of light. Books stand in precarious towers, and papers cover every surface—the functional disorder of a war room.

She pulls back her hood. I expected a scarred vigilante or a middle-aged hacktivist. But she's just...a girl. No older than thirty. Blonde hair, cropped close on the sides, longer on top. Three silver hoops line her left eyebrow, with a small stud beneath her bottom lip. A geometric tattoo spreads across the back of her right hand, disappearing under her sleeve.

Andromeda drops into the chair behind the desk and motions for me to sit opposite her.

For a long moment, she looks at me. Not speaking, not moving, just...observing. She tracks across my features like she's memorizing them, or comparing them to something. The silence stretches until it's uncomfortable.

Then she laughs, a sound both soft and sharp. "Luna was right." She leans back. "It's remarkable."

"What is?"

She ignores my question, folding her hands on the desk. "So, I suppose we can dispense with the cloak-and-dagger. You are Star, yes?"

I nod, sinking into the chair. A thousand questions are burning in my mind, but something tells me to wait, to let her lead.

"And you have information implying the Family was targeted in a government sting operation that resulted in the death of a Sister named Melody, is that right?"

"Yes." Hearing it laid out so plainly stings.

Andromeda tilts her head. "Tell me, Star, what do you know about my organization?"

The question catches me off guard, and I fall back on what I've been told. "You're disgruntled ex-Sisters with an axe to grind. You couldn't hack it in the Family, so—"

She cuts me off. Not cruel, but dismissive. "Sounds like your information is a little one-sided." She leans forward, elbows on the desk. "We do much more than that."

"Like what?"

"We rescue women. We expose predators. We build new lives for girls who have been chewed up by the system," she says forcefully. "And we're going to bring the Family down."

"Why?"

Andromeda sits back. "We were founded by someone who escaped that prison. Most of us have escaped it. She learned the truth of the Family and refused to be part of it." Her face softens into something like reverence. "A visionary. A leader. And my friend."

She stretches behind her to a shelf I hadn't noticed, pulls down a framed photograph, and places it on the desk with the back facing me.

"Her name is Nova," Andromeda says, her fingers lingering on the frame. "She started all of this." She pauses, holding my gaze. "But I think you knew her better as...Amelia."

She turns the frame around, and there they are—Andromeda and Amelia, arm in arm, smiling at the camera. Amelia's hair is shorter than I remember, but it's her—bright, alive, unmistakable.

My sister.

The room melts around me. My lungs seize. I can't look away from the photo—from Amelia, older, but so achingly familiar. I stare until my eyes sting, refusing to blink. If I blink, she might vanish.

"Isn't that right, Esther?"

THE GLOW of the streetlight caught the fresh ink of Amelia's tattoo and made it shine. Esther looked at it and reached out gently to touch it.

"Did it hurt?"

"Like a son of a bitch, yeah," Amelia chuckled. "But I love it."

Esther ran her finger over the lines.

"It looks like a star."

"It's a supernova," Amelia said proudly. "The brightest object in the universe. That's what I'm gonna be, Sprout. At least I'll try."

Esther gazed up at her big sister with adoration. "I know you will. You'll shine like Mr. Peeper's lighthouse when—"

"—when the ships come back to the bay," Amelia joined in.

Esther tucked in closer, laughing at their shared memory.

Her eyes stayed fixed on the tattoo, fingertips still gliding over the design. "You're gonna shine so bright that I'll always be able to see you, no matter where you are."

Amelia let out a soft laugh and bumped her shoulder against Esther's. "I don't know if following me is such a good idea." She stared out at the city lights, dropping her tone. "You need to find your own path, something that speaks to you."

The words hung between them, heavier than they should have been. Esther pulled her knees in close, cold despite the warmth of her sister's body. A siren wailed somewhere in the distance, then faded.

"Am I gonna see you again?" Esther asked, her words almost lost in the city's hum.

Amelia turned to her, moonlight catching the edges of her face, which flashed with something sharp and haunted before vanishing, swallowed by her usual protective smile.

"Oh yeah, Sprout. Of course." Amelia wrapped an arm around her shoulders, pulling her close. "Someday, when everything is all better, I'll come back for you."

Esther studied her sister's face, searching for the truth. She'd gotten good at reading people—had to, with their mother's moods shifting like weather patterns. But Amelia had always been an open book to her until now.

"Promise?" Esther pressed, needing more.

Amelia laid her head on top of Esther's, the scent of her hair a calming balm. "Promise."

They sat that way for what felt like hours, with the city pulsing beneath them. Esther wanted to freeze time—to stay in this moment with her sister, secure beside her.

A car alarm went off down the block. Amelia flinched.

"I should get you back inside," she whispered. "It's late."

Esther nodded but didn't move. If she stayed perfectly still, then morning would never come, and Amelia wouldn't leave.

"Hey," Amelia said, lifting Esther's chin with her finger. "Look up. You can see a few tonight."

Esther glanced toward the sky, at the faint pinpoints of light visible over the city.

Amelia squeezed her shoulder. "They're always there..."

Esther swallowed hard. "...even when you can't see them."

"That's right." Amelia smiled, and for a second, she was her old self. "And so am I."

THE SOUND of my real name is a blow. "How do you know who I am?"

"Nova talked about you all the time," Andromeda says. "Her little sister. Her Sprout."

"Sprout," I repeat blindly.

Another shot to the midsection. No one has called me that in over five years. My tears blur the photograph. I blink, sending them spilling down my cheeks, but I don't wipe them away. I'm afraid to move, afraid this moment will shatter if I do.

My mind assembles fragments of memory: Amelia's laugh on the fire escape. Reading my stories aloud in our shared bedroom. The supernova tattoo I touched with my fingertips.

That's what I'm going to be, Sprout. At least I'll try.

Nova. Amelia. The brightest object in the universe.

"She always looked after you," Andromeda says. "Even after she escaped the Family, after she built all this"—she gestures around us—"she made sure you were safe."

I stare at the photograph, at my sister's face. The same eyes that watched over me, the same smile that made everything better. She wasn't gone. She was here. Fighting, building something.

Caron.

It hits with terrible clarity.

He knew. He must have known who I was when he recruited me.

The betrayal burns inside me, alongside something else—a wild, desperate hope that somewhere in this building, behind some door, my sister is waiting.

"She's alive?" The question comes out small and broken, like a child's.

Andromeda pauses. Her face softens, and the hope she's about to take from me hurts before she ever speaks.

"In our hearts, yes." She taps the photo. "This is from two years ago."

The light in the room leaches away, the air thickens, presses in—hard to draw breath. Andromeda speaks, but it's coming from the end of a long tunnel, drowned out by the thudding in my ears, loud and slow like a funeral drum. Rainbows cloud my vision, and the colors and faces smear across it like paint. The only thing that's sharp, that's real, is the smiling face in the picture frame.

There's a hand on my back, muffled words—"water"—but the ringing in my head, high and thin, distorts it, and my connection to reality severs.

In our hearts. Two years.

She's dead. My Amelia. My sister is gone.

Everything's dark, just an empty void.

WHEN MY EYES OPEN AGAIN, I'm on the floor, and my face is wet. My head is resting on Luna's lap, her hand in my hair. Andromeda is squatting down beside us, holding a bottle of water.

"Esther, are you okay?" she says, offering the bottle.

Luna takes it and puts it to my lips, where I draw a little in.

"I'm sorry," Andromeda says. "I shouldn't have put that on you so soon."

"What happened to her?" I croak, uncertain if I even want to know.

Andromeda studies me, weighing something. "That's a complicated story. One I think you deserve to hear." She leans in. "But now isn't the right time."

They lift me and place me back in the chair. My throat tightens, and I examine the photograph again. This is her legacy. Logically, I should weigh all the risks carefully. Rationally assess what I'm getting myself into. But I don't. How could I?

My voice is erratic. "Amelia started this fight. I want to help finish it."

The words feel right the moment they leave my mouth. Like I've been walking toward this my entire life without knowing it. All those years waiting for her, and now I've found her right when I needed to.

Andromeda's smile is soft, almost proud. "You look just like her, you know?"

A slow nod is all I can give without shattering again.

"Luna came back here totally shook. She swore you were Nova. I had to see you for myself."

She extends her arm across the desk, palm up. I place my hand in hers, and she closes around me.

"She'd be so proud of you, of what you're doing. Are you okay to get started?"

I continue nodding through tears and say, "I have to call someone first."

"—AND pull the backup into the off-site cloud instance," Luna says, sketching on the whiteboard. I stare and nod like I understand.

"I've tried getting into those transfer records before," Jeremy's voice crackles through the burner phone. "They're locked down tight —Natalia's access only."

The faces around the table are a gallery of newfound allies—Luna with her funeral-black hair and resting bitch face, Vega's classic spy impression behind her mirrored glasses, and Andromeda appraising me like she's already read the last page of my story. The scene is surreal. A week ago, I was frantically googling *how to remove makeup stains from expensive fabric*. Now I'm plotting against the place that may have saved my life.

"Nova's prior intel showed that Natalia keeps certain sensitive data off the main servers." Andromeda drums her fingers against the tabletop. "Everything compromising stays on her personal computer."

Vega nods. "Illicit financial records, client blackmail material, communications with her outside contacts—it's all there."

"We've never had someone with your level of access before, Jeremy," Andromeda adds. "This is a legitimate opportunity."

Jeremy sighs. "Look, I appreciate the vote of confidence, but I'd need physical access to her computer while it's unlocked. Even when I install updates, she stands right over me, watching everything. She doesn't trust anyone."

Luna turns from the whiteboard. "So, you need a distraction?"

All eyes shift to me. The implication in their gaze is unmistakable.

"Ten minutes is all I'd need," Jeremy says. "If I can get her off me, I can install the monitoring software."

"Esther's the wild card," Luna says. "Natalia wants a confession. You should give her one."

"Wh-What do you mean?" I stammer.

"She's right," Vega says. "It might be the one thing Natalia's more invested in than security right now."

My fingers twist through my hair. "You want me to confess that I wrote the Cinderella post?"

"No," Andromeda says calmly. "She just has to *think* you're going to. Keep her attention long enough to give Jeremy ten minutes."

"And if she figures out what we're doing?" I ask.

"Then we're all screwed," Luna says bluntly, capping her marker. "But especially you two."

"Thanks for the pep talk."

Andromeda covers my hand with hers. "This is more than exposing the Family now, Esther. This is about justice for your sister. For Melody. For all the girls who never made it out."

"What would I say to her?" I ask.

"Lead her on," Vega suggests. "Talk around it, then apologize and say it wasn't you. He only needs ten minutes."

"Are you sure about this?" Jeremy says, clearly concerned. "If something goes wrong—"

"It won't," I interrupt, more confident than I probably should be.

My eyes return to the picture, to Amelia, who built this resistance from nothing. All these girls, all this equipment. The question needs asking.

"How do you"—I gesture around the threadbare room—"stay afloat?"

A proud smile crosses Andromeda's lips. "Nova was a master of acquiring assets. One of her last clients in the Family wasn't a mark— he was a convert. They'd see each other privately, off-book. He understood what we were fighting against and agreed to help. When she vanished, he made a promise to us, and his money has been funding what she started ever since."

Pride and sorrow pull at me from opposite directions. Amelia, industrious and passionate, persuasive to the end.

On the way out, each of them stops to embrace me. Luna hands me another water bottle and runs her hand along my back.

"Welcome aboard," she says with a hint of a smile.

"Let's do this." I meet the eyes of each member of this unexpected alliance. "For Nova."

CARON

The city looked like a galaxy of fractured constellations laid out at his feet. From his penthouse office atop the Family's Fifth Avenue building, the jagged spine of Manhattan glittered in the late evening. The silence was broken only by the soft fall of his custom-made shoes across the Persian rug as he walked to the wet bar. He slid a heavy crystal tumbler across the top and poured two fingers of bourbon, a small-batch Kentucky brand he had no intention of drinking. Health concerns had required that he give up the indulgence years ago—but not the ritual.

The amber liquid swirled in the glass as he raised it not to his lips but to his nose and inhaled. Oak, vanilla, and a touch of burn. A proxy for the pleasure he could no longer afford.

The scent acted as an anchor, but on nights like this, the past had its own gravity. Carrying the glass to the window, he admired the view stretching over Central Park. The boy who'd arrived here forty years ago, blinking at the clouds from the deck of a Turkish freighter, would not recognize the man who owned this view. He'd been Fredek Juhász then, a name buried along with the Greek pharmacist whose identity he'd stolen. A boy who swore he'd never wear a uniform like his father's, which was always splattered with another man's blood. His new name, Caron, was a deliberate choice. Solid. Permanent.

His gaze swept from the window to the shelves of leather-bound tomes that lined one wall. Books he'd bought for their aesthetics, not their words. They represented an order he hadn't known then. In those first few years, he made his office in a tiny room above a

Brooklyn bodega where he had his own little prostitution ring, staffed entirely by Slavic girls. They called him "Mr. Caron" and trusted him almost as much as they feared him. It ran on the same principles he'd learned running flesh in Romania. Respect. Order. Silence.

A practical system, small and clean, it worked until it didn't. The memory came unbidden, as sharp as the alcohol in his nose: the metallic scent on the morning air, the four girls stacked on the fire escape, throats cut with a butcher's indifference. Not a message. Just a lesson, delivered in blood by the Russians, who still ran the show in Brighton Beach. Slamming his fist into the wall that night had cost him two knuckles, a fair trade for the knowledge gained. *This city plays for keeps.*

A hint of cherry floated up from the glass this time as he glanced toward the old map of Manhattan on the wall. After the attack, he had regrouped, stopped seeing streets and started seeing appetites. He learned the city's hungers, borough by borough. Discretion became his commodity. That day, he stopped thinking in terms of hustles and started thinking in terms of empires. Systems so large, so insulated, that no one could ever leave a lesson on his doorstep again.

His office door pushed open, and Kari poked her head in. "I'm heading out for the night. Do you need anything?"

"No, my dear. Thank you."

Kari was one of the earliest. When she'd aged out of the field, he'd kept her on. She had proven more useful as his assistant than she ever did as a Sister.

"You have an eight thirty with Natalia tomorrow. I left it in your calendar. Good night."

Natalia. Well, still Nadia then.

He inhaled his bourbon and recalled their first meeting at a party in Tribeca. Another survivor, but one who wore her past like a tattoo, not a bruise. She was drinking champagne from a shoe when he first saw her. They talked for two hours, and he learned very little about her. They'd fucked in a bathroom because it was the only room with a lock, and she'd told him her plans for a dot-com startup that never got off the ground. Two weeks later, he'd offered her half of everything he'd built—she'd countered that she would run it all, including him. He'd agreed.

She transformed his grimy operation into an *experience*. She designed the velvet trap, doubled the prices, and brought in a new class of girls. Her idea of offering comps to the VIPs changed everything. Men so enthralled by the luxury they never stopped to realize: *If you're not paying for the service, you are the product.* A lesson he'd learned with blood that she had codified in spreadsheets and Italian marble.

The photos on the wall, sun-faded and covered in dust, spoke of more hopeful times. An 8x10 of him, Nadia, and their small staff of twelve standing outside this glass mansion on Fifth Avenue, the day they moved in.

Nadia—Natalia by then—had written new rules. No girls under twenty-one or over thirty, and zero tolerance for violent clients. He chuckled, remembering the heated discussions about calling the girls "Sisters" and the feeling of victory when she'd finally acquiesced and let him have his Family metaphor. A requiem for simpler times.

His circuit of the room complete, he arrived back at the sprawling mahogany desk and set the un-sipped bourbon down. He loved her, he supposed, the way you love a beautiful storm—with awe and a healthy dose of terror. She called him "old man," and he called her "boss," and in the quiet of a shared bed, they both knew who truly held the power now.

The Family had grown, just as she'd planned. Metastasized. He became a shadow in his own house, a king in a court that no longer felt his authority. The world had changed beneath him, and his ability to change with it was no longer certain.

The four girls on the fire escape, a lifetime ago. A lesson delivered.

Perhaps another was due.

TWENTY THREE

The top floor of the Family HQ is unnervingly quiet at 6:40 a.m. The stairs are a better bet than the elevator—less chance of running into someone. It's early, so Kari won't be at her post yet, but late enough for Caron to be at his desk with his morning tea like nothing in the world has changed.

But everything has changed. The truth about my recruitment, about my life here, about Amelia.

A perfunctory rap on the open door, but I'm walking straight in.

"Caron, we need to talk."

He looks up from his leather-bound planner, his pen suspended midair. He's already dressed for the day in a charcoal suit, his salt-and-pepper stubble perfectly groomed. For a moment, surprise flickers across his features before settling back into familiar calm.

"Star." He sets the pen down softly and picks up his teacup from its saucer. "You're up early. Something on your mind?"

My hands find the edge of his desk as I lean in close. "Tell me about Nova."

His teacup clinks as he sets it back down. Nothing else changes—not his breathing, not his posture—but something shifts in the air between us.

"So," he exhales, "you finally know."

The way he says it makes my ears burn with fury. Not surprised, not defensive—almost relieved. He's been waiting for this conversation.

"Were you ever going to tell me?" My voice cracks. "That my sister was…a Sister? That you were looking for me?"

Caron picks up his tea again, inhaling the bergamot steam before taking a slow sip. When he sets the cup down, his movements are careful, controlled, like he's buying time.

"Who else knows?" I demand. "Natalia?"

"Natalia suspects," he admits. "She commented on your resemblance when you first arrived. But I don't know if anyone else has made the connection."

"So, this whole thing? My being here, everything that's happened…" I tilt my head. "You planned all of it?"

He raises the teacup to his lips. A calculated pause.

"Yes."

The single word ambushes me. No explanation, no justification. Just the simple, devastating truth that my entire life since joining the Family has been a charade.

But then, something unexpected: He exhales through his nose, and a raw, genuine pain surfaces on his face.

"Please." He gestures to the chair across from his desk. "Sit down. Let me explain."

My instinct is to stay standing, to keep the anger boiling, but his face gives me pause. I sink into the leather chair.

"I found your sister much the same way I found you," he begins, settling back in his own chair. "Living rough, with no one to care for her. It started small…" He turns his teacup. "A brief conversation, a warm meal. So bright, I found myself caring for her. She deserved better than what she had. I gave her a home, a purpose. For a time, she was happy here."

"For a time," I repeat.

Something flickers across his face and he steeples his fingers, choosing his words carefully.

"Nova was intelligent. Curious. Like you." He pokes his finger in the air. "She began asking questions about our work. About aspects of what we do."

My throat tightens. "What questions?"

"The kind that put her in contact with the wrong type of people," he says. "People who filled her head with ideas about exposing the Family. About destroying what we built here. Throwing away the lives we'd saved."

I lean forward and grab the armrests. "And?"

Caron's face clouds over, and the shadows of his years sculpt his features. "She chose to leave us. I begged her not to. I told her the people she listened to would use her, manipulate her anger for their own purposes. But she wouldn't listen."

He pauses, his gaze fixed on the window. "She used to eat those little…" He looks at me. "What are they called? Gummy bears? She was always chewing on them during conversations." His mouth twists into something like a smile. "Drove me mad."

Right in the feels. Amelia loved those things, especially the red ones.

His melancholy catches me off guard. This isn't the cold indifference I'd expected. This is genuine remorse.

"Then she started speaking out. First to the girls she kept in touch with. Then louder. Online. I tried to reach out to her, to make her see reason, but…" He trails off, shaking his head.

"But what?"

"The people she worked with used her, as I warned they would. They pushed her to take bigger risks, to make bolder moves. And eventually—" His breath catches. "—it cost her life."

The words hit me like ice water.

My nostrils flare as I lock eyes with him. "What happened? Who killed her?"

He breaks our sightline to glance at the window while he runs his hand over the stubble on his chin. "In truth, Esther…I do not know."

Before I can call him a liar, he raises a single finger and continues. "I do know *why* it happened."

I swallow my words for now.

"Your sister carried a righteous fire inside her. But the ones she listened to stoked that fire until it became all that she was—and fire without control eventually consumes everything, including itself." His face is sullen and drawn, as if he's reliving the loss.

I came here prepared for a fight, armed with accusations and ready to demand he pay for his manipulation. But I don't have any fight left anymore. My head falls into my hands, palms against my eyes willing away the sudden, horrific image of her in flames.

The light clink of porcelain floats through the air.

"You think you've found the truth." He cuts through my thoughts. "You've found their version of it. Just like Nova did, she fought with her heart, but she didn't understand the extent of what she was fighting."

A villain's monologue is what I expected. Instead, I got the weary king from a long-forgotten tragedy, lamenting the princess he couldn't save.

"I don't know what to believe anymore."

Caron stands and moves to the window, his reflection ethereal in the glass. "I made a promise to myself after she left. If I ever got a second chance, I wouldn't make the same mistakes. I wouldn't let the same thing happen."

He turns to face me, and his vulnerability is heartbreaking.

"But here we are," he continues, "and history is repeating itself. The people who pushed her are now filling your head with the same nonsense. Using your anger, your desire for justice, like they used hers."

The ground shifts beneath me. Every supposed truth, every alliance, every fact I'd accepted—it all fractures.

"Why should I believe you?" I ask.

Caron returns to his desk and drops his entire weight into the chair.

"Because, unlike them," he says, "I don't have a hidden agenda. I don't need you to fight my battles or die for my cause. I want to keep the promise I made to someone I cared for dearly and let slip away."

The sincerity silences me.

There's no monster here to fight. Only a man haunted by the same ghosts that haunt me. I came to throw punches, but right now I'll settle for getting my balance back.

"Have you been…protecting me? Sheltering me?"

He shrugs, and it's not a denial.

"What am I supposed to do now?"

Caron's smile is resigned. "That is entirely up to you. But make your choice thoughtfully. Your decisions carry consequences now. Nova found that out too late."

There's nothing more to say. A single nod is all I have left.

Rising from the leather chair, I walk out of his office and into the unknown.

"Dɪᴅ ʏᴏᴜ ᴋɴᴏᴡ?"

Jeremy spins around, chair casters squeaking in the quiet office, his face sharp with concern.

"Know what?"

The words are like stones in my throat. "That Nova was my sister."

Jeremy goes completely still for a moment, like his brain's rebooting. His mouth opens, closes, and opens again.

"Not until the call, I swear. I mean, the resemblance is clear now, but I spend most of my day staring at giant monitors, so…"

"But you remember her?"

"Of course I remember her." He runs both hands through his hair, squinting at me like I've just revealed I'm an alien. "This explains… Wow, this explains so much."

My legs give out, and I sink into the chair across from him. "What do you mean?"

Jeremy leans back, looking almost wistful. "You're so much like her, I feel dumb that I didn't see it."

"What was she like?"

"Caron treated her differently than other Sisters. He had me give her access to his office so she could go in there anytime, day or night. No other Sister had that, not even Sage. I thought it was odd how much he trusted her."

Trusted her. The irony makes my insides knot. "What did she do in there?"

"Hell if I know. They'd be in there for hours sometimes. Looked like he was showing her the guts of the operation, not just the glamour."

This version of Amelia—confident, trusted, sitting in Caron's office making decisions—it's so far from the sister I made up stories with that my brain is waterlogged.

"There was always this tension between her and Sage too," Jeremy says, and something cold cascades through me. "Nothing obvious, but you could feel it. Natalia had Sage, and Caron had Nova. They were polite, but…" He clashes his fists together. "It was like they were two projects competing for funding."

Of course they were. Sage's reaction every time Step-Sister comes up makes so much sense now.

"How was she with you?" I have to know if any part of her I remember survived in this place.

Jeremy's face softens. "She was friendly, which was…nice. Most Sisters barely acknowledge me, you know? But Nova would say hi any time she saw me, ask how things were going."

There's something reflective in his cadence that makes my heart ache. At least some part of Amelia's kindness was real.

"She was curious about the technical stuff too." He pushes his glasses up. "How the systems worked, the security we used. I was flattered, honestly. She wanted to understand the business side of things and asked a lot of questions."

Unease washes over me. "What kind of questions?"

"Stuff like…how we backed up data, which encryption methods we used, network architecture—" Jeremy's eyes go wide as the realization dawns on him. "Oh. *Oh.* She wasn't just making conversation, was she?"

I shake my head slowly. My brilliant sister, gathering intelligence piece by casual piece.

"When was this?"

"About two years ago. And here's something else—right around that time, Natalia came to me with a weird request." He's getting animated now, pieces clicking together. "She wanted me to monitor Nova more closely. Track her system access, flag any unusual activity. Said it was routine security, but…"

"But what?"

"The timing. It was right after the Step-Sister blog launched." He stares at me with growing amazement. "Your sister was gathering intelligence while Natalia was aiming a microscope at her. She was planning something."

I'm drowning in the revelations. This calculating woman Jeremy's describing—is this who Amelia was? Or who she had to become to survive here?

"That's not the Amelia I remember," I whisper.

"Maybe she couldn't be," Jeremy says. "Maybe that's how she survived long enough to fight back."

She was playing both sides. She had to. And so do I.

"Star, your sister was smart. She was three steps ahead of everyone, including me, clearly." He chuckles. "I can't believe I didn't make the connection sooner."

I can only nod. The enormity of everything Amelia built settles on my shoulders, a mantle I never asked for. She started this war against the Family from the inside. She gathered the intelligence, built the network.

Now, Andromeda wants me to finish what she started—even if it means becoming someone my sister wouldn't recognize.

THERE'S a small outdoor terrace just off the cafeteria with a few tables and one of those giant canvas umbrellas you see in every movie set in Paris. I need some air and a place to think, and this fits the bill.

My tablet is on my lap, but I haven't turned a page in twenty minutes. Caron's words are tumbling and twisting with everything Andromeda said and what Jeremy told me, like a Gordian knot in my brain.

Unlike them, I don't have a hidden agenda.

Isn't that exactly what someone with an agenda would say?

Setting the tablet aside, I look out over the gloomy city.

"You look like hell," Aura says from behind me.

"I'll take that as a compliment."

She doesn't laugh, just studies me, head tilted, as she walks over and leans against the railing. "That blog post's causing a lot of waves."

"You think I wrote it?"

"No." She smirks. "I *know* you did."

I drag my hand down my face. So much for my brilliant disguise. "How?"

"Please," Aura scoffs. "It's your week off, and yet you disappear for hours. You're always writing in your notebook, and you slam it shut whenever anyone walks by." She shrugs. "Plus, that post sounded like you when you get all fired up about something."

"It didn't name names."

"You didn't need to." She plucks a thread from her sleeve. "People are pissed. Natalia's not used to being surprised. And Sage...girl looked like someone just kicked over her altar."

That lands harder than it should.

"What happened with her, anyway?" Aura asks. "We could hear you two screaming from the hallway."

Heat rushes to my face. "It was a long time coming. Some back-burner things boiled over."

She snickers to herself. "Okay. So, you just gonna let the rest of us deal with the fallout?"

"I didn't mean for it to go this far."

"Do you know I'm losing my stipend because of this? And the veterans?" She smacks her lips. "They're getting pissed."

"Aura—"

"No, listen." She holds up a hand. "I like you, okay? But there's one group here you don't want as enemies. Spoiled bitches who can't have what they're used to having. Trust me."

The threat is soft, cushioned by genuine concern.

"If you're gonna start fires in this house, don't let other people burn for you." Pushing off the railing with a dancer's grace, she heads toward the door—but stops halfway. "I can't keep defending you, not when their designer shoes are on the line, you catch me?"

I nod slowly, but I can't look at her.

"For what it's worth," she says without turning around, "some of what you wrote? Needed saying."

A flutter rises in my chest.

"I'm not saying I know who's behind Step-Sister," she adds. "But if I did, I'd guess she appreciates having someone else in the deep end."

Her tone raises the hair on my arms.

"Eventually, though…admit you lit the match."

She glances back, one corner of her mouth tipping upward. "Be smart, Estrellita. Bright is pretty. Smart keeps you breathing."

And then she's gone.

Twenty Four

My lines are rehearsed, but they keep slipping away. What waits ahead is a walk into the lion's den with nothing more than mediocre acting skills and hope. Jeremy's Remote Access Trojan is our only weapon. A digital spy planted in Natalia's computer. He called it a RAT. Cute name for something that could get us both killed.

What if she knows the second she looks at me? Natalia doesn't miss a thing. One look is all it'll take.

My phone buzzes, sending a jolt right through me.

JEREMY

5 mins

Kora's breathing exercise does nothing for me. Grabbing the strategically selected notebook pages, I arrange my face into the expression of someone with nothing to hide. I'm failing miserably.

Ten minutes. That's all he needs. Ten minutes of me not screwing up.

I don't like my chances.

The last few yards to Natalia's office feel like a walk toward my execution. The solid glass door might as well be labeled *Abandon all hope, ye who enter here.*

The door is heavier than it looks, but it swings open in one motion—no time to chicken out. Jeremy sits at Natalia's massive desk, fingers poised on the keyboard. Natalia stands behind him, both of them staring intently at one of her three monitors.

"Not now. I'm in the middle of—" Natalia begins without looking up, her voice clipped with irritation. Then her head turns, and her eyes lock onto mine. She shifts from annoyance to sharp curiosity in a microsecond. "What are you doing here?"

Don't look at Jeremy. I fix my gaze on Natalia's face, and my mouth goes dry.

"We need to talk," I say, proud that the words come out steady. I close the door behind me, and the latch clicks like a lock on a prison cell.

"Are you here to confess?" she asks, crossing her arms. "This is not the best time."

"It's about that, yes," I say.

She exhales, and I can practically see the gears whirring. Her gaze flicks from Jeremy to me and back again before she waggles a finger at him.

"Get up and stand over there for a moment. This shouldn't take long."

Goddammit.

My brain locks. This wasn't the plan. Jeremy should be at the keyboard, not standing by the desk like a kid caught with his hand in the cookie jar. We need a new strategy.

"May I sit?" I ask, gesturing toward the leather sofa against the wall.

Natalia waves her hand dismissively.

Sinking onto the sofa, I cross my ankles like a proper lady, as if that might gain me brownie points.

"About what you said at the meeting," I begin, hands folded in my lap. "About loyalty. The Cinderella post is a concern—of course it is. Trust is everything in the Family, right?"

I sound like I'm auditioning for a cult recruitment video.

"I admire how you've built something so…protective." The words taste like toothpaste and OJ. "A haven for women who desperately need it."

Natalia's perfectly sculpted eyebrow arches higher with each word. She's getting impatient.

"I know some people might think I wrote it, and I wanted to set the record straight—"

"Just tell me you wrote the fucking thing so we can move on," Natalia barks, her Russian accent thickening with irritation.

"I—" I swallow hard, buying seconds. "I wanted to explain my side of things."

Ten minutes. That's all we need. And I've wasted at least two of them already.

"What's to explain? You wrote it. Admit it, and then we'll discuss your punishment," Natalia snaps.

It's now or never. My knees are jelly, but I straighten my spine and meet her gaze.

"That's the thing, Natalia. I didn't write it."

Her eyes narrow to dangerous slits, and waves of anger radiate from her.

"I don't have time for these games, child," she hisses, taking a step toward me. Her heels clack on the marble like tiny hammers driving nails into my skull.

"No games, Natalia, I swear. I—"

"Natalia, please," Jeremy cuts in, and I nearly choke on my spit. What is he doing? "If it's okay with you, I have a lot of machines to update today. Could I just...?" He points to the computer with a nervous half smile.

He's a genius, and this is his brilliant move?

"I know who did write it, though," I say, pulling Natalia's attention back to me.

Her head snaps between us so fast her earrings sway. Wrinkles form on her brow as confusion melts into pursed lips.

"May I?" Jeremy asks again, gesturing toward the keyboard.

Natalia makes a guttural sound—between a growl and a sigh—and waves her hand dismissively at him. "Fine. Be quick."

Son of a bitch, it worked!

She turns her attention back to me, crossing her arms. "So, who wrote it? Enlighten me."

My mind whirls like a hamster on an espresso binge, searching for something real, something plausible—anything to keep her focus on me. Pulling out the notebook pages, I try to shield the tremble in my hand.

"I've been doing research on Step-Sister," I say, spreading my notes on the coffee table.

Natalia looks baffled. "Research?"

"Yes, I've been analyzing the posts. The time stamps form a schedule—late nights, Sundays and Thursdays. The writing style changes too. Here, and here." I point to the highlighted sections. "It's subtle, but it's there."

Natalia flicks down to my notes, then back to my face. She's guarded—confused but interested.

"It's smart, really," I add, tapping one page for emphasis. "Using language to divide people. Whoever wrote this knows how the Family works—how close the girls are. They knew a single spark would be enough to start a fire."

Natalia cocks her head. "And you think this is deliberate?"

I nod. "Yes. You're not dealing with a spurned ex here. This is someone strategic. Disciplined." I glance up and give her a faint smile. "Someone like you, actually."

Her face doesn't move—no flicker of recognition at all. I push on anyway.

"Almost had it figured out," I say, "but now I'm not so sure. What if it's somebody we don't know about? Somebody close?"

I lean in, like I'm sharing a secret. "Is there anyone on the inside you've had doubts about?"

Natalia deadpans, "Besides you?"

"Right," I laugh too quickly. "Besides me."

"No."

With a hard swallow, the last piece of the lie forms on my tongue. "Well, I think I know who's behind it. At least, who's coordinating all of it."

Her head snaps up. "Who?"

"Someone called Nova," I say, the name falling from my lips like a penny off the Empire State Building.

Natalia's face transforms in an instant. The cool executive melts away, replaced by something raw and feral. The intensity pushes me backward into the sofa cushions.

"Where did you hear that name?" she demands.

"She's a top member of Step-Sister as far as I can tell, and she used to be in the Family." I mold my face into the most earnest look I can muster. "Truth be told? I think she's the one behind it all. I think she's *the* Step-Sister."

My shoulders square back as the corners of my mouth lift—channeling that golden retriever energy, tail practically wagging.

Look what I found. Aren't I clever?

Natalia's motionless. Her expression doesn't shift—it drops off her face entirely.

"Nova is dead," she says flatly.

The words push me back, and I want to lean across the table to slap her.

"What?" The shock in my tone is partly genuine. "How do you know that?"

Natalia waves her hand dismissively, like she's swatting away an annoying fly. "This is old news, girl. You're giving me nothing new."

Jeremy's fingers are moving across the keyboard in a blur. How much longer does he need?

Switching tactics, I drop my head down, face crumpling into a mask of disappointment.

"I'm so sorry," I blubber. "I thought I was doing good work. Something that would help find out who's trying to tear us apart."

Natalia is beyond irritated now. She's...done.

"You waste my time with this nonsense?" she snaps. "You assume I'm not aware of every person who has ever betrayed the Family?"

She paces in front of me. Each step sounds like dynamite.

"I thought—"

She cuts me off with a sharp gesture. "You didn't think. That's the problem." She stops pacing and stares a hole through me. "You want to prove your loyalty? Stop playing detective and do what you're told. No more games."

Jeremy gives me the slightest nod from behind Natalia's back.

It's done.

Relief floods through me, but I project chastened regret.

"I was only trying to help," I murmur, staring at my hands.

Natalia sighs heavily. "Get out of my office. And next time you come in here, have something meaningful to say."

"Yes, ma'am," I say meekly.

Turning to leave, I catch Jeremy's eye. His face is blank, but triumph is hiding beneath the surface. My knees almost buckle. Laughter, tears, and vomit all fight to be the first one out.

JEREMY CLICKS THE MOUSE, his head darting between monitors while I hover behind him, close enough to read the text but not enough to crowd him. Every time a new window pops up, a shot of adrenaline runs through me.

"What about that one?" I point to a folder labeled *Acquisitions*.

Jeremy clicks, then dismisses it with a shake of his head. "Just business records. Nothing we don't already know about."

Another folder—*Client Profiles*. "That has to be good, right?"

"Already checked. It's just the stuff in the system." He clicks through a few more directories, each one making me hold my breath until he moves on.

"I can't believe this worked," Jeremy says, adjusting his glasses. "I honestly thought she was going to throw you in a dungeon."

My laugh comes out strained. "Oh, I definitely pissed her off. And she doesn't buy my story for a second."

"She didn't have to believe you. She just had to be annoyed enough to ignore me." He grins, then sits up straighter. "Wait—look at this."

He points to a folder labeled *N1*. It sits alongside the other folders in the directory, innocuous yet somehow ominous in its simplicity.

He double-clicks it, and a security prompt appears immediately asking for an authentication scan.

"This folder is locked down, almost certainly with biometric protection. She's not screwing around."

I lean closer, squinting. "What does that mean?"

"It's only accessible when authorized by her fingerprint or facial scan. I can't get in there unless she unlocks it first."

"Great. What are we going to tell Andromeda?"

"As little as possible."

ANDROMEDA'S VOICE crackles through the single earbud, short and cold enough to frost the inside of my ear. Jeremy is hunched over the phone wearing the other.

"Let me get this straight," she says, her tone dangerously calm.

"You have it installed, but you can't see anything until she trips the lock?"

"Right, the sensitive stuff is behind biometric authentication. Fingerprints, facial recognition, the works. I can only access what she unlocks while I'm observing," Jeremy answers.

Silence. Then, "So you're a baby monitor, not a burglar."

"Unfortunately, that's pretty accurate."

Luna chimes in, "Can we help babysit?"

"The access only works from inside the Family network, so, for now, this will have to do," he explains.

A sharp exhale of breath in my ear. Then Andromeda clips, "Fine. Keep us informed."

The line goes dead.

Jeremy takes his earbud out. "That went well."

I give his arm a sympathetic pat on my way to the door. "You're doing great. Don't worry about her."

He doesn't face me, but there's a hint of a smile visible.

"Shit!"

Jeremy flinches. "What is it?"

"I forgot to ask her about post thirteen again."

He clicks his tongue. "Pretty sure she wasn't in the mood to answer questions anyway."

My footsteps are loud in the empty stairwell as I head up from the tech floor. Loyalty is splitting me in two. Andromeda's truth could mean my sister's work saved lives. Caron's could mean it got her killed. For now, playing both sides is the only path forward, the only way to find out.

A buzzing in my pocket dismisses the thought. It's not the burner, but my Family phone. Fishing it out, I chuckle to myself. "One more phone and I'm gonna need cargo pants."

A glance at the notification halts me mid-step. It's from Sage. The tips of my ears flush as my legs give out, and I sink onto the step. The message glows up at me.

SAGE

> Star, I'm sorry for how I acted yesterday. Fighting with you wasn't what I wanted, and I'm hoping you'll let me make it right. Have dinner with me in my room tomorrow night, just the two of us, so I can properly apologize.

I read it three times; it doesn't make sense. Yesterday, Sage was ready to feed me to Natalia on a silver platter, convinced I was Cinderella. Now she wants a cozy dinner? Is she trying to make peace before she turns me in? Or does she actually mean it?

The phone goes on the step beside me, and my gaze fixes on the concrete wall. The elegant script of the Family's logo is stenciled there, mocking me.

"What are you doing, Sage?"

Dinner. Her room. Just the two of us. It's everything I've wanted. She knows that.

It's stupid. It's a risk.

I'm going to take it.

Twenty Five

Poor Richard's Playground on Third Avenue is pure chaos—exactly what you'd expect from three acres of Manhattan real estate pretending to be a suburban paradise. Kids shriek from every direction, their voices bouncing off the rubber-coated jungle gym and plastic slides. Pushing through the throng of harried parents and overstimulated children, I do my best to blend in. It's the perfect place to disappear in plain sight. No wonder he picked it.

Jeremy is sipping an iced coffee near the water fountain, and I give him a flat smile. He returns it before handing me a coffee as well. "What's a little more caffeine between friends?" His tone is wary.

"I got your coordinates," I say, taking him in. His face is drawn and pale. "You look like hell. Did you even sleep?"

He takes a long sip. "I wasn't planning on staying all night. When I grabbed my bag to go, one of my alerts went off." His eyes dart around the playground, paranoia etched on his face. "I sat down to look…and that's when I noticed she was on."

He leads me to an empty bench tucked away in a corner of the playground. "She opened the folder."

We sit down, not too close but close enough to maintain a semblance of intimacy amid the sea of chattering adults and oblivious preschoolers. He looks exhausted, locked in a permanent squint. My hand finds his arm, offering what little comfort I can muster.

"What is it?" My grip on the cup tightens.

Jeremy glances around the playground, tracking a group of nannies pushing strollers past us. When he speaks again, it's so low I have to lean in to hear him over the shrieks.

"Star…I saw something I wish I hadn't." He runs a hand through his hair, making it stick up at odd angles. "The information the Sisters gather from clients—Natalia's selling it."

I frown. "We know that already."

"No." He looks away and wipes his nose. "Not just the corporate gossip or business intel. She's specifically targeting government clients. Defense contractors, State Department officials, Pentagon liaisons…classified data."

"What?"

Jeremy nods. "She drafted a message through an encrypted terminal they have set up. High-grade stuff, way beyond what the Family should have access to. She was uploading files into a write-only folder—the kind spies use for dead drops."

"And you read the files?"

"One of them. She opened it to make a last-minute redaction. Schematic plans for a communications satellite. The kind the government uses for secure transmissions."

I'm going to be sick. The playground spins around me, all those happy families oblivious to the conversation happening on this bench.

The look on his face is answer enough, but I still have to ask. "To who?"

He takes off his glasses, cleaning them on his shirt with shaky hands. "She's sending state secrets to Russian intelligence."

"Oh my God." The cold coffee cup against my head does nothing to ground me. This is so much bigger than simple corruption. This is…this is fucking treason.

"There's more," he sighs. "The folder had dozens and dozens of files, dating back years. What looked like client names, recorded conversations, photographs, and financial records. She's been building a database of compromising material on half of D.C."

"Did you take any screenshots? Any proof at all?"

He nods slowly. "Yes, but it's not much. I put them in a secure location, an encrypted drive I keep for emergencies." He glances around, as if federal agents might materialize from behind the monkey bars. "I don't think she knows I was in there."

A mother walks by pushing a double stroller, and we both fall silent until she passes. My hands are trembling.

Jeremy takes the lid off his iced coffee and downs a huge swig, chomping on an ice cube. "It's not just government stuff either. There was a file named *Contingency Planning*. It had procurement orders for custom chemical compositions."

Confusion must be written on my face, as he clarifies, "Poisons. Even notes on administering antidotes. It's like a playbook for 'handling' problems quietly."

"We have to tell someone. The FBI, the CIA—"

"With what proof?" Jeremy interrupts. "I can't walk into a federal building and say, 'Hi, I hacked into someone's computer and found evidence of treason—here are some screenshots.' They'd arrest me before I finished the sentence."

He's right. We're a part of this now too.

Jeremy hangs his head and takes off his glasses. He's not anxious or awkward; he's genuinely broken. His hands shake as he sets down his coffee cup.

"I didn't sign up for this," he whispers. "I could overlook some bullshit corruption, corporate intelligence trading. Not..." He trails off, unable to say it out loud.

"Jeremy—"

"I'm an accessory to this, Star. Do you know what that means?" He looks up at me, and behind his frames, his eyes are damp. He doesn't say the word out loud, just mouths it: "Treason."

A cold, heavy feeling settles in my gut. The moment right before the car crashes.

A group runs past us, their laughter sharp and jarring against our hushed conversation. We pause.

The throbbing in my head intensifies. "What about Step-Sister? We have to tell—"

"Tell them what?" Jeremy's laugh is bitter. "That their little revenge plot became a matter of national security? That we're all looking at federal prison if this goes sideways? No. Andromeda means well, I think, but she's a little too Rambo to handle this kind of intel."

I grab his hand, squeezing it. "Hey. Look at me."

He does.

"We're going to figure this out," I say. "We have to. For Melody, for all the girls who don't know what they're really part of."

"And if Natalia finds out what we know?" His delivery leaves no ambiguity. "Star, people who cross Russian intelligence don't get fired. They vanish."

My head leans against his shoulder. "We're going to be okay." The lie is for me as much as it is for him. "Whatever happens, we've got each other's backs."

His hand tightens around mine, warm and steady despite everything.

The kids chase each other across the playground, and a cold realization settles in. I'm so not equipped for this. I'm just a broke girl from Queens who couldn't save her own mother. Who couldn't hold on to her sister. Who couldn't find the words to make her best friend stay home that night. Who's been pretending to be someone else for so long, I barely recognize myself anymore.

And now I'm tangled up in this shit? Treason? God, what would my mom think if she could see me now? What would Amelia?

Well, Sprout, you really screwed the weasel this time!

Jeremy's thumb traces circles on my hand, and I wonder if he can feel the way my heart is beating.

BACK FROM THE PLAYGROUND, a quick lunch is in order. The dorm sounds far too cheerful for the bomb ticking inside me. My head is swimming in a pool of Russian intelligence, military secrets, and treason. There's not enough chlorine in the world to make this water clear again.

So lost in thought, I nearly collide with Kora as she rounds the corner.

"Whoa there, speed racer." She steadies me with both hands. "You're in a hurry."

Forcing a shallow chuckle, I reply, "Sorry, head's in a fog."

"Tell me about it." She squints at me. "You know what you need? An intense sweat session. Clear you right up. Come to the gym."

"I have to—"

"I'm wearing my old Nikes." She lifts one foot, showing off a barely used sneaker. "Since my stipend's been frozen, I'm back to the bargain-bin life. We can be broke bitches together."

The sarcastic mention of the situation I've put my Sisters in stings more than it should. Swallowing hard, I push down the hurt.

"Rain check? I'm pretty beat right now."

"Tomorrow night, then. Hot yoga." She playfully flexes her bicep.

"Can't, sorry. I have plans."

She purses her lips. "Hot date?"

"Sage invited me to dinner."

Kora's smile freezes on her face. "Sage?" Her bubbly demeanor pops. "Didn't you two just have a blowout? Like, nuclear level?"

"Yeah, but she sent a note apologizing. Wants to make up over dinner."

Her face contorts—confusion, perhaps—before she masks it with a smile.

"Sage doesn't apologize." Her tone is light and brittle.

"Well, she did to me."

Kora's jaw flexes, and she fiddles with her water bottle, twisting the cap on and off. "Interesting."

"Is something wrong?"

"Wrong? No, no." She laughs, but it sounds forced. "It's just—Sage isn't the dinner party type. Especially not private ones."

A tiny muscle twitches in her cheek. "Kora, is everything okay?"

"Yeah, fine." She takes a step back, adjusting her gym bag on her shoulder. "Have a good time. Really."

She walks away before I can respond, her shoulders stiff, the bouncy stride noticeably absent as she turns the corner. One more mystery for the growing collection. What was that about?

Shannon Maroney

NOVEMBER 9, 2018

Shannon folded another cashmere sweater with pure muscle memory. The fabric, retailing for more than she made in a day, felt mocking against her fingertips. A lifetime removed from the polyester blouse itching her skin.

Her manager's voice sliced through her thoughts. "Maroney, customer."

Shannon's jaw tightened as she put on her retail smile. The woman standing before her wore Hermès like a uniform, thrusting a $3,000 dress at her without looking up from her phone. It was the same demanding, dismissive air as her mother's friends, women who saw service staff as furniture.

"Size two," the woman clipped.

Shannon assessed her quickly. No way she was getting into a size two—but the customer is always right.

"Of course," Shannon said with a careful blend of deference and distance.

In the stockroom, Shannon grabbed a size four off the rack and swapped the tags. This wasn't unprecedented; she knew who the big spenders were. She took the dress and returned to the woman, who waved her dismissively toward the fitting rooms—just another invisible helper, but the commission was hers.

At six o'clock, Shannon left through the employee entrance, emerging into an alley that reeked of garbage and city grit. She stopped at the corner when the traffic light turned red, and a convertible pulled up across from her. A Porsche Boxster, sage green. *The exact shade.* Her father had told her it was a custom paint job. In an instant, she's seventeen again, at her family's home in the Hamptons, standing in the six-car garage. Her father beamed as he revealed the Porsche with a giant bow on its hood to a chorus of "Happy Birthday." Her hand felt the heft of the key fob. It had meant freedom, a future that gleamed. The world had made a promise: She would always have the best.

The light changed, and the Porsche growled away, leaving her and the remnants of her past on the curb. The silent tour of the city that no longer belonged to her continued, with each new block holding more phantoms—the hotel bar where her father had taught her about scotch, boutiques where he'd given her a platinum card and told her to practice managing her finances.

The N train took forty-three minutes. She counted every day for months. Two keys and three separate locks—a necessity after the second break-in—and she shouldered the door open. The apartment building held a stench of mildew and whatever the neighbors were cooking. She climbed the four flights to her 280-square-foot studio with the clanging radiator and the peeling walls.

Shannon kicked off her sensible flats and sank onto the twin bed that doubled as her couch. The springs groaned. Everything in this place groaned—the pipes, the floors, her spirit.

Her phone buzzed. A text from her mother: *Can you send money? Just $200. I promise I'll pay you back.*

Staring at the screen sucked her back into the one memory she'd tried to suppress. Home from Cornell, standing in the grand marble foyer. Her mother, Elizabeth, face blotchy and stripped of its mask, rushed to embrace her, stale perfume in a cloud around her. "The FBI showed up at his office," she sobbed. "With cameras. Like he's a criminal."

Shannon deleted the text without responding. Her mother was drunk by noon these days, working her way through cheap wine in the one-bedroom apartment she'd kept after the government seized everything else. They sentenced her father to twenty-five years, the trial burying their life under terms like *racketeering* and *securities fraud*. The world reneged on its promise.

At 8:17 p.m., the front-door buzzer rang. She'd been expecting it. Shannon pulled herself up and walked over to the wall, pressing the button. "Yeah?"

"I'm looking for Sage," a voice crackled through the decrepit speaker. "Thirty minutes?"

She buzzed him in. *Sage.* Her new identity and a stupid, sentimental tribute to the only thing she'd ever loved. She'd posted the ad a few months ago when even scraping the bottom of the barrel came up empty. Rent was due, and in this way, she could let Sage do what had to be done to claw back toward the life that had been torn away from her.

Two minutes later, a soft, unassuming knock. Through the peephole, she saw him—middle-aged in a suit that would have been choice five years ago, hair transplant plugs still healing. He didn't belong here any more than she did.

She cracked the door to the length of the chain and took the envelope he passed through the gap—two hundred dollars. More than she earned in a full day at Bergdorf's. Rent, groceries, something for her mother.

Shannon—no, *Sage*—undid the chain. The metal scraped like an accusation. She took his clammy hand, noticed the pale band on his finger where a wedding ring usually sat, and led him toward the bed.

She knelt on the stained rug, her hands steady as she worked his belt. He stank of drugstore cologne and cowardice.

"You're so beautiful," he mumbled, fingers tangling in her red hair.

She didn't respond. Talking cost extra.

The cheap shag scraped against her knees, and for a moment, she felt the thick, bristly rope wrapped around her taped hands. She was back in Ithaca, back in the mud, sweating, the students cheering behind her.

Lock in and breathe! Find your rhythm!

She would yell from the anchor position, shoulders screaming, rope sliding against blistered palms.

The man grunted, pressure on the back of her head. She focused on the pain. In her knees now, in her hands then, as her teammates executed a perfectly strategized *yank*. The shriek of the rival Kappas tumbling ass over ponytail into the mud brought cheers and soothed the burn.

Here in the silent, grim apartment, she was also executing a strategy. Still a steady anchor, pulling her life back from the brink, one humiliating inch at a time.

Afterward, alone again, she stood under a weak shower, lukewarm water washing over skin that wasn't hers. The girl in the Porsche is gone. The sorority anchor a faded myth. There is only Sage.

Sitting on the bed, she counted the money once more—rent, utilities, food. Nothing left. There never seemed to be enough.

Her phone buzzed—another text from her mother.

Shannon stared at the words until they blurred. Tomorrow, she'd return to Bergdorf's, folding sweaters for women who looked through her.

Tonight, she pulled her knees close, shut her eyes, and tried to forget her own name.

TWENTY SIX

What does one wear when you're not sure if your crush wants to make up or feed you to a predator?

I settle on a sleeveless black dress that hits above the knee and pair it with low ankle boots. Anything higher than two inches and I walk like a newborn giraffe. Besides, if tonight goes sideways, I want to be able to run.

"Perfect," I tell the mirror. "Like a spy who might get lucky. Or kidnapped." I lick the palm of my hand, then give it a whiff. Questionable, so I pop a stick of gum into my mouth to be safe.

At 6:02 p.m., with my heart drumming in my ears, I gently tap on Sage's door. It opens, and there she is, backlit by a soft lamp, her pale green dress the color of celery, with a slit up the leg so bold I bite my cheek. Her hair is in a severe French braid, and her lips are painted a shade of red that makes me want to forget every bad thing in the world. Eleven-year-old me would think she's a princess. Twenty-one-year-old me thinks the same.

"Hey, Star," she says, her tone somewhere between silk and smoke. "You look...wow. Come in."

She steps aside, and I shuffle past her. Her scent hits me: spring rain with a side of citrus.

Her room is immaculate. No stray shoes, no piles of laundry, no evidence that anyone as alive as Sage could live here. On a small table in the center of the room sit two place settings, an actual candle, and a tiny green succulent in a little glass pot.

"Nice table," I say, because I have the social skills of a neurotic hamster.

The first awkward silence settles. Sage glides past it, gesturing for me to sit. I do, wishing my knees wouldn't bounce. Two goblets of red wine land on the table as she places them down, then sits. For a moment, we study each other over the flicker of the candle.

I take a breath and fake a smile. "What are we doing here, Sage?"

She wants to start with a speech—her spine straightens, gaze locking onto mine as her mouth opens—but I bulldoze right through it before she can say anything rehearsed.

"I know what your note said, but the last time you saw me, you were pretty upset. So, why am I here?"

She smooths the hair at her temple. "I overreacted. That wasn't—you didn't deserve that. Natalia's been on my ass to sniff out Cinderella, and I let her get in my head. I shouldn't have taken it out on you."

"And you thought it was me."

Her eyes flick away. "I still do, but I don't want to fight anymore."

My arms cross, and I lean back in the chair. "So, what do you want?"

She looks at me and then at her wineglass. "To just be Sisters again. Like before."

"That's it?" I push because I can't help myself.

Sage crosses her legs, the slit in her dress parting so smoothly that it reveals most of her thigh, all the way up. My eyes follow the line of her leg—of course they do—and there's no mistaking it. It's an orchestrated move, the same one she tried last time. Disappointing.

I take the wineglass, needing something to do with my hands. The goblet is cool against my fingers as I lift it.

Sage's expression shifts momentarily, a flicker of something I can't quite read. I pause, the rim touching my bottom lip. "Everything okay?"

She blinks, and whatever I saw is gone. She reaches for her goblet as well. "Yes. Fine."

My glass goes back down onto the table, and I sheepishly spit my gum into my hand. So ladylike. I'm already off to a great start.

The door explodes inward, and Kora stands in the threshold, puffy-eyed and wild-haired, cheeks blotched red. Sage shrieks—a quick, animal sound—and then, "Kora, what the fuck are you doing?"

I jump out of my chair, but she's already crossed the room, standing between me and Sage with her hands clenched into furious little fists.

"You didn't answer my texts," she slurs with a cocktail of rage and heartbreak. "Why?"

Sage's shoulders tense. "Kora, I'm with someone—"

"No, you're not," she snaps, wagging a finger at me. "You're replacing me. That's what you're doing. Is she your new project now? You got tired of me because I screwed up, because I'm not good enough, so you…" Her face melts; she fights it.

Sage tries to keep her tone calm, but her hands tremble as she moves forward. "No one is replacing anyone, babe. You're acting crazy right now."

"I'm acting crazy?" Kora chokes up and her whole body trembles. "You haven't talked to me in days. I was your best friend. Now I'm nothing?"

My one wish in this moment: to be swallowed by the wallpaper. I have never been less equipped for a situation in my life, and that includes the time I got caught trying to shoplift tampons at a Walgreens. But Sage is a different animal; she switches seamlessly from attack mode to rescue and goes to Kora to fold her up, just like that, arms around her and face buried in her hair.

"Hey. Hey, I love you, okay? I love you, babe. Shh, shh." Sage rocks her softly, the way you would calm a panicked horse. Kora sobs into her dress, and the green silk darkens with salt and snot.

I try to be invisible, but Kora lashes out through the hair and fabric. "Do you love her?" She jabs a finger behind her head, straight at me. Her voice is twisted up with something ugly. "Do you love her more than me?"

Sage glances at me, then back at Kora. "What are you talking about?"

"Don't bullshit me. You wanted a new toy. That's what happens— every time." Kora sniffles. "Why can't it just be us?"

Sage doesn't answer right away. She keeps holding her and rocking, whispering, "You know I love you. Nothing changes that."

There's a long, wet silence. Kora's breath comes in sharp, broken gulps; her whole body is shuddering.

Sage pulls back and wipes away Kora's tears. "Babe, I'm so sorry. I should never have let you feel like that. I fucked up, okay? You're family. I love you. That never changes."

Kora wipes her nose with the back of her hand. She glances at me, cheeks bright scarlet. "I'm sorry," she mumbles.

"It's fine," I say, and mean it. If I move, my entire body might collapse like a pillar of salt.

Kora exhales a ragged breath and falls into the nearest chair like a marionette with cut strings.

Sage steps back. "Let me get you some tissues," she says and heads toward the bathroom, leaving the two of us alone in awkward silence.

Kora's eyes find me again, shame coloring her face. "I really am sorry."

I wave my hand as if to say, *No problems here.*

She looks at the wine. "Do you mind?" she asks. Before I can answer, she grabs it and starts drinking.

Sage emerges from the bathroom, a bunch of tissues in her hand. When she sees Kora with the wineglass on her lips, the sound that tears from her throat isn't human—it's primal, a cry of pure horror that sends a surge of cold through my veins.

"No! Don't!" Her voice is distorted, like in a nightmare.

She launches herself across the room as if she's been fired from a cannon. The tissues scatter everywhere as she swings her arm in a vicious arc, connecting with the goblet, which flies out of Kora's hand, sending wine and shards spraying across the wall in a violent splash. Kora cries out, recoiling from the explosion of glass so sharply that the chair tips over, sending her sprawling. I scramble along the wall to avoid the carnage.

"What the hell are you doing?" Kora gasps from the floor.

Sage is already on her, grabbing her head with both hands. The look on Sage's face—God, I've never seen anything like it. Wild. Unhinged. Like seeing someone's soul shatter.

"Did you drink it?!" she screams, her hands cradling Kora's head.

Tears stream down her face as she pats Kora's cheeks. Blood is seeping through the silk of her dress, turning it red, like the wine on the wall.

She's heaving now, with these awful, wrenching sobs that sound like they're being dragged from her throat, and she's turning even paler.

This isn't shock—it's terror. None of this makes sense, but one thing is brutally clear: Kora was never supposed to drink that wine.

"Sage," I say, strained, "what's going on?"

"Stay with me, babe," she mutters, tapping Kora's cheek—soft, then harder. "Stay with me, okay? Do you hear me?"

Kora's face shifts from confusion to dawning horror. "Did you do what I think you did?"

It's like I'm stuck in a fever dream of inside jokes.

Scrambling to her feet, Sage stumbles to the dresser. She snatches her phone, her voice tight and clipped. "This is Sage, Room 303. Code Nightingale. Repeat, Code Nightingale." She flings the phone onto the bed and collapses to the floor, pulling Kora's head onto her lap to resume her frantic rocking.

Kora closes her eyes and smirks.

"What the hell is a Code Nightingale?" I plead.

Kora is eerily calm, like she's already accepted something I can't grasp. "It's a medical emergency."

"What medical emergency?"

She looks at me, expressionless. "I've been poisoned."

The room folds in on itself like a carnival mirror. Sage presses desperate kisses to Kora's cheek, apologizing over and over through her sobs. Blood drips onto the carpet from the gash in her thigh. My thoughts are a useless jumble, a white noise of pure disbelief.

Kora cups Sage's face with one trembling hand. "Why, Shannon?"

The name—her private name—destroys something in Sage. She crumples like paper, curling into herself on the floor, keening.

Two enormous men in gray jackets, like rhinos, fill the doorway, bags in hand. Sage doesn't look up, just points a shaking finger toward Kora. They slide over to her, one checking her vitals while the other prepares something I can't see. Within seconds, they've lifted her between them and are carrying her out.

"Wait—" I start, but they're already gone.

The room falls silent except for Sage's broken breathing. She's still curled on the floor, blood pooling beneath her leg.

I should do something. I don't move.

"Was that supposed to be me?"

SAGE HASN'T SAID A WORD, hasn't moved. She's still curled on the floor, the split of her dress soaked through with blood, mixing with the wine on the carpet. Her braid has completely unraveled and her makeup is streaked and muddled. She looks like a Renaissance painting that's been left out in the rain.

The candle on the table casts shadows that dance across the wreckage, and her entire body heaves with each sob. The impulse to run, to scream, surges within me, then dies, leaving only numbness behind.

"You were going to poison me?"

She flinches, and her breath comes in shuddering gulps, as if she's drowning above water.

"Yes." The word cuts me like another piece of broken glass.

There has to be more—but she's struggling to find it. Her lips part with no sound, and fresh tears spill down her cheeks.

The wall holds my weight as I slide down to the floor, knees up. A rivulet of wine dribbles down my leg.

"Natalia ordered this?" The question seems absurd.

"Not exactly."

Aghast really doesn't begin to adequately describe my state of mind. "Not...exactly?"

"Natalia knew." She sniffles. "That you were Cinderella. She told me to handle it."

"Handle it how?"

"She didn't say." Sage's head drops. "But I couldn't let her investigate."

"Why not?"

"Because she'd dig. And she'd find the logs." She's rambling, the words spilling out of her. "This was the second time. Natalia wouldn't forgive that. Not twice. She'd know I lied, and then—" Her breath hitches. "We'd be done. Not fired. Done."

"Sage." I cut through her spiral. "Slow down. What are you talking about?"

She looks up at me, eyes bloodshot. "Kora."

"You said second time. What's the second time?"

"Melody. And Sparrow."

"Sparrow? What about her?"

"She died two years ago on assignment. Kora vouched for her, pushed her into it, said she was ready. It went bad." Her voice cracks. "Natalia never forgot. Gave her one last chance. Kora's been on borrowed time ever since."

Just like Melody. Everything locks into focus, sharp and awful.

"They're both dead. Kora's little Sisters." Sage wipes her cheeks, heaving for breath. "If Natalia found out, Kora would be blamed. She'd be handled."

"So, you covered for her."

Sage nods furiously. "I signed the ledger and took responsibility. Natalia thinks I'm to blame."

"You protected her?"

"Yes," she says, like the word costs her everything. "If Natalia knows I lied—that we both lied—" She shakes her head.

"So, when Natalia told you to handle it…"

"I panicked." Her voice is hollow. "If she found out…about Kora…"

"And you thought murder was easier?"

"I thought—" She collapses into herself, sobbing. "I thought if you were just gone, the problem would go away. No investigation. No questions. No discovery. Kora would be safe. I'd be safe. It was the only way."

Sage crumbles, shoulders curling inward like she's trying to disappear into herself.

"What now?" I ask.

She wipes her face, but it only gets dirtier. "I don't know. Natalia will find out what happened." More sobbing. "And Kora. God, Kora."

"Is she going to die?"

"No." The word comes out fierce, desperate. "No, they're good. They'll save her. They have to." The tremor in her words betrays the doubt. The not knowing.

"You've lost her anyway," I say.

Sage nods, tears sliding silently down her cheeks. "I've lost everything." She wipes at the blood on her leg. "Natalia won't forgive this. A messy attempt, betrayal, medical involved… I'm done."

"Maybe being done is what you need."

She says nothing.

We sit in the wreckage of her room, her perfect space, her imperfect plan. The candle has burned lower, wax pooling on the table. Outside, there are sirens in the distance. Maybe for Kora. Maybe not. The city doesn't care about our personal calamities.

Sage shifts and my legs tense, but she's just turning to face me. Raw and real and stripped of everything. She looks at me, wanting to say something, but I don't give her the chance.

"I can't look at you right now," I say, and her head falls back to the floor as she heaves into the rug.

Pulling myself up, glass grinds under the heels of my boots. The woman who'd rather kill me than risk expulsion from this fucked-up cult lies in a heap at my feet. This is what the Family does. It turns people into weapons without regard for who they're aimed at.

I step over the destruction and walk out the door, leaving her to drown in who she's chosen to become.

Twenty Seven

This ceiling has been my whole world for hours, the scene in Sage's room replaying on a loop, each pass making it harder to believe any of this is real.

Three gentle taps on my door, hesitant. No need to guess who it is. The first instinct—to throw something—gives way to the second. Hauling myself off the bed, I cross the room and open up.

Sage is a wreck. Her hair hangs limp around her face, eyes swollen, black rings beneath them. My eyes wander from the plain gray sweatshirt to the black shorts, then the haphazard bandage on her thigh. Dressed down like this, she isn't a princess any longer, but a regular college girl after hell week.

Her mouth opens, but only a short, broken sound falls out. Down the hall, two Sisters peek around the corner, pointing and chattering. Just perfect—an audience for my attempted murder reunion tour.

"Get in." The last thing I need is to be part of any more Family gossip.

She slips inside, keeping her distance like I might lunge at her. Fair assumption, honestly. After closing the door, I lean against it, arms crossed.

"What are you doing here?"

Instead of answering, Sage stands in the middle of my room, looking lost. There are more bandages wrapped around her shaking right hand.

The silence lingers until I can't take it anymore. "Is Kora okay?"

"They pumped her stomach." She sobs. "Stable, but they're keeping her overnight for observation." She takes a shuddering breath. "She won't talk to me."

"I can't imagine why."

Sage flinches like I've slapped her. "I deserve that."

"You deserve a hell of a lot worse," I snap. "You tried to kill me."

"I know what I did." The bed sags as she drops onto it.

"Do you?" I push off from the door but keep my distance. "Tell me, is it quick? That poison? Or was I supposed to suffer?"

Tears spill down her cheeks. "Just...sleep. That's all."

"Just sleep." The words twist into a bitter laugh. "What was the plan after I passed out? Throw me off a balcony? Or watch me die and then go get a fucking manicure?"

Her breath comes in desperate gasps, but she doesn't move.

"Forgiveness isn't on the table, by the way." Pacing to the window and back is the only thing keeping me from exploding while Sage stares blankly into her lap. "Say something! You were going to kill me to save Kora—how does that make sense?"

She wipes her runny nose with her sleeve, and it's such an un-Sage-like gesture that it momentarily throws me off. "It wasn't just about Kora... You have to stop." There's a fragility to her, as though she'll shatter with the slightest touch.

"Stop what?"

Her hands play with the cuffs of her sweatshirt as she rocks on the bed. She looks at me with pleading eyes. "The questions. The poking into things. You don't get it. I can't let it happen again."

"Again? What are you talking about?"

"My life! Everything I've built here." Her volume rises with each word. "You're going to destroy it. Take it away from me. I can't go back to being nothing. And you—"

Spittle flies from her mouth as she points at me with a shaking finger. "You're exactly the same. The questions, the notebook, that look in your eyes, thinking you can fix what isn't broken."

The tendons in my neck pull taut, and a cool shiver rises up my back as I fight to keep calm. "The same?"

She ignores my question and steers directly into hysteria. "You were going to do it! Take it away. I can't go back, Star!" Her hands slam onto the mattress. "I can't fucking go back! Why can't you leave things be?! Why are you just like her?!"

I dart over and grip her shoulders to calm her down. "Like who, Sage?"

Bloodshot eyes, manic and horrified, bore into mine. "Nova."

The name drops between us like a falling bomb.

Her head sinks. She inhales slowly and exhales through pursed lips.

"When you first got here, I didn't see a new recruit. I saw a ghost." Her eyes flick back to mine. "I saw Nova's little sister."

I wait for her to take it back, to say it's just a joke.

"You…you knew?"

Her chin is trembling again. The mania has faded into despondency.

"She was my friend, Star. I saw her fight this place and almost destroy it. Destroy me. Destroy herself. And then you show up with the same notebook and the same fire. And I could see it happening all over again."

There's a strange buzzing sensation in my head, not quite a tremor but more subtle—like my nervous system is quietly rerouting itself around this new information.

"I tried everything," she continues, raspy and raw. "Became your Big Sister, thinking I could guide you, keep you away from the rabbit holes Nova fell down. Tried to be your friend." A glance at my face, then away, as if she can't hold eye contact. "I saw the way you looked at me and thought I could use that to keep you close. To control you."

A fresh heat rises up my neck. Not anger, but humiliation. My pathetic schoolgirl crush. She'd seen it, dissected it, and tried to weaponize it. I wasn't someone she was interested in; I was a problem with a simple solution. The burn runs all the way to the tips of my ears. What a fool I am.

Oblivious to my shame, she throws her hands up. "But nothing worked. You kept slipping the leash. You have the same infuriating need to know. That drive. You kept digging about Melody, and then Cinderella…" She shakes her head and a tear breaks free, landing on my leg.

The muscles in my throat contract, and a part of my heart breaks —not for who she is, but for who I wanted her to be.

"I couldn't let it happen again." She cradles her head with both hands. "When Nova fought back, everything fell apart. Girls got hurt. Sparrow died. The whole place nearly collapsed." She sniffles. "I can't go back."

"So, you 'handled' it?"

"I tried to. I thought I had no other choice."

We sit in silence, trading breaths.

"She played us both," I say.

Sage looks up, confused.

"Natalia. She knew what you'd do. Knew you'd break yourself into pieces trying to stop me. She wanted to test your loyalty, see if you were willing to become a killer. Is that who you are, Sage?"

"I don't fucking know anymore!" Her cry is punctuated by the flat *thump* of her fists against her thighs. "I don't know what to do."

And here it is—my opening.

A violent cocktail of hate and pity churns in my gut, but getting out of this place means I need her. She knows the weaknesses, she has the access, and trying to take this place down without her is impossible. I could let her live with her own choices, but there's no time to process right or wrong. She's broken. Useful. It has to be now.

"I do."

Her head snaps up.

"We burn it all down," I say. "We take Natalia out."

Sage stares. "That's ridiculous. She's untouchable."

"No one's untouchable." I move closer. "And you know every weak spot in this organization."

"She'd kill us both."

"You're almost a murderer already. What's left to lose?"

She rises and walks to the window. "You don't understand. This is all I have. Without it, I'm nothing. I can't go back—"

"Bullshit." I stand beside her. "The Family is what's keeping you trapped. It's what made you this way."

"I can't go back."

"If Natalia tosses you out, you'll be back on the street. At least this way, you'll have a chance to set your own path."

We lock eyes in the window's reflection, and the broken soldier gives way to the petrified girl underneath.

"Be free, Shannon."

The sound of her name makes her flinch. "I don't even know who Shannon is anymore."

"Let's find out," I challenge. "Help me do this, and we both get our lives back."

Doubt crosses her face as she shakes her head. "Why do you even want my help? After what I did?"

"Don't mistake this for forgiveness." I glare at her. "But you're the only person here who can do this, and I'm not stupid enough to try it without you."

Turning away, she runs her hands over her arms and walks in little circles, sniffling as her focus darts around the room.

"I need you." The words are bitter, wrong and true all at once. "And you need me. Because your plan to save yourself is lying in a hospital bed deciding whether to ever speak to you again. You didn't solve a problem. You became one. I'm not the one you need to worry about anymore."

Sage stops her frantic pacing and stares out the window, her back to me. The silence stretches, and her breathing settles down. When she turns back, her face is focused and aware.

"If we do this, there's no going back. For either of us."

"Would you want to go back?"

Her shoulders slump with a weary sigh. "You won't throw me to the wolves when this is over?"

"We protect each other," I say. "That's the deal. You follow my lead."

A long, shaky breath shudders out of her like a final surrender, and she accepts. "Okay."

"All right," I agree, not offering my hand to shake. The wound is too fresh.

"I don't understand how you think we can do this alone," she says.

"We're not alone."

TWENTY EIGHT

We've been in Jeremy's office for the past hour while Aura offered to clean Sage's room. The precious look of appreciation Sage gave Aura prompted a mental note: *That girl deserves some new shoes.*

"How long have you been planning this?" Sage asks, folding her arms.

All the time we've spent bringing her up to speed about Melody's journal, the secret folder, and Natalia sending secrets to Russia—and this is her first question. Not disbelief. Not panic. Logistics.

"Not planning. More like...staying afloat," I say with a shaky breath.

Sage listened to everything without flinching and stared at the floor as if it all confirmed something she'd long suspected. In her sycophantic devotion to this place, she'd chosen to simply overlook the parts that made her uncomfortable.

Kora is going to live, but no one knows if there will be any aftereffects. Jeremy intercepted the medical report and rewrote the reason for the Code Nightingale into a plausible *alcohol overdose*. It bought us time, and right now, time is oxygen.

"So, what's the play with Natalia? She wanted me 'handled,' so why would she accept less?" I ask.

Sage turns to me, and the strategic lieutenant is back. "Because my clean exit turned into a Nightingale circus."

I look at her with snide disappointment. "Clean exit?"

She sighs lightly. "I didn't mean it that way. I'm sorry."

I cluck my tongue and scribble in my notebook.

"Look," she says, leaning forward. "That mess, the gossip—Natalia hates that more than failure. It creates questions. So, I give her a solution that makes the questions go away."

"And that is?"

"Tell her the pressure worked. You're in shambles—my personal project, leashed and declawed. She gets control without the liability of a body. It's clean, it gives her the win, and for Natalia, that's everything."

Jeremy looks at her. "What if she doesn't bite?"

"Then we're on borrowed time," Sage says.

The hem of my skirt frays from my picking at it. "There's one more thing."

They both turn to me. Surprise flashes across Jeremy's face—which makes sense, since I haven't run this past him.

"We need to tell Caron."

I hold my breath, waiting for their reactions—it takes an eternity. They stare at me like I've suggested we invite Natalia for brunch to discuss treason over mimosas.

Sage, who had been folding her arms, lets them drop to her sides.

"No," she says sharply. "Absolutely not. Are you insane?"

"He's the top of the food chain, Star," Jeremy adds. "He's not on our side. I don't think he has a side."

"We talked the other day, before everything went to hell." I pick at a ragged cuticle. "About Amelia."

Jeremy's forehead wrinkles, but he stays quiet.

"I'm telling you, he was different. The way he spoke about her wasn't a performance. He looked sincere."

"Star, he's had decades to perfect that act," Sage says, her tone gentle. "It's how he reels everyone in."

"Maybe. But I don't think he knows what Natalia's doing. He talked about the Family like it was something better."

Sage rolls her eyes. "He's not senile. He's directing the whole thing."

"I don't think so." My certainty is a surprise. "This isn't the sort of thing you can bribe away, right? Why would he risk losing everything he's built? How does Caron benefit from betraying the country? Money? He's already got more than he could ever spend."

My palms rub against my knees. "He's not even Russian; it doesn't add up. Amelia trusted him once, and I'm following her thread."

Sage's lips flatten, and she sighs.

"Gut instinct is risky." Jeremy scratches his nose. "However, Natalia went to extreme lengths to hide these transactions. Everything else—blackmail, intel, corporate espionage—that's all visible in the system."

"Your point?" Sage snipes.

"Why go to this trouble if Caron was on board?" Jeremy turns his screen to us, showing a web of data flows. "Why hide *only* this?"

Sage crosses her arms. "Plausible deniability. She's protecting him."

"Possibly," Jeremy concedes, pushing up his glasses. "But there's enough in plain view to put everyone away for a century. Only hiding the Russian intel would be unusual if he were in on it."

Sage opens her mouth, then shuts it. She grabs a pencil from the desk and fidgets with it.

"Because he wouldn't approve," I say. "This crosses a line even for him."

Sage looks between us, her face pale. "So, what then? We waltz into his office and announce his right hand is a traitor?"

"No," I say. "We show him proof."

Jeremy swallows. "It's not proof. More like very suspicious evidence."

"It just has to be enough to make him doubt her," I counter.

"It's not," Sage says with a finality that sinks me.

"Agreed," Jeremy says. "We need more than this to go to Caron."

I drop my head into my hands and try to run this over again in my mind. "Why can't you copy the files when she opens the folder?"

"I could, but her computer will show the copy activity. If she notices it, she might realize she's been compromised and—"

His face goes slack, his eyes unfocused and staring into the distance. His fingers don't stop, though. They dance over the keyboard while his mouth moves, tapping out the silent commands he's writing in his head. This is the wizard conjuring his magic.

Sage starts to say something, but I grab her hand, shaking my head. *Don't break the spell.*

A moment later, he blinks, and his focus is back. A slow smile spreads across his face. "Unless I don't execute the copy through her account, and I do it with a system daemon and no user-facing notifications."

I exchange a look with Sage. "English, please."

He's almost smiling. "I can hide a program payload as a macro in a normal file. When she opens it, as long as she has the protected folder unlocked, it'll silently copy the contents over. No trace."

"Like a virus?" Sage asks.

"Not a virus. Think of it as a Trojan horse. The file itself is real—a financial report, something she'll expect. But when she brings it inside the gates, so to speak, and opens it, the code I've hidden inside will get to work and copy the files."

Sage nods. Does she actually understand, or is she just playing along?

"Great," she says. "We can email it to her."

Jeremy's demeanor sinks. "The file can't be emailed. The scanner will flag it for malicious code."

"The scanner you wrote," I remind him. "That's twice now."

He gives a weak chuckle. "The file has to be opened on her computer, by her, while she has the protected folder unlocked."

"No pressure, then?"

"I can do it," Sage says. "She wanted to discuss an account overage. I'll use that as a pretext."

Jeremy bounces a little in his chair. "Okay, great. I can give you a USB key with the file. As soon as she's unlocked the folder, I'll message you. Get her to open the file within two minutes—the sooner, the better."

"Why two minutes?" I ask.

"That's how long we have before the authorization expires and the folder locks again."

"Okay, I'll do it," she agrees.

"Let me get to work." Jeremy spins to his keyboard.

I release Sage's hand, and my palm is damp. So much for staying cool.

IN THE BACK room of the Step-Sister safe house, Andromeda sits at the main table, while Luna leans against the wall, and Vega types on a laptop in the corner. The clacking keys are the only sound.

Andromeda looks up as we enter. "What have you got for me?"

"Unfortunately, not as much as we'd like," Jeremy says, opening his laptop. "Her access patterns indica—"

"Patterns?" Andromeda cuts him off. "I don't need patterns. I need proof. Something concrete."

"It's not that simple," he explains. "I'm handcuffed until she accesses the protected folders. We're getting pieces but—"

"No smoking gun," she finishes, slamming her palm on the table. "You two are on the inside. You have access we've been trying to get for years, and you still have nothing?"

A hot flash washes over my face. After everything we've risked, she acts like we aren't trying.

"We can just walk away right now," I say sharply. "Go back home and you can figure this shit out on your own."

The room goes still. Vega stops typing, and Luna looks up. Jeremy cringes.

Andromeda's eyes narrow. I've made a terrible mistake.

Then the corner of her mouth twitches.

"You sound just like her."

"Like who?" I ask, and then it hits me.

"God, I miss that fire," Andromeda says, her tone calmer. "I'm expecting you to be her, and that's not fair. Not yet."

"Thanks," I say. "We have some good news, though."

She sits forward, curiosity replacing frustration. "Like?"

I take a breath. "We've got Sage on board."

The statement lands in silence. Andromeda's face goes slack.

Luna breaks it with a sharp bark. "There's no way you flipped Sage. Perfect soldier Sage? No way." She crosses her arms, looking to Andromeda for confirmation.

Andromeda doesn't speak, but her eyes say she doesn't believe me either.

My cheeks burn with the familiar sting of being doubted. Fine. The burner phone lands on the table between us with a thud, and I tap on the screen.

It rings twice before connecting.

"Hello?" Sage's voice is cautious.

"Sorry to call you this way, Sage. Jeremy and I need you to say hi to someone."

Luna leans forward, her tone laced with suspicion. "I'm supposed to believe this is really Sage?"

A pause stretches on the other end. Then, "Violet, is that you? I had no idea you'd joined Step-Sister."

The name hangs in the air like smoke. Luna's face drains of color, and Andromeda clutches the table. No one says a word. Luna's lower lip shakes, and she rushes from the room.

"Thanks, Sage. Talk soon." I end the call.

"Well, that was unexpected," Vega quips.

I turn my head to follow Luna out. "Is she okay?"

"They were pretty close but had a falling-out." Andromeda offers a wry smile. "She'll get over it."

Vega takes her sunglasses off. "How?"

Andromeda's smile widens as she leans the chair back, the front legs leaving the ground. "If you just pulled this off...you changed the entire game."

"It's a long story. But do me a favor and I'll forget you doubted us." I grin.

"And that is?"

"We need a new blog post. Something to make Natalia panic."

"Bait?"

I nod. "Make it sound like Cinderella's been cut loose. She was charming, but pumpkins rot. Time for a fresh voice."

"Sounds good. Natalia's jumpy. Paranoid about leaks."

"Exactly. She'll waste resources chasing ghosts."

"We'll get it out tonight," Andromeda says.

"One more thing?" I ask sheepishly.

"Yes?"

"There was an old blog post. Well, it was deleted, but we found a version of it and—"

"Entry thirteen," she says, flat and emotionless.

"Yes," I answer. "It was never republished on the new server. Why?"

Vega and Andromeda share a glance. Jeremy and I do the same.

A shadow passes over Andromeda's face. The floorboards creak as she hoists herself from the chair and crosses the room to an old filing cabinet. Reaching inside the top drawer, she pulls something out, returns to the desk, and tosses a weathered notebook onto the surface. It lands with a soft thump.

"Because that post is the reason your sister is dead," she says.

A sickening slurry of fear, pain, and sadness blends in my stomach.

"She wrote it," Andromeda continues, "and it was going to be her final move. Her last effort to expose Natalia."

My lip trembles. "What happened?"

"Truth be told, I don't know the details. We'd moved locations just a week prior after we'd been burglarized. Nova stayed back to finish up, and we assume Natalia learned about the post, about our location, and took it all down."

Blinking away tears, I turn to Jeremy with a silent plea: *Please don't have anything to do with this.*

He reads my expression and shakes his head. "I know nothing about that. It's not in any of the reports. If it was Natalia, she must have used someone from outside. Untraceable."

His ignorance isn't the comfort I'd hoped it would be.

"The whole place was trashed, every computer taken, and Nova was nowhere to be found." She gestures at the notebook. "There was a hidden spot where we kept things. This was inside. She must have known what was happening and stashed it. We never saw her again."

My fingers hover over the cover—Amelia's notebook. The worn cardboard is solid under my hand—the last genuine piece of her I might ever touch.

"That's everything she worked on," Andromeda says. "In the Family and here. Entry thirteen was the last thing she ever wrote. We were offline for months afterward, trying to rebuild."

Opening it sends years of missing her crashing into me all at once. Her cramped, angled handwriting. Meeting minutes, client notes, long passages, and doodles in the margins. My finger glides over an indent where she'd pressed the pen hard, imagining her here—alive, breathing, real.

I hand it to Jeremy, unable to read it right away. "Scan every page."

"When we rebuilt the blog, we made a choice," Andromeda continues. "We didn't want to lose anyone else. We fight a different way now. With survivors, not martyrs."

"Thank you."

She's given me more than a notebook. She's given me a purpose.

And a lot of fuel to get a fire started.

A FREIGHT TRAIN of rage slams through me, sending me pacing between the spring riders and the slide. My hands shake, and the tang of blood fills my mouth from biting my cheek. The playground at 110th Street is barren, but the swings creak in the wind, chains dancing like spirits.

"She killed her," I say for what must be the fifth time. "Natalia murdered my sister, and I'm supposed to what—play nice?"

Jeremy stands next to a bench, holding out his phone. Sage's voice comes through the speaker, tinny but clear.

"Star, listen to me," she says. "I get it. I do. But charging into HQ like some avenging angel is exactly what she'd want."

"I'm going to kill her." The words come out flat, certain. "Tonight. I'll walk into her office and—"

"And what? Strangle her with your bare hands?" Sage says, dripping with sarcasm. "Very strategic. I'm sure that'll go well."

"I don't care."

"Yes, you do." Jeremy steps closer, phone between us. "You care about Melody. About the other girls. About—"

"They're all dead!" My chest heaves. "Just like Amelia."

"Listen to me," Sage says, her tone shifting. "Natalia is no joke. You won't get within ten feet of her."

"So I die trying."

"Christ, Star." Sage exhales sharply. "You think that's what Amelia would want? Her baby sister bleeding out on Natalia's marble floor?"

She's right, and it hits like a splash of ice water. My knees can't hold me upright, and I drop onto the bench.

"You think I don't want justice?" Sage continues. "Melody was my friend too. But revenge isn't justice, and suicide isn't heroic—it's just stupid."

Jeremy sits down next to me, phone still in hand. "Star, your sister didn't fight so you could follow her into a grave. She was trying to expose the truth."

"And look how that worked out for her."

"She was building a case," he says. "Be smart about it. Patient. You can pick up where she left off."

My teeth grind together, and the rage still seethes inside, but something else eases its way in. Logic. Strategy. They're right, and I hate it.

"Amelia would want you to win," he says. "Not just strike back."

My balled fists pound into my knees. "I want to destroy her."

"Then do it right," Sage's voice crackles. "Make it stick. Natalia's survived this long because people underestimate her. Don't be the next person on that list."

"Fine," I grumble. "But when we burn her down, I want to be the one holding the match."

Natalia Czarina

Natalia stepped into Pristine Waters, the exclusive day spa hidden on the thirty-ninth floor of a Midtown high-rise. The hushed waterfall in the corner cast its mist over river stones. Orchids bloomed from recessed shelves, and the air was filled with sandalwood and lavender.

She hated all of it. But some pain required regular attention.

Before walking in, she'd received an intelligence update that confirmed her fears. She barely remembered the Sister who'd installed the tracker—a false defector sent over months ago for this specific purpose. And now, that investment had flagged a critical threat. Nova was planning another blog post. A big one that would compromise everything. And it was going live tonight.

Shut her down, or shut her up?

The decision sat in her chest like a debt coming due.

"Ms. Czarina, wonderful to see you again," the receptionist said with deference.

Natalia nodded once. "Ana is ready?"

"Yes, suite three."

She followed the stone path to her room, methodically removing her jewelry—diamond studs, gold Cartier watch, two rings—placing each piece in the small velvet pouch she kept in her handbag. She undressed with military precision, and the cool air caressed her skin as she lay face down on the heated table, arranging herself beneath the crisp white sheet.

Temporary solutions often bred permanent problems. She'd learned that in Moscow, watching her father's colleagues vanish for half measures. How many *comrades* had she met for dinner and then never seen again?

The door opened.

"Good afternoon," Ana said.

Natalia didn't respond. This was their understanding: No small talk. Just hands doing what they were paid handsomely to do. Ana wasn't an acquaintance; she was a tool.

Ana's fingers pressed into Natalia's shoulders. The tension there had solidified into pebbles beneath the skin. As the pressure increased, her mind drifted.

Taking Nova offline would be surgical. A hack, maybe—wipe the servers, destroy the infrastructure, scatter her meager network of rebels.

But Nova was smart. She'd have backups. Contingencies. The blog would resurface like a hydra, heads multiplying.

Ana's thumbs dug deep into the tight cords of muscle along her shoulder blades, a precise, disciplinary pressure. A flash of controlled pain, and the fragrance of sandalwood in the air soured, morphing into the pungent bouquet of the old state-run gymnasium and its decades of little girls' sweat. She stood at the barre, foot pointed in an exquisite arabesque while the elderly teacher's cane rapped time against the hardwood floor. "You are rushing, Nadia Czarina."

Her father had enrolled her at three. By seven, she could pirouette until Moscow dissolved into a blur of windows and light. Even then, she'd felt superior to the soft girls with their dreams of prettiness and western materialism. She heard it sometimes from the others, from the grown-ups at home: *prodigy.*

No. She pushed the memory back, forced her mind to the present crisis. Nova. The choice.

But the memories wouldn't cooperate.

Ana's hands moved lower, working across Natalia's shoulder blades in firm, sweeping motions.

"Deeper pressure here?" Ana asked.

"Yes."

Her father's face appeared as Ana worked into the muscle. His stillness. The rare times he sat rigid in full uniform on a cold steel folding chair while she danced, never applauding. His flat smile amid the scent of unfiltered cigarettes and gun oil stood as a silent coronation. But afterward, his palm on her head: *"Молодец, маленькая женщина."* *Well done, little woman.* It was enough—it was everything.

What would he tell her now?

Weakness invites attack, Nadi. You know this.

The heat of the table spread through her body as Ana's hands glided along her spine.

The sheet shifted, and it felt like the stiff corner of a linen napkin, the ones her mother had taught her to fold into swans. *Charm is a virtue, darling. Men love a mystery, but not an assassin.*

That memory faded quickly, replaced by the cool, grooved steel of a Makarov pistol's grip, its heft solid and serious on the kitchen table. Her father nodding as she reassembled the firing pin with the delicate touch of a watchmaker. Her mother's lips pressed tight, witnessing her daughter choose a side.

She'd chosen then. She could choose now.

Tools or weapons, Nadi. Everybody is one or the other.

Another solution presented its cold logic to her. One decisive action. Tonight. Neutralize the liability.

But this was Nova, Caron's pet project. He'd never admit the depth of the attachment, but it'd been apparent since the girl had arrived broken and starving years ago. One of the many strays the old man brought in but failed to housetrain. She had been brilliant, promising even—until she discovered a conscience. If she were to be put down, there could be no loose ends for him to connect, no trail leading back.

Ana's hands moved to Natalia's right leg, working down from hamstring to ankle, and the memory came as sharp and uninvited as Ana's deep tissue pressure—a Friday evening, the recital. She'd leapt from the stage's lip, meant for a grand jeté, but the slick of her own sweat on the polished wood stage splintered every intention. Tibia. Spiral fracture.

Her breath hitched.

"Too much?" Ana asked.

"No, continue."

Months in a cast. Glaring from the window of their seventh-floor flat as other children played. Burning at the unfairness. Ballet stolen from her forever.

Stop. She didn't need this distraction. Not now. But the ache lingered. It lived inside her, nestled in the space that the girl who loved to dance once occupied. Natalia swallowed to suppress the twinge and recalled how she had redirected her discipline.

Education became her new barre, every test a recital to be flawlessly performed. She finished high school two years early, and on graduation night, as Moscow spun in a drunken summer of change, her father poured her a single shot of vodka. His voice was rougher than the whiskers on his face. "Are you ready for the world now, Nadi?" It was a challenge. She met his gaze and downed the vodka in one swallow.

"Turn over, please," Ana said, intruding on the memory.

Natalia flipped onto her back, settling onto the warm table as Ana worked along her legs and up to her hips.

Her thoughts wandered to Moscow and Lomonosov University. Her mother crying with joy when she was accepted. She'd relished the game with her professors—a war of points and praise. The calculus of ranking herself above the slackers and the lazy beauties. Nights alternated between studies and the shooting range. Running track at dawn, pushing her body until it threatened revolt. The library at 3 a.m., languages stacking like ammunition. English for opportunity, French for seduction, Arabic for strategy.

Every skill a weapon. Every weakness eliminated.

Nova's weakness was sentiment. Her righteous anger and the need to save the lost lambs made her predictable. Targetable.

Ana dug into her arms, kneading away the tension, and for a moment, Natalia could almost feel her father's hands. The ones that typed the letters she still kept inside a strongbox: *They cannot break you unless you let them. Never show them your tears until you need to. Remember who you are and what has been sacrificed for you.* The advice was her armor, and at the bottom of each page, the single handwritten word was a crack in his own: *папочка—Daddy.*

Ana applied pressure to her trapezius, and it wasn't pain that blossomed there so much as a familiar, heavy feeling across her shoulders. She carried a similar feeling on her graduation day, her father's voice shaky with rare emotion. "Now, you are ready for the world, Nadi. Make it yours."

And she had. With every calculated step, every decision, every manipulation, she had carved her place. *She'd lost ballet. She'd found a purpose.*

The choice crystallized.

Half measures were for those who couldn't stomach the cost of power.

Ana's hands stilled. "We're finished, Ms. Czarina."

Natalia opened her eyes, returning fully to the present—to the waterfall sounds and lavender air she despised. "Same time next week." It wasn't a question.

She rose, wrapped a towel around herself, and headed toward the showers. Along the way, she stopped to grab her handbag. Taking her phone out, she typed the message.

Then sent it.

Some pain required permanent correction.

Twenty Nine

Amelia's notebook. It's almost like holding a piece of her soul. Jeremy dropped it off a few minutes ago, saying nothing, just a half smile and a nod.

Now it's me and her words. The cover is worn where her hands once held it, the edges soft from use. Five years of emptiness and now this—proof she existed beyond my memories.

"Let's see what you had to say, sis."

The notebook is classic Amelia—organized chaos. Client notes bleed into personal thoughts. Sprawling paragraphs are interrupted by doodles. Some pages have neat bullet points; others are frantic scribbles that crawl up the margins. Flipping slowly, savoring each page, I notice an entry in faded ink.

I never had a father, not one I cared about. My real one walked out on me and Esther when we were kids. I check on her from time to time but can't bring myself to see her. Soon, I keep telling myself, when I get my life back in order.

I think I'm getting closer to that. I'm 21 now and joined a group I think I fit in with. I can't say what we do in case Mom reads this someday, but it's safe, and it's good for now. The old man who runs the show here has taken a liking to me. I don't know why, but he's funny, and I like talking to him. He tells me stories about his younger days in the city, and it's real crazy ~~shit~~ stuff. Like gangsters and everything. We sit up nights sometimes and play canasta. It's a dumb European card game he loves. I suck at it and barely understand it, but he plays with me anyway. I think he likes the company. And truthfully, so do I.

Caron wasn't lying. They had a relationship. They played cards and told stories. Like Jeremy said, he trusted her, and she liked him. What happened?

Laughing at the crossed-out curse word conjures visions of when Mom would chastise us when we swore. Even in her private journal, Amelia couldn't help but edit herself.

More pages flip past: her first week in the Family, client nerves, doubts about the work. Small things, but they add up. Then—

Sparrow.

Her name is circled. An arrow points to one word scrawled in all caps: DEAD.

Below that is a list. Dozens of names. Initials. Locations. A page alive with arrows and cross-outs and panic.

I press my palm against my mouth, trying to steady my breathing.

In the margins, there's a phrase: *Elegant Leverage.* I have no idea what it means, but something about it makes my skin crawl.

Some of these entries read like she was losing her grip on reality. The handwriting gets messier, the thoughts more fragmented. What happened to her?

The last entry in the older, faded ink appears just a few pages later. It's short.

I know me and the old man don't get along anymore like we used to, but I can't imagine he's okay with what's going on. I think Nat's playing him. I'd go to him directly, but I don't think he'd believe me now. Not after what I did. Still, if all this blows up—I hope he's not caught in it.

What does she mean by *"what I did"*?

Step-Sister?

Turning the notebook over, I open it from the back and swipe past a couple of pages until I see it. The missing blog entry scribbled out in shaky handwriting.

Blog Entry #13

Time to Bring it Down

Let's get this out of the way: The Family isn't an escort

service. It's an intelligence operation disguised as luxury companionship.

They don't just sell sex—they harvest information, manipulate powerful men, and ruin lives with a wink and a kiss. The beautiful girls, the designer clothes, the illusion of seduction—packaging for the actual product: intimate access and elegant leverage.

I watched them turn a girl from Wisconsin into a honeypot operative with nothing but a vial and a smile. "Just slip it into his drink, sweetie." She cried for three days after. Then they gave her some diamonds and told her she was special.

The girls they find are already broken—homeless, desperate, or running from something worse. They offer salvation through transformation. A new name. A new wardrobe. A new family. Then they erase them, turn them into perfect anonymous weapons: Special Assets.

Sex and secrets are yesterday's news. Today, it's compromise. Classified intel. Corporate espionage. Political blackmail. Not escorts—weapons leased to the highest bidder. The Chinese, Saudis, Russians, Wall Street psychopaths.

To the old man, if you ever read this, I want to believe you didn't know. But if you did—if you let her use us this way—you don't get to call it a Family anymore.

I'm done being quiet; it's time to be loud. To blow it up, to bring it down. And if I go down alongside, then so be it.

—Your Step-Sister

The words warp as my tears hit the page. *Classified intel. Corporate espionage. Political blackmail.*

Special Assets.

Amelia knew everything. She saw it all and went nuclear instead of strategic. Why did she call out Caron directly? Why didn't she wait? Build a case? Find allies?

Because she was furious and couldn't stand watching them turn girls into weapons for one more day. She didn't have the mistakes of others marking the path for her.

Like she left for me.

My finger runs along her words: *If I go down alongside, then so be it.*

I have to be stronger. For her and Melody, for Jeremy and Sage.

I riffle through the pages of the notebook, leaning down to inhale the musty scent of paper and ink. And when the doodle flashes by in the margin of a page, absurd and beautiful, my heart does that flutter thing.

A chicken. In a cape. Holding a sword.

Prince Eggward the Third.

Written beneath him: *He Lives!*

"You remembered." My throat closes, but a sob claws its way out. Somewhere underneath all the scribbled notes and scrambled clues about the Family, my sister was still there—still the girl who made up stories with me about magical chickens and talking sandwiches until Mom yelled at us to be quiet. Our secret language, our shared universe. The doodle is like a message across time: *I'm still here, Sprout.*

I put the notebook in my lap and close my eyes.

I'm wearing the cape now.

There are two truths: Amelia wanted to save these girls from becoming weapons for the Family, and Caron wanted to save me from Amelia's fate.

It's the same story, told from different sides of a broken mirror.

I'll find out what happened, I promise. I'll follow this all the way down into the dark, where the real truth lives.

FOAMY TOOTHPASTE SWIRLS down the sink drain. My electric toothbrush buzzes against my molars, the vibration oddly soothing— like a tiny sander whittling away at my anxiety. A few hours' sleep had been a mercy, and I'm thankful for it.

Sage tried to kill me. Now we're allies, sort of. She'll maintain Natalia's trust while we try to take her down from the inside. It's a fragile arrangement built on mutual desperation. Do I trust her? Not even close. But when you're drowning, you don't get picky about who throws the rope. This morning is the first test for both of us.

My tablet is propped up on the counter next to me. The latest Step-Sister post glows on the screen. Andromeda came through.

Blog Entry #40

The Slipper Didn't Fit

Listen up, darlings. Let's talk about amateur informants and their adorable attempts to play whistleblower.

Cinderella had her moment. All sparkle and sass, dropping breadcrumbs like she aspired to be some grand revolutionary. Cute. But revolutions need more than dramatic blog posts. They need substance.

Our little princess thought she could blow the lid off something big. News flash: She was just another prop in a much larger performance. Charming while she lasted, but pumpkins rot. And this one? She's wilting fast.

We've got a fresh voice now. One that matters. One with actual insight, not recycled rumors and teenage angst.

To our fallen heroine: Thanks for the entertainment. The Family eats its own as it always has.

Stay sharp, Stay free.

—Your Step-Sister

My Family phone buzzes, and I glance down, toothbrush still humming between my lips.

SAGE

Natalia's office. Now.

That was fast. Even though we planned for this, my nerves are still on edge. My fingers tremble, and I nearly drop the toothbrush. I tap the phone with my free hand, careful not to drip toothpaste onto the screen.

Be there in 5.

"You can do this," I say out loud. "Just act nervous. Shouldn't be hard."

NATALIA'S OFFICE should be in a magazine spread with the caption "Intimidation." My blood pressure spikes the moment I cross the threshold.

"Sit down," Sage barks, her voice slapping me across the face. She's wearing an all-black power suit that adds a sinister edge to her performance.

With appropriate remorse, I slink over to the chair and drop into it.

"You have been disloyal, reckless, and frankly stupid," Sage begins, each word precise and cutting. "You're lucky Natalia has a warm heart and is willing to let you stay rather than putting you out on the street where you belong."

My head dips—a picture of penitence.

"You put the Family at risk with your irresponsible behavior," she continues, pacing now. "Anything like this again will not be tolerated. Do you understand?"

My chin quivers on command, a trick I learned from every sad movie I've ever seen and perfected by begging on the street. "Yes. I'm sorry."

Sage crosses her arms. "As punishment, for the next week, you will see no clients, your stipend will remain suspended, and you'll be on cleanup duty, starting with the bathrooms."

Wait, what? We didn't discuss this part. My face is a thin mask over my internal screaming. *Bathrooms? Are you kidding me?* Blowing our cover is not an option, so a nod is the only safe response.

"Caron never should have brought you into the Family." Natalia stares through me. "He's stubborn and soft. I am not. From now on, you will do what you're told and stay quiet. *Понятно?*"

That last word sounds like *potato*, a detail I file away for a less terrifying moment. "I'm sorry. I never meant to cause so much trouble."

"I don't need sorry," Natalia says, leaning forward. "I need discipline. Your Big Sister is putting her neck out for you. Do not make her regret it. This is your last chance." She snarls, "Get out of here."

My legs move on instinct, but my ribs feel constricted. I risk a glance at Sage on the way out the door, and her chin gives an almost imperceptible dip.

What's up with the bathroom duty?

TWENTY MINUTES LATER, the cafeteria doors open, and I'm met with spontaneous applause—Sisters, their faces filled with mock support, are clapping and cheering. My cheeks burn hot.

"Thanks, Cinderella! I got my stipend back," someone yells from the back, and laughter fills the space.

Mortified, I duck my head and make for the food line. My usual breakfast goes on the plate: scrambled eggs, bacon, and toast. Nothing fancy, just fuel for whatever fresh hell today brings.

A corner table provides enough cover. I sink into a chair and run the fork through my food. The eggs taste of nothing, but I force them down anyway.

"So, you did it?" Aura slides into the seat across from me. "How mad was she?"

I shrug, playing casual. "Pretty upset. I'm on bathroom duty for the week."

She throws her head back and laughs, drawing more attention our way. "Well, *chica*, if that's the worst of it, then you did okay."

It's nice to have someone who thinks I'm not entirely insane.

"How's Sage?" Aura asks.

"She's okay," I lie.

"Good."

"Thanks for cleaning up her room," I add. "You're a lifesaver. I owe you some new shoes."

"Damn right you do," Aura says, grinning. "Looked like there was a bullfight in there. I don't even wanna know."

If only she knew how close to the truth she was.

The buzzer sounds, and we part ways. I'm on lockdown for this week, but after that, how am I supposed to go back to clocking in like none of this ever happened?

I head through the door, and a voice calls out, "Star?"

I turn around, and it's Manolita from cleaning services, her gray uniform crisp in the early hour. She's holding a mop and bucket, and her face is a mix of sympathy and duty.

"Miss Sage told me to supervise you," she says, her accent thick as she pushes the cleaning equipment toward me. "Bathrooms, *sí?*"

My Cinderella story comes full circle. Though somehow, I skipped the part with the prince and the castle.

Manolita's smile is friendly and inviting. "Come. Third floor first."

The bucket sloshes with each step as I follow her into the service elevator. Does Sage sending Manolita mean she's still upset, or is this part of the ruse? Anger is a luxury I'm too tired to afford.

"You know," I say as the elevator doors close, "I used to help my mom clean our apartment. She'd say, 'Cleaning helps you focus. Dirt tells stories.'"

Manolita nods. "Smart woman, your mother."

"Yeah." A genuine smile warms my face. "She was."

ESTHER HOLLAND

Esther had a theory that mops were the devil's preferred instrument of torture, not pitchforks. Barefoot on the kitchen linoleum, her muscles burned as she used all her strength to push it across the floor while her mother scrubbed up dead skin and tomato sauce like it was an art form.

"Esther, sweetie, you're not fighting a snake. Let the mop do the work." She wore a bandana over her dirty-blonde hair and sleeves rolled up past her elbows, exposing arms as thin as broom handles and marked with scars of habits long forgotten.

Esther, aged twelve and at the height of her drama phase, brandished her mop like a bayonet. "If we left the dirt alone, it would form a crust and become a new rock layer. Someday archaeologists could study us."

Mom smiled in a way that meant she was both proud and annoyed—a rare trick. "Dirt tells stories. That's why we clean. You wouldn't want some stranger excavating our secrets, would you?" She pointed at a thumb-sized brown smear. "That's the cider spill from New Year's Eve, remember? The bottle exploded."

"You said it just fizzed a little," Esther said, trying not to smile.

"I said that to keep you from crying." Mom leaned in and sniffed the stain theatrically. "Still smells like apples. It's a memory, fossilized." Dabbing the spot with a ragged towel, she passed it across. "Go on, clean your history."

Esther rubbed the patch until it lightened, hoping traces of laughter were trapped in the fibers. She imagined the apartment as a living thing, its walls full of stories.

"Your grandmother used to say, 'Cleaning isn't just about making things pretty—it's about knowing what you have.'"

Esther paused, resting her chin on the mop handle. "What does that mean?"

"It means when you clean something, you touch every part of it. You notice the chip in the counter. The loose floorboard. The places where things are breaking." She ran her finger along a hairline crack in the tile. "Life's the same way. You can't fix what you pretend not to see."

She sat back on her heels. "When everything's a mess, your mind gets messy too. But when you clean one small corner, you remember you have control over something." She smiled. "That's why I make you help, even though you're terrible at it."

"I am not terrible," Esther protested, but she was smiling too.

"Maybe not," Mom conceded. "But you need the practice."

AUGUST 12, 2018

The shouting had been going on for twenty-three minutes. Esther knew because she'd been counting the ticks of the old black wall clock.

"This place is killing us, Mom!" Amelia pleaded. "Look around you. The mold in the bathroom. The roaches. The heat barely works. We deserve better than this."

Esther pulled her knees in tight, making herself as small as possible in the corner of their sagging couch. The springs dug into her thighs, but she didn't move. If she stayed still enough, they'd forget she was there.

Their mother slammed a dish into the sink. "And how is walking out supposed to make that better? That's not how family works, Amelia. We help each other."

"Help each other do what? Slowly drown?" Amelia gestured wildly around the apartment. "I'm twenty years old. I should have my own place by now, not sharing a bedroom with my kid sister in a building where the stairs are held together with duct tape and optimism."

Amelia's face flushed with anger. As siblings, they were so alike—same sandy blonde hair, same thin frame—but Amelia had something Esther didn't: fire.

"There are opportunities out there," Amelia continued. "I've met people who can help me, help us."

Mom's laugh was harsh. "What kind of opportunities? What kind of people? The kind who want something in return? There's always a catch, Amelia."

"Not everyone is trying to fuck you over, Mom!"

"Language!"

"Esther's fourteen, not four. She knows what's happening here."

Esther wished she didn't. Wished she could plug her ears and transport herself anywhere but where the two people she loved most were at war.

"I've given everything for you girls," Mom said, dropping her voice. "Everything. And this is how you treat me?"

Amelia went silent, then walked to the closet and pulled out her backpack—the one Esther knew she'd packed two days ago. The one Esther had pretended not to notice.

"So that's it?" Mom yelled. "You're just abandoning Esther?"

Amelia froze at the door, her hand on the knob. She turned and found Esther huddled on the couch, and something softened in her expression.

"No," she said, her backpack sliding from her shoulder. "I'm not abandoning her."

She crossed the room with quick strides and knelt, her face level with Esther's.

"I'm coming back for you, Sprout." She grabbed Esther's hand. "I'll call. I promise."

Esther wanted to launch herself from the couch, wrap her arms around Amelia's legs, and beg her not to go. To drag her sister back into the bedroom to invent another story, this one about how family doesn't leave. But something deeper inside her, raw and exposed, wanted to scream, to make Amelia feel even a fraction of the pain that was breaking her apart.

Amelia let go, turned away, and walked out the door, leaving Esther to watch her childhood follow right behind.

NOVEMBER 3, 2023

The antiseptic odor of the hospital room couldn't mask the fetor of finality that hovered in the air. Esther sat in the hard plastic chair, her fingers intertwined with her mother's paper-thin hand. A steady beep from the heart monitor provided a metronome for their shared silence. The call had come six weeks ago, during her sophomore year of college. Cancer. Not much time.

"You look tired, sweetie," Mom said, her voice worn to a rasp by pain and medication.

Esther forced a smile. "Says the woman in the hospital bed."

Mom's laugh turned into a cough that shook her frail frame. Esther took the water cup from the side table and guided the straw to her cracked lips.

After a moment, Mom caught her breath. "College must be keeping you busy. Tell me about your classes."

Esther shifted in her seat, guilt twisting inside her. She hadn't been to class for almost two weeks, spending every possible moment at the hospital instead. "You know, challenging but good."

A feeble smile crossed Mom's face. "I'm so proud of you, you know. First one in our family to go to college. You're going to make something of yourself."

The words hit Esther hard. If only she knew the truth—that Esther was failing most of her classes, her academic scholarship in jeopardy.

"Mom, I—"

"No, let me say this while I still can." Mom's grip tightened with surprising strength. "I didn't do right by Amelia. I know that now. I was too strict, too afraid of what people would think. I pushed her away." Tears slid down her shadowed cheeks. "And now she's gone, and I never got to tell her I'm sorry."

Esther's throat clamped tight. Amelia had been missing for years, but Esther still clung to her sister's promise to come back, long after everyone else had given up.

"Mom, you can't blame yourself for what happened with Amelia."

"But I do. Every day." A sob leapt out of her. "I should have listened more and judged less." She shook her head weakly against the pillow. "I wish I'd been a better mother to both of you."

Esther couldn't hold back a sob of her own. She crawled onto the narrow hospital bed, careful of the IV lines and monitoring cables, and laid her head on her mother's shoulder like she used to as a child.

"You were the best, Mom," Esther whispered fiercely. "You kept a roof over our heads. You made birthdays special even when there was no money. You read to us every night, no matter how tired you were." She snuggled in closer. "You loved us with everything you had."

Her voice grew thick with regret. "I should have come home more. Called every day, not just weekends. I should have—"

"Shh." Mom's trembling fingers stroked her hair. "You're here now. That's all that matters."

They stayed that way for a long while, Esther listening to the labored rhythm of her mother's breathing, memorizing the touch of her fingers, knowing these moments were precious and dwindling.

When Mom's eyes closed, the morphine granting some relief, Esther returned to her chair. She pulled out the small, worn notebook she carried everywhere and wrote, her pen a silent blur across the page.

Mom stirred a short time later, her gaze finding Esther hunched over the notebook.

"Still writing, I see," she rasped, a faint smile on her lips. "You've always had a gift with words. I used to read your stories over and over. It made me so proud."

Esther looked up, tears threatening again. "I write to keep things with me." She took her mother's hand. "It's the way I'll remember you."

Mom's fingers tightened around hers. "Then write me better than I was."

"I'll write you exactly as you were," Esther promised. "Perfect."

Thirty

"We've been sitting here forever. It's almost eleven." I'm twisting a USB cable around my wrist for entertainment, which has elicited a few odd looks from Sage. Jeremy's gone through three energy drinks in the last two hours, and Sage left and came back with juice. "She's in her office, right?"

"Yes," Sage affirms, her usual confidence replaced with something tighter, more brittle. "Working late, like always. Her lights are on. I checked before I came down here."

Jeremy types faster than I can think. He finishes up, clicks his mouse, and pulls a tiny USB key from his computer.

"This is the file," he says, holding it out to Sage. "To her, it should look like a normal spreadsheet, but once she opens it, it'll copy the folder to a network location I've set up."

Sage takes the drive from him. Her fingers are steady, but a slight tremor in her thumb betrays her calm demeanor as she closes her fist around it. This tiny weapon against Natalia's empire.

"She won't notice anything?" Sage asks.

"No," Jeremy says. "It'll run silently in the background. Get her to open it while that folder's unlocked, and we're golden."

"And you're sure this will work?" I tighten the cable around my fingers.

"As sure as I can be without testing it," he replies—not exactly the reassurance we were hoping for.

Jeremy brings the remote window front and center on his monitor—no activity on Natalia's computer.

The silence is killing me. "Hey," I blurt out, "what do you call a fake noodle?"

They both stare at me blankly while I twist the cable around my arm.

"An *impasta!*" I grin.

Crickets. Then Sage, bless her heart, actually chuckles.

"She's on!" Jeremy shouts, and there's movement on the remote window.

Sage stands up, straightens her shoulders, takes a quick breath, and mouths a silent pep talk before she heads out the door.

Natalia checks her email: Saks Fifth Avenue is 20% off tomorrow, Denali is upset about the planner for the Armstrong gala, and a spam message from a discount liquor store.

Then she opens a terminal window, and Jeremy shifts in his chair, adjusting his glasses and leaning in. "This might be it."

Natalia types a long string of gibberish into the terminal, and a line of text appears.

—CONNECTION ESTABLISHED—

We both follow the mouse cursor like we're cats as she clicks the folder. Something pops up asking for authentication, then vanishes, and the folder opens.

Jeremy sends the message to Sage and starts the timer on his phone.

"I'm starting the server daemon on my side. When the code runs on Natalia's machine, it'll log its progress here."

I squint at the screen. Are my eyes playing tricks on me?

"Did…did you name the program *Eggward?*"

He looks at me sheepishly. "He lives."

My heart.

TIMER: 1:45 remaining

Natalia is scrolling through the folder. Jeremy is taking screenshots as a contingency. No message from Sage. We wait.

TIMER: 1:30 remaining

Natalia stopped scrolling. Nothing's moving.

"Is something wrong?" I ask.

"Sage is probably there. I don't see the USB drive attached yet."

TIMER: 1:18 remaining

Jeremy points to the screen. "She plugged it in."

The cursor floats over to the drive icon, and it opens.

The file is there. She's not clicking it. Why?

TIMER: 1:07 remaining

Jeremy is getting frustrated and certainly blaming himself. I touch his shoulder as something flashes onto his terminal window:

```
[INITIATE_LOG_START]
[PAYLOAD_EXECUTE_SUCCESS]
[TEMP_INSTANCE_CREATED]
[COPY_INITIATED]
```

The spreadsheet file opens in the remote window.

Jeremy smacks his desk with his hand and turns to me with a huge smile.

"It's working?" My voice lilts.

"It's working."

Now it's a matter of time. Can his program copy the files before the access runs out?

One little dot appears in the terminal window, followed by another. Jeremy is transfixed.

TIMER: 0:53 remaining

A few more dots.

"How many dots until it's done?" I ask.

"I don't know. I didn't have the total size, so I put a dot for every megabyte."

I can't tell if he's happy.

TIMER: 0:40 remaining

Dot. Dot. Dot. It's like watching a life raft inflate one gasp of air at a time.

TIMER: 0:24 remaining

We've got a couple more dots. That's good, right?

"What happens if it doesn't finish?" I ask.

"Hopefully, the half we get is enough."

Hopefully.

TIMER: 0:18 remaining

The spreadsheet closes, and the USB drive icon disappears.

Jeremy makes a noise, and not a good one.

"What happened?"

"She pulled the drive out. That may have killed the copy process."

We stare at the screen.

TIMER: 0:04 remaining

```
[COPY_COMPLETE]
```

[TEMP_INSTANCE_REMOVED]
[TERMINATING]
"Does that mean...?"

"It finished," he says.

We jump from our chairs, and I pull him into an embrace. This time, he hugs me back—a brief, comforting squeeze.

Jeremy disconnects from her machine and checks the network.

The door to the office flies open, and Sage storms in.

"Tell me you fucking got it."

Jeremy turns to her and smiles. "We fucking got it."

The stress drains from her face, leaving her features slack with exhaustion. She drops into the chair, kicking her heels off.

"She didn't want to open it at first—asked why I didn't email it, and I had to improvise. Told her it was too big, and I got an error message. I was pissed, like I just wanted to get it over with, and that wasn't acting. When she took the drive from me, my heart nearly stopped."

"Did it run okay?" Jeremy asks.

"She saw the file, clicked on it, and it opened. I didn't see anything else. We went over the numbers, and she complained like she always does. Chastised me for not catching the error and then pulled the drive out. When she did that, I thought it ruined everything."

"It didn't," I say. "We got the whole folder."

"You're a genius," she says to Jeremy, and I swear he blushes.

"We couldn't have done this without you," I tell her. "She wouldn't have trusted anyone else."

Sage exhales heavily, as if the pressure of the entire night had been held in her lungs. "Yeah."

As I look at the two of them, a swell of pride lifts me. If that folder has what Jeremy thinks it does, we may have enough to pull Caron to our side. I cross my fingers in a silent prayer.

THE FLAGSTONES ARE cool beneath my bare feet as I trace their geometric patterns. Back and forth. Six steps this way, turn, six steps back. The wisteria hangs above us, draping the pergola of the Conservatory Garden in purple shadows that dance with the breeze.

It's so damn pretty here, like we're extras in some period drama about rich people's garden parties and not planning a coup against the place we call home.

Sage is sitting on a bench, hair catching the morning sunlight, like she's posing for a photo shoot. Her eyes haven't left the ornate iron gate at the garden entrance for the past ten minutes.

"The one who called the meeting shouldn't be late," I mutter, resuming my pacing.

"He'll be here," Sage says. "Stop walking in circles."

My comeback dies on my tongue. Jeremy is power walking up the path, dodging elderly tourists and nannies with strollers. He's wearing khakis and a blue polo, his tech-bro camouflage that does little to hide him in this sea of sundresses and linen pants.

He doesn't say hello, just ducks under the wisteria, his breath coming in ragged bursts. It smells like coffee and panic, and his first words are a gunshot: "She knows."

A couple walking nearby burst into laughter. The sound is like glass shattering across my skull. Sage's hand, which had been resting casually on her knee, curls into a fist.

"Knows *what?*" I hiss, dropping beside him.

Jeremy leans in, forcing us to huddle like we're planning a heist. "Not what. *Who.*" He swallows hard. "Natalia cornered me. Not in the office. In the server room, an hour ago. No witnesses." His tone turns colder. "She wants me to implement a 'proactive threat-detection system.' Her words."

Sage shifts closer. "For what?"

"For who," Jeremy corrects. "For you two."

The warmth drains from my face. "What does that mean, exactly?"

"Location pings every five minutes. Keyword flags on every message, every search query." He's rambling. "She wants to know if you order a salad or a sandwich for lunch. A digital cage custom-built for both of you."

My hand goes instinctively to my bag, where my notebook is tucked away. Suddenly it's heavy, like a brick of evidence. All my thoughts, my real ones, live on those pages.

Sage's demeanor hasn't changed, but her jaw is tight. "And she came to you to build it."

Jeremy nods, looking like he might throw up on his Kenneth Coles.

"I don't think she suspects me. At least not yet. That's the only reason we're having this conversation and not being tossed into a white van."

The fountain at the center of the garden gurgles cheerfully, mocking us. I turn away from them, my mind miles ahead of my mouth.

"That's it, then. We're out of time." A strange calmness overtakes me, like I'm in the eye of the hurricane. "We have to go to Caron. Right now."

Jeremy's head snaps up. "That again?" He waves his hand like he's trying to erase my words. "I'm only maybe 20 percent through the data we collected. We can't prove she's the sole actor. What if Caron is in on it? That'd be walking into our execution!"

"If we wait to go through all of it, she'll have us handcuffed!" I shoot back. "We'll never get to him. This is our last chance to move freely."

"Moving freely into an execution is not a plan!"

Sage holds up her hand, silencing us both. She turns toward Jeremy.

"Forget the what-ifs. Give me facts," she says in a measured tone. "In the 20 percent you've reviewed, is there any direct link to Caron? His name, accounts, authorizations—anything?"

Jeremy takes a shaky breath and concentrates, sorting through the data in his mind. "No. Nothing direct. The money flows through myriad shell corporations and offshore accounts, but I saw nothing implicating him." He frowns. "It's almost...aggressively clean. Like she's built a firewall around herself."

"It *is* a firewall," I say, grabbing onto his words. "She's not protecting him—she's *hiding* it from him. That's our angle, how we frame this." My gaze alternates between them. "We can't wait until we find his signature on a check. It needs to be now."

Sage cranes her neck up to the wisteria vines and releases a slow, controlled exhale. "Jeremy's right that waltzing in and accusing Natalia won't end well." She squints at us. "So, we don't accuse. We present evidence of a threat. A threat to his Family."

Jeremy and I exchange glances.

"How long can you stall her on this?" Sage asks.

The question grounds him. "I can buy us a day, max, by telling her

I need to shift processes around to free up compute for the new services. It's flimsy, but she's arrogant. She won't question the tech."

The three of us share a glance. No handshakes. No high fives. Just the silent acknowledgment that we've pushed all-in on the biggest gamble of our lives.

I stand up, brushing a leaf from my skirt, and fix my attention across Fifth Avenue to the gleaming glass and steel of our building. Our prison. Our battleground.

"Then we don't waste a second of it," I say, finding a strength I don't recognize. "Jeremy, package what you have. A presentation for the CEO. Clean. Professional." I look at both of them. "I'll set up the meeting."

BEING UP HERE IS A MISTAKE, especially after getting chewed out by Natalia, but this is too important to put off. Everything is riding on an old man who might already be lost to the same rot that's eating the rest of this place. All I can do is hope that the person Amelia trusted is still in there somewhere.

Kari sits at her desk outside Caron's office, manicured nails clicking against the keyboard like tiny insects. Her face is a mask of professional disinterest when she looks up at me.

"Can I help you, Star?"

"Is he in?" I lean against the corner of her desk.

"He's stepped out." A glance at her screen. "He'll be back shortly, but he's swamped today."

I pass a cream-colored envelope across to her. Inside is a letter written this morning after our impromptu meeting in the garden. There's enough information in it to pique Caron's interest without giving away our entire hand. It's an invitation to a meeting at the café a few blocks away. My signature is the only one on it; if this goes sideways, the others are safe. My fingers leave damp prints on the paper as I hold it out.

"Could you please give this to him the moment he gets back? It's important."

Our eyes meet, and I will her to understand the significance.

"I promise," she says, taking it from me. "I'll put it directly in his hands."

"Thank you." I turn away, already second-guessing my decision.

LUNCH IS a luxury I can't afford right now. In the wizard's cave, Jeremy is alone, poring over the documents we copied. He turns as the door clicks shut behind me, and his face says this will not be a playful romp through treasonville.

"Find anything else?" My attempt at casual is betrayed by my heart, which is doing the cha-cha against my ribs.

"You don't want to know."

"How bad are we talking?"

"Death penalty bad." Jeremy grabs his frames and adjusts them. "If this went to trial—which it wouldn't, because Natalia would never let it get that far—but if it did? They'd melt the key after they locked the cell."

My jaw drops. "Holy shit."

"Yeah." He rubs his eyes beneath his glasses. "We need to be careful with this. It isn't dirty laundry—it's nuclear waste."

Sage whirls into Jeremy's office like a tornado in stilettos, the door banging against the wall. I jump in my seat, but Jeremy doesn't flinch.

"I've got five minutes, tops," she announces. "Natalia is riding me already."

Jeremy spins in his chair to face us. "I've cataloged some more data. Probably a third of what we've got."

"What about Caron?" Sage cuts in. "Is he implicated?"

He shakes his head. "No. From what I'm seeing, he hasn't been involved in actual ops for years."

"So, he's just a figurehead now?" I ask.

"I won't know for sure until I go through everything," Jeremy says, turning back to his screen. "But there's no time to do that before we meet, so we go with what we have."

Sage paces the small office. "Star, you should be the only one he sees at first." She points between herself and Jeremy. "If Caron sees us, he may think it's a setup and leave. We'll wait at the back of the café. If he chooses to listen, then we'll come forward."

My mouth is dry. "Do you think he will?"

"Just tell the story," she says.

Sage heads for the door. "I've got to go. I'll be there ten minutes prior. We only get one shot at this."

She leaves, and I slump in the chair. "No pressure or anything."

Jeremy glances at me. "Remember, we're not accusing. We're presenting evidence."

"And if he doesn't believe us?"

He turns back. "You don't need me to answer that question."

My mind fills with scattered thoughts: Amelia's notebook. Caron's face when he talked about her. All the things that have led to this moment.

One shot.

Jeremy Tallinder

The walls were lined with leather-bound books that looked decorative, not read. Persian rugs covered hardwood floors that were impossibly shiny yet still gave off an antique vibe. The man —who had introduced himself as Caron—wore a perfectly tailored charcoal gray suit with subtle pinstripes. He picked up Jeremy's CV from his desk for the third time. Then he dropped it, drumming his fingers on the leather desk pad.

"On paper, you're just right for this role," he said in a calm, measured cadence. "But I need to know if you're just right in the flesh." He pulled what appeared to be a network diagram from his drawer and slid it across the desk.

"Your predecessor claimed he was qualified, but within six months, he folded like a cheap card table and had to be shown the door. Do you think you can work with this?"

Jeremy shifted in the chair, the supple leather making him acutely aware of how out of place he felt. He eyed the diagram. Salvageable for sure. Amateur mistakes, but nothing that would require a complete wipe.

"Yes, sir. I think I can fix this. There are a few issues, but I don't believe you need to start over."

Caron seemed pleased with his answer. "The level of responsibility is immense." He leaned back in his chair. "Besides fixing this, you'll oversee the development of our internal systems, databases, dark web portals, mobile applications—everything. You'll be the primary architect. I'll give you direction, but you'll have complete freedom in how you implement things."

The scope of it all made Jeremy's pupils dilate. At Google, he was one programmer among thousands, working on fragments of larger systems he'd never fully understand. This sounded like building an entire organization from the ground up. Exciting and terrifying in equal measure.

"I want no secrets between us," Caron said, his focus fixed on Jeremy. "We have to trust each other completely if this is going to work out."

Jeremy nodded. "I understand."

"Your primary directive—above everything else—is to protect the Sisters." Caron's voice took on a cautionary quality. "Keep their information safe, their identities hidden. The Sisters change their names when they join the Family, you see. For their protection and to allow them the freedom to be someone else."

He paused, studying Jeremy for a long moment. "Have you ever aspired to be someone else, Jeremy?"

The question caught him off guard. Had he? Sometimes, late at night when he couldn't sleep, he wondered what it would be like to be the kind of person who walked into rooms and commanded attention instead of shrinking into corners. "I suppose everyone has."

Caron smiled. "Indeed."

"Would I be doing anything illegal, sir?" The question tumbled out.

Caron's laugh was rich and genuine. "Everything we do here is aboveboard, I assure you. The deep level of security and surveillance is strictly for the Sisters' protection—to keep the company off the radar of those who would seek to do us harm."

"Like who?"

Caron waved the question away with a dismissive gesture. "Someone with your talents shouldn't concern himself with such mundane matters. That's what people like me are for. The NDA we ask you to sign is admittedly lengthy, but coming from Google, I don't expect it's something you've not seen before."

Jeremy nodded. "I have no problem with that, sir."

Caron opened his drawer again and pulled out a white envelope, sliding it across the desk. Jeremy hesitated before taking it, the paper heavy and expensive between his fingers.

"This will be your annual compensation," Caron said. "There is potential for a bonus in the right circumstances. Unlike Google, we are not and never will be a public company, so I cannot offer you the promise of stock. However, I feel you will find the offer more than satisfactory."

Jeremy opened the envelope and stared at the number typed under the letterhead. His brain stuttered, unable to process what he was seeing. "Is this a joke?"

"No."

"There are...there are two commas in this number."

Caron's smile widened.

Thirty One

I fidget with the paper napkin in front of me, tearing tiny bits off the edges and arranging them in a neat pile. This café is exactly what we needed—small, unassuming, with enough noise to mask our conversation but not so much that we can't hear each other. The morning rush has thinned out, leaving mostly empty tables, and the lingering air holds the scent of coffee and pastries.

My knee won't stop bouncing, and the tightness in my shoulder is complaining again. I've rehearsed what I'm going to say a dozen times, but the words are still clumsy and inadequate. How do you tell someone their empire is crumbling from within? That the person they trusted most is betraying them?

A check of my phone: 11:27 a.m. Sage and Jeremy should be in position, waiting for my signal. A sip of coffee confirms it's lukewarm, a fact I barely register.

Through the window, he appears. Caron, traipsing with measured steps, a gray fedora tilted on his head. He belongs in an old movie—all class and composure. Does he suspect what he's walking into?

After stopping to check the sign, he steps inside. The bell over the door jingles, and for a moment, our eyes meet across the tables. Something flickers on his face, too quick to read, before settling back into careful neutrality.

This is it. Everything we've done comes down to the next few minutes.

Removing his hat, he makes his way toward me. Without a word, he pulls out the chair and tosses the envelope I gave Kari onto the table between us.

"What is the meaning of this?" His voice is low, controlled, but there's an edge to it.

"I want to show you something." I open my bag and withdraw Amelia's notebook, dropping it between us. The page is marked with a Post-it note, and I flip to it.

"This was my sister's," I say. "Nova's."

I twist the notebook around, and he looks at the page where Amelia wrote about their late-night card games, their chats, their bond. His eyes soften, and a subtle smile curls onto his mouth, as though for a second, he could see it in his mind.

"She trusted you. I think you trusted her once too. Now, I'm asking you to trust me."

Caron stares at the notebook for a long moment; then his eyes flick up at me, guarded. "I don't understand. Why are you showing me this? What is it you want?"

" The Family is in danger. Not from the outside, but from within."

The words cause him to lean back, posture stiffening. "What are you talking about?"

Flipping to another marked page, I let him read for a moment before speaking. "Nova wrote about assignments that…never made the official schedules. These were off-book operations, and they didn't seem right to her, but she couldn't see the entire picture." Our eyes connect. "She suspected these missions were putting the Sisters, and the Family itself, at significant risk."

His bushy brows crease, pinching his forehead as he stares through me.

Another page turns. "And this is evidence that Sparrow died during one of these operations."

Caron's face darkens. "What are you implying here, Esther?"

He used my name. This has gotten to him.

Keep going. Don't accuse. Present.

"What Nova was seeing was just the beginning. There's a pattern targeting clients with government or military connections where information is being extracted."

I take a breath, letting that hang in the air.

"There is a money trail," I continue. "Payments routed through shell companies designed to be untraceable."

A muscle in his jaw twitches. "And where does this trail…lead?"

"To accounts with confirmed ties to Russian intelligence."

"How could you possibly have proof of such a thing?"

My nostrils flare involuntarily. This is it. "Jeremy?"

From a corner table, Jeremy rises and makes his way over. Caron's head whips around, his eyes opening wider.

"Jeremy?" he says.

"Sir, when you hired me, you said no secrets between us. Do you remember?" Jeremy is surprisingly steady. "This is me keeping my end of the deal."

Opening his laptop, he sits down and walks Caron through what we found: client records, data collection, silent auction reports, and crypto transaction logs. With each new piece of evidence, Caron's body falls in on itself a little more. The wrinkles on his face deepen, and he grips his hat, slowly twirling it in circles.

"Sir, this is a fraction of what we've uncovered." Jeremy pulls up another document. "In this most recent drop, a government satellite—"

"Enough," Caron says, his gaze fixed somewhere between us, a thousand-yard stare.

We let the silence hold, giving him whatever time he needs to understand.

"How," he speaks deliberately, "did you get this information?"

I glance at Jeremy.

"I planted a remote tracker on Natalia's computer," he admits.

Caron's lips tighten.

"We needed to know for sure. We couldn't come to you unless we were certain."

"And she just let you put this...tracker on her computer? She's smarter than you think."

Without being asked, Sage steps around the corner, and Caron's entire demeanor changes. His mouth drops open, his shoulders fall, and his hat lands on the table.

"I helped them, Caron. Everything they're telling you is true." She stands next to me, and her presence—her confirmation—is what finally makes this real to him.

"Sage..." His breath fails him for a second. "You? If you knew of these things, why didn't you come to me?"

"I didn't know. Not for sure. I knew what the Sisters were being asked to do, but not the endgame." Sage looks down as she clasps her hands. "Forgive me, Caron, but I thought it was being done with your approval."

Looking every one of his years, he puts his elbows on the table, exhales like a grizzly bear, and rests his head in his hands before regaining his composure.

Caron shifts between the three of us, the calculations clear on his face—his tech guy, a trusted lieutenant, and his newest Sister all working together, keeping secrets from him. "How long?" he asks. "How long have you three known this?"

"We came to you as soon as the threat became clear," I say.

His nose twitches, and he nods slowly. "What is it you want?"

I flip to the back of the notebook—to the blog post. Number thirteen.

"Nova never got to publish this, but she planned to." I drag my finger along the paper, lifting off near the bottom.

His eyes scan the page, and I study his face as he reads the words Amelia meant for him.

To the old man, If you ever read this, I want to believe you didn't know. But if you did—if you let her use us this way—you don't get to call it a Family anymore.

A long silence stretches between us, and when he finally looks up, the certainty that was on his face when he walked in is gone. Replaced by the fragile countenance of someone realizing they've inadvertently become the villain of their own story.

He glances between the notebook and my face, and his lips take a rueful turn as he places his hand on the page.

"You look like her, you know. Your sister." He gives me a quick smile. "She tried to tell me something was wrong once. I didn't listen."

His admission hangs heavy over the table. This is the man Amelia trusted. Is this enough to get through to him?

"I know," I say. "I think she hoped you'd listen eventually. She documented all of this so she could bring it to you, but..."

Caron's hand moves across the notebook. "But she ran out of time," he finishes.

"We may be running out of time as well, sir." Jeremy brings up a new document on the laptop. "The other side is pushing back."

He points to the briefing. "This is a report of a botched operation. A Sister, Amber, was caught during an unauthorized attempt to access a client's device."

Jeremy pauses, but Caron doesn't react.

"The client let her go after she said she was only curious about it," Jeremy continues, "but they became suspicious. I assume you weren't aware of this?"

Caron lets out a blast of air, a half snort, half cough. But it's his silence that answers the question.

"We believe the operation in which Melody died was a deliberate attempt to entrap the Family during the commission of an illegal intelligence breach."

This allegation hits him hard—the way his nose twitches, the subtle flaring of his nostrils. His grip tightens around his hat, wrinkling the band.

"They must have realized that the Family uses the Sisters to obtain classified information from their clients."

Caron's full attention is on Jeremy.

"So, they booked an engagement using a falsified identity. A honeypot they knew the Family would bite on. Something went wrong, and Melody wound up dead."

Caron stares at the screen, his face ashen. "How are you so sure of this?"

Sage speaks up. "Because I ran point for the mission. In hindsight, it's easy to see the red flags. I made a terrible misjudgment."

She takes a shattered breath, and I take over.

"We're uncertain about what happened that night. The DoD isn't in the habit of killing escorts, so something must have gone sour. We need the actual story. If there's anything you can do..." I trail off, a knot of emotion stealing my voice.

Caron looks as if he's been hit by a dump truck. He bites the insides of his cheeks as his gaze arcs over the three of us. "Do you understand what you're asking me to do? Natalia built this place with me."

"And she may take you down with it," I say.

He spins his hat in a circle on the table, a mindless, repetitive motion. He's just going to walk away and pretend this intervention never happened, isn't he?

"It took courage to do what you've done today—to come to me." He looks my way. "Give me a little time, and I'll be in touch. Yes?"

The three of us nod in unison. Caron picks up his hat, plants it on his head, and walks out of the café.

We let out a collective exhale that I'm surprised doesn't blow the utensils off the table.

We did it. We're okay.

Right?

🦐

THE THREE OF us sit in silence at the back table of the café, wedged into the corner farthest from the windows—three conspirators with nowhere to hide. I shred another corner off the napkin. It's basically confetti now, little white snowflakes in the saucer where my cappuccino foam used to be. Across the table, Sage keeps twisting her pearl earring—round and round in a dizzying hypnotic motion—while Jeremy taps his phone screen so relentlessly the glass should crack. We've been silent since Caron's shadow disappeared past the window.

"We just signed our death warrants," Sage says, voice as flat as the empty plate in front of her.

The words land with a wallop. I open my mouth to protest, but she keeps going. "Powerful men don't thank messengers. They bury them. Caron will wrap this up in a bow and hand it to Natalia with a polite smile." She yanks her earring free, a tiny bead of blood on her lobe like punctuation.

My throat tightens. She doesn't get it. Caron cared about Amelia. He wouldn't do that. But the doubt creeps in like cold air under a door.

"I don't think he'll betray us," Jeremy mutters, rubbing at a coffee stain on the table with his thumb. "But that doesn't mean we're safe. He's going to try to handle Natalia himself, and she'll figure out we're the source in about five minutes."

"You don't know that," I snap, forcing a breath to soften my tone. "He built this whole thing. He knows what he's doing."

Why are they being so negative? We finally did something.

Sage snorts. "He built it with her. That's the problem." She leans in, hair falling across her face. "When push comes to shove, men like Caron protect themselves and their legacies. We're collateral damage waiting to happen."

Jeremy twirls his coffee cup in a slow circle. "I'm more worried about operational security. If he confronts her without proper precautions, she'll trace everything back to the breach."

Jesus, these two should open a funeral parlor together.

"Stop it." I slam my palm on the table harder than necessary. The sugar packets jump. "Both of you. We made the right choice."

Sage wipes the blood from her ear, smearing it across her thumb. "He'll choose the Family. He always chooses the machine."

Jeremy's phone buzzes, and we all flinch involuntarily as if it's already the call from Natalia.

"Just a weather alert. Sunny all week." He lets out a shaky chuckle that sounds like a sob.

"What other choice did we have?" I say. "Keep letting Natalia get away with this? Let Melody's death mean nothing?"

"Star's right. Statistically speaking, doing nothing guarantees a negative outcome," he says.

Sage runs a hand through her hair, tugging at the ends. "It doesn't matter now anyway," she sighs. "We crossed the Rubicon the moment we showed him that laptop. If he doesn't help us, we're dead. If he bungles it, we're dead. If he does nothing…" She shrugs. "We get to live a little longer."

"So, we wait," Jeremy says, putting his phone down. "Stay low. Act normal."

"Normal," I repeat. The word has no meaning anymore.

The café walls close in on me. The air thickens, and my vision blurs.

The wooden chair groans as I push it back and shoot to my feet. "I need some air."

Sage looks up. "Star—"

"I'm fine. Just…need to think. I'll meet you back at the dorms."

I push through the café door, and the bell jingles overhead, cheerful and oblivious to the enormity of what's taken place. Outside, the air tastes like exhaust.

We did the right thing. We had to.
Now we have to survive it.

$$\mathfrak{J}$$

SLUMPED AGAINST THE HEADBOARD, I have my legs crossed, notebook balanced on my knees. What comes next? We've played our hand, exposed ourselves. Now we'll see if our bet was big enough.

We confronted Caron. And somehow, we're still breathing.

I scribble the words down in my notebook, then cross them out. Too dramatic, even for me. But damn if there isn't some truth in it.

Tallinder & Sage: Funeral Emporium

A chuckle, but I scratch that out too, then doodle a tiny fedora in the margin.

Caron didn't listen to Amelia; will he listen to me?

A knock at the door interrupts my spiral.

I snap the book shut. "Come in."

Aura walks in, but it's not her usual saunter; she moves deliberately with slow steps. Her face holds an unfamiliar intensity.

"*Chica*, you got a minute?"

"What's up?"

She drops onto my bed, slumping against the pillows. "I'm leaving."

"Leaving where?" I give her a full smile. "Did a client offer to take you to Cabo?"

Aura laughs quickly, but there's no soul in it. "No, Star. I'm leaving the Family."

Her words pull the air from my lungs, and I sit up straighter. "What do you mean?"

"I asked out. Got my walking papers a few minutes ago. You're my last stop." She twists her hands together in her lap. "I need a change. Need to do something for me, ya know?"

The mattress bounces as I fall back onto the bed. "So, you're abandoning me in my time of need?"

Aura chuckles, and this time, there's a hint of her old self in it. "If I know what you've got cooking, there won't be a Family for me to stay with anyway, am I right? Get out now while I'm still intact, know what I'm sayin'?"

Of course she knows—she's seen me stumbling around like an amateur spy for weeks.

"Anyway," she continues, "you'll know how to reach me. I'm just moving to a new constellation."

She's confirmed the answer to a question I've had for some time. I flip onto my side and ask, "How long have you worked with Step-Sister?"

"Ah, long enough." She shrugs. "They appealed to my sense of 'fuck this place,' ya know? I drip-fed them some bullshit—a one-liner from the meetings, stuff like that. It was never that serious."

Never that serious. Unlike me, apparently, who's turned everything into a five-alarm fire.

Her hand is small when I cup it in mine. "I need you to do me a favor, Aura."

"Call me Maitea. I don't need the nickname anymore."

The finality in her voice pulls at my heartstrings. "Nice to meet you, Maitea. I'm Esther."

She crinkles her nose and makes a face. "Esther?" A deep howl flows out of her. "Girl, I pegged you as a Jenny or some shit."

We slap each other's arms, dissolving into laughter—part hysteria, part relief. For a moment, we're not Star and Aura—just two girls saying goodbye.

"So, what's this favor?" She eyes me suspiciously.

"I need you to be my insurance policy."

"What kind of insurance are we talking about here?"

"I've put together a lot of information for Step-Sister. Like, a lot. Stuff that could bury the Family in some deep shit. Financial records, client lists, blackmail." I fidget with the corner of my notebook. "But it's all encrypted."

Her dark eyes narrow, like she's reading the fine print on my soul. "And you're not going to give them the password."

I snap my fingers. "Exactly. You're going to be my password. If this whole thing goes pear-shaped, I need you to pull the pin. Can you do that?"

She stares at me for a moment and nods firmly. "Absolutely."

Relief floods over me as I pull her into a hug. It isn't one of our usual quick embraces; this one is solid, grounding. My face buries in her shoulder, trying to absorb her strength. Her arms wrap tightly around me, quieting the buzz in my head.

"You'd better be careful," she mumbles. "You might be walking right into something, ya know?"

My hands stay on her shoulders as I pull back. "I know. That's why someone I trust has to hold the key to this truth bomb."

Leaning in close to her, cheek to cheek, I whisper the password.

She looks at me like I've told her I can secretly talk to squirrels. Then she laughs, really roars, doubling over with it.

"You a crazy bitch, you know that?" she gasps between giggles.

Despite the fear, I join her. We collapse into another hug, this one tighter, more desperate.

When she pulls away and stands up, a part of me goes with her. Aura stops at the door and looks back.

"Keep it real, Estrellita. And good luck."

And then she's gone again—for good this time.

Caron

Caron flipped through the financial statements, his reading glasses perched on the end of his nose. Numbers usually told a simple story —money in, money out—but these figures made no sense. An incoming transfer of $350,000 marked only as "operational income" with no corresponding documentation.

He removed his glasses, pinching the bridge of his nose. The Family's finances had grown complicated over the years, but he'd never lost track of how the money flowed until recently.

Caron gathered the papers and walked down the hallway to Natalia's office. In the corridor, he stopped beside a painting—a Baltic seascape she'd hung last month. The signature in the corner read "V. Petrov." She'd been collecting Russian art lately. Small changes. Little adjustments. Pieces shifting on the board.

With one knock, he pushed her door open without waiting for a response.

"Nadia, what is this?"

She looked up from her computer, blonde hair framing her face, and glanced at the paper in his hand without a trace of surprise.

"You'll need to be more specific, old man."

Caron placed the document on her desk, stabbing at the mysterious entry with his finger. "Three hundred fifty thousand. No origin. No tracking." His tone is even. "Money doesn't make itself."

She barely glanced at it. "Unreported expenses that came back to us. Richardson's account finally paid what they owed."

"Richardson's final payment posted on March 3. I signed off myself. This is new money."

"Then it's from the Wakefield project. Diamond did exceptional work there." A professional smile. "I'll take care of it."

Caron studied the pulse of her carotid artery—steady, but the left corner of her mouth twitched, almost imperceptibly. He'd seen that twitch in bed, in boardrooms, in the moments before she lied to senators.

He turned as if to leave, took two steps toward the door, and pivoted back. "Look at me, Nadia."

She met his stare, clear and hard.

"Are you doing anything that could burn us down?"

A flush came across her face. "How dare you ask me that? After everything we've built?"

He studied her unblinking eyes—the same winter blue that once looked at him across a bathroom sink and said, "We could own this city." They hadn't blinked then either.

"I asked you a simple question," he said, his face blank.

"And I've given my answer." A firm response, her stillness matching his own. "I've done nothing we haven't agreed to."

Caron studied her, his expression going cold. "Are you selling what the girls collect? To anyone outside our circle?"

The air between them hardened.

"No." Flat, direct.

Years ago, he'd believed he loved her. Perhaps he still did, in the wounded way old soldiers love the wars that broke them. He wanted to believe her words now, but the Romanian street boy in him—the one who survived on instinct—kept whispering caution.

A twitch of his nose, a small tell from his childhood he'd never eliminated.

"Okay."

On the way back to his office, he stopped at the painting again and ran his thumb along the frame, feeling the grain of the wood.

She was lying. But about what, exactly?

THIRTY TWO

Jeremy's office door opens, and I stop short. Sage is perched on his desk, one leg crossed over the other, examining her nails like she doesn't have a care in the world.

"Well, look who joined us," she says without looking up.

"I came as soon as I got the—" Jeremy's face stops me. He's clicking a pen obsessively, his usual nervous tic dialed up to eleven. "What happened?"

"Caron stopped by." *Click.* "No warning. Just showed up."

Sage looks at me. "He has a contact."

"At the DoD," Jeremy finishes. *Click.* "Someone inside who's been protecting the Family."

A sharp laugh. "Of course he does."

"This isn't a joke, Star." Sage slides off the desk. "I know this guy. We ran some things together years ago."

"You know him? How well?"

Click.

She waves her hand dismissively. "Well enough, let's leave it at that. The point is, he's agreed to meet. Tomorrow night at the Plaza."

The small office is like a cage, and I pace between the door and Jeremy's desk. "So, Caron snaps his fingers, and some government official comes running?"

"He called in a favor, I'm sure," Sage says.

Jeremy pushes up his glasses. *Click.* "He'll only meet with Sage."

I stop mid-step. "Absolutely not."

"Excuse me?" Sage's voice falls into the dangerous register I've learned to fear.

Click.

"You're going to walk into some hotel room alone with a guy who could make you disappear? After everything that's happened?"

"I've done this before, Star. Many times."

"Yeah? When was the last time? Yesterday? Last week?"

Sage's lips flatten. "Two years ago."

"Two years ago?!" I throw my hands up.

Jeremy clears his throat. "I have an idea."

We both turn to him. He's stopped clicking the pen, which somehow makes me more nervous.

"I've been thinking about what Sage said when we were in the park." His eyes flick between us. "About how the best revenge isn't killing Natalia—it's ruining her."

"I said that?" Sage's eyes widen in surprise.

"We may have a chance to do that." He spins his monitor toward us, revealing a technical diagram that might as well be hieroglyphics. "If Sage can get him away from his satellite phone—"

"Satellite phone?" I interrupt. "What is this, *Mission Impossible*?"

"Just listen," Sage says, shifting on the desk.

Jeremy bends around the scattered printouts and energy drink cans to grab a small black gadget with two cables hanging off it. "Sisters have been using tech like this, Natalia's tech, for years to obtain information for her. What if we used it against her?"

Sage and I stare, waiting for him to answer his own rhetorical question.

Jeremy's cadence picks up. "If I can send a message through his phone—a memo that looks as though it came from official channels—there's a chance Natalia's Russian contacts will think she's been turned."

I glare at him. "You want to trick them into believing she's working for *us*? That's your plan?"

"Yes," Jeremy says, a grin spreads across his face. "We'll send a memo planting a seed of doubt so potent they'll have to cut her loose. In their world, loss of trust is nonnegotiable."

"How do you know they'll even see this memo?"

Jeremy pulls up another screen full of numbers I don't understand. "The Russians are monitoring these communications. They have to be, with the encryption keys Natalia gave them. All we're doing is giving them something to find."

"Are you sure?" Sage asks.

"We've seen the satellite schematic Natalia sent to them. What else would it be for?"

I squint at the screen, which doesn't help me understand it. "So, you're what…prank-calling the Kremlin?"

Jeremy gives me his patient half smile. "Think of it as a two-part magic trick. Part one: We craft an official memo, accidentally-on-purpose revealing Natalia has been flipped and is a cooperating asset. Part two: We send another memo, panicking so much about the first memo being 'leaked' that no one questions its legitimacy in the first place."

"This sounds like something from one of those spy novels you're always—" I stop. "Oh my God. This *is* from a novel, isn't it?"

His cheeks flush. "Some of the brightest intelligence minds of the twentieth century wrote spy novels, Star. The concept is sound. Make it read as though someone has made a career-ending mistake. The fear in the second memo validates the claim in the first."

He smiles like the Cheshire Cat.

"That's…diabolical." I lean on the desk. "And if they trace it back to us?"

"Impossible. It's his phone. It'll look like an internal leak, not sabotage."

Sage studies the screen as if she's memorizing every pixel.

"You're going to seduce a government agent to do this?" I ask.

She stands, hand on her chin. "This guy has a thing for me, has for years. I don't think there will be much seduction necessary. He's…predictable." She stares at the back of the office, lost in thought.

"By the time they trace the breadcrumbs, Natalia will already be under a microscope…or worse," Jeremy says.

She moves around his desk. "How long would you need?"

"Sage, no." I move toward her. "This isn't—"

"How long, Jeremy?" She doesn't turn around.

"Five minutes. Maybe ten."

The room quiets except for the hum of Jeremy's computers. Sage's focus is absolute as she stares at the far wall.

"I can get him away from the phone. Then you come in and do what you have to do fast."

"This is crazy." I bounce between them. "You're both nuts. What if he catches on? What if he has security? What if—"

"What if it works?" Sage turns to face me. "What other plan do we have?"

"You want to play spy games with someone who plays them for real?"

"He'll be…occupied."

"So, we're risking your life on a Tom Clancy plot?"

"It wasn't Tom—" Jeremy starts, but Sage cuts him off.

"It's my risk to take, Star."

Sage holds my gaze, not asking for permission, but for trust. Jeremy is a kid playing with matches that could burn everything down, but he's *our* kid. Sage must have walked into rooms like this a dozen times and come out fine. Maybe I'm overthinking things. The fear is still an icy knot inside me, but beneath it, I believe in them.

I unclench my fists. "Okay," I say, the word tasting like both surrender and victory. "I hate it. But I trust you." Maybe this is what courage feels like. "But I'm going too."

"Star, there's no reason for that," Sage says

"Yes, there is." I cross my arms. "You don't get to be the only idiots in the room. I'm your lookout."

Sage rolls her eyes. "Fine."

Jeremy adjusts his glasses again. "We could… You could wear a wire. I mean, not a wire exactly, but a small mic."

"Where?" Sage asks simultaneously as I say, "No! A wire? Are you serious?"

Am I the only sane one in the room?

"It's a tiny microphone, no bigger than a dime," he explains. "We could stick it in a hair clip."

I sigh, loud and theatrically.

"We can have a code word you say when he's…you know, indisposed?" Jeremy cringes a little.

"Okay," she says.

Jeremy looks at us both. "So, we're doing it, then?"

"You're sure this will work?" I ask more for me than him.

"There are no guarantees. But it's playing the odds. And I think that's better than doing nothing, right?" he says.

Our eyes make a triangle, the decision settling in. Sage is the first to move, her face hard and emotionless.

"Good," she says. "Let's get to work, then."

THE CAFETERIA BUZZES with morning chatter. Three tables over, a group of Sisters laugh at something, their voices rising and falling in harmony. I used to sit at a table like that—full of noise and belonging. Three weeks ago, this corner table was a circus: Melody laughing too loudly at something Aura said, Kora swiping food off everyone's plates, Sage sipping tea and parsing out wisdom we'd all lean in to hear.

Now it's just me and the echoes of conversations past.

The empty chair across from me was Melody's. And Aura—no, Maitea now—out there somewhere, hopefully safer than she was here. I haven't seen Kora since the night in Sage's room, when everything went sideways.

"This is what winning looks like," I mutter to myself.

I open my notebook to a fresh page. Writing is the only thing that still feels normal.

If we pull this off tonight, what happens next?

The question hangs there, unanswered. The plan has never extended past burning Natalia. Never a consideration for what the Family becomes without her—or what I become without the Family.

Or what happens if the whole thing implodes and she finds out.

The cafeteria doors swing open, and a flash of red hair brightens the room. Sage glides in, perfectly poised in a pale yellow blouse and pressed slacks. She doesn't look my way—hasn't for days. It's all part of the plan, this cold war between us. I still haven't forgiven her, but my anger has softened. She's caught in this web too, and perhaps we can help free each other starting tonight.

If Jeremy's plan works—and that's a big *if*—we might finally have leverage against Natalia. We might get answers about what happened to Melody, about what happened to my sister.

Closing the notebook, I sweep the cafeteria one more time—all these women living double lives, some knowing it, some not. All the empty chairs where my friends used to sit. Where a future once seemed possible, before it all went down the drain.

Speaking of which, it's time to find Manolita and get my supplies. There are some toilets with my name on them.

Thirty Three

They're practicing in our King Room at the Plaza, and I channel my nervous energy into the only productive thing I can do: document everything. It smells like expensive carpet cleaner and that specific hotel air freshener that's supposed to be calming but only gives me butterflies. We're two floors below where the meeting is going to happen with Caron's contact.

"Again," Jeremy says.

Sage slides the thin mica sheet between the door and frame with practiced grace. She's done this six times already, each attempt smoother than the last.

"Better," he murmurs, adjusting his glasses. "But you're still letting the door close too hard. The sheet could slip if you're not careful."

Sage huffs, blowing a strand of hair from her face. "I know what I'm doing."

"Do you? Because two attempts ago, you almost dropped—"

"Children," I interrupt. "Play nice."

Watching them practice is twisting me up inside. Each time the plastic sheet slides between the lock, the reality of what we're about to do crashes into me. In less than an hour, Sage will use this trick when she enters the room with Caron's contact. Then we'll slip in behind her when she says the go phrase.

Simple. Except nothing about this is simple.

"One more time," Sage says, resetting her position outside the door.

Her black dress makes her look straight out of a Bond film. A gold hair clip she wears hides a miniaturized microphone Jeremy rigged to feed us her audio.

My focus returns to the notebook. If this goes wrong—*when* this goes wrong—at least there will be a record. My handwriting gets shakier with each line.

Plaza Hotel – Room 1604 – 7:14 p.m., Sage is practicing the door trick. Jeremy is nervous-eating Tic-Tacs. I'm pretending to be calm.

"Star, you're panicking," Sage says without turning around. "I hear your pen scratching from here."

"It's called documenting," I say, my pen still moving. "There's a difference."

"Is there?"

The door slides open again, and Sage steps through, the mica sheet in her right hand. She makes a show of looking around, impressed, while she slips the sheet against the latch. When she pulls the door closed, there's the faintest click—not the complete latch engaging, just the barest contact.

"Perfect," Jeremy says. "Just like that."

Sage turns to me with the hint of a smile that doesn't last long.

"How's the audio?" she asks, touching the clip.

Jeremy pulls the headphones from around his neck. "Crystal clear. Can you repeat the go phrase?"

"I could stay a while." The sensuality in her voice raises goose bumps on my arms.

"And the pull phrase?"

Sage sighs. "It's a little chilly in here."

"Better to have one than not, right?" he says.

Sage heads to the bathroom to finish her makeup while Jeremy taps away at his laptop.

Needing a distraction, I ask, "Hey, did you know Aura was leaving?"

He looks up and adjusts his glasses. "Yeah. A couple of days ago. The account deactivation order came in."

He swallows, like he's deciding whether to say more.

"What is it?"

He glances down, then back at me. "When I collected her badge, she put it in my hand and said, 'You take care of her, okay?'" He looks away. "I don't think I was supposed to tell you that."

"I'm going to miss her."

The thought of Aura—tiny and fierce, with her big hair and bigger attitude—makes my throat clench. She'd know what to say to loosen everyone up.

Jeremy nods, fingers pausing over the keyboard. "I always liked her, but she scared me."

"That's just because she called you 'tech boy' and threatened to put your glasses somewhere uncomfortable that one time."

"Twice, actually," he corrects with a smile.

Sage steps out of the bathroom, and the hotel lighting catches the copper undertones in her hair. Her black dress wraps her like a shadow, enhancing her elegance and mystery.

"What do you think?" she asks, turning in a circle.

She's as stunning as High Queen Estrella from my favorite fantasy series, but it takes a hard swallow simply to manage a casual "Amazing."

Jeremy's eyes dart between us, and he smiles nervously.

Sage walks to the center of the room and extends her arms. We rise from our seats to join her and clasp hands. Hers finds my right, Jeremy's my left.

Her palm is cool against mine, steady where I'm trembling.

"Let's get this done and get out of here," she says, focused and calm. "Quiet, simple, safe."

We squeeze a silent promise and then release. Sage gives us one last look and heads out the door.

THIRTY-FIVE MINUTES IS an eternity when you're waiting for something to go wrong. I check my phone for the tenth time, jiggling my leg so fast I'm practically vibrating off the chair.

"It's fine," Jeremy says, not looking up from his laptop. "The audio cutting out is normal with this kind of distance."

"Is it? Or are you saying that because you don't want me to freak out?" I twist a strand of hair around my finger, tighter and tighter, until it hurts. "What if they took her? What if she's in the back of some black SUV heading to New Jersey right now? Do you know how many bodies they've pulled out of the Meadowlands?"

Jeremy looks over his glasses. "You watch too many mob movies."

"And you don't watch enough!" I snap, then sigh. "Sorry. I—"

The laptop speakers crackle to life with a burst of digital static, and then Sage's voice filters through—distant and warbly.

"—think it's adorable—" *static* "—unicorn pajamas—" *static* "—would love—"

My heart stops. "Did she say *unicorn pajamas?*"

Jeremy leans forward and adjusts his laptop. "I…don't know."

The audio cuts out. I'm walking in the small space between the bed and the window.

"What happened? Why can't we hear her?" My palms press against my eyes. "This is bad. This is so bad."

"Star, relax. They're probably in the elevator. The signal can't penetrate—"

"Or they're in a soundproof room. Or he found the mic. Or—"

"Or they're in an elevator," Jeremy repeats, firmer now, tapping at his keyboard. "These old buildings have notoriously poor reception in the—"

The audio bursts back to life, much clearer this time. Sage's choreographed laugh fills the room.

"You should see it in the winter. It's just as nice," a deep male voice says.

"I'm sure it is," Sage replies, honey-smooth. "Maybe someday."

My legs go weak with relief. "She's okay."

A small smile plays on his lips. "Told you. Elevators."

I grab my notebook and scribble down the time and what we heard. My handwriting's still shaky, but at least now it's from relief instead of panic.

Plaza Hotel – Room 1604 – 8:41 p.m. : Unicorn Pajamas.

"This is us," Deep Voice says, and a door clicks open.

"Come on, Sage," Jeremy mutters under his breath.

"Oh wow, what an amazing room. Look at that view," Sage says, on her game.

The deep voice is distant now but still clear. "Can I get you a drink?"

A click—the door locking? It's hard to tell for sure.

Jeremy turns to me, a hopeful smile on his face. "So far, so good, yeah?"

I nod, biting at my cuticle.

For the next few minutes, Deep Voice talks about his cabin in the Adirondacks while Sage makes all the right impressed noises. There's a clink of glasses—he's relaxing. Trying too hard, but relaxing.

"So, this thing must be pretty important for the elusive Sage to come out of hiding," Deep Voice jokes.

"I wasn't in hiding, Tim. I do a different job now." She plays along smoothly.

Deep voice's name: Tim. Has a nice cabin. Won't shut up about it.

"Well, it's great to see you again either way," Tim says. "Let me give you what you came for."

There's a rustling noise, followed by what sounds like scratching.

"She's touching the hair clip," Jeremy murmurs.

"So, what's on this?" Sage asks.

"The truth about what happened that night," Tim replies. "It's shitty that it went down that way. I'm sorry."

"*Shitty?*" The word burns in my mouth like acid. Melody wasn't an inconvenience—some footnote in a DoD report. She was my best friend.

I grip the chair so hard my fingers turn red. "*Shitty,*" I repeat "That's what he calls it?"

Jeremy's hand covers mine—warm, steady. His touch startles me, but I don't pull away. For once, the anchor is welcome as rage and grief twist inside me.

"Easy." He squeezes my fingers.

There's the slight rustle of fabric, followed by the tiny *click* of a clasp—her purse. She must be securing whatever Tim gave her.

"Just be sure it gets to the right eyes," he says.

"Not my first rodeo, Tim," Sage retorts.

"That's for sure. Remember Georgetown?" he asks. "That senator's aide thought he was clever."

"Until you found his offshore account," Sage laughs. "He cried, didn't he?"

"Like a baby," Tim chuckles. "Those were simpler times."

"They were," Sage says. "Before Caron put you on permanent retainer. He knows which assets to keep close."

Tim chuckles again. "Hey, the old man's checks still clear. He takes care of the ones who take care of him. You know that better than anyone."

Jeremy leans forward in his chair, staring at the laptop. The audio is crystal clear—every breath, every clink of ice in a glass.

Tim + Sage laughing. He likes her. I hate him.

"You always were the best at getting what you needed," Tim says. His voice has that edge to it—the one men get when they've tag-teamed from the big brain to the little one.

More rustling. The sound of a glass being set down.

"Well, I guess I should go," Sage says, neutral and professional.

There's movement—fabric against fabric—and I imagine Tim standing, getting closer.

"You're still as incredible as you were back then, Sage."

The silence that follows seems endless. Jeremy's gripping his pen so hard it's bending. I hold my breath.

Then, Sage, silky and deliberate:

"I could stay a while."

My heart skips.

That's the go phrase.

BOUNCING up the stairs as fast as my legs will carry me, I use the handrail for balance as Jeremy rushes ahead. The go phrase keeps repeating in my mind—*I could stay a while, I could stay a while*—on an endless loop.

"Right here," he says over his shoulder, his laptop tucked under one arm, a small black device in his other hand. His glasses are sliding down his nose, but he doesn't have a free hand to push them up.

We ease the stairwell door open onto the eighteenth floor. The hallway stretches before us, all plush carpet and old-world charm. Everything about this place screams opulence. I should be used to it by now.

"Room 1811." I point down the corridor.

We walk as casually as we can—which isn't casual at all. My legs are tingling and weak, and he's got that hunched-over tech-guy walk, his shoulders pulled up to his ears as if trying to shield his laptop from the hotel's security cameras.

When we get to the door, he stops for a moment and pops in his headphones, straining to hear.

"There's lots of rustling," Jeremy says. "Tim asked her to sit—"

He frowns, looking at his phone.

"What?"

His eyes snap open, and his brows pull closer. "The audio went dead. There's nothing."

The base of my throat tightens. "What do you mean, nothing?"

"I mean *nothing*. Complete silence."

"Oh God." My hand swings out, grabbing his arm. "Sage—"

Jeremy exhales slowly. "Tell me you got it, Sage," he murmurs, like a prayer.

He extends his hand toward the door, pressing it gently. The door slides forward without resistance.

The mica sheet worked.

He pushes it open just enough for us to slip inside. The suite is larger than I expected, with a partition wall separating the entry area from what must be the bedroom. We creep in, and the door closes behind us with the barest click.

From beyond the partition comes the sound of light music and giggling.

He crouches down carefully, placing his equipment on the carpet. His fingers are steady as he pulls up a program on his laptop, but sweat beads at his temples.

"Find the phone," Jeremy says.

Scanning the room, I see Tim's blazer folded across a chair. Sage knows what she's doing. My knees carry me across the floor as I shimmy over. Lifting the blazer—it's heavier than expected—I surgically slip a hand into the breast pocket, extract a thick smartphone, and bring it back to Jeremy.

He taps out a few incantations on the keyboard, connects the device to Tim's phone and then to his laptop. His lips move, counting something under his breath, and there's no interrupting him when he's in the zone like this. The glow from the screen carves out the sharp lines of his face, a mask of focused relief. He looks like every renegade hacker from the movies, and for a second, I believe we could be that cool.

But it's not his magic show that has my attention right now; it's the sounds from beyond the partition wall. A moan? My mouth goes dry, heat crawling up my neck.

Not now. Focus.

Another moan, louder this time. The inside of my cheek takes the bite of my teeth, my nails digging into my thigh—anything to force the thoughts away.

Jeremy glances at me, eyebrow raised, then back at his screen. "Connecting now," he whispers.

The sounds from the other side of the partition are getting more intense. I squeeze my eyes shut, fighting the urge to—

BZZT BZZT.

The phone in Jeremy's hands lights up, vibrating violently. We both freeze, staring like it's a live grenade.

BZZT BZZT.

"Shit." Jeremy fumbles with it. He taps the Decline button.

We both exhale in relief, and he starts typing.

BZZT BZZT.

It starts again.

"Son of a…" He looks at me with panic on his face. "Answer it."

"Are you insane?" I hiss at him just as the music from the bedroom quiets.

BZZT BZZT.

A voice—it's Tim. "Is that my phone?"

Jeremy's face contorts like he's cosplaying a monitor lizard. "Answer it."

"Forget about it; they'll call back," Sage says. "Let me show you something much more interesting."

A part of me dies inside, but there's no time for fantasies. The music picks up again.

Jeremy shoves the phone into my hands. "Bluff them. I need to focus."

The buzzing is impossibly loud.

My fingers tremble as I take it from him. I manifest my Penny's Pleasure Palace voice and answer. "Hey there."

There's a pause. Then a confused man says, "Tim?"

Jeremy makes a frantic hand gesture at me.

"Oh, hi, Tiger," I purr, as I recall every femme fatale movie I've ever seen. "Timmy's going to be...tied up for a while, if you know what I mean."

I glance at Jeremy, and he's nearly choking.

"Who is this?" the man asks.

"Say room service," Jeremy mouths frantically.

I shake my head at him. "I'm the reason Tim can't answer his phone, sweetie."

"What?"

Jeremy looks like he's about to have an aneurysm. He points to the laptop where a progress bar shows 60%.

"Look, Timmy's got his...hands full at the moment," I continue, gaining confidence. "That's it. Right there, baby."

A weird thrill shoots through me—I'm enjoying this.

All the color in Jeremy's face is gone. He focuses on the laptop.

"I can take a message," I offer sweetly, "but he's got a lot of work to do still." I pull my face away from the phone. "Isn't that right, Timmy? Be a good boy for Mama."

I smile and shrug.

"Hang up," Jeremy mouths, eyes full of terror.

"I'll just...call back later," the man says, and the line goes dead.

We both stare at each other for a long moment, and then Jeremy lets out a shaky breath.

"That," he says, "was actually brilliant."

"Thanks," I whisper back, my hands shaking so much I almost drop the phone. "Next time, I'll be the hacker, you talk sexy."

He grins. "Deal."

The progress bar on the screen gets to 100%, and Jeremy

disconnects everything from his laptop and Tim's phone. "Put it back exactly as you found it." He hands the phone back to me.

I take it and creep back toward the partition, careful to stay focused on the blazer draped over the chair. The sounds from the bedroom are louder again, and I force myself to block them out. This isn't about Sage. This isn't about my stupid, irrational feelings.

The phone slips back into the breast pocket, arranged just as it was. Behind me, Jeremy is already packing his equipment. I sneak back across the room to join him, and we slip out the door, taking the mica sheet with us.

Leaving Tim in expert hands.

NATALIA CZARINA

Natalia sat in her father's bedroom, holding his weathered hand between her own. The red-eye from New York had left her body weary, but her spirit remained strong. There were no machines here, no doctors. This was how he wanted to go: dignified, on his terms. His once-powerful frame had withered, his skin translucent over blue veins, but his eyes—like a storm over the Baltic—were unchanged. She'd worn her most expensive suit today, a black Chanel with gold buttons. He would notice. He always noticed.

"Nadi," he called out, a shadow of the commanding tone that had guided her through adolescence. "Come closer."

She leaned in, her blonde hair falling forward. The room carried scents so familiar—paper, tobacco, and something distinctly him that she'd recognize anywhere.

"Papa," she managed, forcing the word past the tightness.

He strained for her cheek, hands trembling. "Look at you, my Nadi. So strong. So pure."

A hot sting surfaced behind her eyes, and she locked her jaw against it, focusing on the sharp crease of the bedsheet. Even now, she wouldn't disappoint him by showing weakness.

"Don't weep for me," he continued, each word costing him breath. "I cared for your mother as I cared for you. I served Russia in her glorious days, and I served her when she was broken. My ledger is clean. That is all a man can ask for on the day of his death."

Natalia nodded, unable to speak. The room darkened around them until there was nothing but his face and the warmth of his palm against her skin.

"Our name. Our blood. It dies as it lived." His fingers tightened on hers with a grip that belied the frailty of his frame. "But the flag, Nadi, the flag is eternal." His eyes filled with intensity. "Protect it as your family."

A quiet shudder went through her as his words locked into place, a new and permanent piece of her foundation. Not a request. A final command. A sacred trust.

The light shifted across his features, and she took in every line and hollow. How many times had she stood before him seeking approval? How many flawless performances, perfect exam scores, and strategic victories were laid at his feet like offerings? Yet here, at the end, Natalia understood that she'd been chasing his peace as much as his pride. She could carry what he'd built. His life's work wouldn't dissolve with his final breath. She would be the keeper of his flame.

"I will, Papa," she promised. "I will make you proud."

His lips curved in a smile as his eyelids drifted shut. "You already have, Моя крошка. You always have."

His breathing slowed, each rise of his chest shallower than the last. She didn't move. Didn't call for the nurse. This moment belonged to them alone.

As he slipped into sleep, Natalia stood and squared her posture. She would carry his legacy forward. The world would bend to her will, just as he'd taught her.

This is what he would leave her—not money or property, but purpose. Duty. Power.

Three days later, Natalia stood at attention as they lowered her father's casket into the frozen ground. Snow dusted her black coat, melting against the wool. The SVR captain approached, his uniform immaculate, his manner somber yet purposeful.

"Nadia Czarina," he said, "I would like to speak to you regarding an opportunity—"

She silenced him with a sharp look. "This is his day, not the time for such matters."

The captain nodded, retreating. As he passed, his hand brushed hers, leaving a small, stiff card in her palm before he disappeared into the crowd. Natalia turned back to view her father's legacy disappearing beneath Russian soil.

This was her true awakening.

MAY 24, 2022

The quarterly revenue report was the best one yet. Since she'd taken over day-to-day operations from Caron, the Family's profits had nearly tripled. What had begun as a high-end escort service now extended its reach into information brokerage, blackmail, and strategic corporate infiltration. Following the upward trajectory of the graph, with each peak representing another milestone in her ascension, she allowed herself a smile.

The leather portfolio closed, and she gazed around the office—all clean lines, Italian marble and glass—a far cry from Caron's old-world aesthetic with its heavy wood and European chairs. Redesigning this office had been her first executive decision. The past had its place, but the future required clarity, determination, and transparency.

A television mounted on the wall played CNN on mute, the footage of President Putin standing stone-faced at a summit in Moscow. Something stirred in her—a familiar ache she couldn't quite name.

She unmuted the set and observed Putin in his element, his expression inscrutable as European leaders shifted uncomfortably beside him. The ticker underneath announced new sanctions against the country. "Russia's invasion of Ukraine enters its third month," the reporter said. "Attempts to negotiate a halt to aggressions have thus far proven unsuccessful."

"Look at you," she whispered in her native tongue. "Playing the long game."

Natalia poured herself a glass of thirty-year-old scotch, remembering her father's words: *Drink nothing you cannot taste the struggle in.* He had preferred vodka—harsh and unforgiving—not this amber liquid that slid down her throat like silk.

Her phone rang—another CEO requesting some of her girls for an executive retreat. The details were confirmed mechanically while she fixated on the television. Russia was moving, risking, while she…

what? Arranged dates for wealthy men and collected secrets that rarely mattered beyond quarterly board meetings?

She glanced at her Cartier watch, her pale pink Jimmy Choos. So polished. So American.

Her father had lived in a three-room apartment until the day he died. He maintained the same lifestyle for forty years and considered meat at dinner a luxury. Yet he'd shaped history, moved invisible levers of power while men like these Manhattan millionaires slept soundly in their beds.

"I've become a businesswoman," she said to the empty room, the words bitter on her tongue.

Setting down the glass, she slid her shoes off and stood in first position. Her father hadn't raised her to count money. Her feet shifted into second and then third positions. She wasn't brought up to wear pretty things. Fourth position. He'd raised her to bend the world, to matter. Fifth position. Her legs lowered into a demi-plié, and the burn rose inside her.

The ornate lacquered box sitting on her credenza called out to her. A gift from her father when she left for America, it held treasured memories and reminders of him. She lifted the top and dug through the old medals and photographs until she plucked out a single business card inscribed in Cyrillic. The SVR captain had pressed it into her palm after the funeral. "Should your path ever align with ours," he had said.

Natalia opened her laptop and began typing. There were connections to be made, old contacts to resurrect. The Family provided her resources, but resources without purpose were just decorations.

This was her true calling.

JUNE 17, 2022

The café was quiet, just as she preferred. Natalia stirred her tea methodically, watching the clouds swirl in circles. Across from her sat Dmitri Volkov, a cultural attaché whose actual position she'd deduced within minutes of their introduction.

"Your father was a great man," Volkov said. "I worked with him briefly in '92. The collapse was difficult for patriots like him."

Natalia kept her face neutral. "I didn't arrange this meeting to reminisce about my father."

Volkov smiled. "Direct. Like him." He slid a plain manila folder across the table. "Russia is rebuilding, Nadia Czarina."

She opened the folder, riffling through its contents. A list of American defense contractors. Names of officials. Code names: *Aegis Phoenix* and *Thunder Guard*.

"The Family has access to powerful men," Volkov continued. "Men who speak freely after liquor and…companionship."

"You want me to spy?"

"I want you to serve," he corrected. "As your father did."

Her father's voice, firm but gentle in her mind: *Never betray your principles, Nadi. A man can survive anything but the death of his honor.*

"My father would never sell secrets."

"This is not a transaction, Nadia Czarina. This is duty. Purpose." He caught her eye. "The world that your father believed in is returning. Help Russia reclaim her dignity."

Natalia's fingers tightened around her teacup. Was this betrayal? Or only fulfilling what her father had asked of her?

Bend the world, Nadi.

"The men change. Governments rise and fall. But Russia—Russia is forever," Volkov said.

She saw her current life—arranging escorts, collecting trivial corporate secrets, amassing wealth that meant nothing to history. What would her father think of that?

American money has made you soft.

She took the folder. "I'll need certain assurances."

Three weeks later, Natalia dead-dropped her first intelligence package—schematics for a Spitfire missile gleaned from a senator's aide during a weekend in the Hamptons. As the confirmation came through her handler, pride washed over her—a feeling she hadn't experienced since childhood, a pride in service to something greater than herself.

This was her true inheritance.

JANUARY 11, 2023

The ticking of her father's antique clock was the only sound in her office. The report sitting in front of her detailed Sparrow's death during the operation; how the girl had been caught accessing files from a lieutenant colonel's laptop—a simple job gone wrong. Security had been unexpectedly upgraded. Sparrow panicked and hadn't made it out of the room.

"Such a waste," Natalia spat, running her finger along the edge of the paper.

Sage stood in front of her desk, hands clasped behind her back.

"This was a major lapse in judgment." She glared at Sage.

"I'll talk to Kora, make sure she understands."

"You're giving her too much rope. One day she'll end up hanging herself." She slid her glasses off and deliberately laid them on the desk. "Or you. I trust this will be handled."

Sage nodded.

"What about the body?"

"Already taken care of, ma'am."

"Good. She served with honor. The other Sisters should know that." Natalia picked up her glasses and slid them back on.

Sage gritted her teeth. "This won't happen again, ma'am."

"No, it won't." Sage was dismissed with the wave of a hand.

Natalia walked to the credenza, where her father's photograph stood in a simple silver frame. He looked out at her, proud in his impeccable uniform.

"You understand, don't you, Papa?" she whispered, touching the glass. "The part serves the whole."

The dossiers covered her desk, with the names of the parts embossed along the top: *Jade, Denali, Rose.* She had access to the best technology in the world, but she liked to hold the individual components in her hands, rearranging the paper folders like pieces of her majestic machine.

Sparrow had been a vital, but ultimately replaceable cog. Her father's words came back to her: *The watchmaker does not mourn the spring. He exchanges the broken for the new and winds the clock.*

"We make them into something," she said, "or they are scrap."

The Family was no longer Caron's simple business but her grand complication, a timepiece of immense power. And if one gear failed, a careful hand could always replace it; it was a mechanism of perpetual progress. The Sisters were the gears and springs that she assembled in perfect synchrony.

Her father's clock ticked—a steady, unfeeling rhythm—the sound of purpose.

This was her legacy.

Thirty Four

Cross-legged in Sage's desk chair, I bounce my leg in a nervous rhythm against the wood as she pulls her laptop closer. The scent of jasmine tea is in the air, and it's remarkable how much better it looks than the last time I was here. The wine stains are still faint on the wall, but otherwise, it's immaculate.

"Ready?" she asks, tucking her hair behind her ear.

"No."

Tim gave her a USB drive with documents about Melody's final night. My best friend, reduced to just a DoD incident report.

"Jeremy went through everything." She taps on her keyboard. "There was a ton of bureaucratic bullshit, but he made a summary of both reports—the official one and the internal one."

I pick at a hangnail until it bleeds. "And they're different?"

"Of course they're different." She looks up. "What 'happened' versus what *actually* happened."

Sage turns the screen toward me, and there's a presentation with neat bullet points and highlighted sections that make my palms sweat. Jeremy's work is always so organized, so clinical, even when it's documenting the worst thing imaginable.

"You sure you're okay?" she asks, softer now.

I nod, though I'm not. But the not-knowing is worse.

Sage scrolls through the document, and I lean forward, a fist inside my guts, squeezing them tighter—the truth about Melody.

"So, the official report is a complete whitewash," Sage says. "No mention of the agent's misconduct. Just calls it an 'accident involving a hired escort.'" She scrolls down, her finger pointing to the screen. "And they kicked it to local police, knowing full well it would go nowhere."

I dig my nails into my palm. "Of course they did."

"But the internal report…" Sage pauses. "Jesus…"

"She was caught, wasn't she? Trying to get the data."

Sage nods, somber. "He woke up during the process. Identified himself as a federal agent and told her not to move."

Melody panicked, her hands fumbling with the device, the raw fear when everything went wrong—the visions won't stop coming.

"She ran down the hall," Sage continues, her breath catching. "He chased her."

"Did he have a gun?"

She scans the document. "It doesn't say. But she ran into an empty room that was under renovation."

The scene flashes in my head with terrible clarity: Melody, frightened, cornered, looking for any way out. The agent pursuing her, his footsteps right behind her.

"The balcony."

Sage's chin quivers. "According to the agent, she slipped and lost her footing. Fell backward through the broken balcony railing."

My hand flies to my mouth, but a sob still pushes through, a choked, ugly sound. The image burns in my mind: Melody stumbling, arms windmilling, the moment of horrible realization as she tipped over the edge.

"The agent looked over the railing." Sage holds back a sob. "But she'd fallen too far. He could see her body near the service entrance."

The room swirls around me. I squeeze my eyes shut, but that only makes it more vivid—Melody's body, broken on the concrete, the red dress she loved so much spread around her like spilled wine.

"They escorted Jade out. Dismissed her and told her nothing." Sage scrolls down. "Then they approached hotel security and demanded the footage be erased. When the employees refused—" She gasps, her face pale. "They drew their weapons. Forced them to delete everything."

"What the hell?"

"Then they just left. Left her there." Sage's voice breaks.

The laptop slides off her knees as she covers her mouth with her hands. Her entire body shakes with silent sobs.

Moving from the chair, I slide onto the bed and wrap my arms around her. Sage buries her face against my shoulder, her tears soaking through my shirt.

"It's my fault," she wails against my neck. "I should never have sent her."

"No," I say, my guilt choking me. "This is on them. The fucking government. The Family. The entire system."

I stroke Sage's hair, remembering how Melody used to braid mine when I was nervous. The thought squeezes my heart.

"Caron's team must have arrived right after," Sage says, pulling back. Tearstains trail down her cheeks. "That's how they recovered her pendant. But they were too late."

"She was alone, Sage," I say, the words like acid.

She takes my face in her hands. "She didn't die for nothing, Star. We're going to make this right."

Right? What does right look like anymore? How do you make a senseless death meaningful? How do you balance the scales when someone you love is gone forever?

She pulls me in again, and we cling to each other, two broken people trying to stay afloat in the wreckage of it all.

"She deserved better," Sage says into my hair. "She deserved so much better than this."

All I can picture is Melody's smile, her stupid jokes, the way she'd always save me the last piece of bacon at breakfast. Her silly seahorse. How we pinkie swore we'd always be there for each other.

I wasn't. How do you make that right?

"THAT'S THE THING," Jeremy says with rare confusion in his voice. "There's no way this would have been on DoD servers with the other files. Tim must have put this here on purpose. Maybe as a warning?"

My arms cross as I lean against his desk. Tim's USB drive contained more than just Melody's files.

"And you're sure this is legit?" I ask. "Sage and I just looked at what you sent over."

Jeremy straightens his glasses. "As far as I can tell, yeah. The file structure, the formatting, the signature—it all matches legitimate FBI documents I've seen before. I missed it when I went through the first time."

"So, the FBI is planning to raid us? Raid the Family?"

"Yes."

"In three days?"

"Yes."

"And there's nothing we can do about it?"

"No."

The room gets a little swirly. "So, what does this mean? We're all going to prison?"

Jeremy's hand messes up his hair, and it would be cute if we weren't discussing the end of days. "I don't think that's realistic. But it won't be good for Caron and Natalia."

Something clicks in my brain—a half-formed thought, dangerous and tempting. My face contorts, torn between loyalty and justice.

He leans forward. "What?"

"Do we tell them?" The words fall out of my mouth. "Isn't it good if the feds come in and bust them?"

Jeremy scoffs. "It's not just them, Star. It's me, it's you, it's every Sister out there."

"You said we weren't all going to prison!" I yell, throwing my arms in the air.

"I said it wasn't realistic, but it's still possible." He takes his glasses off and cleans the lenses.

His words land. This isn't a surgical strike that would only remove the corrupt leadership. It's a sledgehammer that would crush everyone in the Family—guilty or innocent—girls who have nowhere else to go. Girls like me.

"We need to tell Caron."

Jeremy nods. "I think you're right."

"Let Sage know we're heading up. And print that out." I head for the door.

THE SECOND THE elevator doors open, the shouting from inside the office echoes off the marble floors and wooden walls. Not just any shouting—the kind that bristles your skin because you know you're not meant to hear it.

Jeremy and I approach Caron's office cautiously. Kari is standing frozen by her desk, her face drained of color. She widens her eyes and shakes her head at us—sign language for *Turn around and run.*

"—*years* of my life!" Then a slam on the desk. "While you sat there playing father figure to broken dolls!" That's Natalia.

"You think your twisted games are helping them?" Caron. Raw with a rage I've never heard from him. "This was not about power or politics. We were supposed to protect them."

"Protect them?" Natalia laughs. "From what? Reality? The world uses people. I just made sure we were the ones doing the using!"

Jeremy is practically vibrating with the need to flee. I see the sheer panic in his eyes and realize he's a liability here. Natalia can't know he's been plotting against her.

I jerk my head toward the narrow stairwell past Kari's desk—the one Caron took me down when he recruited me. "Go," I whisper, giving his arm a firm squeeze.

He doesn't need to be told twice. He gives me a quick, grateful nod and flows into the shadows, melting out of sight as the argument escalates.

"You turned my family into a weapon." Caron's voice hardens. "My girls into soldiers."

"Your family?" Natalia says. "Your girls? I built this empire while you played cards with your favorites and turned a blind eye. As long as the money came in, the details didn't matter."

The elevator dings behind us, and Sage steps out, her eyes widening as she takes in the scene. She hurries over, asking quietly, "What's happening?"

"World War Three," I say.

"You turned this into your twisted political crusade," Caron shouts, and something hits the floor. "Selling everyone out, and for what?"

"You were fine with selling information for years!" Natalia shrieks. "Suddenly, the buyer makes a difference?"

"Do you honestly believe your father would approve of this?"

"Don't you dare judge me. I did what had to be done. My father was twice the man you are. You stand for nothing. You're weak."

"Weak?!" The crash of shattering crystal punctuates the word. "I protected you! When they came looking, I protected all of you. You lied to me."

Sage moves closer to me, her shoulder pressing against mine. We stand in a little huddle of dread as the argument rages on.

"You're living in the past," Natalia says. "The world changed. I changed with it."

"I should have stopped you years ago," Caron says, "when I first suspected."

"But you didn't," Natalia barks. "Because deep down, you wanted it too. You needed the power, but you didn't have the balls to do what was necessary."

"I had lines I wouldn't cross."

"Lines are for losers. For those who stand for nothing."

The office door flies open, and Natalia emerges in a blaze of blonde hair and fury. She stops short when she sees us clustered together. But it's not *her* presence that makes my jaw drop—it's Kora standing right behind her. Kora—who hasn't spoken to me since Sage almost killed her—glares at me now with a stony stare.

Natalia scowls as she takes us in. "Well," she says, "it appears the children have arrived to witness the divorce."

Kora steps up beside her, arms crossed—she's thinner, but not weak. "You."

Sage steps forward. "Kora, I—"

"Don't." Kora raises her hand. "Just don't."

Natalia turns back to Caron, who's standing in the doorway of his office. He appears smaller somehow: hunched over, cheeks slack.

"You don't know how to recruit girls who can do the work anymore." Natalia's gaze slides to me. "Instead, you bring in wayward orphans."

My cheeks burn. I open my mouth to snap back, but my tongue is glued in place.

"Girls with no skills, no value. Is this a business or a daycare?" She surveys me. "Just another mouth to feed, another body to clothe. Pathetic."

"That's enough, Nadia," Caron says from the doorway, his face ashen.

"No, it's not nearly enough." She turns back to him. "You've grown soft. We require strength, not sentimentality."

"The Family was never meant to be this," he says.

"The Family was nothing but a whorehouse"—Natalia points to her chest—"until I made it powerful. Made it matter."

Sage shifts beside me, her hand finding my elbow in silent support.

"You were always afraid of the spotlight. Always hiding in shadows. That's why you're being left behind." She turns to Sage, her face cold. "And you. Did you think I wouldn't find out about your little meeting with him? Your failed attempt to play both sides?"

Sage doesn't flinch. "Natalia—"

"*Nyet!*" Natalia raises her hand. "I trusted you. Groomed you. And you betrayed me for this…fossil."

"She's not the only one who feels betrayed," Kora says, stepping forward.

Sage wilts. "Kora, please—"

Kora's gaze sweeps over us, landing on Sage with purpose. "Your problem, Sage, is you want everyone to love you. You can't stand to pick a side, so you play games with all of us until we break." She gestures to herself. "Guess who broke first?"

"That's not fair." Sage pounds her fist into her hip.

"No?" Kora tilts her head to the side. "You used me. For years. And when I became inconvenient, you tossed me aside for a new toy."

Sage flinches.

"I understand loyalty." Kora moves closer to Natalia. "Not whatever game you've been playing."

Natalia places a hand on Kora's shoulder, a gesture that's both protective and possessive. "Some of us know where we belong."

They move to leave, and Natalia pauses directly in front of me. "You have no place here. You never did."

They disappear down the hallway, leaving me stunned.

Caron sinks into the chair behind Kari's desk, running a hand over his face. "Come in," he says finally, gesturing toward his office. "All of you."

Jeremy reappears from the stairwell, clutching the printout, his face pale but resolved.

We file in after Caron. The office is a mess—papers scattered across the floor, a chair on its side, the crystal decanter shattered in the corner, aged bourbon wafting through the air.

"I apologize that you had to witness that," he says. "It was… unprofessional."

"What happened?" I ask.

Caron picks up the overturned chair. "The truth happened." He looks at each of us. "Natalia has been using the Family for years. Not just as a business, but as her political cudgel."

Jeremy steps forward, clearing his throat. "Sir, we have something you need to see."

He places the printout on Caron's desk. The top page has "Federal Bureau of Investigation - *Classified*" stamped across it in bold red letters.

"What is this?" Caron asks, grabbing the paper.

"They're coming for us in three days," I say.

Caron looks up sharply. "Where did you get it?"

"It was part of Tim's intelligence," Jeremy says.

"How?"

"I asked the same thing. He went out of his way to include this."

"As a warning," I say.

"And it's authentic?"

"Yes, sir. The signature, the formatting—it all checks out."

Caron leans back, staring at the ceiling. Then he cackles like a man dancing on the edge of a cliff.

"Caron?" Sage says, stepping toward him.

His laugh fades as he slumps forward and taps his finger on the paper. "I should show this to Nadia, just to see her face when she realizes it's all over."

He pushes the paper toward me on his desk and rubs his face. "But what would she care? She'll be on a private jet to Moscow before the first agent kicks in the door. Leaving us to pick up the pieces and start over."

A heavy silence envelops the room. Jeremy stares at his shoes. Sage stands still, her posture belying her uncertainty. Caron falls back into his chair, glancing at the paper and then at me.

I snatch the printout off the desk and turn toward the door.

"Star, what are you doing?" Sage asks, but I'm already moving.

"Sitting around all gloom and doom ain't gonna fix this," I say, heading for the door. "I'm done waiting."

"Where are you going?" Caron asks.

With the paper clutched in my fist, I turn around. "To do something stupid. Or brilliant. I'll let you know how it turns out."

Jeremy catches my eye through the doorway, and his face shifts with realization. This is what we planned for—the Plaza, the satellite phone, the messages—the trap we set.

I want to hear it snap.

Thirty Five

The paper crumpled in my fist is a verdict. Ghosts walk with me down this hall: Melody's smile, her body broken on the concrete. Amelia's face, her last words scrawled in a journal. All the girls that the Family used up and threw away. This ends now. Or I do.

My heart tries to batter its way out of my ribs. Every breath is gasoline, waiting for a spark. Grief and fear are gone. All that's left is the burning.

"Star! Wait!" Sage yells, her footsteps scrambling behind me. "There's something you need to know!"

I don't slow down. Don't look back. I'm done with hesitation, done with careful planning, done with being Star.

I slam through Natalia's office door, and the sound cracks off the marble. She's standing behind her broad glass desk, and her head whips toward the door.

"How dare you—" she starts.

"No!" The word comes out raw, visceral. "You don't get to play Queen Bitch anymore."

Fire crawls up my spine. "You're over," I say, the words pressing out of me. "The girls you've used, the lives you've crushed—now you pay for it."

Natalia gestures in my direction, emotionless. "Remove her."

Kora starts toward me, but something inside me cracks wide open. All the fear, all the hesitation, all the times I've bitten my tongue—no longer.

"You're such a fucking coward," I spit at Natalia. "Hiding behind these girls, using them as shields while you cower up here. When's the last time you got your own hands dirty? Afraid of getting blood on your manicure?"

Natalia's posture slips for a moment. She darkens as if she's never been spoken to like this.

"You ignorant child." Her accent is thick with contempt. "You have no idea what you're poking at. Go back to your gutter before you get hurt."

The door swings open behind me, and Sage rushes in. Kora steps away from me toward Sage, and her face is a stop sign.

But I'm not done. Not even close.

"Is that what you told Amelia before you had her killed?"

The words tear out of my throat like razors. The air goes still, as if everyone has stopped breathing.

Natalia's face tightens, and her lips curl into a snarl. The mask has slipped off, and what's underneath is so much darker than I expected. Her eyes are like a hurricane.

She places both hands on the desk and leans toward me.

"Yes." Her voice is pure frost. "That's what I told her."

The force of her "yes" travels through the floor and up into my legs, which threaten to give out, my knees locking to keep me from collapsing right here on the cold marble.

"She never knew when to stop pushing," Natalia continues. "Clearly, it runs in the blood. Her idiot misfits—always digging and pushing, writing that fucking blog, post after post." Spittle flies from the corner of her mouth.

My vision blurs at the edges. Amelia. My sister. Dead because she wouldn't stop fighting.

"They had to be taught a lesson," Natalia says with a shrug.

Every cell in my body is screaming. The pain is so absolute it could drown me, but I shove it down, lock it away. I can fall apart later. Right now, I have to finish this.

"You think you're some perfect soldier, but you're just a monster who uses lost girls as ammunition in your little war. No more." My face is alight with an inferno of rage as I glower at her.

I slam the FBI report down on her desk so hard her candy bowl rattles.

"They're coming for you, bitch."

The paper spreads across the glass like a wanted poster. Three days. That's all she has left before the walls come crashing down around her little empire.

Surprise crosses her face as she scans the document, then fades as she reads with increasing urgency. Her laughter, when it comes, is crystalline and cruel—the sound of something precious shattering.

"This is your fault," she snaps, looking at Sage. "You always were shit at recognizing talent. Sending a child like Melody to do a woman's work."

Sage's face is stoic and unreadable.

"The one who couldn't follow simple instructions." Natalia's irritation level is rising. "She was supposed to be invisible. You sent her to die."

"No!" rips from my throat like a battle cry. "This is *your* fault! You used Melody! For what? So you could play spy from a Fifth Avenue mansion while these girls died for you? You couldn't even see you were being set up. Your fucking ego killed her!"

Rage nearly steals my voice, but I push through. "You're a traitor. You should rot for what you've done."

"I am a patriot!" Natalia slams her hand on the desk, seething. "Americans don't understand the word. You play pretend with it. I sacrifice for it!" She snatches a crystal paperweight and hurls it at the wall to her left, where it explodes into glittering shrapnel.

I flinch but don't look away.

"Do not lecture me about honor, child. I know courage. What it means to fight for something real. You're just an infant playing at revolution." She picks up the report and shakes it. "This means nothing to me."

Her body shakes; her composure is shattered. This is who she truly is—a woman who'd die for an idea but wouldn't help the person next to her. She screams about honor while the people who trusted her bleed out at her feet. All that brilliance, all that power, wasted on abstract concepts instead of actual human beings. I almost feel sorry for her.

"I don't need this anymore," she snarls. "I don't need any of this."

She crumples the raid order into a ball and fires it straight at my chest. It bounces off me and lands at my feet like a grenade.

"This is your problem now," she spits. "I hope they fry you all."

I take a step toward her, but an arm locks around me from behind. It's Sage.

"Star, don't. Let her run."

Natalia walks to the far corner, her footsteps like a countdown. She presses her palm against a black panel, and a section of the wall slides away, revealing a safe. The electronic lock beeps as she presses her thumb against it.

"You have no idea what you've done." She turns her back to us and begins emptying it.

A maroon leather bag comes out first, then stacks of cash—more than I've ever seen in one place. Bills bound with paper bands, thick as novels. Next, her hand emerges with something that weakens my legs.

A gun. Small and silver. She places it on her desk with the casual indifference of someone setting down car keys.

My throat constricts. Every instinct screams at me to run, but my feet are welded to the floor. A stupid thought flashes in my mind—*she wouldn't, not in front of everyone*—but the truth crashes in before I can finish. This is Natalia. Of course she would.

"Years of my life," she says, opening the bag, "spent building this place. Keeping you all safe, fed, and relevant."

She cradles the antique clock from her bookshelf—ornate, old-world. She looks at it like a favorite child's toy before placing it carefully inside. "Just to have you piss it away. None of you deserve this life."

The cash disappears into it in neat stacks. Followed by files, a red passport, jewelry that glitters like captured starlight.

"I was the glue," she continues, eerily calm, as if she's narrating for herself. "The spine that held this Family upright. Without me, you would all be back on the street where you belong."

She taps on her laptop, and the enormous monitor above her desk flickers to life, mirroring the screen. Her fingers skip across the keyboard effortlessly.

"But now?" She laughs, cold and sharp. "Now I get to go home. Where loyalty means something."

A terminal window opens—black background, green text. Command prompt blinking.

"And in six months, when I'm sipping tea in Gorky Park, I won't remember this place existed."

She types a string of numbers and letters into the window that mean nothing to me but everything to whatever system she's accessing, then pokes the Enter key.

"You don't realize how good you had it."

"Why?" Sage asks. "Why did you do all this?"

Natalia doesn't look up from the bag. "You wouldn't understand. You think your father was a player? No, just an incompetent criminal who couldn't launder money properly." She zips the bag, and it sounds like a record scratch. "Legacy means nothing to people like you."

Sage's jaw tightens, but she doesn't respond.

"I owe you nothing." Natalia slings the bag over her shoulder, and the gun disappears inside her jacket like a magic trick.

Something on the monitor changes, and it catches my eye. The terminal window has updated.

She takes a piece of hard candy from the bowl on her desk and pops it into her mouth.

"You might want to make alternate plans," I say steadily.

Natalia's head snaps toward the screen. Her face drains of color, features falling slack.

Glowing on the monitor, in bold green letters against the black background:

[SESSION TERMINATED] – [ASSET DEACTIVATED]

"What?" Her eyes widen as she flops the bag down and lunges for her laptop, fingers flying across the keys. "No, no, no…"

She types frantically—passwords, commands, anything. But the same message keeps appearing, repeating like a digital death knell.

[SESSION TERMINATED] – [ASSET DEACTIVATED]

Kora moves behind her, staring at the screen over her shoulder.

"Th-This isn't possible," Natalia stutters. "I have protocols, assurances—"

[SESSION TERMINATED] – [ASSET DEACTIVATED]

The message blinks like a heartbeat, then stops. Flatline.

Natalia whirls around, her face feral. "What did you do?" she growls.

Joy surges through me, pure and fierce. We did it. *He* did it. Jeremy's brilliant, insane plan worked. We burned her on both sides. A genuine smile spreads across my face—the first in months—and the expression it puts on hers is worth every sleepless night since Melody died.

"No country for old spies, huh?" I pick up the crumpled FBI order at my feet.

My smile is the last straw. Natalia's face loses all expression as the light behind her eyes dims. Her hand moves into her jacket as if swatting a fly, and there's a gleam of metal.

The gun.

The world narrows to the space between us. The silver glints as her arm lifts with unnatural slowness, the dark barrel growing larger as it fixes on me. My body knows to move, but my muscles are frozen by the impossibility of it all. This is how I die—not from cancer or old age or in a blaze of glory, but from a woman who can't take a joke.

"Star!" A full-throated scream from beside me.

Sage hits me like a linebacker, her shoulder driving into my ribs. We go down hard, my hip cracking against the marble floor as a gunshot thunderclaps through the office, so loud it steals the air from my lungs. There's only silence after, then a high, metallic whine that bores through my brain.

I'm not dead. We're a tangle of limbs on the floor, and Sage's body presses down on me while something warm and wet soaks through my jeans. The room stinks like the firecrackers Amelia and I would toss out the window on the Fourth of July.

"Sage?" I croak out.

She tries to say something back, but all that comes out is a choked breath. A patch of dark red is spreading across her blouse on the right side. It's blood. Her blood.

"Sage!" I shriek, rolling her gently off me. Crimson blooms through her blouse and runs onto the floor, onto me, pooling around us as if her very essence is draining away. The taste of triumph sours as she lies there. All our planning, all our cleverness—for what? So my friend could bleed out on the floor?

Natalia leans over her desk and adjusts her aim. The gun swings toward me again, and no one's left to push me out of the way. I close my eyes and wait for the blackness to come.

A blast.

But it's not a gunshot. The office door bursts inward, and I look over as Caron rushes through it. It's his body, wearing his suit, but the person inside isn't him any longer. His eyes are orbs of black fire, burning with a fury so intense it's completely erased the man I knew.

Natalia swings the gun away from me and toward him. I'm frozen as she takes aim. Something moves behind her.

Kora—a flash of decision.

Her eyes snap, and in a blur of motion, she lunges—not at Caron, but at Natalia, grabbing Natalia's wrist and pushing it toward the wall as she fires. The bullet ricochets off the marble column, sending chips dancing through the air.

Natalia can't regroup before Caron is on her. His hand closes around her throat like a vise, and the gun clatters to the floor.

"No more lives, Nadia!"

He lifts her clean off the ground, her feet kicking vainly in the air before he brings her head down on the desk with the dreadful sound of shattering glass. The candy in her mouth flies across the office.

"Killed my Sisters, tore my Family apart!"

"Caron, no!" The scream is trapped in my throat, no idea if I'm making any sound. A nightmare. Move. Speak. Nothing works.

"Betrayed me!" His voice is guttural, almost howling.

Another slam. Natalia's head bounces off the glass, and something wet spatters across it, speckling the papers. Her left eye bulges from her horrifically discolored face.

"No more lives!" His crying is a startling mix of rage and devastation.

The next slam is the worst. Something shatters—bone or glass? The sound is sickeningly final. Natalia goes limp, her head lolling at an impossible angle. Blood pools beneath it, mixing with the scattered documents and shards.

Caron lets go, and she crumples to the floor, a broken doll in a heap of tailored wool.

The violence ends, leaving a vacuum in its place. Sage's labored breathing and the distant hum of the ventilation system fill the void. Natalia isn't moving. At all.

Kora sprints around the desk and drops to her knees beside Sage. Her hands shake as she cradles Sage's head, and the sound that comes from her throat is raw and savage, like something is dying inside her.

"Nightingale!" she screams. "Call in a Nightingale!"

I'm floating, as if this is happening to someone else. The world fractures into a series of stuttering images, sounds muffled by the ringing in my ears. Natalia's body. Sage's blood. Kora's sobbing. Caron, standing over the wreckage, looking at his hands. The question rises out of the devastation.

What the hell just happened?

The world comes back in fragments—sounds first, then streams of light through my blurry vision. My ears are clanging like church bells, but Caron clears the haze. "Code Nightingale in the executive row. Now!"

He bites off the words, breaking at the end. The order is sharp, but underneath it, he sounds like a man calling the fire department while watching his own house burn down.

I turn my head, and the movement sends lightning through my skull. Kora is there, cradling Sage's head with shaking hands while blood spreads across the white marble like spilled paint.

"Stay with me, Red, please," Kora says, voice thick with tears. "I got you."

From behind me, Caron again, in fragments: "…extract sensitive materials…"

Kora holds her hand over Sage's side, blood oozing through her fingers. "She came to me in the hospital," Kora says, "said you'd need someone to have your back."

The words don't make sense at first. Hospital? Back? Then it clicks—the way Kora moved when Natalia raised the gun. No hesitation. Pure purpose.

Sage glances at me. That's what she was trying to tell me in the hall.

Kora kisses Sage's forehead, stroking her hair. "Shannon, I'm sorry I wasn't fast enough."

"Shh" is all Sage can manage, her voice like air.

The sound breaks something inside me. This isn't the end I envisioned. I told Caron it would be stupid or brilliant. Looks like it was both.

When I turn back, Caron's face is wet with tears. His hands are shaking as he stares down at what's left of Natalia, what he's done.

Kora and I huddle around Sage as the medical team pours out of the elevator. We step aside as they surround her.

"Go," Caron says, not looking at us. "All of you. Let me take care of this."

Before we leave, Caron kneels beside Natalia's broken body, his hand resting on her head, gentle now, almost tender. He's crying—great, heaving sobs that shake his entire frame.

He'd created this place with his own hands. Now they were covered in the blood that might tear it all down.

THIRTY SIX

Coiled into the chair across from Caron's desk, I pull my knees up to make myself feel smaller. The tang of bourbon and something else I don't want to think about right now hangs in the air.

Caron is sitting on his desk, phone pressed to his ear. He's aged a decade in the last few hours. "That's great to hear. Thank you so much," he says, his voice hoarse. "Yes, please let me know right away."

He hangs up and looks at me, a hint of relief softening his features.

"Sage is out of surgery. The bullet hit her hip bone. She'll have trouble walking for a while, but she'll be okay."

The knot in my midsection loosens just enough for me to breathe again. "That's great news."

We sit in silence for a moment, heavy with the reality of it all.

"So, what now?" I ask. "With the raid coming and all—"

"There is no raid, Esther."

My face goes blank. "What do you mean, there's no raid?"

Settling back against his desk, he folds his hands in his lap like a priest at confession and lets out a long breath.

"I asked Tim to plant the raid order," Caron says. "It's not real."

The room tilts. My hands clench the arms of the chair. "You… What?"

"Tim has been a friend of the Family for many years, so I asked him this favor. I knew you would discover it and bring it to me." He studies his hands. "Natalia only responds to overwhelming force. I needed her to have a reason to run, not fight."

"You planned this?" It comes out strangled.

A sheepish look, like he's been caught with his hand in the cash drawer. Except the currency is people's lives, and the bills are soaked in blood.

"I prefer *engineered*," he says.

"But I—we—" The fragments slam together in my mind like a car crash. "You let me take that paper. You let me go to her office because you—"

"Thought she would run, yes." He nods. "But when I heard the gunshot, I ran to her office as fast as these old legs would carry me. I thought I would find you dead, Esther. In my rage..." His chin trembles. "I only wanted her to leave, not..." He gestures at the blood on his cuff. Her blood.

The room starts to spin faster. Our plan. Jeremy's brilliant, stupid plan with the satellite phone and the messages. We'd undermined everything without knowing it. If we hadn't made Natalia's handlers think she was turned, if we hadn't forced her into a corner—

"Oh God." My hands shake. "It's my fault."

"Esther—"

"Sage got shot because of me." I feel dizzy, can't breathe. "Natalia is dead because of me. We ruined your plan, we forced her hand, we—"

My vision tunnels, heart hammering rapidly. I slide off the chair onto the floor, fetal position, choking, trembling.

"I killed her." I wheeze between desperate gulps. "I almost killed them both. If I hadn't—if we hadn't—"

Caron is beside me now, his hand on my back. "Breathe, child. Just breathe."

But I can't. It's all closing in—Melody, Natalia, Sage bleeding on the floor, all the lies and people I've hurt because I thought I was so damn clever—crushing down until nothing is left but the thundering in my head and the certainty that everything is my fault.

The world goes black.

THIRTY
SEVEN

The Holland kitchen measured roughly eight feet square, a space that could accommodate four people only if none of them needed to move very much. The aroma of tomato sauce—prepared from a recipe card yellowed with age and grease—filled the air with something that might have been comfort, if not for the underlying current of urgency. Ruth Holland moved through her domain with the practiced efficiency of someone perpetually behind schedule, her cell phone wedged between shoulder and ear while she conducted the wooden spoon like a frantic baton.

Esther stood in the doorway, all of nine years old, her bare feet flat against the cold linoleum despite knowing better.

She clutched a notebook against her, its purple-inked cover already softened from being hugged and opened too many times. The edges bore the telltale creases of something treasured.

Her mother's voice cut across the small space, sharp with familiar frustration. The insurance company again—the same weekly battle over claims and coverage that never seemed to end. Mom jabbed the Mute button and began sorting laundry with her free hand, never pausing in her stirring. The performance was impressive, if exhausting to watch.

"Esther, baby, not now." The dismissal came without eye contact. "Can you check the oven timer, please?"

Three minutes remained. Esther relayed this information to the space between her mother's shoulder blades and received no acknowledgment.

She waited for the inevitable pause, that brief moment when Mom would lower the phone and pinch the bridge of her nose, a gesture she had memorized as thoroughly as her Crayolas.

When it came, Esther stepped forward. "Can I show you something?"

Mom's eyes, dark-circled and glassy, focused on her daughter. "Let me guess: You need me to sign your reading log."

Esther shook her head and extended the notebook. "It's my story. I finished it. The whole thing."

The wooden spoon was balanced across the pot, and Mom wiped her hands on denim already stained with the day's minor disasters. "Esther, honey, you know I love when you write. But right now…" Her gesture encompassed the chaotic nature of it all: the laundry basket, the oven, the tower of bills beside the microwave. The glance she gave her daughter contained no coldness, only the weight of too many obligations. "Rain check, okay?"

Esther nodded and slunk to the kitchen table, where her chest receded like someone had let the air out. She placed the notebook at the edge, then withdrew to the hallway while her mother returned to the call.

The notebook remained on the table, its purple lettering catching the late-afternoon light slanting through the single window. From her bedroom doorway, Esther could see it amid the dinner preparations, a small square of hope in the beige landscape of their apartment. She waited, hoping for the moment when her mother might notice what had been left behind. But the sauce continued to bubble, the phone continued to ring, and only the angle of the sunlight changed, growing longer as the day slipped away.

Amelia's yell announced her arrival before she appeared—booming up from the street and preceding her like a herald. Esther tracked her sister's approach by sound: the building's entrance door, the bassy escape of music from headphones, the rattle of keys, and finally the volcanic "Yo!" that marked her entrance.

She materialized in the kitchen seconds later, fifteen years old and carrying herself with the confidence of someone who expected the world to step aside when she entered a room. Her hoodie hung off one shoulder with studied carelessness, her hair arranged in a topknot which looked both intentional and accidental. She leaned over the bubbling pot, inhaled deeply, and pronounced, "Smells like tomatoes and dreams. Nice."

She helped herself to the bread as her mother scolded—Amelia recognized no boundaries when it came to food—and only then noticed Esther hovering in the hallway, waiting.

"Hey, Sprout." The nickname carried its usual mixture of affection and authority. "What's this?" She had already spotted the notebook.

"It's nothing," Esther said, moving closer with deliberate casualness.

Amelia cleared a small corner of the table and pulled two of the chairs close together. "Come here, show me what 'nothing' is."

She patted the seat beside her, and when Esther walked over and slid into it, Amelia leaned in closer, her shoulder a safe barrier between them and the havoc of the kitchen.

She opened the notebook and read aloud with theatrical emphasis: "The cat looked at me like it knew all the secrets of the world, but it wasn't telling." Her laughter filled the small space. "Very mysterious, Sprout. Why is the cat so shady?"

Esther's cheeks burned. "It's just a story."

Amelia continued reading, her tone gradually losing its mocking edge. She turned pages with increasing attention, her lips moving silently over the words. Occasionally, the corner of her mouth would twitch upward. Esther sat next to her, twirling a magnet she took from the refrigerator door, waiting for the inevitable dismissal.

Instead, Amelia's face registered an emotion Esther had never seen directed at her before—something approaching respect.

"You know this is good, right?" She poked at the page. "Like, *actually* good."

Esther blinked. "I thought you were going to make fun of it."

"I mean, yeah, you used the word *perambulate* three times on the same page, but it's funny. And sad. And kind of genius." She flipped backward through the pages, found a passage, and read: "The tree in the backyard was like a grumpy grandfather, always dropping things and refusing to move." She snorted. "That's gold."

The compliment landed like something in a foreign language, requiring translation. Amelia was rarely generous with praise.

"You're just saying that."

"No, seriously. This part where the kid hides in the laundry basket to listen to the grown-ups? Did that happen, or did you make it up?"

Esther shrugged. "I don't know. Maybe both?"

Amelia closed the notebook and set it upright like a small monument. "You know what I love most?"

Esther shook her head and bit her bottom lip.

"When you write, you're not little Esther from apartment 2D anymore, right? You can become anyone you want to be."

Esther let her lip go and looked at her sister. "I guess so."

"Your writing is your superpower, you know? Being able to transform your life with words. You gotta keep writing this stuff. For real. Like, you might be famous someday if you get out of this dump."

Esther hadn't thought about it that way before. When she was writing, she wasn't the girl whose clothes came from the Salvation Army, or the kid the teachers never called on. She was whoever she needed to be, whoever she could imagine herself to be.

The words settled between them, a promise neither of them acknowledged directly. Esther felt her mouth pull into a reluctant smile, caught between hope and disbelief. She felt something shift around her, like a door opening in the walls of their kitchen—a door to a world of possibility.

Amelia tore off another piece of bread. "If you ever get rich, you owe me a house." She paused, considering. "Or at least a lifetime supply of gummy bears."

"Deal," Esther said, her smile now impossible to suppress. She wanted to grab the notebook and run into her room to write a hundred more stories before the feeling faded.

Amelia picked up the pen and scrawled her name in the notebook's margin, underlining it three times before adding a slightly imperfect five-pointed star.

"There," she declared, "now it's got my blessing. That means it's sacred."

Esther touched the doodle with her fingertip, and the ink bled onto it.

The moment solidified—bold and bright, a secret that belonged only to the two of them.

Amelia tilted her chair back dangerously. "I gotta put this laundry away before Mom screams at me." She tapped the notebook once more. "This is great, Sprout."

She disappeared down the hallway, headphones back on, leaving behind the creaking chair and the still-warm ink of her benediction.

Thirty Eight

My eyelids flutter open to a familiar ceiling. My ceiling. Someone is jackhammering against my temples, and for a blissful second, there's nothing to remember. Then Caron's voice plays back in my mind like an old recording.

There is no raid, Esther.

He'd been playing a separate game all along, moving pieces on a board of his own making. The false FBI raid was his opening, and I was his pawn, pushed forward to threaten the queen into retreating.

But our counterplay was real too—our plan, the one Jeremy and Sage risked everything for at the Plaza. We hadn't just unnerved Natalia; we'd dismantled her, cutting her off from her handlers with a few well-timed radio waves. Caron had intended to flush her out, but we burned her to the ground without regard for the collateral damage.

Natalia is dead because of me—no sugarcoating it. No victory, no triumph, only a hollowed-out space where solace was supposed to be. Caron hadn't won, and neither had I. We both just used the ghosts of two dead girls to get what we wanted. There can't be a winner in a game like that. Only regrets and the people they haunt.

When I try to sit up, the room spins like one of those carnival rides that makes you puke. Something moves in my peripheral vision.

Kora is at my desk, legs crossed at the ankle, thumbing through my notebook. She looks up and tucks a curl behind her ear. "Hey, kid, you okay?"

I blink twice, my mental jigsaw still missing pieces. "How did—"

"Caron carried you here." She sets my notebook down. "Asked me to watch you until you woke up. Said you had a panic attack."

That's one way to look at it.

"How long?" My throat is like sandpaper.

"About an hour." She hands me a glass of water. "You should drink."

The water goes down in gulps. "Caron?"

"Had to take care of things, as you can imagine." Her crooked smile makes a brief appearance. "He'll be back."

My head falls onto the pillow, and the enormity of everything sits on top of me.

"I told you the first month was the hardest, didn't I?"

I roll my eyes at her, but her smirk makes me smile.

"Have you heard about Sage?"

Kora's lips twitch. "Yeah. She's going to be okay."

"That's good. Really good."

"She's tough," Kora says, fidgeting with her sleeve. "Always has been."

"I used to think I knew what tough meant."

"Sometimes the strongest people are the ones who ask for help." Kora stands and stretches her back.

"I thought… I was so sure you were on Natalia's side. When you grabbed her arm like that—" I say.

"That was the point." She glances down at her hands, still lightly stained with blood. "Sage came to see me in the hospital after… everything. We had a real heart-to-heart. She asked if I'd do this for her, play the double agent. I couldn't say no."

"The way you were around her—"

"Acting classes at Yale." A shrug, but it doesn't quite hide her pride. "Plus, I learned from the best. Sage has been playing parts her whole life."

"You missed your calling. Broadway could be next."

Kora laughs, a genuine sound that's out of place. "God, no. I'm done pretending to be someone I'm not."

"You're leaving?"

"Yeah, I mean, they were going to age me out anyway, so I figure, why not get some early retirement in."

For a moment, we're quiet. And then I ask, because I have to. "That morning in the cafeteria, after the Cinderella post. You knew it was me. Why didn't you turn me in?"

She looks toward the door, all traces of her usual bravado gone.

"Because I already had two Sisters' memories on my conscience. I wasn't going to add another."

The plural throws me off for a moment, but then it's clear who she means.

"Melody and…Sparrow?"

There's wounded surprise on her face. "You knew?" A chuckle, then, "Right, Sage. Of course you knew."

Her voice drops as she looks down at Mr. Ribbit, sitting on my bed. "I could have been smarter with both of them."

"We all could have been smarter."

She's quiet for a moment, then leans down and picks him up, turning him over in her hands like she's searching for answers in the stitching. "I pushed them too much. Told Mel to handle it herself. Thought she was ready." She shakes her head. "Then I saw you, fighting in your own way, and I knew I couldn't make the same mistake again. Now I have to live with that."

"Yeah."

"I don't think either of us knew what was coming." She hands Mr. Ribbit to me and turns to go. My hand catches her arm, and she spins around.

"When you see Sage…can you tell her…" My chin trembles, and heat rushes to my face.

Kora comes back, sits on the bed, and throws her arms around me. It's the best hug I've had in a long time.

"I will."

We hang on to each other for a while before our embrace breaks. Halfway out the door, she turns back and smiles. "You still owe me a gym day."

I don't know whether to laugh or sob, so I do both.

STILL REELING from Kora's visit, my muscles tense up when the door to my room opens—no knock, just a casual intrusion like I'm on exhibit.

It's Barbie. Not the doll-like, manicured Barbie who struts around the dorms with her nose in the air, but dressed down, stripped of pretense. Her hair is pulled into a messy ponytail, and she's wearing jeans and a plain T-shirt. No makeup. No glitter. No attitude.

"Did you win?" she asks, leaning against the doorframe.

"What?"

The door closes behind her as she steps inside. "Caron carried you in here, so either you lost, or you won, but it cost you everything." The mid-Atlantic affectation in her voice is gone, replaced by something warmer.

"I don't understand."

The strut is still there as she walks over and sits on the edge of my bed like we're having a sleepover. "Sweetie, I'm not as dumb as I play. I've been waiting for this day since you walked through the door." Her eyes find mine, serious and searching. "Is she done?"

The question hangs in the air, and I can't tell if this is real or if I'm having a lucid dream. "How did you know?"

"Sugar, your sister almost torched this place single-handedly." She chuckles. "When I saw you at the ceremony, I figured you were here to finish the job."

"You knew Amelia?"

She throws her head back in raucous laughter. "Child, everyone knew her. She was the backbone of this place back in the golden days." She looks down at her hands. "You don't last as long as I have without a keen sense of smell. I play the game that works for me, but don't for a second think that I don't hurt for those girls and what happened to them."

Staring at her, I struggle to reconcile this woman with the walking stereotype I've been avoiding since day one.

"So, all that—" I gesture in the air, trying to capture her usual persona.

"Is what keeps you safe in a place like this," she finishes. "The less of a threat they think you are, the less attention they pay."

She's disarmed me completely, and I choose to trust her.

"Natalia won't be running things anymore," I reveal.

The tension leaves her jawline. "Well, can't say I'm heartbroken about that, but I suppose some mighty big changes are coming, then?"

"Yes, pretty big."

She nods, understanding. "The girls should know. Not everything, but enough so they don't panic."

"Could you…?" I catch her meaning. "Could you talk to the other Sisters? Let them know so they aren't caught off guard?"

Barbie squeezes my hand. "It'd be my pleasure, sugar. I'll start the telephone tree before the vultures circle."

The doll that I'd seen before was a character, a performance. The woman who played the role is a survivor.

"Sis would have been proud of you. You're more like her than you know," she says softly before walking out.

Lying back down on the bed, my head crashes into the pillow. I surrender to the dark, my mind turning over the decision I've already made.

Thirty Nine

It's 6:40 a.m. and the elevator doors slide open with a soft chime that is far too cheerful. The executive floor looks different—same marble floors, same fancy artwork, but the air is lighter, like someone cracked a window after years of stale breath.

I tug at my gray sweatpants. What a sight I must be. My hair is still wet from the shower, and my threadbare T-shirt has seen better days. Twenty-four hours ago, I would've been mortified to be caught looking like this up here. Now? I couldn't care less.

Funny how watching people die puts fashion in perspective.

My bare feet splat across the cool floor, toes wiggling against the marble, savoring the sensation—one last memory to take with me.

Yesterday, I was knee-deep in blood and secrets. Today, I'm walking away. Walking back to nothing, back to nobody, should be terrifying—but instead, it's almost serene.

The door to Caron's office lies ahead. Behind it sits the man who saved me from the streets, who showed me a world of unimaginable luxury. But also the man who's responsible for this entire monstrous construct.

There's only one thing left to say.

"So, what will you do now?" Caron asks.

I shrug, picking at a loose thread on my sleeve. "I don't know. But I managed before."

His face falls when he looks at me. "Don't manage like before. Start a new life."

He opens his desk drawer and removes a stack of cash—crisp, new bills bound with a paper band—and holds it out to me. An attempt to smooth things over with money, as he's always done—but some scars can't be sanded out with hundred-dollar bills.

"I can't accept that."

"You can, and you will," he says firmly. "I won't take no for an answer. Your sister said no all the time. I won't let you do it to me as well."

My throat tightens at the mention of Amelia. "Tell me about her. In the Family, I mean. Before things went bad."

Caron softens as a glow ignites in his eyes.

"I cared deeply for her," he says. "When our paths first crossed, she was homeless, bitter, and suspicious of everyone. She took a chance on me, and we got along marvelously. She had such intelligence, such wit and humor. I miss her terribly."

"Thank you for that."

"She talked about you."

My head snaps up. "What?"

"She was so proud." He smiles. "She'd tell me stories of the things you two would do."

"Why didn't you tell me that before?"

"Would you have listened?"

He's right, and the admission is a bitter pill. Before, I would have twisted his words into another manipulation. Now I see the memories.

He leans forward. "I was just fulfilling my promise to her."

I tilt my head to the side like a dog.

"She came to me, Esther, when things had gone bad and Natalia was on the warpath." He shifts behind his desk. "I was not happy with her for the things she said about the Family, but she seemed desperate. She asked me to look after you…if something happened to her."

The words crush me. She knew. Amelia knew she was in danger. And instead of running, instead of saving herself, she spent her last moments thinking about me, trying to protect me.

"When I'd heard that your mother had passed, I knew I had to find you," Caron says. "You hid yourself well."

I can't speak. Can't even think. The truth is sand beneath my feet.

Whenever I've found my balance, it shifts, and I have to regain my footing all over again.

My body moves on its own, rising from the chair and carrying me toward him. His arms open, and I fall in. He holds me close, one hand stroking my back as I shake with silent sobs.

"I'm sorry." The words are muffled against his shirt. It's not enough.

"Go now," he says. "Be who your sister wanted you to be. Don't worry about me. I'll be all right."

I release him, stepping back. My eyes fall one last time on the pile of cash beside him. The answer to a prayer a very different girl once whispered from a park bench.

I turn and leave, closing the door on the man, the money, and the life that could never have been truly mine.

THE CENTRAL PARK Conservatory Garden is peaceful, with the morning dew still clinging to the petals of the vibrant flowers. Jeremy is on a bench, fidgeting with his watch, when he spots me. His face lights up with that awkward, genuine smile I've grown to love.

"You made it." He springs up.

"You sent me coordinates. It's our thing."

He shrugs. "After everything that happened, I wouldn't blame you for disappearing without a trace."

We sit down, and an elderly couple strolls past. A breeze passes over us, leaving the scent of jasmine in the air.

"So, you're leaving?" Jeremy asks. "Will you be okay?"

I nod. "I've got enough money to get started again. Who knows, maybe I'll write a book about all this someday."

"Just change the names," Jeremy says with a half smile. "And mine better be cooler."

"'Wizard' is already pretty cool." A playful tap lands on his knee.

"Caron told me about the false raid, how he planted that document for us to find."

My head sinks into my hands. The memory is too fresh to relive.

"Don't beat yourself up." His hand almost touches my shoulder before settling back in his lap. "We made the best decision we could with the information we had available."

"Yeah, that's what I keep telling myself. Doesn't make it any easier to swallow."

"I wish he'd let us in on it, though." He adjusts his glasses. "We could have helped instead of…you know."

"Accidentally blowing the whole thing up?" I offer with a bitter laugh. "Yeah, but I guess he needed us to believe the lie too."

He peers behind him, still paranoid. I can't blame him.

"Caron is going to shut it down."

I stare at him. "You're serious?"

"I am. He came to see me last night and asked me how we could do it so no one gets exposed."

My eyes widen. "What did you do?"

He shifts in his seat. Here comes the tech talk glow again.

"He understood it was just a matter of time before the FBI came calling for real. So he thought, 'Why not get ahead of them?'"

"What do you mean?"

"I sent over the final dossier to Step-Sister," he says. "Everything we had on Natalia, the operations, all of it."

He looks at me, his mouth twitching.

"What?"

"Did you need to make the password *AuraHasASexyAss* with an exclamation point?"

"Yes!" I exclaim, and we crack up. "Absolutely necessary."

"Well, they'll have a laugh when they open it."

"Why bother sending it now?"

"Because they'll leak it to the FBI. It'll make them feel like they won."

My head tilts. "And that's a good thing?"

"It is when you've rigged the entire system with false data." The shit-eating grin on his face is precious.

"Spill," I demand.

"I wrote a batch program that scrubbed all the information in the Family database and replaced it with random data I generated with AI. So, all the records are still there, and everything looks legitimate. But the identities are phony, totally conjured up. Except for Caron and Natalia of course."

"Like a wizard!"

"Caron will get arrested, but they'll have nothing concrete to prosecute him with. Eventually, he'll walk free with no more FBI or Step-Sister to worry about. It's kind of brilliant, actually."

"And all the Sisters' stuff?"

"Untraceable. They may as well be fictional characters."

"Will they be okay?"

"We'll send a message through the portal, explaining what's happening. Caron ensured they'd all get a 'substantial severance.'"

Glancing down, he tries to hide the smile spreading across his face.

"What if they find backups or something like that?"

"What backups?" He's being coy. "Unfortunately, they were all corrupted. Blame it on the tech guy. His name is Randy Mize."

We share a laugh, and my admiration for his genius grows. He shakes his head, a small, tired smile remaining. As our laughter fades, he adjusts his glasses, a familiar habit, but the frantic energy that usually surrounds him is gone, replaced by a profound calm. The reality of what we've done settles in.

"We never would have been able to do any of this without you."

Jeremy's cheeks redden. "It was an honor being a spy with you, Star."

"Esther." My correction is soft, but firm. "My name is Esther."

We stand, and Jeremy opens his arms. I step into them without hesitation, feeling his heart drum against mine. This isn't like our previous embraces—quick, nervous, charged with adrenaline. This is real. Honest. Warm.

"Thank you," I say, pressing into his shoulder. "For everything."

Reaching into the pocket of my jeans, I take out the burner phone and hand it to him. "Almost forgot this."

"Hang on to it," he says. "Never know when it may come in handy."

We share a final nod, an unguarded smile, and a breath that carries all the words we've held inside.

THE SEAHORSE STICKER is still on Melody's door. My fingers trace its outline, and for one stupid second, I expect her to yank the door open, catch me touching it, and laugh at me for being sentimental. The handle turns. Unlocked. Of course it is—why lock an empty room?

I slip inside and close the door behind me, sealing myself in the brittle stillness. The first thing that hits me is the smell. Or the lack of it. No strawberry shampoo. No vanilla body spray. Just stale air and the chemical tang of industrial cleaner.

The bed is stripped down to the bare mattress, but I sink onto it anyway, running my hand across the surface. We sat here so many times—her cross-legged, me sprawling beside. Chatting about this life, about Sage, about what we'd do once we aged out. She always said we'd leave together. She promised.

There's still a Dr Pepper in my mini-fridge. The last one she brought me. I can't bring myself to drink it. Can't throw it away either. It's just sitting in there, gathering dust. An absurd aluminum monument to someone who deserved so much more.

My throat closes up, and I press my hands to my eyes, but the memories come anyway—Melody teaching me to dance in the common room, laughing when I tripped over my own feet. The notes she'd slip under my door with terrible puns just to make me smile. The way she'd grab my hand when I was spiraling and squeeze until I came back down.

She should still be here. We should be plotting our escape together, scheming about the lives we'd build once we were free. She wanted to show me Rocky River—promised she'd take me to her favorite diner where they served chocolate-chip pancakes the size of dinner plates. Said we'd road trip to the Florida Keys, just the two of us, no assignments, no responsibilities, no one watching. We were supposed to get matching tattoos. Something goofy and meaningful that only we'd understand.

Or maybe we'd have stayed in New York. Found some cramped apartment in Queens where we'd split the rent and complain about the neighbors. She'd drag me to open mic nights, and I'd force her to stay in and watch old movies. We'd order too much Chinese food and fall asleep on the couch mid-conversation.

Instead, she's gone. Scrubbed away. A memory cleaned up and covered over.

I open my mouth to say goodbye—that's what you're supposed to do, right? Say goodbye, get closure, move on.

But I can't. The word won't come. It feels like a betrayal, like I'm giving up on her.

"I'm sorry." My voice cracks. "God, Mel, I'm so sorry."

I don't know what I'm apologizing for. For not saving her. For still being here. For the fact that her last moments were terrified and alone, and I can't undo any of it.

The tears come, hot and endless. I curl onto my side of the bare mattress, in the room that used to be hers, and I let myself break.

Strong tails in stormy waters.

But what do you do when there's nothing left to anchor to?

Mr. Ribbit sits propped against my pillow beside the open mouth of the unzipped backpack.

My hand closes over his worn head. "You're coming with me, buddy. She'd want you safe."

The doors of my wardrobe pull open and spread like giant wings. Row after row of designer clothes I never properly organized—my Family uniform. Each piece a glittering promise of a woman I never became.

I trail my fingers across the fabric. "I don't want a single thing from this place. Not one damn thing."

But the blue cashmere sweater—the one Melody said I was beautiful in—caresses my hand. The softness is a memory against my skin. Was that feeling manufactured too?

Off the hanger it comes, and I stuff it into my backpack.

The black ankle boots are next. "It's just practical," the lie whispers. "They fit so well, I'd be stupid not to take them."

Next comes the red skirt I never got to wear, then the cardigan, puffy and warm with its extra-long arms. With each item, my justification grows thinner.

The truth sits heavy on me: Parts of this life weren't all bad. Parts of it are mine to keep.

My mother's voice sounds in my head. *Some things can be both a poison and a medicine. The trick is knowing when to take them and how much.*

Backpack zipped, Mr. Ribbit's head peeking out the top, my throat clamps. For the last time, I take in the room that was both my home and my cell.

I toss the backpack over my shoulder and close the door behind me. I don't look back.

EPILOGUE

The radiator in my studio apartment hisses and clanks, providing the soundtrack to my typing. It's not much—this little place in Brooklyn—but it's mine. Clean. Safe. No one watching. No one expecting anything from me.

Abandoning my laptop, I shuffle to the kitchenette. The kettle's handle is cracked, but it works—kind of a metaphor for my life. My tea of choice is ginger and cinnamon today, and while it steeps, the mail pile needs to be cleared. Bills, flyers for restaurants out of my budget, and what I've been waiting for: a freelance check from *TrendSpotter*. Three hundred bucks for five articles about "summer fashion must-haves" I researched on the internet. What a joke. This should be deposited before it expires, like my writing career.

Tea in hand, I walk to the window—a narrow pane of glass that pretends to be a view. Three floors up means the bodega's neon sign and a sliver of sky are visible between buildings. Some slush still clings to the street corner from the snow last week. It's not exactly the panorama my room with the Family had, but I don't wake up sweating anymore, so that's something.

My walls are mostly bare; decorating requires both money and the belief that you'll stay somewhere long enough to make it worthwhile. But one thing I did print out and tack up: the *Step-Sister* blog post that appeared the day after the Family was raided. I've posted it above my desk, edges curling, but the words still cut with truth. It hangs over me while I write my book—not as a trophy, but as a warning. Some stories need telling, but at what cost?

Blog Entry #42: The Final Chapter?

The Family is Dead. Long Live the Truth.

Caron sits in a federal detention center, but how long he'll be there is anyone's guess. The FBI raid was spectacular; they came in not with guns blazing, but with search warrants and subpoenas. They're frustrated, though. All those servers, all those databases, and what do they find? Nothing. My sources tell me that all the records are phantoms.

Natalia? Gone. Vanished like a spirit, leaving behind nothing but rumors. Some say Russia; some say she's hiding in plain sight. Me? I'm just glad she's no longer pulling strings.

The Sisters have scattered. Not dramatically—no tearful goodbyes or bombastic exits. Just quick departures. A final gift slipped under a friend's door. A whispered "Take care of yourself" in the elevator. They're rebuilding. Healing. Starting over.

But me? I'm still here. Watching. Waiting. The Family might be gone, but the systems that created it? They're still very much alive.

To every Sister who survived: You are more than what they told you. More than a transaction, more than a performance, more than a prop in someone else's story. You have a place here...if you want it.

The truth has teeth now. And we're only getting started.

Fare thee well, Cinderella. We hope your castle awaits.

Stay safe, Stay strong.

—Your Step-Sister

A teacup toast to Andromeda and the work she's doing to keep Amelia's memory alive. Someday I'll take her up on that lunch offer. This place certainly isn't a castle, but it's mine.

The news reports said Caron went quietly when they came for him—sitting in his office, probably in one of those impeccable suits, hands folded on his desk. No drama, no chase. Just a nod and a calm walk to the waiting cars. *Extremely cooperative,* the papers called him.

Without Jeremy's handiwork, they'd have had enough to put him away forever. But after? The prosecutors kept promising bombshell evidence that never materialized. The case is still going on, but it's built on sand, and everyone knows it.

Is he in there right now, teaching the other inmates to play canasta with that patient half smile? *No, no, you must discard after drawing,* he'd say in his accent. I'll never forgive him for building the machine. For creating a world where girls like Melody could be used up and tossed aside. But he did pull them off the streets, and in the end, when it mattered most, he regretted leaving the door open for the monster to get in, and he remembered what was important. I hope he finds a worthy opponent.

My phone chimes from the desk, breaking my reverie. I pick it up, smiling at the notification—our little group chat, where we keep each other entertained with updates and random thoughts. We named it *Survivor's Club* as a joke, but the name stuck.

The new message is from Maitea. She's sent a selfie of her sitting cross-legged on the polished wooden floor of Caroline and Shannon's yoga studio, surrounded by little strips of colored tape marking dance positions. Her hair is pulled back in a messy bun, and she's making an exaggerated, exhausted face that doesn't hide how happy she looks.

MAITEA

These white girls think they can salsa after ONE lesson. Pray for me!

I laugh out loud, typing back a quick prayer-hands emoji. The studio has been open for three months now, and it's become something special. Caroline used the money her parents left for her, handling the classes while Shannon manages the business side. They somehow convinced Maitea to teach dance lessons twice a week, which has turned out to be their most popular offering.

I scroll back to a picture of the grand opening with Caroline cutting the ribbon while Shannon stands beside her with her cane. She'll probably always need it, but she's thriving in ways I never expected. The injury altered her physically, but it changed her inside too. She's softer now, more genuine. When she smiles, it hits you in your soul. A part of me will always see her as High Queen Estrella, a lingering *What if?* But for now, just having her as my friend means the world to me.

Flipping through our chat history brings a familial warmth. Those three women might be the best thing that came out of this entire ordeal. We were Sisters in name with the Family, but that moniker feels much more appropriate now.

The picture of me and Caroline at the tattoo parlor spreads a silly smile across my face. She's pretending to hold me down while I howl in pain. Amelia was right, though—it did hurt like a son of a bitch, and I do love it. It's a little seahorse on my left ankle with a banner underneath that says *Strong Tails in Stormy Waters*. Better scroll away before the tears start.

A soft chuckle helps push back the sadness when the one and only post from the fifth member of our clique scrolls in. Jeremy doesn't say much in the group chat—he still gets nervous talking to women, even in text, which is both endearing and ridiculous considering everything we've been through. He was so excited when he landed a job at an AI startup in Williamsburg. Something about "ethical machine learning" that he tried to explain over coffee, his hands flying as he described algorithms and safeguards with the same passion he used to save dozens of women from fates unknown.

We meet for breakfast every Sunday at this little diner, where the eggs are perfectly fluffy and the coffee is much too strong. He updates me on his latest projects, and I tell him about my book. Neither of us talks about the Family directly, but we don't need to. The understanding is there in the comfortable silences, in the way he always sits facing the door so I don't have to, in how he still encrypts every message he sends me out of habit.

Turning from the window, I settle in at my desk. It's time to complete what I've been working toward for the last eight months. The document on the screen stares at me: *Losing My Families* by Esther "Star" Holland.

Typing the last period was like dropping a stone into still water— a tiny action with ripples that might never stop. This is the hardest thing I've ever done in my life, and that's saying something, considering everything that happened with the Family. Some days, the words wouldn't come. Other days, they poured out like blood from a wound that wouldn't mend. But it was a story I had to tell, even through all the pain.

Writing it down helped me process the grief. Not heal—at least not yet—but try to understand it. I don't have a publisher yet, and the literary agent I spoke to a month ago told me, "Misery memoirs are a tough sell," but admitted that he was interested in reading it when I was done.

I click on the page titled "Dedication," and my fingers pause for a moment before I type:

To my Seahorse and my SuperNova. You didn't get the chance to tell your stories, so I'm telling mine for all of us.

Pushing the chair back, I take a sip of my tea. It's gone cold, but I finish it anyway. I pick up my phone and open messages.

> I finally did it. It's done.

The response comes back right away.

JEREMY

> I knew you could. That's amazing.

I smile, and before I can put the phone down, he follows up with another.

JEREMY

> Celebrate?

I glance around the room and land on Mr. Ribbit, sitting on my bed with his perpetually surprised expression.

"What do you think?" I ask.

His wide eyes stare back at me.

"I agree."

> Yes!

A Note From The Author

If you made it all the way to this page, that means you stuck with The Family to the end, and that alone means more than I can fit into a paragraph. Thank you for spending your time with Star, Melody, Sage, and the rest of this crazy world that emerged out of the strange corners of my mind.

This story lived with me for a long time before it ever had a title, a cover, or any hope of becoming something tangible. Finishing it and putting it into your hands is one of the rare moments in life where the dream actually matches the outcome.

Since you've come this far, perhaps you'd allow me to ask one small favor.

Reviews—even short ones—make a world of difference for authors, especially those of us taking our first steps into this intimidating world. They help new readers decide whether to give a book a chance, and they keep this whole writing life rolling forward. A few honest words on Amazon, Goodreads, or wherever you purchased this book have far more power than most people realize.

And if you'd like to keep up with what I'm writing next, or you're curious about the odd collection of stories, musings, and questionable decisions that make up my day-to-day, you can always find me at www.ricperrott.com

Thanks for sharing a bit of your time with me. I'll meet you again soon… at sunset.

—Ric

Acknowledgements

Writing a novel might seem like a solitary act from the outside, but *The Family* grew out of a small constellation of people who kept me steady and honest along the way. Alex was the first to see these pages take shape and the one who kept reading them long after she had every right to pretend she was busy. Her support, patience, and willingness to listen to me ramble about plot points while walking Milo made this book possible.

Kristin, my editor, took the rough, partially correct words in my head and coaxed them into the shape they were always meant to be. She made this story clearer, sharper, and more faithful to what I always imagined. Donna and Sharron at Hot Tree Editing brought the professional polish that every book needs but few authors talk about. Working with them was a pleasure from start to finish.

My first beta reader, Babs, read early drafts with honesty and clarity, never shying away from the notes I needed to hear. That early feedback nudged the story onto its glide path. Diren, who designed the cover, gave me the gift of seeing Star for the first time outside my own mind. From the moment I saw that first image, I knew it was her. Matt and Jane at 100Covers, thanks for making the back look as good as the front.

To my family for being so supportive of my new "hobby," and offering to read everything I write even if it's absolutely not your vibe. That means the world to me, thank you.

To everyone who read advance copies and shared thoughtful feedback: you helped shape these final pages more than you know. Early readers are the quiet backbone of any novel, and I'm grateful for each of you.

And finally—to you, the reader, holding this book in your hands. Thank you for stepping into this world and spending your time with these characters. You're the reason I sit down to write the next one.

— Ric Perrott
November, 2025

About The Author

Ric Perrott has been spinning tales for as long as he can remember. First as a kid scribbling stories into composition notebooks, then as a programmer shaping logic into narrative, and now on the page where the characters disobey as often as the code did.

A longtime musician, gamer, and unapologetic fan of anything with a gripping story at its heart, it was time to give the ideas that had been following him around for decades a place to live.

He is the author of the short story Pick Up the Pieces, and The Family is his debut novel with Mirelune Press.

When he isn't writing, Ric can be found with a guitar in his hands, a controller nearby, or his nose buried in a book. He lives in Florida with his family, a Goldendoodle named Milo, and enough half-finished ideas to last several lifetimes.

You can follow him on social media at:

Also By
Ric Perrott

PICK UP THE PIECES